THE VISCOUNT'S WALLFLOWER BRIDE

LAUREN ROYAL
DEVON ROYAL

June 2021 Edition
SWEET CHASE BRIDES

THE VISCOUNT'S WALLFLOWER BRIDE by Lauren Royal & Devon Royal

Published by Novelty Books, a division of Novelty Publishers, LLC, 205 Avenida Del Mar #275, San Clemente, CA 92674

COPYRIGHT © Lauren Royal & Devon Royal, 2016, 2021

June 2021 Edition

Cover by Kimberly Killion

Learn more about the authors and their books at www.LaurenandDevonRoyal.com.

ISBN: 978-1-63469-179-6

MORE SWEET CHASE BRIDES BOOKS

∾

For June & Lærke,

our first mother-daughter readers

ONE

England
July 15, 1673

S T. SWITHIN'S DAY. Well, it was fitting.

Ford Chase stared out his carriage window at the miserable, wet landscape. According to St. Swithin's legend, if rain fell on the fifteenth of July, it would continue for forty days and nights. Not that Ford believed in such superstitious swill. But today it seemed almost plausible.

This was shaping up to be the worst day of his life.

The carriage rattled over the drawbridge and into the modest courtyard of Greystone, his brother's small castle. Cold raindrops pelted Ford's head when he shoved open the door and leapt to the circular drive. Drenched gravel crunching beneath his boots, he made his way down a short, covered passageway and banged the knocker on the unassuming oak door.

Benchley cracked open the door, then slipped outside and shut it behind him. "My lord, what brings you here today?"

"I wish to speak with my brother." Ford frowned down at the small, wiry valet. What was he doing answering the door? "Will you be letting me in?"

"I think not," Benchley replied in a surly tone Ford had never heard him use before. "I'll fetch Lord Greystone." And with that, he disappeared back into the ancient castle.

Shivering, Ford stood open-mouthed in disbelief. Well, this treatment certainly fit in with the rest of his day. Rain dripped from his limp brown hair to sprinkle on the stones at his feet. Deciding he needn't ask permission to enter his brother's home, he reached for the latch.

The door opened, and his brother stepped out. He looked haggard, his face a pasty gray, his green eyes and black hair dull.

"Colin? What the deuce is going on?"

"Illness. Measles, we think. Thank goodness you're here."

Ford pulled his surcoat tighter around himself. "Come again?"

"Amy is ill, along with Hugh and the baby. And half of the servants. One of them died yesterday," Colin added grimly.

"Died?" Ford's gut twisted as he thought of Amy—Colin's lovely, raven-haired wife—and their wild four-year-old son, Hugh, and the baby, Aidan...all dead.

"It's not so bad as all that," Colin rushed to assure him. "The poor maid was eighty if she were a day, and the disease went straight to her lungs. Amy and the children will recover."

Ford nodded, noting his brother looked worried, but quite calm. "Good. I'll keep them in my prayers." He shook more water out of his hair. "At least *you* won't be falling ill. Do you remember when all four of us caught measles on the Continent?"

"I could hardly forget." Moving like an old man, Colin leaned gingerly against the doorpost. "But what does that have to do with now?"

"At a Royal Society lecture, I learned one cannot fall ill with the same disease twice," Ford explained.

"I've had measles more than once."

"Not true measles, the one with the high fever. Spotted skin is a symptom of many different conditions."

"If you say so." Colin shrugged, but his face showed a hint of relief. "Still, the fever is dreadful, and Jewel has yet to suffer measles. True measles, as you put it. Will you take her with you —away from here—before she succumbs as well? It would ease my mind, and Amy's too, I'm sure. The worry is doing her no good."

Alarm bells went off in Ford's head. Take his niece? Where? And…how? What was he to do with a little girl? Instinctively, he began backing away. "Uh, I only stopped by to let you know I've left London and will be at Lakefield for the foreseeable future—"

"Perfect."

"—working on my watch design. I…I just wanted to be alone for a while. You see, Lady Tabitha has eloped."

"With the rest of the family off in Scotland, I was at my wit's end deciding what to do. I was about to settle Jewel in the village. But this will be much better—"

"Tabitha *eloped*," Ford repeated loudly, stopping in his tracks.

Didn't his brother *care* that he'd had his heart trampled today?

"She eloped?" Colin blinked, then shook his head. "My sympathies, Ford, truly. But what did you expect, man? After so many years—how long had you been courting her, anyway?"

"Since…well, I was ten when we met. But we weren't 'courting,' as you say, until…sixteen or so? I gave her that little ring—"

"Sixteen! So now, at twenty-three, you've kept her waiting seven years, with nary a whisper of a serious proposal—"

"I *told* her we'd marry someday. In a few years." Tabitha had always been Ford's perfect match—his pretty and spirited childhood friend had grown into a flawless beauty with a sparkling wit. Together at court, they'd reveled in an endless round of lavish balls and entertainments, and while Ford was away at university, she'd busied herself with whatever it was women liked to do, leaving him plenty of time for his pursuits. *Parfait.* Or so he'd thought. "For heaven's sake, she was hardly a spinster at twenty-one. And as you said, I'm only twenty-three—"

"I married at twenty-one."

"*You* were in a hurry to have children."

"No. *I* was in love."

"So was I! So *am* I, that is."

"You really have no idea why Tabitha gave up on you, do you?" Colin rubbed his eyes. "I know you don't want to hear this, baby brother, but it's time you grew up. Maybe Jason and I coddled you too much."

From beyond the passageway, the patter of rain filled their sudden silence. Ford's hands wanted to curl into fists, but his brother was obviously weary, so he thought it best to ignore Colin's unfair remarks. Doubtless the poor fellow had spent sleepless nights watching over his wife and sons—exactly why Ford wasn't ready to settle down himself.

"You look tired," he said. "You'd best get some rest."

His brother heaved a sigh. "I'd rest easier if I knew you had Jewel. You'll take her, won't you? Just for a week or two. Maybe three. Until the illness has run its course." Colin twisted the signet ring on his finger, narrowing his eyes. "Why are you hesitating? I need you."

Ford stifled a groan. What on earth would he do with a five-year-old girl? He loved Jewel, of course. He loved all his nieces and nephews—even boisterous Hugh—and had learned to enjoy the role of uncle. But bouncing a baby on his lap or entertaining a child with a simple card game was one thing. A few moments of fun before returning the little one to its parents. Completely different from being responsible for a child all on his own...

"I'm not hesitating." Ford shoved a hand through his wet hair. "I just don't know how..."

Colin's eyes went wide. "Did you think I'd expect you to care for her on your own? Heaven forbid." His lips quirked as though he might laugh, but he covered it with a cough. "I'll send Lydia along with her."

Ford longed to wipe the patronizing look off Colin's face—but not nearly enough to refuse his offer. With Jewel's very competent nurse at her side, Ford wouldn't have to do a thing.

He could just poke his head into Jewel's room and say hello every once in a while before returning to his laboratory.

"You won't have to do a thing," Colin went on, echoing Ford's thoughts. "You can stay cooped up with your toys all day, if you like."

Irked that his brother had guessed his thoughts, Ford gritted his teeth. "They are not toys, they're instruments of—"

"Relax, brother. I meant no disrespect to your little hobby."

Ford grunted. "Why do I even bother?" he wondered aloud.

"How should I know?" Colin retorted. "I'm just a regular human, incapable of grasping the complexities of your genius. Why, talking to me must be like trying to communicate with a toddler."

"Criminy, I—"

"Maybe *that* was your problem with Tabitha."

Now Ford's fingers did curl into fists. He'd never pretended to understand women. No scientific analysis in existence could decipher *that* code.

But science wasn't the only thing he understood.

And he hadn't *had* a problem with Tabitha!

And he was finished with this discussion.

"Of course I'll take Jewel," he said, hiding his fists behind his back. "Her company will be delightful."

And he wasn't lying. Just now, anyone's company would be preferable to that of his deuced brother.

TWO

*V*IOLET ASHCROFT cleared her throat and held up her book. "'To say that a blind custom of obedience should be a surer obligation than duty taught and understood... is to affirm that a blind man may tread surer by a guide than a seeing man by a light.'"

"What is that supposed to mean?" her youngest sister, Lily, asked, busily stitching her tapestry in the grayish light from the large picture window. Lily probably had little real desire to know what the quote meant, but she was unfailingly kind. And Violet would never turn away from anyone willing to listen.

She hitched herself forward on the green brocade chair. "Well, you see—"

"Why do you care?" their middle sister, Rose, interrupted. Rose cared little for anything that didn't have to do with dancing, clothes, or gentlemen. Tossing her gleaming ringlets, she looked up from the vase of flowers she was arranging. "It's nothing but a bunch of gibberish, if you ask me."

"Nobody asked." Violet aimed a pointed look at Lily. "Did you hear anyone ask?"

"Girls." Clucking her tongue, their mother poured a dipperful of water into the kettle over the fire. "I used to comfort myself that when you all grew up, this bickering would cease. Yet it never has."

Lily's wide blue eyes were all innocence. "But Mum," she said sweetly. Their mother's proper name was Chrystabel, but as their father called her Chrysanthemum, they'd taken to calling her Mum. "It's loving bickering."

"And a poor example for your little brother." With a sigh, Mum began plucking petals from a bunch of lush pink roses. "What *does* it mean?" she asked Violet. "And who said it?"

"It means we should understand why we are doing things instead of blindly behaving as we're told. Rather like our Ashcroft family motto: *Interroga Conformationem*, Question Convention. But said much more eloquently, don't you think? By Francis Bacon."

Violet snapped the book closed, its title, *Advancement of Learning*, winking gold from the spine in her lap. "But I'm wondering," she teased. "When did *my* Mum become interested in philosophy?"

"I'm interested in all of my children's hobbies."

"Philosophy isn't a hobby," Violet protested. "It's a way of looking at life."

"Of course it is." The kettle was bubbling merrily, spewing steam into the dim room. The fire and a few candles were no match for this gloomy, rainy afternoon. "Will you come and hold this for me, dear?"

Violet set down the book and made her way over to the large, utilitarian table she always thought looked out of place in what used to be a formal drawing room. "Did Father bring you those roses?"

"He did, the darling man." Mum's musical laughter warmed Violet to her toes. "Could you smell them from across the room? He rose early to gather them between dawn and sunrise, when their scent is at its peak."

Violet snorted. "Why not let the poor man stay abed, and simply cut a few extra blooms? We have plenty." But leaning in to smell the roses, she found them uncommonly fragrant. It *was* rather darling, the way Father indulged Mum's strange whims. Not that he was without his own eccentricities. Her parents both seemed to be blind where the other's peculiarities were concerned.

And so much the better, in Violet's considered opinion. If she were ever to wed—which was to say, if one of Hal Swineherd's pigs ever sprouted wings—her husband would have to be more than a little blind. The eldest Ashcroft daughter was no great beauty, with her square-jawed face, her heavy eyebrows, and her unfashionably tanned complexion.

And then there were her plain brown eyes, not the mysterious almost-black of Rose's eyes or the fathomless deep-blue of Lily's—just brown. Average. Like all of her. She was neither fat nor thin. Not tall like Rose nor petite like Lily. Medium height, medium figure, medium everything. Average.

And she preferred not to even *think* about her hopeless hair— a drab, weedy brown thicket that could only be contained by twisting it into an unfashionable plait. Well, unless she wanted to spend hours each morning at her dressing table, allowing a maid to laboriously coax it into something resembling a stylish *coiffure*. Many ladies suffered that, every morning, without complaint.

But, honestly, didn't they have *anything* better to do?

In any case, she liked to think that what she lacked in lustrous curls, she made up for in prodigious good sense—for instance, the good sense not to dwell on the disadvantages of being hopelessly average. Instead, she chose to appreciate its one big benefit: average drew no attention, and above all things, Violet hated being the center of attention.

Rose thrived on it, though. "Let me help, Mum," she cried, dropping the stem of blue sweet peas she'd been about to add to her floral arrangement. "Violet won't get the top on straight."

Tact had never been Rose's forte.

But there was still time to learn—Violet believed one could

learn anything, if she put her mind to it. With a tolerant sigh, she stuck a wooden block upright in the big bowl and held it in place while Mum sprinkled in all the rose petals, then turned to lift the kettle.

A slow, careful stream flowed from the kettle's spout, just enough water to cover the sweet-smelling flowers. Quickly Rose popped another, larger bowl upside down on top of the wooden block, using it as a pedestal. The steam would collect beneath and drip down the edges to the tray below. As it cooled, it would separate into rosewater and essential rose oil. Distillation, Mum called it.

A rich, floral scent wafted up, and Violet inhaled deeply. As hobbies went, she didn't mind her mother's unusual one of perfume-making.

"Thank you, girls," Mum said when Rose released the bowl. "Would one of you hand me the vial of lavender essence?"

Violet turned and squinted at the labels, then reached for the proper glass tube. "I read in the news sheet this morning that Christopher Wren is going to be knighted later this year. And he was just elected to the Council of the Royal Society."

Mum took the vial. "An architect in the Royal Society? I thought that was for scientists."

Violet nodded. "Scientists, yes, but there are philosophers as members, too. As well as statesmen and physicians. And, evidently, at least one architect. I so wish I could attend one of their lectures."

"The Royal Society doesn't allow women at their meetings." Mum pulled the cork stopper and waved the lavender under her nose. "Besides, hardly any of the men there are eligible."

"I don't want them to court me, Mum." On the whole, she didn't want anyone to court her, much to her mother's distress. "I only wish to cudgel their brains."

Mum froze with a dropper halfway in the vial, taken aback. "Cudgel their—"

"Talk to them, I mean. Learn from them. They're so brilliant."

"Ah, I see."

"Men aren't interested in *talking* to women," Rose told her, "and the sooner you learn that, the sooner you'll find one of your own."

"Faith, Rose. I'm not yet eighteen. You'd think I was in my dotage, the way you've become set on marrying me off."

"You're expected to marry before I do—and at the rate you're moving, you'll be yet unwed when *I* turn eighteen."

"Rose!" Mum admonished.

The words stung, but Violet decided she couldn't resent her sister for stating the facts. She truly *didn't* intend to be married by Rose's eighteenth birthday, nor by any of Rose's subsequent birthdays. For Violet was smart enough to realize that the eccentric tendencies she'd inherited from her family, together with her plain looks, left her little likelihood of finding—let alone enticing —a compatible gentleman. The knowledge didn't bother her; she'd long ago accepted her fated spinsterhood, with characteristic good sense, and learned to see the advantages of a life spent free to do as she pleased.

But that didn't mean she begrudged her sisters their happiness. Bold, beautiful Rose was only fifteen and already eager for love. And fourteen-year-old Lily, sweet, nurturing, and just as lovely, was born to be a mother.

But Violet was the oldest, and convention dictated the sisters wed in order.

Still, when had the Ashcrofts ever been conventional?

"Hang what's 'expected,'" she said to no one in particular. "We can marry in whatever order we choose." *Or not at all,* she added silently.

"Hmm," was her mother's noncommittal reply. She added three drops of lavender to the bottle of fragrance she was creating, then swirled it carefully.

"Is that a new blend?" Violet asked.

"For Lady Cunningham." Mum sniffed deeply and passed the bottle to her oldest daughter. "What do you think?"

Violet smelled it and considered. "Too sweet. Lady Cunningham is anything but sweet." The woman's voice could curdle milk. Returning the mixture, Violet hunted for the vial of petitgrain she knew would soften it.

Nodding her approval, her mother added two drops, then made a note on the little recipe card she kept for each of her many friends.

"Look," Lily said, her embroidery forgotten. She rose and settled herself in the large, green-padded window seat. "There's a carriage about to pass by."

Mum and Rose hurried to join her at window, while Violet returned to her chair and opened her book. "So?"

"So…" Lily brushed her fingers over one of the flower arrangements that Rose left all over the house, sending a puff of scent into the air. "Carriages hardly ever pass by here! I wonder who it could be?"

"The three of you are too nosy for your own good." Violet flipped a page. Imagine being more interested in someone's mundane exploits than in the sage wisdom of a great mind!

"It's our occasional neighbor," her mother said. "The viscount."

Violet's attention strayed from her book. "How do you know?"

"I recognize his carriage. A hand-me-down from his brother, the marquess."

"How is it you know everyone's business?" Violet wondered aloud.

"It's not so very difficult, my dear. One need only take an interest, open her eyes and ears, and use her head. I believe the viscount is in tight straits. Not only because of the second-hand carriage, but heavens, the state of his gardens. Your father nearly chokes every time we ride past."

"I'm surprised Father hasn't made his way over to set the garden to rights," Lily said.

"Don't think he hasn't considered it." Mum leaned her palms

on the windowsill, studying the passing coach. "Why, I do believe Lord Lakefield isn't alone."

Despite herself, Violet rose, one finger holding her place in the book. "And how do you know that?"

"The vehicle's curtains aren't drawn." Mum gave a happy gasp of discovery. "There's a child inside! And a woman!"

Idle curiosity brought Violet out of her chair—Francis Bacon could wait a moment, after all. She wandered toward the window to look out. But of course the carriage was only a blur.

Everything more than a few feet from Violet's eyes always looked like a blur. It was one reason she preferred staying at home with her books and news sheets, rather than going about to socialize with her mother and two younger sisters. She was afraid she'd embarrass herself by failing to recognize a friend across the room. Or by tripping. Which she did. Frequently.

"Well, well, well," Mum said. "I must go bring the lady a gift of perfume and welcome her to the neighborhood."

"You mean find out who she is," Violet said.

Her mother's second hobby was delivering perfume and receiving gossip in exchange. Not that anyone begrudged her the information. To the contrary, Chrystabel Ashcroft never needed to pry a word out of anyone. Warm and well-loved, she barely walked in the door before women began spilling their secrets.

On the rare occasions her mother had succeeded in dragging her along, Violet had seen it happen, her bad eyes notwithstanding.

"I wonder if the viscount has married?" Rose asked.

"I expect not," Mum said. "He's much too intellectual for anyone I know." As the carriage disappeared into the distance, she turned from the window. "Why, he's a member of that Royal Society, isn't he?"

"I believe so." Violet watched her mother wander back to the table, wishing she'd never mentioned wanting to attend a Royal Society lecture. The last thing she needed was Mum plotting her marriage. "Perhaps he would suit Rose or Lily."

"I think not." Mum sniffed the perfume in progress, then chose another vial. "I cannot imagine whom he would suit, but certainly not your sisters."

"It's just as well," Rose said, "since you're forbidden from matching us."

"You know the rules, Mum," Lily added.

The three sisters had a pact to save one another from their mother's matchmaking schemes. It was one thing—perhaps the only thing—they all agreed on.

"Heavens, girls. It's not as though I arrange marriages behind my friends' backs." *Everyone* Mum knew was her friend. Literally. And they all adored her. "All of my brides and grooms are willing—"

"Victims?" Violet broke in to supply.

"Participants," Mum countered.

Lily sat and retrieved her handiwork. "How many weddings have you arranged this year, Mum? Three? Four?"

"Five," their mother said with not a little pride. She tapped her fingernails on the vial. "Only seven months in, and a banner year already."

The sisters exchanged a look. "And all five of these couples," Violet ventured, "were fully cognizant and enthusiastic participants in your plans?"

Mum cocked her head. "I'm not sure what *cognizant* means. But enthusiastic, yes, all of them. And now blissfully happy, I might add."

Rose plopped back onto her own chair. "Bliss or no, you're not matching me up, Mum. I can find my own husband."

"Me, too," Lily said.

"Me three," Violet added.

"Of course you all can." Mum's graceful fingers stilled. "I wouldn't dream of meddling in my own daughters' lives."

THREE

"**N**URSE LYDIA SAID if it rains today, it will rain for forty days more." In the dim cabin of the carriage, Jewel cocked her raven head. "Do you believe that, Uncle Ford?"

"Of course not. It has no scientific basis in fact."

"I know a poem about it, though."

"Do you, now?"

A smile gracing her heart-shaped face, Jewel nodded. "Nurse Lydia taught it to me last year. And I still remember."

Ford threw a glance at the woman sitting across from them, but she was leaning against the window, sound asleep. "Will you quote it for me, then?" he asked Jewel.

She cleared her little throat.

> "St. Swithin's Day if thou dost rain
> For forty days it will remain
> St. Swithin's Day if thou be fair
> For forty days 'twill rain nae mair."

"That sounds more like something your Aunt Caithren would have taught you," Ford observed, thinking of his brother

Jason's lively Scottish wife with all her stories, superstitions, and verses.

"Maybe she did." Jewel turned to her caregiver. "Nurse Lydia, did you teach me the poem, or did Auntie Cait?" When Lydia didn't answer, the girl rose and reached across to poke her shoulder. "Nurse Lydia?" A frown creasing her forehead, Jewel sat down and looked at Ford. "She's sleeping."

"I can see that." Frowning himself, he put a finger to his lips. "Perhaps we should be quieter, then."

His niece surprised him by obediently settling back. He smiled. Maybe having her stay with him wouldn't be as bad as he'd thought. She was adorable, after all. And she seemed an agreeable sort. If only *all* women were as agreeable as Jewel, he thought, brooding over Tabitha's inexplicable betrayal.

Ford rubbed his temples. Women. Baffling creatures. Perhaps he was better off without them.

Rain pounded on the roof and streamed down the windows, an oddly comforting tattoo. Lulled by sound and motion, Ford's lids slid closed—then flew open when the carriage bumped into a rut. The nurse pitched forward, and he leapt to set her aright.

He jerked his hands away. She was burning up.

Her eyes opened, looking glazed, the pupils huge black voids.

"Nurse Lydia?" Ford raked his fingers back through his hair, his mind racing. If she was ill, what on earth would he do with Jewel? The nurse *couldn't* be ill. "Are you feeling unwell?"

"Hot," she mumbled. "Tired." Her eyes shut again.

Criminy, she *was* ill. An all too fitting development for an all too abominable day.

He had to get Jewel away from her.

Trying not to panic, he reached to shake Nurse Lydia awake. "Where are you from?"

She blinked, swayed, then managed to hold herself up by planting both hands on the bench seat. "G-Greystone, my lord."

"No, before that. Have you family, miss? Parents? Brothers or sisters?"

"Mama," she murmured. "In Woodlands Green." A soft, prolonged snore followed, nearly drowned out by the relentless rain.

She hadn't gone far from home to find employment, then—Woodlands Green wasn't more than half an hour south. Ford knocked on the roof, barely pausing for the carriage to stop before throwing open the door.

Without waiting for the steps to be lowered, he lifted Jewel and jumped down.

She let out a little squeal. "What are you doing, Uncle Ford?"

"Lakefield isn't far." He balanced her on a hip. "We're going to walk from here."

"In the rain? Mama says not to get cold and wet. You could fall ill." Her little forehead furrowed. "We could get measles."

"Staying with Nurse Lydia could give you measles. Besides, it's not cold. It's summer." Never mind that Jewel's teeth were chattering. Surprised to find himself feeling protective, he held her closer. "Can you tell me Nurse Lydia's surname?"

"Her what?"

"The part of her name that comes after Lydia." Huge drops splotched his brown surcoat and dripped from the brim of his hat. He shifted the girl on his hip. "Like in your name, Chase comes after Jewel."

She only cocked her small head, which was rapidly becoming soaked.

Taking a deep breath for patience, he tried again. "Your name is Jewel Chase. Nurse Lydia's name is...?"

"Nurse Lydia. Two names, just like mine."

He rolled his eyes heavenward before looking to his coachman. "Spalding, take the nursemaid to Woodlands Green and find her mother." Woodlands Green was tiny—even without a surname, it probably wasn't an onerous request. "And tell the woman to send for a physician, courtesy of the Earl of Greystone." He set his niece on her feet. "Lady Jewel and I have decided to walk home in this fine weather."

Jewel promptly slipped in the mud.

With a sigh, Ford picked her back up, wondering if things could get any worse.

FOUR

*T*HE NEXT MORNING, Ford awoke with an elbow in
his ribs.

"Hey!" Blinking blurred, itchy eyes, he pushed a little arm off
him for what had to be the dozenth time. He was exhausted.
Jewel had wiggled the entire night. When not nestled up against
him, or half on top of him, she'd been attacking him with various
limbs—she seemed to have at least eight of the things. Her tiny
toenails had left scratches in the vicinity of his knees. "Lie still,"
he growled, pressing the heels of his hands into his eyes.

He heard a whimper and suppressed a groan. Not the tears
again!

Tears were what had landed Jewel in his bed in the first
place. He'd breathed a sigh of relief after tucking her in last
night, only to find himself awakened by heartfelt sobs. Between
her hiccups and gulps, he'd gathered that last night had been the
first she'd ever spent away from her mother and father.

Ford couldn't blame a little girl for missing her parents. But if
he'd had any doubts he wasn't ready for marriage and a family,
they were gone by morning. Long gone.

His mind was made up: he was swearing off women. Even
the agreeable ones were a headache.

When Jewel sniffled, he turned his head to see her heart-shaped face cradled on the pillow beside him, her rosy cheeks damp with tears. More tears threatened to spill from her emerald-green eyes.

He pushed a clump of her thick black hair aside and felt her forehead. No fever, for which he was tremendously thankful. Illness was the last thing either of them needed.

"Come now, Jewel. It's morning, can you see?" He waved a hand toward the window, where yellow light shone through spaces between the crooked shutters. One more thing on his repair list.

At least the rain had stopped. So much for St. Swithin's prophecy.

"We'll have a nice day together, you'll see." One day. He could survive one more day. First, of course, he'd dash off a message to his brother, informing him Nurse Lydia had come down with the measles. Colin would send a replacement. Someone who knew Jewel. Someone who knew what to do.

Did you think I'd expect you to care for her on your own? Heaven forbid.

Ford realized his hands had fisted around the counterpane. He remembered Colin's sneer, the dismissal in his face. His brother thought so little of him. Thought him too irresponsible to entrust with his precious daughter. What did he think Ford would do? Forget to feed the girl? Perform an experiment on her? He wasn't an imbecile.

Meanwhile, his twin Kendra—also aged twenty-three—cared for two children of her own, *every single day*. Surely Ford could care for one measly child for a few short weeks. What did Kendra have that Ford didn't have?

He'd hated the feeling of being dismissed by a brother he looked up to.

And blast him if he'd prove the scoundrel right!

No, he wouldn't give Colin the satisfaction. He and Jewel would manage on their own. Somehow. It was only for a short time. If he was clever enough to invent a new type of watch, surely he could figure out how to handle his niece.

And next time, Colin would know better than to underestimate him.

With an ingratiating smile, he turned back to Jewel's sad little face. "Come now, baby."

"I'm not a baby."

"Of course you're not." He hadn't consciously used the endearment; it had simply slipped out of his mouth. "If you stop crying, I'll give you a shilling."

That did the trick. The tears ended, and she struggled to sit in his rumpled bed, apparently smarter than he'd given her credit for.

Thank goodness. A girl bright enough to be reasoned with. Never mind that his estate was in sad shape and he could ill afford to throw around bribes—he'd give Jewel his entire meager savings if it would ensure her cooperation.

He stared at the canopy above him, wondering when his blue bed-hangings had faded to gray. And if the old ropes that supported the mattress would hold, since his niece was jumping up and down on it now, exacerbating his headache.

"A shilling," she chanted in a sing-song voice, timing her words to her bounces. "A shilling. Will you take me shopping?" she asked breathlessly.

Not yet six years old and already eager to shop, he thought with an inward smile. Where did women learn this inclination? Was it in their chemical composition? "There aren't any shops nearby, but if you're good, after breakfast I'll show you my sundial."

She bounced once again to land on her bottom, then sat there in her twisted white nightgown, looking dubious.

"And later this week, I'll take you to the village."

"To shop?"

"Yes, to shop." The way things were going, she ought to have amassed a small fortune by then. He rolled over and swung his legs off the side of the bed, rubbing his face.

"Uncle Ford! I can see your knees!"

Blinking, he cast a glance over his shoulder. "Have you not seen your father's knees? And your brothers'?"

"Yes." She giggled. "But they're my family."

"I'm your uncle, which is family, too." Standing, the shirt covered him to mid-thigh. Should he have left his breeches on as well? He normally slept bare, but he supposed, for her sake, he'd have to keep himself clothed while she was here. He held little hope that she'd stay in her own bed at night.

Meaning he'd best brace himself for more long hours of nocturnal pummeling.

What had he done to deserve this?

As the youngest of four, he'd never had much to do with children, save as a charming uncle who bestowed the occasional coin or pat on the head. Whatever compelled people to desire these strange beings—and the headaches that went with them—was beyond him.

His clocks struck noon before he managed to coax some breakfast into her and get her dressed in a miniature pink confection of a gown whose fastenings he found perplexing. He was itching to work on his watch design, but she hadn't forgotten about the sundial.

Although St. Swithin's clouds and rain would have better matched his mood, the day was warm and sunny when they finally stepped outdoors. A fluffy white rabbit blinked at Jewel, then took off toward the Thames. She bounded after it, but Ford followed more slowly, feeling the effects of the sleepless night.

Perhaps he would have to hire more servants. He gave an inward sigh, knowing such an expense would *really* push his budget. Although he'd been granted the title and Lakefield estate as a boy, shortly after King Charles's restoration, he'd never really lived here. By the time he'd come of age to set up his own household, the neglected manor house had deteriorated enough to send him running in the other direction. The mere idea of such an enormous renovation project was overwhelming. So, between Oxford terms, he'd lived in the family's London town house or at Cainewood Castle with his older brother Jason, the Marquess of Cainewood, which left him free to pour what income the estate produced into his laboratory. Someday he'd have to fix up Lakefield House, most likely when he succumbed to marriage. But "someday" had always seemed far, far in the future.

He hadn't left the manor unoccupied, of course, but the elderly couple who cared for the place—and cooked for him on the rare occasions he visited—was no match for a five-year-old's energy. If he wanted assistance, he was going to have to hire it. Perhaps the "shopping" trip to the village would come sooner rather than later. He could shop for a nursemaid and household help while Jewel shopped for whatever little girls bought with their shillings. Ribbons, he imagined, already dreading the daunting task of fixing her hair.

"Uncle Ford! Where is it?"

He looked up, noticing Jewel had wandered back while he wasn't watching. He hadn't been watching at all, as a matter of fact. She could have fallen into the river.

He heaved an internal sigh. He would have to be more vigilant.

"Have you lost the rabbit?" he asked.

"No." She giggled. "Well, yes, but I meant the sundial. I cannot find it."

Egad, where had it gone to?

He paced the garden, which was utterly overgrown. Green and wild, plants and vines intertwined with weeds, all semblance of order gone. Jewel ran after him, her short legs no match for his long strides. The sundial had been in the middle of a circle of hedges and wooden benches...

"Ah, here it is!" He pushed his way through a ring of bushes that seemed to have grown together. The benches he'd remembered were covered with vines. In the center of the mess, he yanked at some greenery and brushed dirt off the carved stone surface of the sundial. "Under here."

He turned to see her beaming up at him as though he were a genius, melting his heart. "How does it work, Uncle Ford?"

He reached to lift her over the bushes. "Well, you see—"

"Good afternoon, my lord."

A warm, melodic voice. He turned and frowned at the owner, who stood at the edge of the hedge circle. Although he had a feeling the pleasant-looking matron wasn't quite a stranger, he couldn't for the life of him place her.

She plucked two stray twigs off her bright yellow skirts, then raised a groomed brow. "So nice to have you in residence. Trentingham Manor can seem lonely when all our neighbors are away in the City."

Mystery solved. Trentingham. As in *Earl of*. The neighboring estate.

Still holding his niece, Ford executed an awkward bow. "Pleased to be here, Lady Trentingham."

When her wide mouth curved up, her brown eyes smiled to match. Plainly curious, her gaze flicked to Jewel before focusing again on him. "Will you be staying long?"

"Just while I finish a project." And until he felt up to showing his face in London. He pushed his way back through the hedge and set Jewel on her feet, grimacing as he brushed leaves from his breeches.

The countess shot a glance down the side of the house—he noticed the paint was peeling—to where her carriage waited, a coachman sitting up top. The door was open, and someone waited inside as well, enjoying the sunny day. A lady's maid, if he could judge by the woman's starched white cap.

"Pretty lady," Jewel said, staring up at his neighbor.

"Why, thank you, Miss…"

"Jewel," the girl supplied.

"Lady Jewel," Ford clarified. "My brother's daughter."

"Ah," Lady Trentingham murmured. Some of the confusion cleared from her face. "I'm glad of your acquaintance," she said with a graceful curtsy, for all the world like they were meeting in Whitehall Palace.

Jewel mimicked the motion. "I'm glad of your ac-ac—"

"Acquaintance," Ford said helpfully.

But apparently Jewel didn't take it that way. She fixed him with a malevolent green glare. "I can say it."

"Of course you can." Palms forward, he took a small step back. "Forgive me."

"All right." She turned to the woman, focusing on something in her hand. "What's that?"

"Don't point, baby," Ford said. Though his twin sister forever accused him of being oblivious, he did know his manners.

Lady Trentingham knelt by Jewel's side. "It's a bottle of perfume. I brought it for the lady of the house. And I suppose"— she looked to Ford for confirmation—"that's you?"

He nodded his agreement as Jewel squealed. "For me?"

"For you, sweetheart. Would you like to smell it?"

"Oh, yes," his niece breathed. She waited, dancing from foot to foot while the woman removed the stopper and handed her the bottle.

Jewel waved it under her nose. "It's lovely, my lady!" Tipping the bottle, she wet her fingers and dabbed the potion on her neck, wetting some of the overgrown greenery in the process.

"You must use only a little," Lady Trentingham warned her, "or you'll smell like a field of flowers."

"I like flowers."

"Then you must come and visit Trentingham Manor." She rose to her feet, smiling at Ford. "My husband enjoys gardening."

"I've heard that of the earl." Everyone had heard that of the earl. And standing in his own shambles of a garden, knowing what Lady Trentingham and her husband must think every time they saw it, made Ford want to squirm.

"Who is caring for Lady Jewel?" the countess asked.

"I am, now. Her nursemaid fell ill, so I sent her home."

"Alone?"

"No, with my coachman and two outriders."

Amusement flickered on her face. "I meant, are you caring for Lady Jewel on your own?"

"Oh." Feeling thickheaded, he cleared his throat. "I suppose I am."

"And how are you getting along?"

His neighbor had a straightforward way about her that Ford found refreshing. Heaven knew Tabitha hadn't been so.

"Well, I've had Jewel for..." He twisted around to peer at the sundial. "...it's going on eighteen hours. And no disaster has befallen her yet, so although I haven't managed to find time for anything else, I reckon I'm doing all right."

Lady Trentingham's laughter tinkled through the tangled vegetation. Her gaze turned contemplative. "I have a son."

"Do you?" he prompted, feeling more thickheaded still.

"Rowan. He's six years of age, and his favorite playmate is away from home for the month—perhaps I'll bring him over to play. That might give you a bit of a respite."

"A *boy*?" Jewel interjected.

"A kind one," the woman assured her. "He doesn't have maggots."

Jewel looked dubious. But she also looked lonely. And as far as Ford was concerned, Lady Trentingham could be his savior. An angel sent from heaven. A fairy come to wave her wand and sprinkle magic dust.

"I shall bring Rowan tomorrow," she decided. "He has lessons in the morning, but perhaps after dinner."

"He's welcome for dinner," Ford offered. Breakfast and supper, too. Anything to keep his niece occupied so he could work. He was so close to finishing his design...

He must have looked as desperate as he felt, because his neighbor released a tiny, unladylike snort.

"After dinner," she confirmed, hiding a smile as she turned to make her way back to her carriage.

$\sim$

"*H*OW DID IT GO, milady?" Anne asked Chrystabel as the coach set off for Trentingham.

"Fine," she assured her maid.

Perfect, she added silently.

Now she just had to make plans to keep both Rose and Lily busy tomorrow. As well as herself. Violet—her wonderful, willful, bookish daughter Violet—would be the one to take Rowan to visit Lady Jewel.

Picking dead vegetation off her skirts, Chrystabel smiled. She'd met young Ford Chase before, but this visit had confirmed it. If ever a perfect husband existed for Violet, it was the charming, slightly preoccupied but ambitious Lord Lakefield. These two needed each other.

Her daughters were dead set against her arranging their marriages, and well Chrystabel knew it.

But a resourceful mother could always find a way.

FIVE

"*P*LEASE WAIT, Margaret," Violet told her lady's maid the next afternoon. "If all goes well, I'm going to leave Rowan here and come back for him later."

She stepped down from the carriage and grumbled all the way to the front door of the large, if shabby, Lakefield House. She couldn't fathom how she'd ended up here, escorting her reluctant young brother to play with a strange little girl.

Mum's convoluted explanation had made sense at the time, but how was it that suddenly Rose and Lily both needed to be measured for gowns, and she didn't? True, she hadn't been clamoring for new clothes like they had—she'd never really cared about such things—but Mum had always been careful to treat her three girls evenly.

At the bottom of the chipped stone stairs that led to the entry, she pulled Rowan out of the bushes where he was hiding. He promptly scurried to hide behind *her* instead. With a sigh, she mounted the steps and raised the knocker.

Before she had a chance to bang it down, the door swung open, and she stumbled forward and nearly fell into the house. She was saved from that indignity by someone's hands clasping her shoulders. Warm hands, keeping her upright. They belonged to a young man—a footman?—and when she looked up, his face was only inches from hers. She nearly gasped.

In all her life, she'd seen relatively few men up close—close enough to *see* with her poor vision. And this one was quite literally the most beautiful man she'd ever seen.

A distant part of her recalled that she ought to speak, but the rest was busy sinking into brilliant blue eyes. "I—I'm—" Backing away a little, she cleared her throat and tried again. "I'm here to see Lord Lakefield—"

"At your service." The stranger bowed. "Ford Chase," he added with a wide, winning smile that made her stomach feel odd. "And you are...?"

This was the viscount?

He couldn't be. "You're not wearing a periwig," she said nonsensically.

"Pardon?" He blinked. "I never wear wigs. I don't care for them."

She supposed her father often went wigless out here in the countryside, but—never? She squinted at the stranger, realizing he wasn't wearing a footman's livery, either. She'd been but twelve or thirteen the last time she'd met Lord Lakefield, and all she really remembered of the encounter was long, untidy dark hair and a distracted manner.

This fellow *did* seem rather distracted. He raked impatient fingers through his hair—still dark, but no longer untidy.

And those eyes. She'd never noticed Lord Lakefield's eyes... well, she'd probably never been close enough to properly see them. Aristotle had said that beauty was the gift of God. She wondered what this man could have done to be so deserving of the Lord's favor.

"And you are...?" he repeated.

She shook her head to clear it. "Violet Ashcroft."

"The Earl of Trentingham's daughter?" He looked somewhat perplexed. "I expected your mother."

"Well, you have *me*." She was regaining her equilibrium. She was, after all, a very levelheaded young woman. "And this is my brother, Rowan, who has come to claim the pleasure of meeting young Lady Jewel."

The pleasure of meeting young Lady Jewel? Why, she was babbling like a featherbrained courtier. Drawing a deep breath, she pulled her brother from behind her skirts.

The viscount gave him a proper, grave nod. "Pleased to meet you, Lord...?"

"Tremayne," Violet supplied, since Rowan seemed unlikely to say anything. "He's Viscount Tremayne. But you can just call him Rowan."

Much more stoically than normal, Rowan bowed.

"Uncle Ford!" A little girl came bounding up to the door, skidding to a stop on the dull wood floor. "Who is here?" The moment her gaze fastened on Rowan, Violet knew her brother was in trouble. "You must be that boy the pretty lady told me about." She glanced up at her uncle, appearing both surprised and pleased. "He's like *me*! I like him!"

While the two children did share similar coloring—jet-black hair and deep green eyes—the girl's enthusiasm was enough to send Rowan skittering behind Violet again.

Following him, Lady Jewel poked him on the shoulder. "What're you hiding for, huh? Don't you want to play?"

"No," Rowan muttered. His fingers clawed at Violet's skirts. Sensing his panic, she feared it would be only a matter of seconds before he found his way underneath.

Lord Lakefield also wore a look of panic, though she couldn't fathom why. "Do come in," he urged, taking Violet quite improperly by the arm. Before the door shut behind her, she shot a helpless look back at the blur that was her maid Margaret in the carriage.

She hadn't intended to go inside.

But here she was. Still gripping her arm, the viscount fairly hauled her down a passageway whose paneling was so worn that even with her bad eyes she could tell it needed refinishing.

Behind her, Rowan held on like a drowning man clutching a life preserver. He was literally dragging his heels.

Evidently undeterred, Lady Jewel chattered cheerfully as she walked along beside him. "How old are you? Your mother said you were six. Are you six? I'm almost six. When's your birthday? Mine's next week. Mama said we would have a celebration. But now she's ill."

"I'm sorry to hear that," Violet replied, since it was clear Rowan wouldn't. Her heels clicked on the wood-planked floor. She could feel the warmth of the viscount's fingers through her indigo broadcloth sleeve.

"Papa promised me she'd get well," Lady Jewel said. "And he always keeps his promises."

They turned into a drawing room decorated in various shades of red and pink. Or perhaps they'd once all been matching crimson, but some pieces had faded.

Lord Lakefield dropped Violet's arm and waved her toward a couch. She pried Rowan's hands from her skirts in order to sit, and he dropped cross-legged to the floor, his gaze on his lap.

What were they doing here? Violet wondered, nervously twirling the end of her plait. Rowan was clearly miserable, and she hadn't planned on staying in the first place.

"Make yourself comfortable," Lord Lakefield told her. "I'll go ask for some refreshments. I rigged up a bell"—he gestured toward the wall where she assumed it was placed—"but I'm afraid my staff is getting on in years. They're a bit hard of hearing."

Dazed, Violet nodded. "So is my father."

"Oh?"

"He's half deaf. Although my sister sometimes claims he just doesn't want to listen to whatever theory I'm spouting at the moment."

Faith, she was babbling more than Lady Jewel.

"Theory?" Lord Lakefield blinked. "*You're* interested in science?"

"Philosophy, actually."

"Oh." Something indecipherable flickered in his eyes. "I'm certain whatever you have to say must be fascinating. If you'll excuse me." And with that, he took his long, lanky form out the door.

She rose and wandered over to see where he'd pointed. A pull cord disappeared cleverly into a hole, attached, she assumed, to a bell. Her ears were still ringing with his words.

"Fascinating..." she murmured to no one in particular. Apparently the viscount was trying to flatter her. No man ever thought a woman discussing philosophy was fascinating.

But what could he be hoping to gain?

"Well," she said aloud, glad she had the common sense to recognize an empty compliment, "Jean de La Fontaine has written that all flatterers live at the expense of those who listen to them."

Lady Jewel blinked. "Huh?" She shook her head, then knelt on the floor next to Rowan. "Do you think I'm pretty?" she asked.

SIX

_F_ORD HURRIED to the kitchen, not least because he
had a feeling Violet Ashcroft was poised to bolt.
And he couldn't allow that to happen.

Philosophy. Truth be told, he loathed the discipline—if one
could even call the study of unprovable and oft indecipherable
prattle _a discipline._ But at least this Violet seemed to have a keen
brain in her head, which was uncommon, in his experience. Not
that the ladies he knew were simpleminded, but he tended to
gravitate toward girls of the fun and frilly variety. To be perfectly
honest, after a long day at his studies or in his laboratory, he was
seeking a diversion, not a fellow academic.

Tabitha, for instance, had been a lovely diversion. But a
diversion was the last thing Ford needed just now, and as he'd
come to realize he couldn't avoid all of womankind entirely, he'd
decided to limit his female contacts to those who proved practical. Hilda, for example—his housekeeper—was a useful woman
to have around.

And as for Lady Violet...

With her thick, chocolate-brown plait and eyes the color of
his favorite brandy, Violet was nice-looking, although not the
sort of beauty who would turn heads. Which was fine with him,

since he wanted his head right where it was, thank you: square on his shoulders, where he could use it to concentrate on his work.

If he could convince Lady Violet to stay a while and maybe even come back with Rowan tomorrow, perhaps he could finally sneak away to his laboratory. In which case he'd have to admit that his twin, Kendra, was right—ladies *were* good for more than just flirting and adorning one's arm.

Though not to her face, of course.

As he barged into the kitchen, his housekeeper looked up from polishing the silver, one gray eyebrow raised in query. "Yes, my lord?"

"Are the refreshments ready?"

Hilda never answered a question—she always had one of her own. "Is Lady Trentingham here?"

"No," he said, wondering where Harry, Hilda's husband, had gone off to this time. The two of them might be servants, but their marriage mimicked most of the aristocracy's—which was to say they stayed as far from each other as possible.

"Lady Trentingham is at home," he told her. "The countess's daughter came instead. Lady Violet."

"The sensible one?"

"Come again?" Spotting a tray of biscuits on the kitchen's scarred wooden worktable, he inched his way over.

"The oldest, yes? Lady Trentingham calls her 'the sensible one.' The middle girl—Rose, I believe—is 'the wild one,' and the youngest, Lily, is 'the sweet one.'"

"She has three daughters? All named for flowers?" How absurd.

"Are you not aware that her husband enjoys gardening?"

"Yes. I am." He slid one of the small, round biscuits off the tray and popped it into his mouth. Mmm, cinnamon. Dusting crumbs off his fingers, he clasped his hands behind his back and began to pace. "How do you come to know all this?"

Hilda frowned. "Why shouldn't I know my neighbors?" She

shoved at a gray hair that had escaped her cap, then went back to polishing the silver. "Lady Trentingham, she's a perfumer, you know. Every once in a while, she drops by with a new bottle. Spiced Rosewater, I prefer."

"Spiced Rosewater?" He paused to reach for another biscuit.

She slapped at his hand. "Leave it, will you? I laid them out in a pattern."

He scrutinized the tray, but his mathematical mind could discern no regular design.

"Do you not like Spiced Rosewater?" she asked.

He leaned close to a wrinkled cheek and sniffed. "It's lovely." In truth, she smelled like one of her cinnamon biscuits. But whatever made her happy.

"When Lady Trentingham brings the perfume, she likes to sit a spell and chat. I've heard all the stories of her girls as they've grown."

"Lady Trentingham sits and talks to the household help?"

"And why not? We're people too, you know."

Of course they were—he just didn't think about it much. And he was woefully ill informed about his neighbors. It seemed Lady Trentingham was well-nigh as eccentric as the earl.

"Here comes Harry," Hilda said, watching out the window. "Don't you think it's time to serve these refreshments?" She shoved a steaming pitcher into Ford's hands and, taking the tray of biscuits, hurried out of the kitchen before her husband could make his way in.

Hilda came up to Ford's shoulder and seemed as wide as she was tall. Obediently carrying the hot beverage she'd prepared, he followed her ample behind down the corridor to the drawing room. They stepped inside to see Violet Ashcroft on her hands and knees, her bottom jutting into the air beneath its layers of petticoats and sturdy, serviceable skirts. Which weren't frilly in the least. A fitting gown for The Sensible One.

Even through all that fabric, Ford could tell she had a rather nice bottom. Especially compared to his housekeeper's.

He frowned, mentally clamping down on his thoughts. He wasn't supposed to be noticing *any* female's bottom. He was supposed to be appreciating women for their practical uses only.

Lady Violet's brother was under the low, square table that sat before the couch. "Rowan," she said. "You come out here this minute."

"No." The boy crossed his arms, not a simple feat given he was lying on his belly. "Not until *she* leaves."

"C'mon, Rowan," Jewel cooed, getting down on her knees herself. "Come out and play. I've always wanted to play with a boy."

Knowing Jewel had two brothers at home, Ford choked back laughter. And she wasn't pronouncing *boy* at all the same way she had yesterday in the garden.

His niece was clearly in love.

And Rowan was having none of it.

"We've brought biscuits," Ford declared, announcing his presence. Lady Violet gave a little embarrassed squeal and jumped to her feet. Her pinkened cheeks matched his faded upholstery.

"Biscuits?" Rowan asked. "What kind?"

Ford grinned. Little boys were so much easier than girls. "Cinnamon," he said.

"I'm still not coming out," Rowan said.

"Would you like a drink of chocolate?" Hilda coaxed, taking the warm pitcher from Ford's hands.

"Chocolate?" The boy inched forward. "Real chocolate?"

"He cannot have it," his sister said firmly. "Chocolate gives him hives."

Rowan crawled closer and bumped his head on the apron of the table. "Ah, Violet…"

She reached to grab him by the wrist. "Got you, you little monster." She dragged him out. "Now, I cannot blame you for being intimidated, but you must mind your manners. Guests don't hide under tables."

"I want to go home."

"Guests don't say things like that, either. It's very rude."

Jewel rose, brushing off the mint green skirts that Ford had spent half an hour struggling her into. "Here." She offered Rowan a biscuit, and he reluctantly climbed to his feet. "Eat this, and then I'll show you Uncle Ford's laboratory."

"No you won't," Ford said. Not again. He'd taken her to his laboratory yesterday afternoon, hoping she'd sit quietly while he worked. Ten minutes later he'd hauled her out—just before she'd managed to destroy the place.

"Please, Uncle Ford?"

"No."

"Puleeeeeze?" The look in Jewel's green eyes bordered on pathetic. Chase eyes, like Kendra's. Just what he needed... another Chase lady who could wrap him around her little finger.

She must have realized her feminine wiles were working, because she turned her lavish charm on Rowan. "You must stay," she told him. "Uncle Ford has magnets, and bottles of smelly stuff, and a pen-pen—"

"Pendulum," Ford supplied, remembering too late that she didn't like to be helped.

But she was so intent on convincing Rowan, she failed to take notice. "Yes, a pen-du-lum. And lots of clocks and a telescope. That's a thing to see the stars."

"Is it?" Lady Violet asked, interest lighting her eyes. "I've never really seen the stars."

Scant moments ago, she'd looked like she was ready to haul Rowan home. Not that Ford could blame her, but his own sanity depended on Jewel successfully befriending the boy. He had to keep the Ashcrofts here. Whatever it took.

He wouldn't go crawling back to his brother for help.

"I think Rowan might find my laboratory interesting," he said with an inward grimace. "And although the telescope cannot help you see stars in the daytime, if you stay until dark—"

"I cannot stay until dark!" Violet exclaimed with a horrified gasp.

Criminy, these sheltered country girls. Ford had never met a lady so stuck on propriety—since, of course, such a lady would have been laughed out of King Charles's court.

He kept those thoughts to himself. "Shall we invite your maid in to chaperone?"

She shook her head. "I wasn't planning to stay at all. I had thought to introduce Rowan and then leave—"

"Leave me?" Rowan interrupted, looking even more horrified than she had. "I told Mum I didn't want to come here!" He turned to his sister, burying his face in her dark blue skirts. "Would you really leave me, Violet?"

She patted him on the head. "Of course not. You must have misunderstood me." She glared at Ford as though to say, *This is all your fault.* And he knew, then and there, that his happy visions of working while she and her brother entertained his niece were just that—visions.

Lady Trentingham's fairy dust wasn't going to work. Violet's mother wasn't his savior, and her suggestion that the children play together wasn't the answer to his prayers. As a man of science, he should have known better than to imagine such flights of fancy, even for a moment.

Lady Violet wouldn't prove useful to him, after all.

SEVEN

$\mathcal{T}$HE NEXT MORNING, Ford managed to get Jewel up and dressed by nine o'clock, at a cost of only two shillings. He was getting much better at this child care business. A good thing, because his dreams of hiring additional help had been dashed last night.

A letter from his solicitor had arrived, hinting at financial concerns and asking for a meeting in London at Ford's earliest convenience.

Egad, he thought—it certainly wasn't convenient now. Maybe after his niece went home. In the meantime, the two of them were getting along famously this morning. Having learned what she preferred for breakfast—bread and cheese, with warm chocolate to drink—he no longer had to pay her to eat at all.

Now, if only he could bribe that little Rowan fellow to play with the girl, life would be rosy. True, after he'd suggested they stay into the evening, Lady Violet had hurried her brother home so fast she'd tripped over his threshold on her way out. But today was a new day, and he'd awakened with a new determination.

Desperation bred courage and ingenuity.

Getting the children together hadn't been Violet's idea, he

reasoned, but Lady Trentingham's. Perhaps the mother would be willing to try again. That goal in mind, he settled Jewel in front of him on his horse and began riding toward Trentingham Manor.

"What do you call her?" she asked.

"Why, my lady, of course. I would have to be much more familiar with her to use her given name."

Jewel's little hands tightened on his where he held her around the waist. "You're not fa-mil-i-ar with your horse? That's sad. Papa is friends with *his* horse."

"My horse?" He was feeling thickheaded again. Women always seemed to do that to him, to his constant irritation. "Of course I know my horse. But he's not a her. He's a boy."

"Oh." His niece was silent a moment as they reached the Thames and turned to ride alongside it. "What do you call him, then?"

"Galileo."

"Gali-who?"

"Galileo. Have you never heard of him? He was born in the last century, though he lived into this one."

"Was he a horse?"

"No." Ford choked back a laugh. "He was an astronomer and a physicist and a mathematician."

"That sounds boring."

"Oh, but it isn't." Sunlight glimmered off the water, a beautiful morning to visit. Ford was sure this encounter would end better than yesterday's. "Galileo invented a horse-driven water pump, and a military compass, and something called a thermometer that measures hot and cold. And a much better telescope than the one invented before it."

"Like the one in your laboratory?"

"Well, that one is called a reflecting telescope. It's a newer one, invented by another man named Isaac Newton, only about five years ago. But he wouldn't have invented it if Galileo hadn't invented *his* telescope first. That's the way science works.

And with his telescope, Galileo discovered moons around Jupiter—"

"Auntie Kendra told me about Jupiter. But not moons."

"She was talking about the Roman god." Knowing his twin's love of mythology, she'd likely traumatized the poor girl with bloody tales of Jupiter slaying wretched souls with his thunderbolts. "I'm talking about the planet."

"Like Earth?"

"But much bigger. I can show you with my telescope. And I can show you Saturn, too, which has rings around it. Galileo was the first to notice those."

"That doesn't sound boring."

Behind her, he smiled. "It's riveting, I assure you. Did you know all the planets go around the sun?"

"Mama told me that."

"Well, another man named Nicolas Copernicus thought so first, but Galileo wrote a book to explain it."

"Galileo is lucky," she said. "Your horse, I mean. To be named after a special man." She leaned forward to stroke the animal's jet-black mane, which matched her own dark, wavy tresses. "Rowan is named for a tree."

"Did he tell you so?"

"No. He wouldn't talk to me." Ford could hear the pout in her voice. "But when you were out of the room, his sister told me that in her family, the girls are named for flowers and the boy is named for a tree."

"That's because their father loves to garden," he told her as Trentingham Manor came into view.

A wide lawn studded with shade trees sat between the river and the sprawling, red-brick mansion, its uneven skyline and irregular patterned brickwork the result of a century of alterations. In the extensive gardens set around it, Ford spotted a well-dressed man fiddling with a rose bush.

"In fact," he said, "I'd wager that's Lord Trentingham there now."

Ford hadn't seen the Earl of Trentingham in quite a few years, but as they rode nearer, he could see where Rowan had inherited his looks. The earl's dark hair glistened in the warm summer sun. He looked up, raising a hand to swipe at his receding, sweat-slicked hairline.

"Who goes there?" he asked when Ford reined in beside him.

"Viscount Lakefield, my lord. Ford Chase." Ford slid off Galileo, taking Jewel with him. "And this is my niece, Lady Jewel Chase." The moment he set her on her feet, she raced to a nearby fountain and thrust her hands into the spurting water.

The earl narrowed his green eyes. "Eh?"

"A long time since we've met, my lord." Smiling, Ford held out a hand.

Though the man shook it warmly, he still looked perplexed. "What? What did you say?"

Too late Ford remembered Violet had mentioned her father was hard of hearing. "Ford Chase!" he fairly yelled. "I'm glad to see you!"

Jewel splashed herself in the face as her eyes popped open wide. Then she giggled, and her lips parted in a grin. "Jewel Chase!" she shouted, clearly thinking it was a game.

The earl bowed. "I'm glad of your acquaintance, young lady!" he hollered back.

"Joseph!" Lady Trentingham rounded the corner of the mansion. "How many times must I remind you the rest of us can hear just fine?" Laughing softly, she came close and kissed him on the cheek. "You forgot your hat," she added, plopping a wide-brimmed specimen on his head.

"My thanks, love." Apparently grateful for the shade, the earl clipped a blood-red bloom and presented it to his wife with a flourish.

"Just what I needed," she murmured. But the smile she sent her husband was genuine.

"I'm wearing your perfume," Jewel piped up.

The countess turned to her. "Well, then, come closer, and let me see if it's the right scent for such a lovely girl."

Jewel ran right over, wiping her wet palms on her dress. "Do I smell good?"

Lady Trentingham leaned down and sniffed. "You smell glorious."

A radiant smile transformed Jewel's face. "Will Rowan like it, do you think?"

"She's rather fond of your son," Ford said.

"So my daughter told me." Lady Trentingham's eyes danced as she looked up at him. "She also told me the feeling was less than mutual."

"I'm afraid she was right," he lamented. "And I was so hoping the children would get along."

"I'd wager you were." She looked contemplative. "Men, you know, they sometimes take a while to come around." Her husband had resumed puttering about, but her gaze on him was unmistakably affectionate. "My Rowan takes after his father, I'm afraid, but I'm sure, given time, he'll come to appreciate this delightful young lady."

Ford watched as Jewel went back to the fountain, sighing when she splashed her dress. Another change of clothing in his future. He could already hear Hilda complaining about the additional laundry and ironing. And him having nothing to do but listen, because he couldn't get a stitch of work done with a child running loose.

"Lady Trentingham…" Desperation setting in, he favored her with one of his most charming smiles. "Do you suppose your son might give Jewel another chance?"

EIGHT

*P*ERCHING A KNEE on one of the window seats in the gold-and-cream-toned drawing room, Violet peered out the window at the blur she knew was the viscount and her parents.

"What do you think they're saying?" she asked her sisters.

Rose pressed closer to the panes, fussing with a floral arrangement she'd set in the window niche. "They seem to be discussing that little girl who's playing in the fountain."

"Lady Jewel," Violet said. "The one I told you about who fancies herself in love with Rowan."

Lily's fingers idled over the harpsichord keys, producing a soft, slow melody. "How sweet."

"How absurd," Rose countered. "She's too young to be in love. Unlike me." She patted her deep chestnut curls. "I say, that gentleman out there looks rather fine. Although a bit lanky, don't you think?"

"He's too intellectual for you anyhow," Violet snapped, then wondered why she should suddenly be so short-tempered. " Does Mum look like she's pleased to see them?"

Lily didn't miss a note as she looked up and out the window. "Very."

Rose leaned her hands on the sill. "Now Lord Lakefield has lifted the girl, and Mum is running a finger down her cheek." She turned to Violet. "I think she must like her...do you suppose Mum's already matchmaking for *Rowan*?"

Rose sounded genuinely worried that their six-year-old brother might beat her to the altar. Which only made Violet want to shake some sense into the foolish girl.

Patience. Rose was a master-level course in patience.

"Well," Violet said after a deep breath, "she's not going to get me to take Rowan to Lakefield again. He was miserable." The blurred figures were getting bigger. "Faith. They're coming inside. All of them. Even Father."

The music stopped as Lily stood, looking puzzled. "Why shouldn't they come inside?"

"I...no reason." The sudden quiet was unsettling. Violet drew a deep breath and found herself smoothing her russet skirts, which wasn't like her. She pulled her plait forward to drape over one shoulder and twirled the end fitfully, then dropped her hand as Lady Jewel bounded into the room ahead of the adults.

The girl skidded to a stop on the carpeted floor, backing Violet against the window seat in her enthusiasm. "Lady Violet!" Throwing her arms wide, she hugged her around the knees. "Where's Rowan?"

"Having his lessons." Looking down into that little heart-shaped face, Violet couldn't help but be charmed. "Would you care to meet my sisters? This is Lady Rose and Lady Lily."

"I'm pleased to make your ac-quain-tance," Jewel said quite properly. Violet's sisters exchanged an amused glance as the girl bobbed a curtsy. "This room is very fancy," she said.

It was, Violet supposed, though having lived here most of her life, she didn't think about it much. They stood on a lovely gold-and-cream-toned Oriental carpet. The room's dark oak paneling was studded with gold rosettes, the ceiling's cornice heavily carved and gilded, the furniture upholstered in gold-and-cream silk damask. From where she stood, the details looked fuzzy, but she'd seen it all up close.

"Why, thank you," Mum said from the doorway.

Jewel rocked up on her toes. "When will Rowan be finished with his schooling?"

"Later today, I'm afraid. He has another lesson after dinner."

"Arithmetic," Rose said. "He hates it."

"A *fifth* picnic, you say?" Her father looked to Mum with a frown. "And right after dinner? I know a growing boy needs plenty to eat, Chrysanthemum, but surely—"

"Arithmetic," Mum repeated loudly, laying a hand on Father's arm. "We were talking about Rowan's schooling, and how he hates mathematics." Barely suppressing a smile, she turned back to their guests. "Poor Rowan. I've promised him a sweet after the lesson."

Jewel tugged on her uncle's sleeve. "Can Rowan come to *our* house for a sweet? Oh, puleeeeeze?"

Lord Lakefield grinned down at his niece, a grin Violet suddenly wished were aimed at her instead. It was broad and white and utterly sincere, extending all the way to his brilliant blue eyes. "Excellent idea, baby," he said.

When Mum smiled, Violet could see it coming.

Oh, no.

Trying to look casual, Violet wandered over to a wall and leaned against the dark paneling, then shot straight when one of the gold rosette studs jabbed her in the behind. "I don't believe Rowan will be interested," she blurted out, not nearly as composed as she'd planned.

Mum's smile only widened. "I'm sure Rowan would love to visit for a sweet," she said to Lord Lakefield, as though Violet hadn't spoken. "Will three o'clock suit you? Madame is due here this afternoon for another fitting for Lily and Rose, but Violet will be happy to bring him."

Jewel jumped up and down.

"What?" Father asked loudly. "What was that about gingham?"

When Violet made a pained noise, no one took heed.

NINE

*I*N THE THREE hours since Ford and Jewel had arrived back at Lakefield, his niece had suddenly become very thick with Harry, Ford's elderly houseman. Although Ford knew better than to hope that the old man and girl would become fast friends, he'd jumped at the chance for a brief respite. Now, settled in his attic laboratory, he paused to listen to little giggles floating through the open window.

"Yes," he heard Harry say, "this is perfect. It's the exact color of the upholstery."

Were they redecorating? Ford wondered vaguely.

"Oh, good!" The sound of clapping hands accompanied Jewel's childish voice. "We must hurry, then, so there will be time for it to start drying. And we need something fun to put at his place, so he won't be looking."

"Brilliant, Lady Jewel. I've just the thing..."

Their voices faded around a corner of the manor. Ford shook his head. Whatever they were doing to his house, they couldn't possibly make it look worse. Deciding to ignore them, he refocused on the tiny, intricate gears laid out on his worktable. Finally, he had some peace and quiet.

Watches were so inefficient—the single hand only approximated the hour. Within the last few years, another hand had been added to clocks, one that ticked off the minutes and made time-keeping much more precise. But since watches weren't pendulum-driven, the mechanism that drove a clock's minute hand wouldn't work inside them.

Yet it should be possible to add a minute hand to a watch. A more accurate personal timepiece would be practical, functional —a true benefit to mankind. And after months of trial and error, of scrapped designs and precise calculations and late nights, he was so close to making it work. So close to accomplishing something *useful*...

"Your guests have arrived, my lord." Bustling in, Hilda started flicking a dust rag at his various instruments. "Don't you think you should be downstairs?"

~

*R*OWAN CLINGING to her skirts, Violet followed Jewel toward Lord Lakefield's dining room, wondering how it was that Mum had talked her into dragging the poor boy here again.

And her maid Margaret hadn't even come along this time! Mum had given the woman half a day off. Margaret was being courted, and Mum—who had introduced her to the "nice footman" from a neighboring estate—thought this a perfect chance for the maid to spend some time with her beau.

How very like Mum to risk her own daughter's reputation for the sake of someone else's romance. *Question Convention*, indeed. Sometimes, Violet thought, the Ashcrofts took their motto a bit too seriously.

Most of Lakefield had seen better days, but the dining room struck Violet as particularly dreary. The paneling was so dark it appeared nearly black, and although the built-in cupboards boasted glass in the doors, very few dishes were displayed inside. The room's color scheme was an uninspiring mélange of browns. Everything was clean, though—the viscount had a decent housekeeper in Hilda.

"Here, Rowan," Jewel said brightly as they entered. "Sit here." She pulled out one of the faded tan chairs. "Right here. I put a toy here for you."

"At the table?" Violet asked.

"Uncle Ford lets me play at the table. As long as I leave him to his thoughts."

Violet would lay odds Jewel's parents didn't feel the same way. But she smiled as she watched her brother race to the chair and claim the toy, a cup and ball.

"Rowan..." she prompted.

"My thanks," he murmured absently, making the ball fly up and catching it in the cup with a satisfying—to him, anyway —*bang*. He grinned and did it again. Well, his mood was improved, at least. Perhaps this visit wouldn't go as badly as the first one.

"Oooh, you're very good at that," Jewel all but purred, sidling up to Rowan.

He smiled, making Violet think perhaps she could learn a thing or two from Jewel about flirting.

Jewel touched him on the arm. When he looked up at her, she fluttered her lashes. "Rowan, will you show me how to do that? I'm just a butterfingers. I miss the cup every time."

Faith. *Rose* could learn a thing or two from her about flirting.

But then Jewel reached for the toy, and Rowan jerked away, his frown back in place. "Mine."

"Rowan," Violet scolded, silently cursing her mother for sending her here again. "Behave yourself."

Jewel looked crestfallen. Knowing what it was like to feel awkward with boys, Violet felt for the girl. The sash on her powder blue dress was tied very crookedly in back—the viscount's work, no doubt. Perhaps some female companionship would ease the sting of male rejection.

"Here, let me fix your bow," Violet offered brightly, stepping up to retie it.

"Good afternoon," came a low voice from beside her.

She turned, blinking when she saw Lord Lakefield. Silver braid gleamed on his deep gray velvet suit, rather fancy for an afternoon at home. But she had to admit he looked splendid.

Feeling underdressed in her plain russet gown, she resisted the urge to rearrange her skirts. "Good afternoon, my lord."

"Please, just call me Ford," he said with a smile.

That was so improper, she wasn't sure what to say in return. Should she ask him to call her Violet? Would doing so invite too much familiarity? The oldest of four, she knew how to deal with children, but men remained a mystery. Especially eligible, handsome men the likes of whom usually failed to notice her existence.

She played with the end of her thick plait. Honestly, why was a tall, charming viscount with hypnotic blue eyes and hair that curled just right even *talking* to a girl like Violet, let alone asking her to call him Ford?

Had the world gone mad?

His smile wilted at the edges. Could he read her terror on her face? "Violet?"

Faith, he was calling her Violet already. Perhaps she should just try his name in her head. *Ford.* It seemed to fit. But when she opened her mouth, it felt entirely too scandalous to say aloud. She seemed to have lost her tongue.

This was ridiculous.

Evidently her silence had stretched long enough. "I'm just going to call you Violet," he said blithely. "We're neighbors, after all. Rowan, my man, what have you there?"

"A cup and ball." *Bang, bang.* "Lady Jewel gave it to me."

"Did she? I wonder where she got that old thing?"

Violet tore her gaze from the viscount—Ford—and glanced at the toy. "It *does* look rather used," she said, finally finding her voice. "Ancient, actually."

"Harry gave it to me," Jewel said.

Ford nodded. "My equally ancient houseman."

His housekeeper walked in and set a pitcher of ale on the table. "Is that what my husband was doing with you? I was wondering what you two were up to this morning. That toy once belonged to our son—did Harry tell you that?"

Jewel nodded, then her voice took on that flirtatious quality. "Isn't Rowan good at it?"

"Very," Ford said, sharing a smile with Violet that caught her by surprise. Clearly he was on to his niece's ploys. He waved Violet toward a chair. "Won't you sit down?"

"I'll be back," Hilda said, "after I get my tart out of the oven."

Seating himself beside Violet, Ford reached for the ale and her cup. At Trentingham Manor, servants did the serving. For a nobleman, he didn't seem to have very many. "How was your afternoon?" he asked.

"Fine," she said, watching him pour. He had nice hands, long fingers and square nails. She wracked her brain for a topic of conversation. "I'm reading a book by Francis Bacon."

He filled the children's cups, adding water to both. "Philosophy?" he asked, his tone cool but courteous.

"Yes." *He remembered!*

"And what does Francis Bacon have to say?"

She sipped while she thought of a reply, wondering why she cared so much what he thought of her. "He believes in liberty of speech."

"That's admirable." He drained his cup.

"He thinks knowledge and human power are synonymous."

He smiled vaguely as he refilled it.

"Do you agree?" she asked, feeling more awkward by the moment.

"Oh, yes. Yes, I do."

She sighed with relief when Hilda waddled in with four plates and started setting one in front of each of them. A welcome distraction. Steam from the plain apple tart wafted to

Violet's nose, smelling sugary and delicious. She lifted her spoon.

"I don't like apples," Rowan said. "Do you have cherry tart?"

"Do you have manners?" Hilda retorted with a glare. Muttering to herself, she left the room.

Violet wanted to slip beneath the table. "Francis Bacon says," she rushed out, "that if a man will begin with certainties, he will end in doubts, but if he will be content to begin with doubts, he will end in certainties."

Ford finally looked interested. "That sounds very much like the new science. One puts forth an assumption and then endeavors to prove it."

"So then," she said, warming to the subject, "perhaps philosophy and science are compatible."

"Perhaps they are."

He looked surprised or dubious; she wasn't sure which. She wished she could see him clearer.

"You know," he said, "some philosophers belong to the Royal Society."

Bang, bang.

"Rowan," she said quietly. "We're trying to talk."

For once in her life, she was enjoying a conversation with a man.

Bang.

"Rowan!" Her voice was sharper than she'd intended, and her brother looked up midtoss, the toy flying out of his hand. It hit the wall with a *thwack*, and she grimaced.

"Sorry," Rowan muttered.

"What was that?" Hilda asked, hurrying in to investigate the noise.

"A mistake." Rowan rose to go fetch the toy—or rather, he attempted to. How odd. From where Violet sat, her brother seemed unable to rise. His feet didn't reach the floor, but he put his hands on the seat and pushed, his face turning red with strain.

Jewel burst out laughing.

"Jewel," Ford murmured, rising from his chair. "You didn't."

"Oh-oh-oh, yes, I did," she chortled. "D-don't you th-think he deserved it?"

"Deserved what?" Violet asked. "What did you do to him?"

"She stuck me," Rowan said, and for a moment, Violet thought he meant with a pin. But he wasn't crying—in fact, he didn't even look angry. He didn't look happy, either. He just looked blank. "She stuck me to the chair."

"With what?" she asked, aghast.

"Harry," Hilda muttered dangerously, bustling from the room. "I'll kill the man."

"I stuck him with glue," Jewel explained proudly between giggles. "And mud to make it match the brown up-hol-ster-y. And the toy was to make him sit down without noticing."

Violet felt as blank as Rowan looked. Her mouth hung open. When Ford reached over and pushed up on her chin to close it, she hadn't enough wits about her even to feel mortified by the impropriety. "What—how—why—" she stammered.

"It was a jest," he clarified. "A practical joke."

"A jest," she murmured.

"A Chase family tradition." He turned to his niece with an indulgent smile. "Most especially Jewel's father's tradition."

Jewel hiccuped. "Tell her about one of Papa's pranks. From long ago."

He narrowed his eyes for a moment, deep in memory. "Once, when I was young, Colin tied me to a chair while I was sitting there reading a book." He leaned back, lifting his cup. "In some way or other—to this day I haven't figured out how—he managed to get the rope around my body but not my arms or hands, so I didn't notice."

For some reason, Violet found it all too easy to picture him not noticing.

Rowan stopped kicking. "What happened?"

"He left. The knots were behind the chair, so even after I did notice, I couldn't reach them. I yelled for help, but the only response was the sound of his laughter."

Envisioning that, too, Violet's lips twitched. "Did he rescue you?"

"Hours later. I'd nearly finished the book."

"You just kept reading?" she asked with a barely suppressed smile. Faith, even *she* wouldn't read under those circumstances.

"What else could I do?" he said dismissively. "At least Rowan here won't have to wait so long." After a quick mouthful of ale, he rose, moving to Jewel's victim. "Let me free you, my man," he said, lifting Rowan into his arms, chair and all.

Suddenly, seeing her brother hanging in midair stuck to a chair, and visualizing a bookish young Ford the same way, the smile that had been threatening broke free on Violet's face. Jewel was right. Given Rowan's petulance, he deserved the jest, and a rollicking good one it was, too.

"More stories," Jewel said.

"Later, baby." Carrying Rowan out the door, Ford flashed his niece a grin. "Colin will be proud of you when he hears this one."

And Violet had thought the Ashcrofts were eccentric.

TEN

"*A*LL RIGHT, ROWAN. Let's see what we can do here." Ford set the chair down in his laboratory and turned away to locate a beaker.

"Holy Hades," Rowan said.

Shocked at such language, Ford swiveled back and stared.

"Pardon." But the boy didn't look sorry. "What *are* all these things?"

Ford let his gaze wander the chamber's contents, trying to see it through the boy's eyes. A full quarter of the huge attic space was filled with ovens and bellows, a furnace, cistern, and a still. Mismatched shelves held scales, drills, and funnels. Magnets, air pumps, dissecting knives, a pendulum, and numerous bottles of chemicals sat haphazardly on several tables. More things were shoved into half-opened chests of drawers. A larger table beneath the window—Ford's workbench—was littered with the inner workings of several dismantled watches.

It was Ford's playroom, and he was happier here than anywhere else. "Scientific instruments, mostly." He grabbed a beaker and selected a bottle. "That's a microscope," he added, waving behind him.

"What does it do?"

"It magnifies. You can put something beneath the lens and see it up close." Forgetting the task at hand, Ford reached to a table for a book. "Here, look at this. *Micrographia*. It was written by a man named Robert Hooke." Opening the red leather cover, he set the book on Rowan's lap.

Rowan looked down at the title page. "'Some Phys-phys—'"

"Physiological," Ford said.

"That's a big word." The lad read the next words slowly and carefully. "'...Descriptions of Minute Bodies made by Mag—'"

"Magnifying."

"'Magnifying Glasses with...'"

"'Observations and Inquiries Thereupon,'" Ford finished for him. "The book is drawings of things seen under a microscope."

Unlike Jewel, Rowan apparently didn't mind help. Nodding, he turned to a random page and gawked. "Whatever is this?"

"One of the pictures Hooke drew. Of a feather. That's what it looks like very close up."

"Zounds." Rowan stared for a moment, then flipped the page. "What is this?"

"A louse." Ford unfolded the large illustration, revealing the insect in all its horrible glory. The creature was oddly shaped, with a conical head and big goggling eyes.

Goggling himself, Rowan lifted a hand to his hair. "*That's* what lice look like?"

"Up close, bigger than the eye can see alone." Pleased that Rowan was interested, Ford teasingly pulled an expression of horror. "You don't have any lice, do you?"

"I hope not. I don't think so. Not now." Tugging his fingers from his hair, the boy turned to another drawing. "This is a spider?"

Ford finished filling the beaker from the cistern, then glanced over. "A shepherd spider."

"It's particularly ugly," Rowan said with relish.

Remembering the glue, and his guest waiting downstairs, Ford rescued the book. "This is in the way."

As he set *Micrographia* on a table, Rowan's eyes followed it covetously. "May I take it home?"

"No." Ford sensed an opportunity. "But you can look at it whenever you're here."

"When may I come back?"

"To play with Jewel?" He knelt by the lad's chair and, after removing his shoes, poured the liquid over his lap.

"Zounds, that's cold!"

"It'll dissolve the glue." Standing, he attempted to pull the boy off the chair by gripping him under the armpits. "I thought you didn't like Jewel."

At that, Rowan squirmed.

"Hold still, will you?" Ford put a foot on the chair's lower rung to keep it on the floor. "You've certainly seemed to do your best to avoid her so far. And after this trick—"

"It was clever," the boy admitted.

"Yes, it was."

"Lady Jewel is…different," Rowan said. "I've never met a girl who would plan what she did. My sisters sure would never. Lily cares only for her animals, and Rose only wants to go to balls. And Violet…Violet always has to learn new things. Can you imagine a girl liking to study?"

Yes, Ford agreed silently, Violet was the oddest of the bunch. Certainly nothing like the type of girl he'd be looking for if he hadn't sworn off women altogether.

While he mused on that, Rowan's breeches finally came unstuck with an impressive sucking sound. Ford knelt to unlace them and began to pull them down.

"No!" The lad's hands clenched on Ford's shoulders. "I'll be arse-naked."

"Well, you can't sit or lean on anything wearing those." Ford sighed. "I'll go find you some clean breeches. Stay where you are," he added before taking himself off. "And don't touch anything."

When he returned a few minutes later, Rowan waved a hand at some bottles of chemicals. "What are those for?"

"Alchemy, mostly. Although that one"—he pointed—"helped get you unstuck." Ford made a show of shutting the door behind him. "There. You're safe from prying eyes."

The boy pulled off his breeches and hurried to put Ford's on. "What's alchemy?" he asked, gazing down at the gaping waistband with dismay.

"Alchemy is a science." Ford leaned to tug the laces tighter, but it was hopeless. He scanned the tables and shelves, searching for twine, silently cursing himself for the room's usual state of disarray. "We alchemists—King Charles is one, too—are working to find the Philosopher's Stone."

Rowan clutched the brown breeches with both hands. "Violet likes philosophy."

"Well, the Philosopher's Stone has little to do with philosophy. It's a name for a secret—a way to turn other metals into pure gold."

"Holy Had—" The boy caught himself this time. "I mean... you can do that?"

"No. Or not yet—no one can. But many are trying. It's said that in days past, men have accomplished it more than once, but the secret has always been lost." Finally spotting the twine, he walked over to fetch it.

"Why didn't the men write it down?"

"At least one did, in a book—but the book is lost, too."

"What book? Are you looking for it?"

"It's called *Secrets of the Emerald Tablet*, and no, I'm not. It's been lost for a very long time. Nearly three centuries." He knelt by the boy. "After all that time, perhaps *lost* isn't the right word. It was probably destroyed."

"Maybe in a fire," Rowan suggested, with entirely too much enthusiasm.

"Maybe." Making a mental note to keep the lad far from combustibles, Ford bunched the breeches around his waist and circled it with the twine. "But if the secret has been figured out before, it stands to reason we should be able to repeat that success, doesn't it? That's what half of this equipment is for," he concluded, knotting the twine tightly. "Alchemy."

The crotch of the breeches hung to the boy's knees, and the kneebands to his ankles, but he didn't seem to notice. Evidently relieved to be decently covered at last, he smiled happily and lifted a bottle of bright yellow fluid.

His eyes gleamed when he looked back to Ford. "Can I help you find the philosophy rock?"

"Philosopher's Stone." Ford considered. He could turn this interest to his advantage. "Maybe. Maybe you and Jewel together can help me."

Rowan set down the bottle. "Maybe she'll teach me some practical jokes."

"I'm sure your mother would love that," Ford said dryly. But his spirits took flight. Finally, Lady Trentingham's plan seemed to be working—thanks to Jewel's prank.

Whoever would have thought?

"Let's go down," he said. "Hilda will be mighty vexed if we don't finish her tart."

As Ford led him from the room, Rowan gave a wistful sigh. "What other science do you do?"

"Astronomy, mathematics, physics, physiology…"

The boy jumped down the staircase one step at a time. *Clunk.* A step. "I hate mathematics." *Clunk.* Another step.

"But mathematics can be fascinating. Like a puzzle."

Clunk. "Not when Mr. Baxter teaches it."

"Mr. Baxter?"

"My tutor." *Clunk. Clunk.* "He's boring." Around they went, past the middle level to the ground floor, Rowan clunking all the long way. "Jewel said you can show me the stars."

"Indeed. If you're here of an evening."

"Really?" At the bottom, Rowan pushed past him and ran straight into the dining room. "Violet!"

Arriving in the chamber, Ford saw her gaze sweep the boy from head to toe. She bit her lip—to keep from laughing, he was sure—but her eyes danced with humor as she looked pointedly to Jewel.

"I'm sorry about your clothes," Jewel told Rowan obediently, if not quite sincerely. Clearly Violet had had a talk with her in the men's absence.

Rowan shrugged. "That's all right." Hitching up Ford's too-long breeches, he turned to his sister. "Lord Lakefield says if I play with Jewel, he'll show me science. And the stars. Will you bring me?"

"You're willing to play with Jewel?" A note of incredulity tinged Violet's voice. "After what she did?"

"She's not like other girls. Will you bring me again tonight? To see the stars?"

She looked hesitant, but perhaps intrigued as well.

"You're certainly welcome," Ford rushed to tell her. "It looks to be a clear night."

"Maybe," she said. "I'll think about it."

Ford mentally crossed his fingers. If Rowan could persuade her to bring him back, surely he'd tire of seeing "science" after a short while. Then Violet could take the children elsewhere, and he would be left to work in peace.

At this point, even a couple of hours sounded like heaven.

ELEVEN

"SHE WRECKED his breeches, Mum!" Violet paced her mother's perfumery, skimming a finger along the neatly labeled vials. "It was amusing, I'll admit, but I don't think all that glue and mud will wash out."

"It was a harmless prank, dear." Chrystabel calmly plucked violet petals and tossed them into her distillation bowl. "And you did say Rowan wants to go back."

"Yes, but I cannot understand why." Pacing to one of the window niches, Violet perched a knee on the bench seat and leaned to look out. "How can he like her after this? Especially when he didn't like her before?"

"I've never understood how men's minds work. Does your philosophy give you no clue to that?"

Everything outside was a blur. "'It may be said of men in general that they are ungrateful and fickle,'" she quoted.

"And who said that?"

"Machiavelli." She turned from the window. "Now Rowan wants to go tonight to see the stars. And I fear he'll want to go back again tomorrow."

"Isn't that what we've been hoping would happen all along?

That Rowan would find a new playmate to occupy him while Benjamin is away?" Benjamin was the only boy Rowan's age within walking distance. "What, pray tell, is your problem with this development?"

Violet seated herself at the table and grabbed a bunch of flowers. "He doesn't want to go alone. And I don't want to go with him."

"Now, Violet, who said that thing about being charitable? You read it to me last week."

"Francis Bacon again," she said with a sigh. "'In charity there is no excess.'"

"A wise man. It would be a charity, for certain, if you brought Rowan to play. He's bored here in the countryside without Benjamin." Mum's fingers flew as she pulled purple petals, more graceful than Violet could ever hope to be. "And a charity to Jewel as well, stuck in that house with no other children. And you'd be giving Lord Lakefield some respite. Surely he has better things to do than watch that handful of a girl."

Agitated, Violet began plucking petals. "So I should do it instead? Am *I* not allowed to have better things to do?" The scent of her namesake flower failed to soothe her. "Can't Rose go?"

Mum frowned at Violet's busy hands. "Rose is too young, as I've said." She tossed a bare stem into a basket. "Besides, she has no sense where men are concerned, and we've all heard her jabbering about the 'handsome viscount.'"

"And he'd take advantage of her, but not me. That's what you're thinking, isn't it?"

"Violet—"

"It's true, Mum, and we both know it." She plucked faster. "I'm plain next to Rose and Lily. And gentlemen pretend to be deaf rather than listen to me prattle about my interests."

Mum touched her arm. "Violet, your father really *is* hard of—"

"No one will ever show interest in me unless it's for my

inheritance." Ten thousand pounds. Added to her dowry of three thousand.

For thirteen thousand pounds, many men would be tempted to wed a mule.

"Violet—"

"I'm not a featherbrain, Mum." Her hand fisted, crushing a flower. "I know I'm not the type to turn heads."

Because Violet had seen her parents' marriage—because she would settle for nothing less than their example of true love—she was sure she'd never wed. All the local gentry knew the eccentric Earl of Trentingham had three heiress daughters...and all had tried their clumsy hands at wooing the eldest, who would come into her inheritance first. But she'd never accept a husband who was only after her money. Which was why Violet would never accept anyone.

But as she'd said, she wasn't a featherbrain, so she knew better than to say so in front of Mum.

She sighed, knowing that mere weeks from now, when she turned eighteen and came into the money her grandfather had left her, the offers could very well begin to come fast and furious. She'd have a harder time putting Mum off then.

But she would persevere. And someday—many years from now when she was a content, aged spinster—she would use her inheritance to fund her dream.

"Violet." Her brown eyes filled with concern, Mum gently pulled the bruised bloom from Violet's hand. "You may not look like your sisters, but you're a very pretty girl. Especially to those who love you. Which philosopher said that beauty is brought by judgment of the eye?"

"That wasn't a philosopher. It was Shakespeare in *Love's Labour's Lost*."

"Oh."

"But he was paraphrasing Plato. 'Beholding beauty with the eye of the mind.'"

Mum grinned. "See, dear? Listen to Plato."

Rose and Lily burst into the room. "Look, Mum!" Lily waved a letter. "A messenger just delivered this from Lakefield. And he said he was instructed to wait for an answer."

"The oldest messenger I've ever seen," Rose huffed. "He's *bald*," she added in a tone of extreme disgust.

"That's not a messenger," Violet said. "That's Harry, Lord Lakefield's houseman." As she'd hurried Rowan out the door, she'd seen Hilda's husband cowering in a corner while his wife scolded him for his part in Jewel's prank. The man was quite definitely bald, although Violet hadn't found him disgusting.

Maybe beauty *was* in the eye of the beholder.

She rose and went to her sisters. "Let me see the letter." She plucked it from Lily's hand.

"It's not for you," Rose said, snatching it from Violet. "It's addressed to Rowan." So saying, she slipped a fingernail beneath the sloppy red wax seal and snapped it off.

"Rose!" Mum chided.

"You wouldn't want to give him a letter without reading it first, Mum, would you? It could be improper for one so young." Without waiting for her mother's answer, Rose scanned the page. "The handwriting is rather messy," she commented, then began reading. "'Dear Rowan.'" She looked up. "Rather familiar salute, don't you think?"

"Goodness, Rose," Lily said, uncharacteristically impatient. "Must you criticize every word?" She snatched the letter back from her sister. "'Dear Rowan,'" she repeated. "'I am sorry about your clothes. But it was funny. I hope you will come see the stars. Love, Jewel.'"

"'Love, Jewel?' *Love?*" Violet rolled her eyes toward the elaborate plastered ceiling. The blurry curlicues up there seemed in keeping with the little girl's intricate intrigues, with the five-year-old's plans for...

Well, the only word for it was *seduction*.

Lily smiled dreamily. "Yesterday when you brought Rowan back, you said Jewel was in love."

"I was exaggerating. And to write it down…" Violet couldn't imagine declaring herself so casually on a piece of paper. Writing was permanent, important. Once something was in writing, it was there forever.

That was one of the reasons she wished to publish a book.

"I'm in love, too," Rose declared.

Violet blinked. "With whom?"

"With Lord Lakefield, you goose. To instruct his niece to write a letter to Rowan…well, it just goes to show he's a true romantic." Looking rather theatrical, she laid a graceful hand on the smooth skin exposed by the neckline of her periwinkle gown. "Why, it's almost enough to make me overlook the fact that he's poor as a church mouse."

"What a thing to say, Rose!"

Her hand dropped. "Well, lucky for me, it doesn't matter, does it? Thanks to Grandpapa, when I turn eighteen I'll have enough money to nab whomever I like, rich or destitute."

Violet reminded herself to be patient, but she couldn't help gritting her teeth. "Thanks to providence, that won't be for three years, by which time we can hope you will have grown up."

"Girls," Mum warned. "That's quite enough." She turned to Violet. "Lord Lakefield's houseman is waiting. Will you be taking Rowan to see the stars?"

"I'll bring him," Rose offered.

Taking a cue from her husband, Mum pretended not to hear. "Violet?"

"Yes, I'll do it, Mum," Violet said with an elaborate sigh.

But it was mostly for show. She had to admit, she was curious to see the stars. And for some odd reason, she felt a need to save the viscount from a predatory girl like her sister. Not that she didn't love Rose, but a gentleman of Ford's intellect deserved someone who appreciated more than just his exterior qualities.

Quality though his exterior was.

And it *was* very well done of him to have made Jewel write

an apology, though she wondered how he could have neglected to supervise its contents before sending the letter.

Love, indeed.

TWELVE

*H*ITCHING HERSELF forward on one of the drawing room's faded red chairs, Jewel jumped one of Ford's checkers with hers and palmed her new captive. "Your turn. Will Rowan come tonight, do you think?"

"I have no idea what he'll decide. I don't understand children."

"But Uncle Ford, you like children, don't you?"

He'd never thought he had particularly. But as he looked at his charming niece, he didn't have the heart to say so. "I like *you*." Studying his position on the black-and-white board, he lifted one of his dark-stained counters. "And I'd wager Rowan does, too," he added to put a smile on her face. "He seemed much more fond of you after your jest. That was brilliant, baby. You certainly know your way to a young man's heart."

Click-click-click. Three diagonal jumps over her natural wood pieces, and his darker piece was at her end of the board. "King me," he said with a self-satisfied smile.

Draughts. He was reduced to playing draughts. And she'd beaten him three times already. He couldn't remember the last time someone had beaten him at draughts; he must have been seven years old.

For all his intentions to come home to Lakefield to focus on work and not women, the opposite seemed to be happening. When he wasn't paying attention to his niece, he was fretting over his shabby estate. Rather than unlocking the secrets of the universe, his ingenuity was aimed at persuading a young woman named Violet Ashcroft to spend as much time here as possible.

Jewel crowned his piece with one of the hostages she'd taken. "Do you like Rowan?"

"I do. He's very interested in my laboratory." Too interested. But at least the lad had a good brain and a healthy curiosity.

"Do you think Rowan's big sister is pretty?"

Did he? He'd initially thought Violet was nice-looking at best. But now when he pictured her he saw a bold and vivid face, softened by the thoughtful expression in her brandy-brown eyes...

"She's pretty," he said, surprising himself.

They both looked up as Hilda came in. "Harry seems to have disappeared," the housekeeper said. "Where is he?"

Ford shrugged. "I don't know." There didn't seem to be much he knew these days.

"He went to Rowan's house," Jewel said nonchalantly, jumping two more of Ford's men.

Hilda smoothed her wide white apron. "And why is that?"

"I asked him to take a letter there."

"A letter?" Ford frowned at the board, where his pieces seemed to be disappearing at an alarming rate.

"A letter to Rowan," his niece clarified. "An ap-ap—" She glared at him, as though daring him to help her. "An a-pol-o-gy."

"You wrote a letter?" Hilda asked.

"You wrote a letter?" Ford echoed. "All by yourself?"

"Well, I know how to write, you know. Mama taught me. What's so hard about that?"

Ford took his turn, removing none of Jewel's pieces. "It's not the writing of it, baby, it's thinking to do so in the first place. I'm impressed."

"Mama says even a tomboy should have good manners."

"I like the way your mother thinks," Hilda said.

"Besides, I like getting letters. Nobody ever sends me letters."

Seeing her pout, Ford made a mental note to send her a letter after she went home.

Jewel perused the board. "I thought a letter might make Rowan like me."

"He likes you," came a voice from the doorway. Harry walked in, his florid face split by a big smile.

Suddenly Hilda's face wore a frown. "You could tell me when you leave," she scolded, then immediately bustled out past him.

"Women," Harry muttered. "More trouble than they're worth." He turned to Jewel with a courtly bow. "Present company excepted, of course."

Ford stared. Clearly the girl had won him over. Just as she had Rowan. She looked so innocent in her powder blue gown. So young and vulnerable. Which sat at odds with her fully developed feminine wiles and intuition.

Jewel bounced on the ancient chair so energetically he feared it might break. "What did Rowan say?"

"Well, I didn't talk to him, you understand." Harry relayed the details as seriously as if he were a hired spy. "But his oldest sister came out and said she would bring him after the sunset to see the stars."

Jewel squealed and wriggled in her chair, so excited she botched her next few moves. As a consequence, Ford won the game. And Violet was coming with Rowan.

Things were looking up.

THIRTEEN

*R*OWAN CLIMBED into the carriage and motioned Violet after him. "Hurry, it's dark already."

"The sky isn't going away." Still shaking her head at his astonishing change of heart, Violet shrugged into the forest green velvet cloak offered by her mother. "Where's Margaret?"

"I gave her the evening off, dear. Hilda and Harry will be there. And Lord Lakefield is a gentleman. I'm sure we can trust him to behave."

Especially with the likes of me, Violet thought, biting her lip. That old, familiar truth seemed suddenly distressing.

"I've instructed Willets to come back for you at ten," Mum added. "Two hours ought to be plenty long enough to stare at the sky."

Violet looked up. Except for a milky blur, she'd never seen the stars. "I wonder what I might see there?"

"The stars are beautiful," her mother said. "Like diamonds sparkling on a black velvet gown."

Smiling at the extravagant description, Violet gazed at the heavens. She wondered if the stars really twinkled, and if she might be able to wish on one. Excitement fluttered in her stomach.

"I'll be off, then, Mum." She kissed her mother's floral-scented cheek and followed Rowan into the carriage.

A short while later they mounted Lakefield House's steps. Rowan didn't hide behind Violet this time. Jewel opened the door before Violet could lift the knocker, but Violet had anticipated that and didn't fall into the house.

Which was rather a pity, since Ford was there to catch her.

He was still wearing the fancy suit, making her feel underdressed in her simple cotton gown. But that was absurd—she'd only come to look at the sky.

Instead of ushering her in, he stepped outside, a bit too close for her comfort. "I have the telescope set up in the garden," he said. "Follow me."

For such a tall fellow, he moved with grace. As he headed down the steps, she realized she'd stopped breathing.

She commanded herself to inhale.

This was *really* getting ridiculous.

He was just a gentleman, nothing more. She couldn't remember ever being so nervous around one, but perhaps that was because she'd done an admirable job of avoiding them altogether. Surely this discomfort would disappear once she got to know him better. Which she seemed destined to do should Rowan have his way.

Holding a torch, Ford led her around the side of the house and down a path toward an area so overgrown she'd be loath to call it a garden. More like a jungle, she thought, hiding a smile.

The children tagged along behind, their voices coming out of the darkness. "Are you angry with me?" Jewel asked Rowan.

He seemed to consider for a moment. "Will you help me plan a jest on my sisters?"

"Of course I will."

"Then I'm not angry."

Listening to the exchange, Violet made a mental note to be on the alert for "jests." If Rowan thought gluing someone to a chair was excusable, heaven only knew what he and Jewel would come up with together.

In the midst of a tangle of vines sat a ring of scraggly hedges. Ford guided the group through an opening in the greenery. A new one, from the looks of it.

"Uncle Ford hacked at the plants with an ax today," Jewel proudly informed them. "After Harry came back and said you would come. Wasn't that nice?"

Violet thought she heard Ford emit a strange sound.

A circle of wooden benches looked newly uncovered as well. Apparently he'd been busy. In the center, atop a stone sundial, a long tube sat balanced on three spindly legs.

Ford gestured at it with a flourish. "The telescope."

"How nice," she replied, hoping she sounded suitably impressed. But the telescope wasn't exactly awe-inspiring. It was just a skinny, tarnished thing. Her hopes plummeted. This hardly looked like an object that could work magic.

He set the torch in a nearby stand. "Quarter moon tonight," he said, grasping the tube and maneuvering it to point in the moon's direction.

Curious, Violet moved closer. Over the fresh scent of recently cut plant life, she could smell something spicy. And a trace of scented soap. Patchouli, she decided, recalling the aroma from one of her mother's vials. Some years ago, Father had arranged for a number of the minty shrubs to be brought from India. He'd planted them in his magnificent garden so Mum could distill the leaves.

"A partial moon is fortunate for viewing." Ford had closed one eye and focused the other through the tube. "A full moon can be too bright and make the stars around it fade." He made a final adjustment. "Would you like to see?"

"Me first!" Jewel said.

Rowan jumped up and down. "No, me!"

Jewel stepped in front of him. "Me!"

"Well, normally I'd say ladies first," Ford said, clearing his throat, "but seeing as how Rowan suffered this afternoon, I think he should have the first peek. Hurry, though, or you won't be able to see it."

Since Rowan was too short, Ford lifted him to the eyepiece. "Zounds," Rowan breathed. "There are big, dark spots on it."

"They're called craters." Ford raised a foot to the pedestal of the sundial, settling Rowan on his knee with an ease that drew Violet's scrutiny. She'd never imagined someone as vain and preoccupied with himself as the viscount would behave so naturally with children. "What do you think of it?"

"I wish to fly up there and visit."

"Me, too." Ford laughed. "But I expect neither of us will get our wish."

Now Jewel was jumping up and down. "I want to see. Oh, please let me see!"

"Very well." Ford set Rowan down, then readjusted the telescope before lifting his niece. "Hurry, so Lady Violet can have a turn."

"Oooh," Jewel said.

"Why must she hurry?" Violet wondered. "The moon stays out all night."

"Yes, but the Earth moves, you see—it spins. That's why we have night and then day. And because of the spinning, we're moving relative to the moon, so it doesn't stay in the telescope's sight for very long." He set his niece on her feet and waved Violet toward the instrument. "Your turn."

She stepped forward and put one eye to the end, closing her other eye like he had. "Oh," she breathed. "Stars. Just look at all those stars."

"Can you see the moon, too?"

"No, we must have spun out of range like you said." Against black velvet, lights winked at her. White, and faint yellow, and the palest, most beautiful pink. A wonderland of stars.

"Let me adjust it for you."

"Wait." She was looking at a whole new world. Or a

universe, to be more precise. "I've seen the moon," she told him. "Not up close, but at least I've seen it. I want to look at the stars."

"But they don't look much different through the telescope. They're much too far away for the magnification to make a significant difference."

"But they're beautiful," she said. "Miraculous. What are they, really?"

"Other suns. And some people think there are other planets around them, the same way our planet circles our sun."

The children were chattering behind her, probably planning an outrageous jest, but she couldn't stop staring. She nudged the telescope a bit, and another group of stars burst into view. "'There is an infinite number of worlds,'" she murmured softly under her breath, "'some like this world, others unlike it.'"

"A lovely way to put it."

Startled, she jerked back from the eyepiece. She hadn't meant for him to hear that. "I didn't put it that way myself. I was quoting Epicurus."

"Who?"

"A Greek philosopher."

She felt, rather than saw, him nodding beside her. "A forward-thinking man."

A smile twitched on her lips. "Very. He lived about three hundred years before Jesus Christ came to Earth." She leaned close again, peering through the telescope. "Do you believe that there are other planets?"

He laid a hand on her back. A warm hand that made a warmer shiver ripple through her. "I do."

Giggles erupted behind them.

"My uncle thinks your sister is pretty," Jewel told Rowan in a loud, confidential whisper.

Rowan's response was a disgusted groan.

Violet stiffened, and Ford's hand dropped from her back. "So," he said a bit formally. "Should I adjust it on the moon?"

"In a minute." Of course he hadn't meant anything by touching her, Violet told herself—he was a flirt, just like his niece. The awkward moment passed as she refocused on the sky. "For now, I'm enjoying the stars."

Just then, one of them streaked across her field of vision, and she made a silent wish.

Give me the wisdom to write something worth reading...and the tenacity to publish it.

Her first wish on a star.

"Oh," she breathed, "it's magnificent."

Hearing the wonder in Violet's voice, Ford relaxed and decided to ignore his niece's careless comment. Violet probably hadn't even heard; her velvet cloak had slipped to the ground, and she'd not yet bothered to reach for it. He stared at her arched back, encased in a snug green bodice. Simple and practical, but it didn't hide the distinctly feminine figure underneath. Had she been wearing the same gown earlier today? He hadn't paid any attention.

Pretty or not, Lady Violet was even odder than he'd thought. She was still gaping at the sky, slowly shifting the telescope. "Wouldn't you like to see the moon now?" he asked. After all, the stars looked much the same through the telescope as without it.

"Lord Lakefield." Rowan tugged on his breeches. "Lord Lakefield."

"You may have another turn in a minute. For now, your sister's looking."

"I know." When Ford looked down, the boy's smile looked as wide as the telescope was long. "Violet's never seen the stars before."

"Never?" Baffled, he ran a hand through his hair. "What do you mean?"

"She cannot see very well. She says they all just blur together."

She straightened and turned to face them, her eyes glittering with joy in the torchlight. "Thank you," she whispered. "Thank you for showing me a whole new world."

The way she said it made Ford feel like he had *given* her the world, not just shown it to her.

The feeling was not unpleasant.

He eased her aside to adjust the telescope. "Here, now look at the moon."

When she leaned to peer through the lens, he was rewarded with a gasp of discovery. "It's a sphere," she said. "I can see the outline. Even though it looks like a crescent."

"Depending on our position, the Earth blocks part of the sun, so only a portion of the moon is illuminated. But it's always a sphere, no matter how it appears to us."

"Of course. I've just never thought of it before."

When the moon disappeared from view, he pointed out some constellations—Libra down near the horizon and Pegasus up higher.

"My turn!" Rowan said, and Jewel chimed in. "Let us have a turn!"

Clearly reluctant to relinquish the instrument, Violet stepped back, and the children rushed to see.

"Can you show us a planet?" Jewel asked.

Ford scanned the dark sky. "None are visible at the moment. Another night." But he showed them more constellations, and while they waited to take turns, he entertained them with the Greek and Roman myths that went with each configuration.

All too soon they heard the crunch of wheels on gravel announcing the Ashcrofts' carriage had arrived. Violet let out a little unladylike groan. "Is it ten o'clock already?"

"May we come back tomorrow?" Rowan asked. "Can I go into the laboratory?"

Ford gazed at Violet, thinking about how the telescope had helped her to see, wondering if there might be a way to help her more permanently. "I've something that will keep me busy the next few days," he said slowly.

"In your laboratory?" Rowan asked.

"Yes." He turned to the boy. "If you'll come to play with Jewel until I'm done, I'll take you into the laboratory after I finish. We can do an experiment together."

"An experiment?" Rowan's eyes widened, and he did a funny little dance. "Can we really?"

"Will you be working on the watch?" Jewel asked.

"No, not the watch." That could wait—it had waited ages already. Suddenly this new idea seemed much more important.

"Uncle Ford is making a special watch," Jewel told her new friends. "One that tells the minutes." She looked to Violet. "My Uncle Ford is very clever."

"I'm sure he is." Violet smiled at Ford, a smile that managed to transform her whole face. "Thank you for a fine evening."

"You're very welcome. I hope we can do this again." Surprised by just how true that statement was, he smiled in return as he retrieved her cloak and settled it over her shoulders.

If she'd noticed she'd dropped it, or that she'd almost forgotten it altogether, her demeanor gave nary a clue. "I hope we can do it again, too," she said with a last, lingering glance at the telescope. As she took her brother's hand and began tugging him toward the carriage, that infectious smile still curved her lips.

It felt good, knowing he was the cause of that smile. Wanting to give rise to another one soon, Ford hoped he'd prove as clever as his niece thought.

As he watched the carriage roll away into the night, he lifted Jewel into his arms and pecked her on the cheek.

"What was that for?" she squealed.

"Nothing, baby." It mystified him as much as her, but he would analyze the impulse later. "I just feel happy."

"I'm not a baby," she said. "Put me down."

But she planted a big, sloppy kiss on his cheek before he did so.

FOURTEEN

"WHY AREN'T WE going today?" Rowan demanded.

When Violet looked up from the notes she was making at her delicate desk in the library, it took everything she had not to laugh at her little brother. She hadn't seen a pout like that on him since he was about three years old.

But he wasn't going to change her mind. "I told you—we've been there every day since we looked at the stars. Four days in a row, each afternoon we arrive like clockwork. We're wearing out our welcome."

The pout turned into a glare. "That's not true."

Of course it wasn't. To the contrary, Violet was sure Ford was pacing the floors waiting for their arrival. Waiting for them to come entertain his niece so he could work on his blasted secret project.

Well, much as she liked children, she wasn't a nursemaid, and she didn't intend to take up the career now—never mind that it was a spinsterish thing to do. She hadn't seen hide nor hair of Ford since the night he'd shown her the stars. If he couldn't even make the effort to stick his head out of that mysterious laboratory to say hello and thank her for occupying his niece, she was finished making the effort to help him.

Rose glanced up from her desk at the opposite end of the room, where she'd been conjugating Spanish words aloud, much to Violet's aggravation. "Since you don't like him," Rose said, "I can take Rowan instead."

"I like Rowan fine."

"I meant the viscount. I was leaving you a generous window to take a fancy to the gentleman and get yourself married, but since you haven't, I may as well—"

"You're too young to take Rowan over there unchaperoned," Violet said pointedly. She was sick of Rose always trying to marry her off. *Generously.* And though she knew she should feel relieved that Ford was ignoring her, she was annoyed to find herself vexed instead.

But she shouldn't take that out on her sister. She looked up, examining the fuzzy pattern the dark molding made on the ceiling as she searched for her missing patience. "I'm sorry, Rose." She sighed, wondering what was getting into her these days. "If Mum says you may go, you have my blessing."

Rose snapped the Spanish book shut and ran off to ask their mother, Rowan galloping after her. Leaving *Advancement of Learning* and her notes on the desk, Violet stood and turned to peruse the library's well-stocked shelves. But nothing new caught her interest. All she could think about was the viscount's irritating lack of consideration.

"Lady Violet."

She swiveled at the sound of the majordomo's voice, noting he held a silver tray. "A letter, milady."

"Father is out in the garden."

"It's for you."

"Are you certain?" She couldn't remember the last time she'd received a letter.

Raising the parchment, Parkinson cleared his throat. "'Lady

Violet Ashcroft,'" he read off the back. "I believe that is you." Handing it to her, he turned on his heel and left.

Annoyed all over again, she broke the seal and scanned the childish handwriting. *Dear Lady Violet*, she read, *Why have you not brought Rowan today? Uncle Ford has something for you. Please come. Your friend, Jewel.*

Astonished, she plopped back onto her chair. The nerve of him, asking a six-year-old to coax her into a visit. *Uncle Ford has something for you.* She could just imagine what—probably a nursemaid's uniform.

"Violet, dear." Mum swept into the library. "Why won't you take your brother to play with his friend?" In a show of checking for dust, she ran a finger along the carved marble mantelpiece, then down one of the two supporting columns carved to look like palm trees. Her voice took on the prying tone that mothers must practice behind closed doors. "Did something happen yesterday?"

"Oh, Mum, nothing happened." She was getting tired of Mum grilling her every time she came home from Lakefield. What could possibly happen there that Mum would find note-worthy, anyhow?

"I would just like a day for myself," Violet said. "Is that too much to ask?"

"Of course not, dear." Mum focused on the letter still clutched in Violet's hand. "What's that?"

"A note from Jewel." Violet tossed it onto the dark wood desk. Stark white in contrast, the paper looked entirely too conspicuous.

"How sweet. What did the girl have to say?"

She wouldn't tell her mother that the viscount had something for her—news like that would escalate Mum's maternal prying to record levels. An awkward silence stretched between them while Violet stared at the note, wishing it would disappear.

"Jewel was just asking me to bring Rowan," she finally

admitted. When she looked back up, a tilt of her mother's head was all it took. "I guess I'll go after all," she said with a sigh.

"That's my Violet," Mum said.

And if her cheerful smile set Violet's teeth on edge, she was determined not to show it.

FIFTEEN

*J*EWEL WAS WAITING on the steps when they arrived.

"Lady Violet!" she squealed, running down the long walk to meet the carriage outside the gate. "Just wait till you see what Uncle Ford has for you! He had to find rocks to make it."

Rocks? Violet couldn't imagine. What sort of gentleman made things from rocks and had a little girl write his letters?

A strange one—that much was certain.

"Perfect rocks," Jewel clarified. "They had to be perfect." She turned her attention to Rowan. "Tomorrow is my birthday," she said, "and Uncle Ford promised he would take me to the village to spend my money. He said I could invite you and Violet."

"What money?" Rowan asked.

"He pays me to be good. And not to cry. And other things."

Rowan's jaw dropped open. He turned to Violet.

"Don't even think about it," she said.

Jewel looked toward him sympathetically. "Will you come with us tomorrow? I have enough coins for us both."

Violet wasn't surprised. If Ford was willing to pay bribes, she had little doubt a girl as bright as Jewel could manipulate her way to a fortune.

"Rowan can bring his own money," she said.

He tugged on her hand. "Does that mean we can go?"

"I suppose. Since it's Jewel's birthday." She couldn't imagine turning six years old and being away from home for her birthday. Birthdays were major events for a child. In the Ashcroft home, they were major events into adulthood. Her family was odd that way.

Well, not *only* in that way.

She wasn't looking forward to her own imminent birthday.

"Oh, good!" Jewel's face lit up. Violet was having second thoughts already, but who could deny that smile? She still wasn't thrilled with this nursemaid arrangement, but at least it would be something different to do. She wouldn't just be sitting here. And Ford wouldn't be able to totally ignore her.

She hated being the center of attention, but a *little* attention would be nice.

"Come inside," Jewel said, turning to head up the walk. She looped her arm through Rowan's and leaned close. "I have an idea for a jest."

Violet might have been half-blind, but there was nothing wrong with her ears. "I heard that," she said.

Jewel started up the steps. "Heard what?"

"You're planning a jest."

Opening the door, the girl batted her long black lashes. "Who, me? You must have mis-mis—" She paused for a breath. "Mis-un-der-stood."

Jewel's tone was so innocent, Violet would have believed her had she not known her better. She bit back a smile. Faith, could it be she would miss the girl when she left? She knew Rowan would. Though Ford would only be relieved. She could tell he saw Jewel as little more than a bother—an unwanted distraction from whatever spectacular discoveries he expected to make in his laboratory.

But then the viscount came down the corridor and swept the girl into his arms…

And Violet knew she was wrong. His love for his niece was obvious. There for all to see, shining in his incredible blue eyes. "Have you found our friends after all, baby?"

"I knew they would come if I sent them a letter."

"Did you think of that yourself?"

When Jewel nodded, Violet nearly failed to cover her gasp of surprise. Why, the little girl was even more resourceful than she'd imagined!

"That's my clever Jewel." Ford kissed her on the nose. "And I suppose you got Harry to deliver it?"

"He always does what I ask."

"Doesn't everyone?" With a wry grin, he turned to their guests. "Welcome," he said, sounding like he meant it. "Please come in."

"As you wish," Violet murmured. Maybe she'd been too quick to judge him. Absorbed in noticing that he was even better looking than she'd remembered, she tripped over the threshold —and once again found herself in the viscount's arms.

Curse her deficient eyes!

Not that she really minded her current position.

She couldn't imagine how he'd managed to set Jewel on her feet before catching her, but he'd done so quite handily. He steadied her, then grinned. "This is getting to be quite a habit."

"I'm sorry." His hands felt warm on her shoulders. "I know I ought to be more careful."

"Nonsense. I'm fond of catching you."

That charming smile almost convinced her of his sincerity. But of course he didn't enjoy catching her, or even being in her presence, for that matter—the fact that he'd ignored her four days running certainly proved that.

She not-so-subtly wrenched free of his hands. "Lady Jewel said you have something for me?"

"Did she?" He looked disappointed—as though he'd wanted

to tell her himself. He turned to his niece. "What did you tell her?"

"Just that you made something from rocks. And I invited them to come with us tomorrow." She grabbed Rowan's hand. "Let's go play in the garden."

"Wait." With an outstretched arm, Violet stopped her little brother's headlong rush. She looked to Ford. "Do you think we should let them go alone?"

Ford shrugged. "I'll send Harry after them. And if you'll wait for me in the drawing room, I'll bring the surprise."

She watched the children run off in one direction and Ford in the other. The moment they were all out of sight, a little flutter erupted in her stomach.

A surprise. When was the last time a gentleman had given her a surprise?

Never.

Unless she counted her father. Though most of his surprises involved flowers.

Trying not to get her hopes up, Violet made her way through Lakefield's now familiar corridor to the drawing room. She seated herself on the faded couch. She crossed her ankles. She uncrossed them. She twirled the end of her plait with a finger. For the hundredth time since she'd met Ford, she told herself not to be ridiculous.

It was becoming a litany.

Although it seemed like an eternity, she didn't wait long before he entered, breathing hard, as though he'd run from one end of the house to the other. Which she supposed he must have.

He wasn't holding anything, though. Disappointment welled up inside her—which was, again, ridiculous. Then he drew something from his pocket—something small—and held it out, almost shyly.

"I made this for you," he said.

She took it from him, turning it in her hands. Hardly a thing of beauty, it was two round, clear pieces of glass framed by some sort of wire. A little bridge connected them, and there were metal sticks on both sides.

Puzzled, she looked up.

"Spectacles," he said. He slid onto the couch beside her, acting friendly, familiar.

What little composure she had left completely fled.

His brow furrowed. "Have you not heard of spectacles? They're sometimes called eyeglasses."

That jarred her out of her haze. *Spectacles.* Her mouth dropped open, and her breath caught in her chest. "I—of course I've heard of them, but..."

More words wouldn't come.

"Would you like to try them on?"

"I...thank you," she breathed.

She truly *was* thankful. This was the most thoughtful thing anyone had ever done for her. But the sad truth was, she knew the spectacles were useless.

She bit her lip. "I...I can read just fine. I know Rowan told you I cannot see very well, but it's the distance that's a blur. Printed pages look clear as water. But I sincerely appreciate—"

"No." She'd expected him to look disappointed, but instead he grinned. "These aren't for reading, Violet."

"They're not?" Thrilled as she was at his unexpected thoughtfulness, her brain seemed to be muddled, not half because of his closeness. "What are they for, then?"

"Spectacles for reading have convex lenses—they get fatter in the middle. These are concave, the opposite. The edges are thicker than the center. They'll help you see in the distance."

As she digested what he was saying, her hands began shaking. "What is all this metal?"

"Silver. To hold the lenses on your face. For reading, when a body is still, it's fine to hold a lens or balance a pair on your nose. But after I made these, it occurred to me that you may want to wear them and move around. So I devised the sidepieces to rest on your ears and hold them in place."

He scooted even closer, so close she could smell his clean spicy scent. It made her light-headed. Gently he took the spectacles from her hands, narrowing his eyes as he gauged them compared to her features. "I'll probably need to adjust them. You've a smaller face than I thought."

She'd never thought of herself as small—any part of her. Lily was the petite one.

And she'd never, ever thought she might be able to see like a normal person. "May I try them on?" she asked, struggling to steady her voice.

"Please do. I suspect I may have to play with the lenses as well, to give you optimal vision. The degree of concavity affects the amount of correction."

She hardly understood what he was talking about, but she didn't care. Her head was buzzing. Ford had made her spectacles. And he was handsome and generous and warm.

He lifted her chin with a finger, and she obediently raised her face, holding her breath while he fit the contraption in place. It felt strange there, perched precariously. She closed her eyes against the sensation.

When she opened them, Ford rose and stepped back—and he was still in focus.

"Oh, my," she breathed, unable to tear her gaze from his face.

He stepped yet farther away…and she could still see him. He smiled that winning smile of his, and she could see it all the way from where she sat.

"Oh, my word." Suddenly she was looking everywhere. "I can see the bellpull!" she exclaimed, "and the clock across the room." He had clocks all over his house, and this chamber was no exception. "I can read the time! On that clock, and that one, too!"

It was a miracle. She stood, walking on shaky legs to the window. With the spectacles on, she felt taller than before and nearly tripped.

Nothing had changed there, but it only made her laugh.

"Look." She leaned her palms on the windowsill, aghast at the beauty of the world. "I can see it—I can see everything! The clouds and the flowers and the leaves on the trees. Each individual leaf."

"They're working for you, then," his voice came from behind her. "But odds are I can make them even better. We'll have to figure out whether more or less concavity will be optimal, and then, with a day or two to remake them, I can—"

"No." She whirled to face him. "You're not taking these away from me." She put her hands to the frame, tilting the spectacles crazily.

His laugh was merry and deep. "Let me at least make them fit."

"No."

"A minute, that's all it will take." His lips curved in a smile. "I left the sidepieces straight, you see? If I bend them around your ears, they'll stay in place better."

"A minute?"

His eyes met hers, that brilliant, compelling blue. Something flip-flopped in her stomach. "One minute," he promised.

Reluctantly she released the spectacles, and he slid them off her face. The world immediately blurred.

She hugged herself, a little thrill running through her as she watched his unfocused form begin to manipulate the metal. "What a difference they make! Jewel said something about you needing to find rocks. Perfect rocks. What did she mean by that?"

"I took her up into the hills, hunting for quartz for the lenses. Rock crystal." He glanced up briefly, and she wished she could see his eyes better, see the heady glint of intelligence she knew was there. He returned to his task. "Perfectly clear quartz is difficult, but not impossible, to find."

"They're not glass? They're called eyeglasses."

"True." He smiled as he worked. "But plain glass doesn't have the properties needed for optical lenses."

"How did you know that?"

Making a final adjustment, he shrugged, an unconcerned tilt of his shoulders. "My brothers would tell you I've wasted countless hours filling my brain with useless facts, when I could have been doing something productive."

Her insides rebelled at the thought. "Oh, but it wasn't useless at all. Look what you've done with that knowledge!"

He shrugged again. She couldn't make out his expression. "My family would much rather see me improve this estate, instead of sinking all my income into research and experiments." Finished, he stepped closer to put the spectacles back on her face.

"They just don't understand you, then." She could relate to that, since her family rarely understood her.

"You're generous to say so. Especially since I'm beginning to think they might be right. I should have renovated Lakefield ages ago. I've been living with my oldest brother far too long."

He ran his fingers around her ears, making sure the sidepieces curved to fit. A little thrill whirled through her at the feather-light sensation.

"Comfortable?" he asked.

The way he looked at her made her breath catch. She bit her lip and nodded.

His hands still rested around the edges of her face. Warm fingertips lay along her jaw. "Can you see well now?"

She nodded again, gazing into his eyes, his beautiful blue eyes, realizing she was close enough to see them without the lenses. So close she could feel the heat radiating from his skin. "Thank you," she whispered. "You've changed my life."

With all her heart, she meant it. This incredible man she'd only just met had given her the most amazing gift. And now he was looking at her, really looking at her.

She was the center of his attention.

Blinking at that thought, her gaze dropped to his mouth.

He had a beautiful mouth, too. Suddenly, inexplicably, she wanted it on hers.

And even more suddenly it was.

His lips were soft and pillowy and quite unlike anything she'd ever felt before. And entirely different from how she'd imagined a kiss would feel…

A kiss?

She was being kissed.

Ford was kissing her.

Ford was kissing *her*.

She let out a little yelp, which must have startled him because he sprang away from her immediately. He looked as stunned as she felt, his vivid eyes hazy and unfocused—and gazing at her.

She didn't like the attention so much anymore.

Clearing her throat, she looked down at the unvarnished floorboards. Of course he was stunned. A fellow would have to be daft to kiss a girl like her. Especially when she was wearing spectacles. Her hands went to the sides of her face, feeling the metal that hugged her ears. "I suppose I must look a fright."

"No." His voice was rough. She heard him clear his own throat. "You look lovely, Violet. Your eyes shine like bronze beneath the lenses." When she glanced back up, he appeared as surprised to have said the words as she was to hear them.

She knew he was just being nice. Which was, well, nice of him, but it left her in a swirl of confusion. Was it possible that he liked her, at least a little? Would he kiss her again?

Did she want him to?

It didn't matter. Whatever had driven him to do such an absurd thing—such a *ridiculous* thing—was unlikely to ever recur.

"My eyes are brown," she said, meeting his gaze squarely. She wasn't lovely, and she didn't like being lied to. If she'd been average-looking before, now, with the spectacles, she surely looked hideous.

"Your eyes look bronze to me," he repeated, "though I've also thought they look like my favorite brandy. And truly the spectacles look fine. Better than fine."

Much better than fine, Ford realized with a start.

After seeing her flushed with happiness and awe over his gift, he wondered how he'd ever thought her appearance was unremarkable. His sister often accused him of being oblivious, and for once he had to agree. Violet had a striking, unexpected beauty—and now that he'd seen it, he couldn't unsee it.

He also couldn't stop staring.

He wanted to kiss her again.

But he wouldn't. The kiss had frightened her out of her wits. Having observed that rash behavior usually led to bad outcomes, he wasn't usually given to impulse. The kiss had been no more than a momentary lapse. An isolated incident. He'd been temporarily overwhelmed by her tremendous delight, and his own pride in his work, and that infectious smile…

"Uncle Ford!"

Realizing he'd been unconsciously moving toward Violet, Ford straightened as the children came bounding into the drawing room. "What is it?" he grumbled, then cursed himself silently when his niece's eyes turned misty.

He had to learn to be more patient. "What is it?" he repeated, forcing his lips to curve in a smile.

She smiled back. "There was a spi—"

"*What* is on your face?" Rowan interrupted, staring at his sister.

"Spectacles. Ford made them for me."

Behind them, Violet's brandy eyes still glowed with wonder, and Ford didn't miss the fact that she'd finally called him by his given name. His forced smile turned genuine.

"What for?" Rowan asked.

"So I can see better." The glow spread to encompass her entire face. "I can see things all the way across the room."

"Oh." Hands behind his back, the boy rocked up on his toes. "That's good. But they look odd."

"They look better on her than on me," Jewel said. "Uncle Ford used my face to test different ideas. I think we tested about eleventy of them."

Violet grinned. "Eleventy, hmm?"

"Jewel." Rowan made a funny sound in his throat. "Remember? Remember what we were going to tell them?"

"Gads, I forgot!" She paused for effect. "You won't believe what happened!"

"What?" Ford and Violet said together.

"We found a spider in the garden. A big, fat, hairy one. Rowan saved me from it," she added, beaming at said savior.

"Did he?" Violet said very solemnly.

"Mmm-hmm." Struggling to keep a smile from his face, Rowan whipped his hand out from behind his back. "Look."

Violet screamed. And screamed some more. Then she turned to Ford and buried her face against his cravat, so hard he could feel the metal frame of the spectacles digging into the skin beneath his shirt.

He didn't mind having her pressed up against him, but he wished she would stop screaming.

The spider really was quite impressively enormous. "Get that out of here," he told her brother.

"But it's dead. It cannot hurt anyone."

Jewel erupted in giggles. "Yes, Uncle Ford, it's dead." She turned to her accomplice. "I told you it would work. I could tell your sister is lily-livered."

"I am not," Violet wailed, her voice muffled against Ford's front. As if to prove her bravery, she turned to look, then promptly reburied her face.

Knowing his niece well—or rather, assuming she was like her prank-playing father—Ford sent her a warning glance. "Just get it out of here, will you?"

"Oh, very well." Still giggling, Jewel went to open a window and motioned Rowan over to toss the creature outside. "But it really cannot hurt anyone."

"It wouldn't hurt anyone were it alive, either," Ford said. "It's not a deadly sort." Somewhat reluctantly, he coaxed Violet out of his arms. "But that isn't the point."

"It was ugly," Violet said with a nervous giggle of her own.

She walked to the window and peered at the dead spider dangling ungracefully from an overgrown bush. A delicate shudder rippled through her.

"I can see very well," she declared, "and that is quite the ugliest thing I've ever laid eyes on. Perhaps these spectacles aren't such a good idea, after all."

"Nonsense." Ford stepped up to the window beside her. "Ignore the spider. Look at the clouds, Violet."

"The clouds?" She looked up, and her mouth dropped open. "Oh, my word…"

Ford grinned, and as he watched the glow return to her face, he felt an answering glow inside himself.

SIXTEEN

W HILE ROWAN RAN for the house, anxious to tell their mother all about Lady Jewel and the spider, Violet alighted from the carriage, still looking about in wonder.

The world was magnificent. She wandered around the side of the mansion, stunned by the splendor of her father's exquisite flowers. Such brilliant colors, such delicate petals. She'd seen them before, of course, but only in her own hands or leaning down close. The gardens overall had been blurs of color, never this entire panorama of perfect shapes and rainbow hues stretching into the distance. And, oh, the subtle details were wondrous.

Oblivious to her approach, her father knelt by some roses, patting mulch into place. She touched him on the shoulder. "You've done a spectacular job here, Father."

"Eh?" Engrossed, he didn't look up. "What did you say?"

Sighing, she raised her voice a notch. "Your flowers are beautiful."

"So are you, dear," he said automatically, rising from his knees. At the sight of her, he froze. "Violet. What have you done to your face?"

She grinned. "They're spectacles, Father. Lord Lakefield made them for me."

He blinked. "What do they do?"

"Besides make me ugly?" Despite that fact, a smile bloomed on her face. Throwing her arms out wide, she spun in a circle, looking at everything at once. "I can see, Father! I can really see!"

In her exuberance, she'd yelled it, and he'd certainly heard. When she stopped twirling, he gathered her into his arms—something he hadn't done in quite a while.

He hugged her hard before pulling back, then searched her eyes with his. "Can you see everything? Just like me?"

"Everything." She knelt by his flowers. "This red rose, and that yellow one in the distance. And the hedges over there, and the rowan tree by the river." She rose, turning slowly this time, savoring the incredible view. "I cannot wait for tonight to look at the stars." Facing the house, she stopped. "I can see Lily smiling behind the window." She waved merrily, grinning when her sister waved back.

"Violet!" Rowan came running out, their mother trailing behind. "I told Mum about your spectacles, and she wants to see them!"

"Chrysanthemum!" Father cried, yanking Mum in for a kiss as though they hadn't seen each other in weeks. Normally Violet rolled her eyes at her parents' shameless displays, not to mention Father's cloying nickname for Mum. They were so sickly sweet together as to make her stomach turn.

Normally. But today, their affection only made Violet think of Ford.

And her first kiss.

A tingling weakness spread through her body. What was happening to her?

"Let me see these spectacles," her mother said, taking Violet's face in her hands and turning it this way and that. "Do they really help you see?"

"Immeasurably. They're miraculous. And worth looking hideous, I can assure you."

"You look fine, dear."

Now Violet did roll her eyes.

Her sisters stepped outside, both wearing new gowns they'd had fitted the past week while Violet had been at Lakefield House. Rose's was a rich, dark green, the skirt looped up and caught on the sides to show off the bronze underskirt beneath. Flurries of lace trimmed her chemise, peeking from the scooped neckline and the cuffs of the fitted sleeves. With her shimmering hair and tall, willowy grace, she looked like some sort of ethereal wood nymph.

And Violet could see every detail before her sister even came near. Absolutely miraculous.

"What is that dreadful contraption on your face?" Rose asked. Lady Tact.

"See, Mum?"

"You look fine," Lily said. Her gown was a sunny yellow and quite lovely, too. It had a square neckline and a nutmeg-colored underskirt embroidered with yellow daisies.

"I don't care how I look," Violet told them all. "Only that I can see." She turned to her mother. "When will my own new gowns be fitted?"

"Since when do you care about clothes?" Rose asked.

But Mum just beamed. "Tomorrow. I shall send a note to the seamstress forthwith."

"Excellent," Rose said. "And I'll take Rowan to Lakefield tomorrow, since Violet will be busy."

Last week, Violet would have been relieved to hear that. But now she was just annoyed.

"That won't be necessary," Mum said. "Violet can be fitted in the morning while Rowan has his lessons. She'll be free by afternoon."

Rose's pout was so well done, it could earn her a leading role at the Theatre Royal.

"Lord Lakefield said he would take us to the village for Jewel's birthday tomorrow," Rowan informed them. "Jewel has a lot of coins. May I try the spectacles?"

"If you're careful." When Violet gingerly removed them, her world went blurry. She handed them to her brother, and he slipped them on.

"I cannot see," he said, scrunching up his nose and squinting through the lenses.

"Well, of course not. They're for bad eyes, and your eyes are good."

"Let me see," Lily said. Rowan handed over the spectacles, and she held them up to her face. "Goodness, Violet, your eyes must be really bad."

"Let *me* see," Rose said, grabbing for them.

"Careful!" The metal frames were thin, and Violet didn't want her new treasure broken.

"I won't hurt them." Rose slid them onto her face, then gasped. "Is this what things look like to you?"

"Probably. But not anymore." She took the eyeglasses from Rose and happily settled them back in place, sighing as her view of the family cleared. "I don't care what I look like," she said again. "It's just so wonderful to *see*."

"Truly, you look fine," Lily said kindly. "The spectacles suit your face somehow."

Violet didn't believe her, but she really didn't care.

"Truly," Lily repeated, and when she smiled, her teeth looked whiter and straighter than Violet remembered. "It was thoughtful of Lord Lakefield to make them, wasn't it? He must be a very nice gentleman."

"And handsome," Rose added.

Violet gave an unladylike snort. "I thought you found him *lanky*."

"He *is* lanky. Still and all, he's handsome enough."

For the second time in ten minutes, Violet rolled her eyes. It felt different behind the lenses.

Everything felt different.

"May Jewel come for supper?" Rowan asked.

Mum patted her son on the head. "A grand idea. We'll send an invitation immediately. We all owe Lord Lakefield thanks for restoring Violet's vision."

"Eh?" her husband asked. "Did you say something about a decision?"

Mum set her hand on his arm. "I said vision, darling."

"Hmmph," he muttered half to himself as he plucked a dead head off a hollyhock plant. "The man of the house is traditionally involved in decisions."

SEVENTEEN

*F*ORD RECLINED in in elegantly carved chair at the Ashcrofts' polished mahogany table, fighting the urge to pat his stomach. The supper had been exquisite, especially compared to the plain fare Hilda usually served.

"Thank you kindly for the invitation," he told Lord Trentingham.

"Imitation?" The earl cocked his head. "It wasn't common chicken," he said, not unkindly. "The partridges in that fricassee were hunted today."

"Darling," Lady Trentingham said loudly, laying graceful fingers on her husband's arm. Eschewing convention, she sat beside her husband rather than at the other end of the table. "Lord Lakefield was thanking you for inviting him to dine."

"Yes," Ford all but bellowed, since *he* was at the other end of the table, "it was quite a treat to spend an evening in the company of all your beautiful ladies."

He couldn't help but notice that Rose practically purred. "You're quite welcome—" she began.

"Thank *you* for making my spectacles," Violet interrupted. Her mother had seated her next to him. "This is the most wonderful thing anyone's ever done for me," she added, the words clearly from her heart.

Candlelight from the silver branches on the table glinted off the lenses shielding her eyes. "It was nothing," he told her, meaning it. He'd made the eyeglasses as an experiment—to see if he could devise a lens to help her see her daily world as the telescope had helped her see the stars. He was pleased his idea had proven workable, and her happiness was an unexpected bonus.

Unexpected and more pleasing than he ever would have imagined.

As another experiment, he offered her his most charming smile, then dropped his gaze to her lips. When her cheeks flushed fetchingly pink, he was certain she was remembering their kiss.

Hmm. Perhaps he ought to continue this line of investigation. It could very well lead somewhere interesting.

He'd just have to be careful not to let it distract him…

"Are you finished, milord?"

"Pardon? Oh. Yes." He cleared his throat and shifted to allow the maid to remove his plate. Was she Daphne or Dolly? He liked the way Lady Trentingham addressed servants like they mattered to her, and talked to them instead of just ordering them around, and listened to what they had to say. It was both unusual and admirable, and he was attempting to do the same. But the Ashcrofts seemed to have so many. He couldn't remember this one's name.

"Would you care for tea now, milord?"

"Um, yes. Please," he said, feeling more and more like a half-wit. Darla? Was she Darla?

Some impression he must be making on Violet's family. And though he hadn't yet analyzed why, he did want to make a good impression.

They were neighbors, after all.

"Everything tasted so good," Jewel said as another maid whisked away her empty Delftware plate.

Lady Trentingham smiled at his niece. "We're glad you enjoyed it, sweetheart."

In fact, Jewel had all but licked her plate clean. Though he knew Hilda's cooking left much to be desired, Ford hadn't realized he was starving his niece. It was humiliating.

She beamed at their hostess. "Your house is so pretty."

"You've said that," Ford told her. Six times.

Her gaze swept the magnificent molded ceiling, the gilt cornice, the heavily carved fireplace, the enormous flower arrangements set on every flat surface. "Well, it *is* pretty."

Ford felt his shoulders tense. While Trentingham Manor was opulent beyond anything the Chases owned, Jewel didn't have to keep saying it. She was making him out a pauper. Between the two of them, any hopes he had of impressing the earl and his wife were sinking fast.

"Milk, milord?" the maid asked. "Sugar?"

Ford nodded. "Both, if you please."

Dorothy? he wondered. Daisy? She set a small silver pitcher on the table.

"I have the sugar," Rowan announced. As the boy passed the bowl along with a tiny silver spoon, Ford looked at him and wondered if he'd have been called Daisy were he born a girl.

Probably. Or Daffodil. Or Peony, perhaps.

Jewel tugged on the maid's sleeve. "Dinah, can I have tea?"

"May I please have some tea," Ford corrected her automatically. *Dinah*, he thought with relief.

"May I please have some tea?" his niece repeated obediently. "I love tea, but Uncle Ford doesn't have any."

Tea was still somewhat of a novelty and frightfully expensive; heaven knew he didn't stock it at Lakefield House. Apparently Violet's family could afford anything they wanted. And now, thanks to Jewel, they knew he couldn't.

Violet leaned close. "Children rarely think before they speak," she whispered sympathetically. "Rowan is no different."

He knew that was true. But criminy, was his discomfort that obvious? Avoiding her gaze, he focused across the room on the Tudor linenfold paneling—painted white in the latest fashion—while he waited for his tea.

"Good heavens," Lady Trentingham said. "I almost forgot to tell everyone the news. My maid Anne is getting married."

"That's wonderful, Mum." Lily actually clapped her hands. "Is she wedding that coachman you introduced her to?"

"Of course. I knew they would suit."

Rose sipped from her wineglass. "Her betrothed is from the Liddington estate, isn't he? Where will they live?"

"Here, naturally. We'll hire him on." The countess laced her fingers together atop the mahogany table. "Anyone can replace a coachman, but I cannot do without Anne."

"So that makes six matches for you this year?" Lily asked.

"Just so. But I introduced Lord Almhurst to Lady Mary Spencer last week, so I expect I'll be up to seven soon."

The maid arrived with the tea and poured. "Thank you, Dinah," Ford said, hoping the Ashcrofts noticed how respectful he was of their servants. He lifted the absurdly small spoon and began shoveling sugar into his tea. Though he didn't share his twin sister's habit of eating dessert before the meal, he did share her sweet tooth.

"Seven weddings," Rose said with an impressive sigh. "In case you haven't heard, my lord, Mum is the unofficial matchmaker for all of Southern England."

"I've introduced people from the North as well," Lady Trentingham said a bit huffily.

"How admirable." This talk of marriages was making Ford nervous, so he decided to change the subject. "What time shall I fetch you to go to the village tomorrow?" he asked Violet.

Her hands went to the frames of her spectacles. "Oh, I...well—"

"She cannot go," Rose put in from across the table. "Mum has arranged for her to have new gowns fitted."

Rose graced him with a wide smile, but although she had charming dimples, he didn't find himself charmed. Odd, considering her tall, willowy beauty was reminiscent of Tabitha.

"Perhaps I can accompany Rowan instead," she added. "I know how much he's looking forward to the outing."

"It won't take the entire day," Ford said. "The village is hardly a metropolis." An understatement—Jewel would likely finish her shopping in twenty minutes. He spooned in more sugar—pure white sugar, he noticed, imported from the West Indies, no doubt. Another sign of the Ashcroft wealth. He turned back to Violet. "I can come by for you and Rowan in the afternoon, following your fitting."

Behind her new lenses, her eyes clouded. "I—I..." She shifted on her petit point seat cover. "I'm not certain I'm ready to be seen in public," she blurted. "With the spectacles, I mean. I know everyone will stare and ask questions. Perhaps after I'm more used to them—"

"You goose," Rose interrupted. "Just take them off."

Violet's hands went protectively to the sides of her face, as though she were afraid her sister might snatch them off herself. "I like to *see*," she said. "I don't want to take them off."

"If you're going to insist on walking around with glass and metal on your head, then you'll have to get used to people staring at you."

"Rose." Lady Trentingham's tone was soft, but a warning nonetheless. "Our Violet prefers not to be the center of attention," she explained to Ford.

"Please pass the sugar," Lily asked sweetly.

"I'd like some, too," Rose said. "Put it between us."

Ford sent the sugar across the table. "How about if we go to Windsor, then?" he suggested to Violet. "It's much bigger than the village. You're unlikely to run into anyone you know there, and Jewel will find a larger shopping selection."

Violet looked unconvinced, but Jewel's eyes lit like green beacons. "Good idea, Uncle Ford."

"But—" Violet started.

"Yes, it is a good idea," Rose interrupted. "Except that will take all day, so Violet won't be able to go. But as I said, I'll be happy to go instead."

"Rose." Now her mother's voice sounded more exasperated. "That won't be necessary. I can send a note to Madame and reschedule the fitting for another day."

"But—" Violet tried again.

"A perfect plan," Lady Trentingham concluded.

EIGHTEEN

"*H*OLY HADES," Rowan whispered. "Look at that thing."

As they headed toward the river, Violet glanced at Harry walking in front of them, his bald head shining in the sun. Thankfully he hadn't seemed to hear.

"Hush," she told Rowan. "You don't want me to tell Mum you're talking like that, do you?"

Having expected Ford, she'd been surprised when Harry had come to the door instead. Not that she was sure she wanted to go to Windsor at all. She did want to see the town, really see it, but...

She touched the metal frame of her spectacles. Faith, people would do more than stare. They would laugh at her, she knew it.

"But just *look* at that thing!" Rowan exclaimed.

Harry definitely heard that. He slowed so they could catch up, a crooked smile on his face. "I'd wager you've never seen anything like it," he said, gesturing toward the dock.

"I certainly haven't," Violet agreed.

On the river, Ford and his niece were waving from the deck of a barge so old, she half expected it to sink before her eyes. Flecks of gold on its woodwork glistened, the last vestiges of gilding that must have once graced the elaborately carved boat. Once upon a time, she imagined, it had been a ceremonial vessel for someone very important—if not the king himself.

But now it must be more than a hundred years old.

At least the sails still looked serviceable, if a bit tattered and gray. She waved back, and her brother did, too. Then she stopped and turned him to face her.

"Don't say anything bad about it in front of them. Please." She still remembered him asking Hilda for cherry tart, and she never knew what would come out of his mouth next to embarrass her. "Please," she repeated.

"Bad?" Rowan's green eyes looked incredulous. "It's the most wondrous thing I've ever seen!" With that, he broke into a run and didn't stop until he'd crossed the dock and leapt onto the ancient boat.

Violet was glad Harry's old legs gave her an excuse to approach more slowly, since her fashionable high heels hampered her ability to run. She wasn't used to wearing them. But at least, with her new spectacles, she was confident she wouldn't trip over the uneven ground.

A crew waited aboard, three men she recognized as Ford's coachman and outriders. As she lifted her peach satin skirts, Ford reached a hand to help her up. She smiled and put hers in it. "Good day, my lord."

He grinned, his free hand gesturing at the blue, cloudless sky. "It is, my lady." He dropped his voice as she stepped aboard. "You look lovely today, Violet."

Her own free hand went reflexively to her spectacles. Though her new gowns weren't ready, she was wearing her fanciest day dress and knew it was pretty. But she also knew she was not.

His fingers squeezed hers before breaking contact. "I hope you'll enjoy the day."

She nodded, trying to ignore the strange trembly feeling in her stomach. Or was it closer to the vicinity of her heart? No matter, it was only her nervousness—about Windsor, not about

Ford. Ford had already seen her in the spectacles, so there was no reason to be nervous around him.

"I'm surprised you came by river," she said with all the composure she could summon, "rather than by road."

"It's a beautiful day," he replied, "and Windsor just a pleasant sail down the Thames. I thought the children would enjoy it."

"They are already." With whoops of joy, the two of them were chasing around the cabin perched in the barge's center, jumping over ropes and racing around rigging as though the entire vessel were their playground.

Like Lakefield House, the boxy cabin could have used a coat of paint, but it was obvious the boat had once been elegant and impressive. "Wherever did you find this?" Violet asked.

"It came with the estate. Though a bit the worse for wear, she's seaworthy, I assure you. Or riverworthy, in any case."

"She's magnificent." Twirling slowly in a circle, Violet noted the rich details. Although spotless, the barge was old to the point of antiquity. Just the thought of riding on such a silly thing made her want to laugh. But in its own way, it was beautiful, too. "Are you going to fix her up?"

"Perhaps. I haven't thought about it, really." The boat started down river, and he led her to two chairs on the deck. "Sit with me?" She did, and he took the other chair. "What do you fancy shopping for today?"

"There's nothing I want. This is Jewel's day." They were a long way from Windsor yet, so she relegated her nerves to the back of her mind and stretched out, savoring the light breeze on her face and the warm sun dancing on her skin. And the company. She'd never thought she'd enjoy a gentleman's company much, but Ford Chase was changing her mind.

The barge rocked gently as they made their way down the Thames. Father waved from the garden as they passed, and she waved in return, then stiffened.

Father had seen her. That meant other people could see her. Including neighbors.

Her gaze went wistfully to the cabin. "Can we go inside?"

"It's a sleeping cabin—there's nothing in there but a bed, so it's not really suited for the two of us." He raised a brow, a gleam in his eye, and she felt her cheeks grow hot. "Do you not enjoy the sun?" he asked.

"I worry for my complexion," she fibbed. Her mother and Rose both worried about their complexions, but Violet had never cared a fig. "I much prefer rain."

"Rain?" He looked at her as though she were daft, which accurately described how she was feeling at the moment. Then a smile tipped the corners of his mouth, and she knew he had caught her in the lie. "Fascinating. You really prefer rain to sunshine?" he asked, much too politely.

Seeing a man wander the riverbank, she rose and turned her back. "Well, I love rainbows," she said, digging herself in deeper. "And since rain is needed for rainbows, I do prefer it."

He grinned up at her. "I can make you a rainbow without rain."

"Can you?" What an extraordinary notion!

"Absolutely. I will do so tomorrow. In the meantime…" With great exaggeration and a flourish, he gestured to her empty chair.

She sat back down, and Ford began talking about this and that. She was soon so engrossed in their conversation that she forgot all about her eyeglasses or being spotted wearing them. The sun warmed her skin, and though their journey was a leisurely one that covered several miles, the time passed quickly.

Too quickly. Before she knew it, they were docking at Windsor.

It was a busy town. Windsor Castle had suffered much damage during the Cromwell years, and King Charles was now enthusiastically refurbishing and expanding it, which meant many laborers crowded the streets along with the town's usual inhabitants. Wearing her spectacles here would be worse than just being the center of attention. More like being the center of the universe.

She pictured herself on a bustling cobblestone street, surrounded by tradesmen and gossipy matrons and children underfoot—all of them pointing and laughing at her.

When Ford took her hand to help her down from the barge, that nervous, trembly feeling returned in full, overwhelming force. Her heart stuttered.

Wrenching her hand from his, she pleaded a headache and bolted for the shady safety of the cabin.

NINETEEN

*T*WO HOURS LATER, the others returned to the barge. "I'm starving." Followed by the children, Ford stepped inside the cabin to drop off their latest purchases. "How are you feeling, Violet? Can I tempt you with a meal? I promise to take you into a nice, dark deserted inn."

Violet heard the teasing in his voice and knew he knew she was a coward. He'd accompanied the children around town, where Jewel had purchased ribbons and a hat and a doll. For her birthday, Ford had bought her a lovely silver heart pendant. He'd also kindly bought Rowan some marbles fashioned from pretty stones, and they'd stopped at vegetable stands and a butcher, loading the barge with staples for Lakefield's kitchen.

They'd made three trips back and forth, and in all that time, Violet hadn't set foot out of the cabin.

Now the three of them crowded into the small space, their expectant gazes practically pinning her to the bed where she sat.

She bit her lip. Ford had been more than patient. The least she could do was be honest. "I'm sorry, my lord. But I just know people will laugh at me."

"Will you stop my-lording me?" He swept off his hat and, in a gesture that was beginning to become familiar to her, raked his fingers through his long brown hair. "After yesterday," he said in a low, discreet tone, "you should certainly have leave to call me Ford."

"Ford, then," she said. He was right. And she was miserable.

Jewel tugged on her uncle's sleeve. "What happened yesterday?"

"He gave me these marvelous spectacles," Violet said before he could answer, although she knew he'd been referring to their kiss.

She'd been thinking about that kiss the whole time she waited on the barge, replaying every little detail in her mind, over and over, until her lips tingled and she found herself unaccountably short of breath. She'd alternated between wondering if he'd kiss her again and telling herself not to be ridiculous.

Because she knew the truth: He'd been carried away by the success of his spectacles, and it wasn't going to happen another time. And she was far too sensible a girl to fall prey to the hopeless fantasy that someone like him—someone tall and gorgeous and brilliant and kind—could ever have feelings for someone like her.

Only...well, she'd rather *liked* being kissed. It grieved her to think it might never happen again. Which led her to another truth: She'd never get another kiss from anybody if she hid herself the rest of her life. If she was going to wear the spectacles, she needed to get over this fear of appearing in public.

Not all at once, however. "Can we dine on the way back?" she offered as a compromise. "An inn along the river. Where I won't have to walk a street teeming with people."

He measured her for a moment. "If I cannot tempt you with food, I suppose a bookshop wouldn't work, either?"

"A bookshop?" she murmured.

He jammed the hat back on his head. "Right there on Thames Street. You can see it from here." Without asking for permission, he grabbed her arm and drew her off the bed and out of the cabin. She blinked in the sunlight. "There, see?" he said.

In the distance, a sign swung in the slight breeze. The cracked wood looked a century old, but the lettering was newly painted and visible from the barge: JOHN YOUNG, BOOKSELLER.

Thanks to her spectacles, she could read that.

There weren't too many people on the street. "Maybe just the bookshop," she conceded.

Though he didn't lord it over her with words, his grin told her he knew he'd won.

"I'd like to choose a foreign language book for Rose," she added in a paltry attempt to save face.

"And maybe a philosophy book for yourself?" It seemed he knew her all too well. Jewel and Rowan had followed them out, and he waved them off the barge. "Hurry, before she changes her mind."

As Violet stepped onto the dock, she took a deep breath and lifted her chin. Let people stare. Let them laugh, even. She had to get used to it, and she might as well start now.

"Why a foreign language book for Rose?" Ford asked as they walked.

"A peace offering. I've been short-tempered with her lately."

"Having met her, I suspect she probably deserved it." The street was rutted and uneven, and he took her elbow to steady her in her heels. "But I meant why a foreign language?"

"Oh." She was acting daft again, distracted by the warmth of his hand seeping through her peach satin sleeve, and the trembling inside that wouldn't quite go away. She caught a glimpse of herself in the mullioned glass windows of the Swan, a reflection of her walking with a gentleman. It was difficult to think straight. "My grandfather was a scholar and spoke many tongues. Of all of us, Rose spent the most time with him before he passed on—"

"She doesn't seem the type."

"She'd be pleased to hear you say that." As they passed Bel and the Dragon, music pumped out the tavern's open door. "Although Grandpapa is no longer with us, Rose has kept her interest in languages. She teaches herself now, and she loves new books to puzzle out for practice."

"I would never have guessed it. Rose seems..."

"Empty-headed?" Violet supplied helpfully.

"No. Well, a bit, I suppose, but I don't mean it in a bad way."

"She's constructed a good facade, our Rose." She moved closer to him, avoiding a horse and carriage. "She is of the opinion, you see, that men aren't interested in intelligent women."

"I wasn't," he murmured.

"Pardon?"

Switching sides to shield her from the traffic, he cleared his throat. "I wasn't at all aware of Rose's scholarly tendencies. Philosophy, languages...you Ashcroft girls are surely not the usual sort."

"The Ashcroft motto is *Interroga Conformationem*."

"Question Convention?" Judging from his expression, that seemed to amuse him. "What talent is Lily hiding?"

"Only a gentle heart. She cannot stand to see any being in pain, human or animal." She stopped before the bookshop, which looked blessedly deserted, and suddenly realized that with all the conversation, she'd forgotten to worry about strangers staring at her.

In fact, she'd forgotten about everything but Ford, including her unsightly spectacles—and her little brother.

Fortunately, the children were right behind them. "Do you two think you can behave in there?" she asked sternly.

Ford crossed his arms. "No pranks in there, you hear?"

"Gads, Uncle Ford, of course not." Jewel pulled open the door. "Pretty," she said, looking up. "Like Rowan's house, and Auntie Kendra's."

Entering behind her, Violet bit back a smile. The ceiling Jewel was gazing at was beautifully carved and gilded, although the rest of the shop had seen better days. Row upon row of narrow aisles were crammed with books on sagging wooden shelves. More books sat piled haphazardly on the floor, apparently waiting to be sorted. Dark and well-worn, the place smelled like leather, paper, and ink.

Exactly the way a bookshop should.

A man appeared, looking well-worn like the shop. "John Young, at your service." His hair was salt-and-pepper, and his blue eyes were faded with age, yet lively as he regarded Jewel. "You like the ceiling, little one? If you'll follow me, I'll show you a secret about that ceiling."

He wove through the tall shelves and stopped in the middle of the shop. "Look up," he said.

They all did. A carved molding divided the elaborate ceiling, and although the sides were decorated in an identical fashion, the front half was dated 1576 and the back 1577.

"Why are there two dates?" Rowan asked.

"That's the secret." Mr. Young smiled, revealing a mouthful of teeth with only one missing. "Tell me," he asked the children, "what happened between those two dates?" He waited a beat. "I'll give you a hint. It wasn't the first time it happened, nor will it be the last. It happened again about fifty years later, and yet again in 1665."

"I wasn't born yet," Jewel said. "How should I know?"

Rowan puffed out his chest. "I wasn't born yet, either, but I know anyway. The Black Death."

"Bright boy." The bookseller ruffled Rowan's hair. "The workmen were from Italy and sailed for home when the plague took hold. But they promised to come back and finish, and so they did, a year later. Hence the two dates."

"That's funny." Jewel stared at the ceiling a moment longer, then her gaze dropped to a table against the wall. "A draughts board!" She batted her lashes at the bookseller. "May we play?"

"Of course."

"Mr. Young said I'm bright," Rowan told her. "I wager I can beat you."

Ford laughed. "I wouldn't recommend you bet money. She's the type that goes for the throat."

"I can beat any old girl."

Jewel planted her hands on her hips. "We'll see about that."

She made a beeline for the table, waving Rowan into the chair opposite as she settled herself with a fluff of her pale yellow skirts. Her face was all business as she began to set the markers.

Mr. Young turned to Violet, peering curiously at her eyeglasses. "May I help you find something, milady?"

"They're spectacles. They allow me to see at a distance," she explained, although he politely hadn't asked.

"How very fascinating."

He didn't seem repulsed by her appearance, just honestly interested. "Would you like to try them?" she offered.

"I can see at a distance fine. It's up close where I have trouble. My arms need to be longer." His smile reappeared. "It's a brilliant invention, though, isn't it?"

"Quite." She smiled in return. Perhaps not everyone would laugh at her, after all.

"Have you any books in foreign languages?" Ford asked. "And my lady would like to see some philosophy titles."

"Philosophy I have. This way, if you please." After directing her around the corner to a tall shelf full of books, he scratched his graying head. "Now, as for foreign languages, I'm afraid... ah, yes, perhaps I do have something in the back. If you'll excuse me for a moment."

The instant he disappeared, Ford moved close, so close Violet could smell the warm scent of his skin. Patchouli and soap and fresh air.

He backed her gently against the shelves. "How does it feel to be off the barge?" he whispered.

"Liberating." She gave a nervous laugh. "Will you look for books, too?"

"I'll look for Rose's."

"Would you? I'm hopeless at languages."

"I don't know many. French, having grown up on the Continent during Cromwell's Protectorate." He lifted the tail of her long, heavy plait, and Violet went still, barely breathing.

Was he noticing it wasn't soft and shiny like other girls' hair? Did he think it was hideous?

"Some Dutch," he went on, "since the exiled court spent time at The Hague as well. And Latin, of course." Wrapping the end around his finger, he gave it a gentle tug. "But that's all."

"It's three more than I can claim." Watching his fingers play with her hair, her scalp went all tingly. "If you'll choose some subjects Rose might find interesting, I'd be forever grateful."

"Forever grateful. I like the sound of that." He grinned, and her insides flip-flopped.

The proprietor ambled back, dragging a crate of books behind him, and Ford shifted away. Mr. Young nodded toward him. "I don't know what sort of foreign book you're looking for, milord, but you may have anything in here for a shilling."

"Anything?" Violet asked.

"Take your pick. My son Thomas found these in the attic—never been up there myself. Must've been there since before I bought the shop—from the looks of them, before that curious ceiling even went in," he added, his grin revealing the missing tooth. "Tom wanted to get rid of them, seeing as we don't deal in foreign titles, but I cannot seem to find it in me to throw away books." He dusted off his hands. "If you're not wanting anything else, then, I shall leave you to look."

With a nod, he walked off. They heard him stop and talk to the children, a soft murmur followed by their high-pitched giggles. Apparently the shop had no other customers, which suited Violet perfectly. She turned to the shelves, her heart swelling as it always did when she was in the presence of books.

Ford crouched on the floor and began absently sifting through the crate. "What would Rose like?"

"Anything, really, except perhaps philosophy or science." The two subjects she and Ford would want for themselves. She smiled at that thought as she peered at the titles on the shelf.

Choosing a slim brown volume, she slipped off her spectacles, the better to see up close. She set them on a ledge and began to flip pages without really reading. She could still smell the scent of Ford's skin, feel the slight tickle of him playing with her hair.

"What is that called?" he asked without looking up.

"*Aristotle's Master-piece.*" It looked promising, though she was surprised to find a book about or by Aristotle that she'd never heard of before. "I think I shall inquire about the price."

"Here, I'll hold it for you while you look some more."

She handed it to him, and he set it on the floor, on top of two volumes he'd apparently chosen for Rose. She could understand why the bookseller would let them go for a shilling. Even without her eyeglasses, the foreign editions looked like they hadn't been opened in decades.

Still crouching by the crate, Ford began humming a soft tune as he searched. A lullaby, if she didn't miss her guess; she wondered if he sang to Jewel. She slipped another title off the shelf. The clicks of checkers told her the children were miraculously staying put. Though their voices were a bit louder than she would have liked, they didn't seem to be bothering the proprietor, so she decided not to let it bother her, either.

She'd added two more likely books to the growing pile when Ford sat down with a thud, clutching a book in both hands.

He looked like he'd seen a ghost.

TWENTY

"**W**HAT'S WRONG?**" Violet asked. Sitting on the floor, the viscount looked as pale as her father's prized lilies. "Ford?"

"Nothing." He glanced around uneasily, as though he expected someone to pop up and steal the book out of his white-knuckled hands.

She couldn't help but notice those hands were shaking. The book was small and looked old. No, make that ancient, she decided after she'd reached for her spectacles and slipped them back on. It was handwritten, and the pages sounded brittle, crackling when he gingerly turned them.

"Another foreign title, is it?" Even with the eyeglasses, she couldn't read a word. "Do you expect Rose would like it?"

"No." Still trembling, he stood abruptly. "Not this one."

"Can you read it? Is it French or Dutch?"

"It's no language I've ever seen. Will you get those?" he added distractedly, gesturing to the books on the floor.

As she knelt to collect the volumes they'd chosen, he hurried away to talk to the proprietor.

"Yes, only a shilling," Mr. Young was saying when she joined them a minute later. Gazing down at the book, he lazily flipped a few pages. "It's not English or Latin, though, and difficult to decipher, handwritten as it is. Can you even read it?"

"Well, no." Ford raked his fingers through his hair—not the smooth, thoughtful gesture Violet had become used to seeing, or even the quicker one that indicated frustration. This motion was jerky and convulsive instead.

What was wrong with him?

"I have a friend, an expert in languages," he said. "I thought he might enjoy the challenge." He held out his hand, and she could almost hear him willing the shopkeeper to give him back the book.

The man handed it over, gesturing dismissively. "A shilling will do, then. Truth be told, I feel guilty taking money for the thing at all."

"Appreciate it." Ford turned to Violet, taking the books from her arms. "Add these to the total, please." He passed them over to Mr. Young and started digging out his pouch.

"I brought money," she protested. "I cannot accept a gift from you. It wouldn't look right."

"Rubbish. You've already accepted the spectacles, haven't you?"

Her hands went to her face protectively. "These were different. You made them."

"They're just books, Violet."

Mr. Young looked at each book, scribbling their prices on a scrap of paper, preparatory to adding them up. He paused when he came to Violet's first choice. "Are you certain you want this, my lady?"

"*Aristotle's Master-piece*? Yes. Unless…is it very expensive?"

Frowning, he blinked his pale blue eyes. "No, not particularly."

"We'll take it." Ford selected a few coins and pressed them into the bookseller's hand. "Jewel? Rowan? Are you done with your game?" He looked to be in a terrible rush.

"One more minute, Uncle Ford."

He shifted from foot to foot while they finished playing, then took Jewel by the hand to pull her from her seat. With a distracted "Thank you" called over his shoulder to Mr. Young, he waved Violet and Rowan through the door and followed them out with his niece.

"Is something amiss, Uncle Ford?" the little girl asked.

"No. No, not at all. I'm hoping something is very right." He hastened them down the street, his gaze focused straight ahead to where the barge sat waiting. "Hurry. Quickly."

In her fashionable high heels, Violet had a hard time keeping up, and she completely forgot to worry about who might see her wearing the spectacles. In no time at all, he was ushering them aboard.

"Straight home, Harry." Ford hesitated, though for barely an instant. "No, stop at the first decent inn—but not until we've cleared the town."

The children joined Harry at the helm while Ford hurried Violet into the cabin, apparently forgetting it was unsuitable. He pulled the door shut behind them. When the barge began moving, he let out a long, audible breath and dropped heavily onto the bed.

Since there wasn't any other furniture, Violet seated herself primly at the foot of the bed. "What's going on?" she asked, concerned by this odd behavior.

"I just...I suppose I feared Mr. Young would come running out and take the book back." It was still clenched in his fingers. "It's foolish, I know," he said, offering her a sheepish smile.

"Is it that important, then?"

"If it turns out to be what I'm hoping it is, yes, it's important." He relaxed his grip and, opening the book, turned a page and then another. If she could judge from his smile, the crackle of old paper sounded like music to his ears. "Very important."

"I imagine your friend will be pleased."

In the midst of turning another page, he looked up. "My friend?"

"Your friend who is good with languages."

"Oh." She'd never seen a gentleman blush before. "That wasn't the whole truth, I'm afraid. I just didn't know quite what to say. If the bookseller realized what this was…well, what it might be…but maybe I shouldn't…" He met her gaze. "What am I saying? Of course I can trust you." He sucked in a breath and blew it out. "This book could be extremely valuable, Violet."

Just the way he'd said her name, earnestly, like he cared, made her warm to her toes.

Rowan opened the door and poked his head in. His gaze sought out the book. "That looks very old," he said soberly. "Is it the emerald secrets book?"

"It might be," Ford said. "Everyone thought it was gone. I'm not certain I quite believed it had ever really existed." Light streamed through the cabin's two windows, illuminating the old pages, but they didn't glow nearly as brightly as his eyes. "The book was supposed to have been small and bound in brown leather, and of course it would have been handwritten, as Gutenberg's printing press hadn't yet been invented. And here, look." He flipped to the first page. "The alchemical symbol for gold. And five words in the title. But I cannot be sure. I wish I could read the thing."

If Violet had never seen a gentleman blush before, she'd never seen one so excited, either. About anything. "The emerald secrets book?" she asked. "What's that?"

Her brother smiled importantly. "It tells the lost secret of the Philosopher's Rock. I'm going to tell Jewel." He slammed the door, and she heard his footsteps pound across the wooden deck.

"The Philosopher's Stone," Ford corrected the empty space where Rowan had stood.

Violet gasped. "The formula to turn metals into gold?"

"The very same. *Secrets of the Emerald Tablet* has been missing for three hundred years, and if this is it…"

"Do you think it really is?"

"I don't know. It could be. Everyone assumed it had been

destroyed." He turned a few pages and stared down at the ancient text. "I'm crossing my fingers—and I'm probably the least superstitious individual you'll ever meet."

Suspecting he was right, she smiled at that. "What is the Emerald Tablet?"

He shut the book. "It's a long story."

"It's a long way down the river," she pointed out.

"Very well, then," he said, looking pleased. He stood up and began pacing in the skinny, cramped space around the bed, his hands clasped behind his back. "It all started back in Egypt, some twenty-five hundred years before Jesus Christ. Where the Divine Art first had its birth."

"The Divine Art?"

"Alchemy. An Egyptian priest named Hermes Trismegistus was known to have great intellectual powers. The Art was kept secret and exclusive to the priesthood, but more than two thousand years later, when the tomb of Hermes was discovered by Alexander the Great in a cave near Hebron, they found a tablet of emerald stone. On it was inscribed, in Phoenician characters, the wisdom of the Great Master concerning the art of making gold."

He paused, looking at her where she still sat perched at the foot of the bed. "You look uncomfortable there," he said, reaching to scoop up one of the pillows. "Lean back against the wall." He tossed it to her.

He'd told her it was a long story, so she scooted over to the wall and tucked the pillow behind her back, her legs stretched out on the bed. Noticing their outlines were visible beneath the drape of her peach gown, she fluffed her skirts a little. "Where is the Emerald Tablet now?"

He resumed pacing. "We don't know. But years later, in the thirteenth century, a man named Raymond Lully was born to a noble family in Majorca. He took up the study of alchemy and wandered the Continent to learn more of the science. Many stories have been told of Lully's abilities to make gold, which he claimed to have learned from studying the Emerald Tablet."

"What sorts of stories?"

His mouth curved in a faint smile. "You're really listening, aren't you?"

She cocked her head at him, baffled. "Why wouldn't I be?"

"No reason." Still smiling, he turned the book over in his hands, then opened it again absently. "It's said that the Abbot of Westminster found Lully in Italy and persuaded him to come to London, where he worked in Westminster Abbey. A long time afterwards, a quantity of gold dust was discovered in the cell where he'd lived. Another story has it that Lully was assigned lodgings in the Tower of London. People claimed to see golden pieces he'd made, and they called them nobles of Raymond, or Rose nobles. It was during this period that he is said to have written *Secrets of the Emerald Tablet*, I believe around the year 1275."

"Almost four hundred years ago." Looking at the pages Ford was carefully turning, she could believe the book was that old. "What happened then?"

"Lully eventually left England to resume his travels, but it was thought he left the book behind. It was supposed to have been written in language that's difficult to read."

She held out a hand, and wordlessly, he passed her the open book. She removed her spectacles and peered at the spiky writing. She couldn't read a word. Some of it didn't even look like words, but more like symbols.

"Do you suppose it's Phoenician, like the Tablet?" she asked.

"I have no idea. Legend has it that the book changed hands a few times and then disappeared in the fourteenth century, never to be seen again."

"Until now."

"Maybe." His eyes appeared wistful. "It looks old enough, doesn't it?"

"It would be priceless, wouldn't it?" Imagine being able to

produce gold. Caught up in his excitement, she handed back the book. "You could sell that for a fortune. An unbelievable fortune."

"I'd never sell it." He clutched the book to his chest. "If it's the missing volume, I'll never, ever sell it. Even should it turn out not to divulge a working formula."

"You'd feel the same even if it couldn't help you make gold?" Surprised, and yet somehow not, she slipped her spectacles back on to study his face. "I wouldn't have taken you for a romantic," she said softly.

"Who, me?" he murmured, holding her gaze for a long moment, a hint of a smile tugging at his lips.

Silently, he sat himself on the bed, stretched out his legs, and scooted over until he was right beside Violet, pressed against her from shoulder to hip.

Speechless, she looked down. Unwilling to meet his eyes, her own wandered the length of his legs. They looked lean and athletic, his ankles crossed in a relaxed manner.

With every nerve in her body humming, *she* wasn't relaxed at all.

"Raymond Lully is the stuff of legends," he continued calmly, as if oblivious to their improper proximity. "Any book he'd written would hold an immeasurable amount of historic and sentimental value. It would be an honor to own it, no matter what it said."

When he fell silent again, she forced her gaze to his face, and the expression there told her he wasn't oblivious at all.

He knew *exactly* how uncomfortable he was making her.

This was ridiculous.

And now that she'd met his eyes, she couldn't seem to stop staring at them. She felt trapped in their infinite blue depths.

Faith, she was thinking like Rose. She'd never taken *herself* for a romantic—she was far too sensible!

But currently behaving very insensibly, indeed. The barge

slowed and bumped against a dock, but it didn't jar her from the spell Ford seemed to have woven around her.

She licked her lips.

"And what of you?" he asked, his voice soft but his eyes dancing. "Are you a romantic?" Without waiting for an answer, he leaned forward, brushing a hand over her cheek, and—

Harry pulled open the door.

"Will this do, my lord?" He gestured at the scenery behind him, which included a respectable old riverside inn that boasted tables along the bank of the Thames.

To Harry's credit, he didn't blink when he saw them spring apart. And, thank the heavens above, Ford managed to lever himself into a standing position before the children arrived in the doorway.

"It will do very well," he said. "Thank you."

TWENTY-ONE

"LOOK!" JEWEL pointed to an enormous oak by the river. "There are swings!"

The children bounded off the barge and ran shrieking along the grassy bank. Violet walked more carefully behind, teetering a bit on the unaccustomed high heels. She felt rather lightheaded.

Was it her imagination, or had Ford nearly kissed her again? She wished she could ask him what had happened in the cabin—and why. But the thought of actually voicing such questions aloud made her face burn hotter than the afternoon sun.

She sneaked a sidelong glance at him strolling casually beside her, still clutching his precious book. Struck by the silly thought that he might sleep with it tonight, she smiled to herself.

He put a hand at her back. "What do you find so amusing?"

"Nothing." She could feel the pressure of his fingers through her thin satin gown. "Nothing at all." When his hand dropped from her back, she could swear she still felt its imprint.

By the time the two of them caught up, the young ones had claimed the pair of rope-and-board swings that shared a thick branch on one side of the old tree. They were pumping into the air, racing to see who could get the highest, their laughing taunts floating out over the water.

"That looks like fun," Violet said wistfully. Oh, to be six, flying into the sky on your birthday, instead of almost eighteen and dreading it.

Eighteen. Though plenty of girls remained unmarried by eighteen, to Violet it felt like the official start of her spinsterhood. Perhaps because Rose had been hinting as much for the past several months. Or because Mum had married at sixteen—after being caught in a compromising position with Father, as Grandpapa had always told it.

Not that Violet minded her fate as a spinster. She'd been resigned to it for years—planning happily for it, in fact. An unmarried woman enjoyed freedoms a wife never would.

But the word "spinster" sounded so very old and *final*.

Ford took her by the arm and marched her around the giant tree. A third swing there hung empty. "Sit," he said.

She giggled, feeling silly. "You take it."

"Sit."

With a shrug, she did. It had been years since she'd been on a swing—since the last time her family had stayed at Tremayne Castle. The board was flat and hard beneath her skirts. She wrapped her fingers around the thick, scratchy ropes on either side of her head. When she felt a hand at her back, she gave a little shriek, then whooped as Ford pushed her swinging into the air.

He came around the side to watch her, holding up the book to shade his eyes. "It's nice to hear you laugh."

She laughed again. "I feel like a child."

"Is that bad?" he wondered.

Pumping her legs to go higher still, she considered. The wind rushed by, freeing a fleet of unruly curls from their plait to tangle in the frames of her spectacles. When her peach skirts billowed, she clamped them between her legs. The sun sparkled on the water. Through her miraculous eyeglasses, the landscape looked clear and bright and beautiful all the way to the horizon.

"No," she said at last. "Feeling like a child isn't bad." At nearly eighteen, feeling like a child was a wonderful respite.

Placing the book delicately on a clump of grass, Ford stepped behind her and gave her a shove. She leaned back, listening to the wind whistle through her ears as she went soaring into the air.

"I can go faster than you!" Jewel cried from the other side of the tree.

"No, I can go faster!" Rowan yelled, and the two of them pumped their hearts out, racing toward the sky.

Ford's hands on Violet's back felt solid and warm, his pushes rhythmic and reliable. Her lids slid closed. She didn't want to go faster than anyone; she preferred to blank her mind and enjoy the motion.

With her eyes shut, she imagined she was flying. She imagined she was beautiful, and Ford was her handsome husband, not just an irredeemably flirtatious young uncle who wanted her help caring for his niece.

"Holy Hades," Rowan complained, jarring her back into the real world.

Her eyes popped open. "I've told you not to say that!" she called toward the children's side of the tree.

"No matter how high I get," he panted, "I cannot seem to go faster than her. She swings three times and I swing only two."

Jewel snorted. "Because you're bigger, you goose."

"I'm not a goose," Rowan said, and Violet cringed, suspecting Jewel had learned that insult from Rose. But Rowan seemed to consider Jewel's analysis. "Anyway, you're a girl, so you'll get tired," he decided smugly. "And then I'll go faster!"

"No," Ford said, giving Violet another push, "you won't."

"He won't?" Violet asked. Rowan's theory made sense to her. Well, perhaps not the part about Jewel tiring—the girl was a bundle of energy if ever she'd seen one. "If Rowan pumps harder, he won't go faster?"

"He won't," Ford repeated. "The swing is a pendulum—"

"Like in your laboratory?" Jewel interrupted loudly.

"Just like that." He pushed again. "Only you are the weight at the bottom."

Jewel's dark hair streamed behind her, then flew forward to hide her face. "And he's a heavier weight, so…"

"No, the amount of weight doesn't matter." When Violet swung back, Ford wasn't there to push. She slowed down to listen. "The time a pendulum takes to go back and forth is called the period," he said, walking over to push Jewel instead. "And the period depends on the length of the string. Or in a swing's case, the ropes." He reached to give Rowan a shove. "Jewel's ropes are quite a bit shorter, so Jewel swings faster."

"Are you sure?" Rowan asked dubiously.

"Positive. But test it yourself. Switch swings with Jewel. That's what an experiment is all about."

The children dragged their feet on the ground to stop the swings, and Ford came back to Violet.

Soon Rowan and Jewel had switched sides and were pumping again. And Rowan was going faster. "You're right!" he yelled.

"Of course I'm right." Ford gave Violet another little push. "But I didn't figure it out myself. Galileo first made the observation."

"I know all about Galileo," Jewel told Rowan importantly. "Uncle Ford named his horse after him." She swung back and forth, back and forth. "I want to go faster again!"

"I'll swing a hundred times and then you can," Rowan offered.

"Fifty times."

"As you wish. But we'll switch back after another fifty." In his high young voice, he began counting.

Ford gave Violet a huge shove, and she soared out over the

landscape, swinging back so hard one of her shoes flew off and landed on the grass with a *plop*.

"Oh!" she exclaimed, the word sounding breathless and giddy. "Stop!"

"Why?" He pushed her again, and when she rushed back, he plucked off her other shoe. She heard that one, too, plop somewhere behind her back. "There," he called as she swung away again, "now you'll really feel like a child."

Laughing, she wiggled her toes, feeling free in only stockings. And he pushed her higher. And higher. And higher. "Stop!" she screamed, meaning it this time. "Or I think I might get sick!"

He grabbed the ropes and jerked her to a halt. "Better?"

"Much." Still holding on tight, she gave a shaky laugh. "I guess I'm too old for this, after all."

"No one's too old for this," she heard him say from behind her. And then she felt his warmth at her back, and an armed curved around her waist. He came around to her side.

Her hands clenched the ropes as a delicate shiver rippled through her. "Rowan and Jewel..." she whispered, turning her head, but as soon as her lips were in reach he covered them with his own. She heard the children's chatter and hoped that meant they weren't watching—and then promptly forgot all about them, along with everything else but for one hazy thought...

She was being kissed again!

And it felt just as strange and wonderful and exciting as she remembered. He kept one arm securely around her middle, and when he raised his other hand to her face, skimming his thumb along her cheekbone, she thought she might expire from the incredible niceness of it all.

He drew away slightly, and she felt his fingers moving over her ears, unhooking the spectacles. He slid them off. When she opened her eyes, his face was so close she could see every detail with perfect clarity.

Without her spectacles, he was all she could see. He was all she wanted to see.

She kept her eyes open this time as he slowly lowered his mouth toward hers. But before their lips touched again, a girlish squeal pierced the air, and both their heads whirled toward the sound.

Jewel was fine. But the spell was broken.

Pulling a face, Ford straightened and made sure Violet was steady on the swing before handing over her spectacles. Her hands shaking, she put them back on. As his face swam into view, he flashed her a smile. A secretive smile. A smile she didn't think she had the experience to comprehend.

She leaned her forehead against the swing's rough rope, trying to catch her breath. She could hear Ford rummaging about, gathering the book and her shoes.

"Thirty-seven, thirty-eight," Rowan chanted.

Once he'd collected their belongings, Ford paused for a moment to collect his wits. What on earth had possessed him to risk that in front of his young niece? He seemed to be growing more impulsive by the day.

Someone had left one of the inn's benches near the tree—to sit and watch their children, no doubt—and he dragged it over by Violet's swing and sat. He set her shoes on the grass and the book on his lap.

"Forty-eight, forty-nine…" On the opposite side of the tree, Rowan reached fifty, and the children traded places.

"You're very good with them," Violet said quietly from her swing.

Never, in ten lifetimes, had Ford thought anyone would tell him that. Of course, he'd never thought he'd kiss a girl like Violet Ashcroft, either. A shy country miss who spouted philosophy.

"It was only physics," he said dismissively, gazing at her profile. Her lips were slightly parted. He remembered how they'd felt on his, silky and delicate as a flower petal. How appropriate. "Science. I'm good at science."

Still motionless on the swing, she turned her head to look at him. "You're good with your niece. And Rowan."

He felt totally inept with them, but he didn't want to argue. "Perhaps that's because I never grew up myself," he suggested instead. "My family would tell you that."

"You've said something like that before," she recalled, looking flushed and flustered and beautiful, her eyes large and liquid behind her lenses. The spectacles had slipped down her nose, and she pushed them back up. "What are they like, your family?"

"Loud," he answered with a grin. "I have a twin sister, Kendra, and two older brothers, Jason and Colin. All married. Among the three of them, they have seven children already, and I suspect more to come. Jewel is the oldest."

"No wonder you're good with children, then."

He shook his head. "It's not like that. I've played with them, of course, and when I'm not in London, I live with Jason and his family at Cainewood. Two boys, he and Cait have. But before now, I'd never taken care of my nephews or nieces." They all had nursemaids to see to that. "I've never taken care of *anyone* before."

He'd been the baby of the family. Everyone had always taken care of *him*.

"Well, you're doing a proper job." She shifted to look over at Jewel, who was shrieking with laughter as she soared through the air beside Rowan.

His niece looked happy. Perhaps Violet was right, and he wasn't doing such a bad job after all.

"And your parents?" she asked, turning back. "What are they like?"

"Dead."

"Faith," she muttered, her face going white. "I'm so sor—"

"No need to be sorry." He turned the book over in his hands. "I was all of one year old when they died at Worcester, fighting for King Charles. I don't even remember them. My oldest brother more or less raised me, with the help of the exiled court. It was an interesting life."

Her fingers trailed up and down the ropes. "And a rough life, I'd wager."

He shrugged. "Not for me. Our parents sold most everything to help finance the war, but I was too young to worry about where my next meal would come from. Someone else always took care of that. The court moved from Paris, to Brussels, to Bruges and back...the world was my playground. I suppose things were tight, but a child doesn't need much."

When she met his gaze, the expression in them made something twist in his gut. "A child needs love," she said softly.

Soft or not, he heard a challenge in her voice.

"I had love." Uncomfortable under that gaze, he looked at the sun shining off the river instead. "From my sister and two older brothers. I never wanted for anything."

A short silence stretched between them before he finally looked back. One of her stockinged feet reached for the grass and pushed off. "And after you returned to England?" she asked, swaying back and forth.

How to sum up the last decade in a few short sentences? Why did he care that she understood his past? "By the time Charles regained the throne, Jason and Colin were nearly of age. Cromwell had stolen their childhoods, and both of them had too many responsibilities to attend formal schooling. I should never have owned land—being a younger son—but as thanks for our parents' service to the crown, Charles granted all of us titles and estates...and as soon as I could, I left mine behind and went off to university."

"How old were you then?"

"Seventeen. And spoiled rotten."

He'd never thought of it that way before, but it was true. Between term times during his six years at Oxford, and after completing his studies earlier this year, he'd returned to live with Jason. He'd never had to fend for himself. Never worried for anyone else. Never even had to chase a girl, since he'd always had Tabitha waiting in London.

He gave a rueful smile. "I've led a charmed life, haven't I?"

"I'm sure you haven't," she said quickly, and he remembered how things had ended with Tabitha. That part of his life wouldn't fall under the definition of *charmed*…but already, he realized, it didn't seem to hurt anymore. And it certainly didn't matter.

Odd, that.

Leaning back, Violet stuck her legs out straight and stared at her stockinged feet. "Nothing is that simple."

But it had been. It had always been simple for him.

They fell quiet, and he smiled at the quaint picture she made on the swing, shoeless and wearing his spectacles. He'd never talked with a girl like he talked with Violet Ashcroft—never met one who seemed interested in discussing much beyond fashion and gossip. Never talked with *anyone* who made him reveal parts of himself he hadn't even known.

"What was *your* childhood like?" he asked.

"Boring in comparison." Still looking down, she turned her toes this way and that. "Grandpapa sent money for the cause, but he never went off to fight. He put family before the monarchy. We never went into exile, either. I've never been outside of Britain."

"But he did support King Charles?"

She looked up. "Oh, yes. Of course he did. My family was never anything but Royalist."

"I'm surprised Trentingham wasn't attacked by Cromwell's forces, then. Cainewood was." And had the cannonball marks to prove it.

"They confiscated Trentingham and occupied it, but we weren't there. Grandpapa had a secondary title and property that went along with it. Tremayne Castle, very near Wales. Not helpful for the Roundheads strategically, and I suspect too far away for them to bother with." She glanced over at the children. "Rowan is Viscount Tremayne now."

"So your family stayed there for all the years of the war?"

"And after. All through the Commonwealth, until the Restoration. Besides having an odd penchant for studying languages, Grandpapa was a stickler for safety." She pushed off again, gliding up and then down, slowing immediately when she did nothing to sustain the momentum. "My parents were wed at Tremayne, and I was born there. As were Rose and Lily. I was six before I ever laid eyes on Trentingham."

"Six?" he said, surprised. "How old are you now?"

"Almost eighteen."

From the tone of her voice one would guess she thought eighteen was a doddering old maid. But he'd thought she was older. Not that she *looked* older, but Tabitha was twenty-one, yet Violet seemed so much more mature.

"I'm twenty-three," he told her.

"I figured that," she said, "when I heard you were one year old during the Battle of Worcester."

"Unlike Rowan, you're good at mathematics." He smiled, thinking she was good at a lot of things. "Does your family sometimes live at Tremayne Castle now?"

"Not anymore. We retreated there to wait out the Great Plague—Rowan was born there during that time. But then Grandpapa died, and we haven't been back since." Seeming deep in thought, she gazed out over the Thames, swaying gently to and fro in the swing. "The castle was only ever half built. Mum says it's too far from London, and Father prefers Trentingham's gardens. It's a quiet sort of place, Tremayne..." She met his gaze again with a smile. "See, I told you my childhood was boring."

To his great embarrassment, his stomach growled. Loudly.

"Oh!" she said. "It's been at least two hours since you said you were starving! Before we even bought the books!"

"I haven't perished." He stood and handed her the shoes. "But I wouldn't mind wandering over and taking a table."

While she put them on, he went to fetch the children.

"Not yet!" Jewel yelled, swinging higher. "Another minute!"

"Two minutes!" Rowan countered.

"Three!"

"Five!"

"Ten!"

"Ten," Ford agreed, giving Jewel one final push. "But only because it's your birthday, mind you."

Violet followed Ford to an empty table. As she slid onto the bench, she kept a vigilant eye on the two young ones, who faced away as they soared over the scenic river.

"Relax," he told her. "They'll be safe. If they fail to join us, they can eat their portions on the barge on our way home. And the two of us can dine in peace."

A nice thought, Violet decided. Even more nice after he went inside to order a light dinner, then returned to sit beside her.

He couldn't actually have feelings for her...could he? Everything she knew about men told her no—but then again, she didn't know much about them at all. And his actions seemed to paint a different picture. It was confusing, to say the least. Especially when her hands drifted up to her face and she remembered her unsightly spectacles. For a while there, she'd forgotten all about them.

"No one's staring," he said gently. He lowered her hands and laced his fingers with one of them. It felt intimate, and her heart gave a stutter. "You look fine, Violet. You look lovely."

Through the lenses, he appeared sincere. She surveyed the few patrons seated at the other tables. The buzz of their conversation sounded pleasant to her ears, and he was right: no one was staring.

Besides Ford, no one was looking at her at all.

His gaze dropped to the book, his face brightening at the

sight. "I still cannot believe I may have found *Secrets of the Emerald Tablet.*"

"I'm so happy for you."

"It might not be the right book," he reminded her, although she suspected he was actually reminding himself. He squeezed her hand. "But I thank you for sharing my excitement."

"It's contagious," she told him. Her fingers tingled every place they touched his; she'd never realized her hand was so sensitive.

A serving maid came out and put two tankards on the table, along with a pewter platter piled with fat slices of cream toast. She set down two empty plates, and Ford dropped Violet's hand to take one of them.

Her spectacles seemed to be fogging. She pulled them off, wiped them on her skirt, and put them back on. "Thank you for sharing your dream," she said, lifting a tankard. A bracing swallow of ale seemed just the thing. "I very much hope it comes true."

"It would be incredible, wouldn't it?" He also sipped, regarding her over his tankard's rim. "And what are *your* dreams, Violet?"

"You'd laugh." She'd never told anyone outside her own family. Ever. Avoiding his eyes, she busied herself sprinkling sweet brown sugar on a slice of the egg-battered bread.

"I won't laugh. I promise." He sprinkled extra cinnamon on his. "Tell me," he said, cutting a piece.

"Well, one day…" As a delaying tactic, she swallowed a bite of cream toast, then washed it down with some ale.

"Yes?" he prompted, looking amused.

"I'd like to publish a philosophy book," she blurted out. "Not now, of course, but when I'm older. I still have much to learn first."

"A lady authoring a philosophy tome." Chewing, he considered. "It's an ambitious dream."

He was listening, and he wasn't laughing. "I would publish it under a man's name. Otherwise no one would read it."

"Do you think so?"

"I know so." She sipped, then rushed on. "I have an inheritance coming, you see, enough to print and distribute the book far and wide."

He finished his slice and took another. "What is it you're so burning to say?"

"I don't know yet." Perhaps that sounded rather foolish, but it felt so good to finally tell someone—someone who really listened. "I'm still learning, still changing my opinions. But I believe these things are important. Ideas can change the world. And...I dream of leaving my mark."

"So do I."

"But with science, am I right?" Ford was different, like her. She'd never expected to meet anybody like her. "You want to leave your mark with science. Science can change the world, too."

"Exactly."

He smiled, reaching to touch the back of her hand. She thrilled at the contact—until he opened his mouth again.

"I reckon it's a rare fellow who'd let his wife's fortune go to such a project."

His words cut her to the core.

She'd thought he understood.

Disappointment swamped her short-lived giddiness. He was poking fun at her. Raising her tankard to hide her flaming face, she ordered herself to shrug it off. She focused on Rowan and Jewel still swinging in the distance, their lighthearted laughter floating to her on the breeze. Of course he would think like that, she reasoned—she should expect nothing else.

Ford was different, but not as different as she'd hoped. Men that different simply didn't exist.

With a sigh, she lowered the tankard. "I realize most gentlemen marry for money." And Ford would be no exception, especially given his obvious lack of the same. "But as far as I'm concerned, that isn't a good reason to shackle oneself for life."

She watched him rake his fingers through his hair. "That's not what I said—"

"I knew what you were thinking."

"Did you?" he murmured, lifting his own tankard. A series of emotions crossed his face, but Violet couldn't make them out. He took a slow sip of ale. "Are you never planning to marry, then?"

Perhaps she'd dreamed of it for a minute—one brief, insensible minute. "My family isn't a conventional one."

"Question Convention."

"Yes. I feel no compulsion to lead a typical woman's life."

He just gazed at her for a while. A long while, while she tried and failed to figure out what he was thinking.

"No," he said at last, and paused for another sip. "Nobody would ever call Violet Ashcroft typical."

That hurt, but she only stiffened her spine. "I'm aware of my eccentricities, my lord. And I realize they are the reason no man would want me except for my inheritance."

He bristled. "Criminy, is it that much money?"

She couldn't tell whether he was sarcastic or serious, and she didn't get a chance to find out. Because in the next moment, two voices rang out from the riverbank.

"I dare you!"

"I dare *you!*"

And a moment after that, Jewel and Rowan flew from their swings into the water.

TWENTY-TWO

*V*IOLET JUMPED up from where they were eating. "The children!"

Splashes and screams followed.

Icy fear gripped Ford's heart. Boots and all, he made a running dive into the river.

But the splashes were playful ones—on Rowan's part, at least. And if Jewel's shrieks weren't exactly in fun, they weren't pleas for rescue, either. It was obvious both children knew how to swim.

The shock of cold water helped Ford regain his wits as he gathered Jewel and Rowan to him, one in each arm. He should have given his niece more credit, he thought wryly. She was much too clever to leap to her death. And if she was less than pleased with the outcome of her prank, perhaps it would be a lesson learned.

Moments later he'd hauled them ashore, no harm done. But by the time they were back on the barge and sailing for home, Violet was on the verge of hysterics.

"We shouldn't have left them!" she wailed, wringing her hands. Ford had never seen anybody wring their hands. Not in real life. He'd thought people only wrung their hands in plays.

And they hadn't left the children—they'd been watching them the entire time. He'd been there within seconds, he reminded himself, struggling to hold on to logic in the face of hysteria. There had never been any real risk of drowning.

So why was his pulse still beating double-time?

He drew a deep breath. "All's well that ends well," he told Violet philosophically, wondering if a philosopher had actually said that. But if she knew, she was in no state to inform him.

Jewel was equally hysterical. "There were *fish* in there!" Her entire body shuddered, and not from the wet and cold. "Fish! Slimy fish!"

Rowan was hysterically laughing at Jewel, and Ford...well, if he hadn't felt a need to act as the lone voice of reason, he'd have been hysterical along with the rest of them.

"Of course there were fish," Rowan crowed between snorts. "You *goose*," he added with undisguised glee.

Ford suspected he'd been waiting to call Jewel a goose since she'd called him one on the swings. Pouring water from one of his boots, he rather sympathized with the boy.

Women. Ford would never understand them. For a moment back at the inn, he'd thought he had finally made sense of Violet. He'd seen that she was driven by a deep-rooted ambition not unlike his own. That warm flash of connection had felt so surprising and welcome, he'd made an offhand jest about men and marriage—just a silly jest! But it seemed to have shocked her, or angered her. Or both.

Criminy, why did women have to take everything so seriously?

As they neared Trentingham's dock, he sighed and tipped his second boot. Water ran out, along with a tiny sliver of silver.

"Another fish!" Jewel screamed.

Rowan snickered.

Violet moaned.

And Ford knew he wasn't going to get an answer to his question.

TWENTY-THREE

*T*HE NEXT DAY, Ford paced Trentingham's library. He still had no idea where he stood with Violet following that confusing, interrupted conversation. He'd tried to talk to her before departing yesterday, but here at the Manor there always seemed to be a sister or two around.

Turning the old book in his hands, he sighed, thinking she'd probably already forgotten their discussion, anyhow. Why would Violet be dwelling on it, as he was? The exchange could have no particular significance to her. And her family had let him in the house, so apparently they didn't hold him responsible for upsetting their daughter—not to mention for the young heir's soaking. That was a good sign.

After all, he'd hate to think Jewel might lose her playmate.

"Lord Lakefield?" Jarring him out of his thoughts, Rose sauntered into the room with Violet, fluttering her fifteen-year-old lashes. "My sister said you wanted to see me?"

He bit back a laugh, then fastened his gaze on those bold dark eyes and tried his famous smile on her—the one that sent most ladies tittering behind their fans. "Violet tells me you've a special expertise in languages."

Looking a bit off her stride, she leaned a hand on one of the library's two impressive globes, then jumped when it spun beneath her fingers. "Not truly," she said, glaring at Violet as she brushed the front of her magenta skirts. "I know only a little."

"More than a little," Violet argued. "You know French and Spanish, German, Welsh, some Gaelic—"

"Would you know this one?" Ford interrupted, struggling for patience. So far as he could tell, the book was none of the tongues Violet had mentioned or anything related. He walked to a round wooden table and opened the book on its surface. "Does this language look familiar?"

When Rose didn't make a move, he sent a pleading look to her sister.

"Rose..." Violet said. It was a single word, but uttered in a tone he hoped never to hear directed at himself.

"Oh, very well." Rose unriveted herself from the floor and came to lean over the table. She frowned at the book, reaching to gingerly turn a page, then another. The brittle paper crackled in the silence of the richly paneled library.

"No," she said at last. "I've never seen this language. It may be obsolete." When she looked up, her dark eyes were apologetic. "I know only modern languages, my lord." Her false pretense of empty-headedness gone, she closed the book respectfully and slid it across the table.

Disappointment formed a weight in his gut. Reaching for the book, he sat himself on one of the table's four straight-backed chairs. Violet surprised him by sitting beside him. After yesterday, he didn't know what to expect from her.

"How about the title?" he asked, not quite ready to give up. He reopened the book. No author had signed it, but there, right on the first page, was the alchemical symbol for gold. Of course, the symbol was just a plain circle with a dot in the center, so it could mean something else. Or nothing at all—in a handwritten book, such a mark could be a decoration or a doodle. But the sight of that symbol had set Ford's heart to pounding in John Young's shop.

The title alone could confirm whether or not he'd found the right book. He pushed it back toward Rose. "Can you puzzle out a single word of the title, even?"

"I can try." Rose's reluctance disappeared as she took a seat on his other side and drew the book closer. Clearly warming to the challenge, she ran a tapered finger across the handwritten text. "There are five words."

"Yes." But were they the right words? "Can you read any of them?"

"No." She shook her head. "I think not." She flipped back to the center of the book. "Some pages are stuck together."

"It's old," he said with a shrug. He'd peeled a couple of the pages apart and found nothing of interest, just more of the same. And he'd ripped one of them in the process. "I hesitate to start tearing at it, when I don't even know—"

"This is strange."

"What?" Violet asked.

"Well, I can read this one word here. *Argento*. It means silver in Italian."

Silver. Ford's hopes took an incautious leap. A book that mentioned silver might also mention gold. And Raymond Lully had lived in Italy for years.

Violet reached across Ford to touch her sister's hand. "Are you sure? I never knew you could read Italian."

"I'm sure." A hot blush touched the girl's cheeks.

Rose resembled Violet, but her features had a glossy perfection that was missing from her sister's. Tabitha had been like that, too. They were *too* perfect, Ford thought. Violet's looks were friendlier, more comfortable. Natural.

He could touch her without worrying about messing her up.

"I found an Italian book," Rose explained, gesturing to the shelves that stretched to the high, geometric-patterned ceiling. "It wasn't too difficult to teach myself. The language shares much with Spanish."

Nodding, Violet sat back. A pity—he'd rather enjoyed having

her lean over him. She'd smelled like flowers. Probably violets, he imagined.

Rose looked back down to his book. "Of course, some languages share the same words with different meanings. For example, in French *four* means oven, but in English it's a number. So just because *argento* means silver in Italian doesn't mean it couldn't mean something else in another tongue." Carefully, she flipped another page. Scanning it, she hummed under her breath.

"What is it?" Violet asked.

"It's odd, that's all. That one word appeared to be Italian, but others aren't. There are letters here that are foreign to me, and here"—she looked up—"look at this line, here."

Both Ford and Violet scooted closer, their chair legs rasping on the carpet. "Yes?" Ford prompted.

"This line is written backwards. Even the letters are backwards, like in a mirror. And then this line here"—she drew a graceful finger along some text—"has no strange letters at all." In her enthusiasm, her voice had lost its deliberate seductive quality. "The writing is a bit faded and more than a bit smeared, but all readable, you see?"

Violet shook her head. "I cannot read it."

"You cannot comprehend it," Rose corrected. "But you recognize the letters, don't you?"

"It may be a code," Ford realized suddenly.

"Different languages and patterns. You may be right." Rose looked up at him, her dark eyes excited. Her face looked younger. "Violet said this could be an important book. Was the book you're looking for written in code?"

"I never considered it before, but it could have been." The book had been rumored to be difficult to read. If he were recording priceless secrets, he'd be tempted to do so in code.

And he knew someone who was *very* good at cracking codes.

"If it's a code," Violet asked her sister, "do you think you could puzzle it out?"

Rose shook her head regretfully. "I'm afraid not. There are too few words I recognize."

"And none in the title?" Violet pushed.

"None." Rose turned to Ford. "I'm sorry."

She looked sincere and capable, and although she didn't hold the same appeal as her older sister, he liked her much more than he'd thought. "That's quite all right," he told her, offering a smile. "You've actually helped a lot—"

"Where is Jewel?" Rowan interrupted, running into the room.

"At home," Ford said. "With her new friend Harry."

"*I'm* her new friend." Jewel would positively preen if she saw Rowan's pout. "Is she in your laboratory?"

"She'd better not be."

"You said we could go into the laboratory today. You promised."

"Rowan—" Violet started.

"He's right," Ford cut in.

He *had* promised. And at Lakefield, it would be easier to get Violet alone.

Just to talk to her, of course. To apologize for however he'd managed to offend her yesterday.

Rising, he closed the small leather book. "I did promise," he reminded her. "And a Chase promise is not given lightly. You'll come along, won't you?"

Her hesitation wasn't encouraging.

"Lord Lakefield..." Rose's voice was back to its practiced purr. "What is your laboratory like?"

"Messy," he said shortly. She was plainly angling for an invitation, but he wasn't at all tempted to offer one. Then he noticed Violet was scowling at her sister.

That was much more encouraging.

He graced Rose with another of his famous smiles, adding, "Perhaps sometime I'll show you."

"I'll come along," Violet blurted.

Very encouraging, indeed.

TWENTY-FOUR

"**I**T'S UP HERE, Violet."

"I'm coming." Violet followed her brother up the dark, square staircase and then up some more, the old wood creaking all the way to the attic.

They walked through a corridor lined with books—not the handsome leather-bound volumes that filled the Ashcrofts' impressive library, but books that were clearly well read, jumbled haphazardly on plain shelves. Science books, she assumed.

From what she had seen, which granted was only part of the ground floor and now this attic, it seemed Lakefield didn't boast a proper library. If she were mistress here, she would remedy that.

But of course that was never to be. Just being in this place reminded her of how much money Ford needed to fix it. He was going to have to marry for money, and she would never let that happen to her.

At the end of the corridor, Rowan stepped into a room. As Jewel scampered past him, he waved an expansive arm in a very grown-up way. "Look."

The single word was uttered in an awed tone. Entering the laboratory, Violet could see why.

Ford's workroom was housed in a gigantic open space. Beneath a steeply pitched ceiling of raw beams that exposed the stone-tiled roof above, a profusion of paraphernalia lived in charming confusion. Under the single shuttered window, a jumble of gears and other parts sat among an army of watches and clocks. Their ill-timed ticks filled the air, sounding like hundreds of scampering mice.

"Incredible," she said. There was no other word to describe it.

Ford opened a drawer and took out a shallow pan. "It's nothing compared to my laboratory at Cainewood. Or Charles's laboratory—the man has at least six of everything."

She didn't doubt it. King Charles was known to take his scientific pursuits very seriously and indeed had chartered the Royal Society. She'd heard he attended the regular meetings.

Just then, the clocks began chiming, as badly timed as their ticks, and she burst out laughing at the absurdity of it all. How anyone could accomplish anything in this chaos was beyond her comprehension.

"Look at this," Rowan said, pulling a heavy red book off a shelf. He shoved aside a mortar and pestle to set the book on a table, then opened it with great ceremony. Flipping several pages, he stopped on one and unfolded a large diagram.

She blinked. "What is that?"

"A spider," he said gleefully. "Like the one we scared you with."

Jewel snickered and moved close.

Violet slanted her brother a dubious glance. "That doesn't look like any spider I've ever seen."

"It's as seen under a microscope." He pointed to an instrument across the room, a handsome specimen of chased brass. "The book is called *Micrographia*." Pronouncing the word carefully, he turned to a random page, and the children leaned over the sketches.

They all stared at the patterns of tiny squares and holes. Jewel scratched her head. "What is it?"

"'Cork and other such frothy bodies,'" Violet read. "Fascinating, isn't it?" Even more fascinating than the pictures was her brother's animated face. He treated lessons as a chore; she'd never seen him show interest in anything academic.

"Look at this," he said, unfolding another large drawing. "Snowflakes."

"No, they're not," she said, hiding a grin. "Read it."

He focused on the page. "'Several observables,'" he enunciated slowly, "'in the six-branched figures form'd on the surface of urine by freezing.'"

"Ewww." Jewel made a face.

But Rowan was unruffled. "Can we buy one of these books, Violet? Please?"

"I have no idea where to get one."

"London," Ford said, polishing a small rectangle of mirror on his breeches. "Check the title page."

She turned to it and read. "'Printed by Joseph Martyn and James Allestry, Printers to the Royal Society, and sold at their shop at the Bell in St. Paul's Churchyard.' Hmm." She looked up at Rowan. "I'll talk to Father about it when next we go to the City."

Ford ripped a piece of white paper from a page of scribbled notes. "When will that be?"

"When Parliament is in session."

"I'll see if we can get one for him sooner." He turned to his niece. "Would you and Rowan do me a favor? Run downstairs, will you, and ask Hilda for a pitcher of water."

While Jewel hurried Rowan from the room, sending a pendulum swinging as they went, Ford walked to the single window and threw the wooden shutters open wide. "Three o'clock on a clear and sunny day," he said. "The sun should be just about right."

"For what?"

"Our demonstration. I promised you a rainbow, remember?"

Baffled, she decided to take a wait-and-see attitude. "I'm sorry Rose couldn't help you," she said.

"But she did. Without her observations, I may never have realized the book might be in code. Or in a language so old it's obsolete." He set the paper by the mirror and pan. "I have a friend from my Oxford days, now an expert in ancient linguistics. And codes." He laughed at some reminiscence. "Rand used to infuriate his brother by deciphering his secret journals. I'm going to send for him tomorrow."

"So you do have a friend."

A faint glint of humor lit his eyes. "I have many friends."

"I'm sure you do." More than she had, she'd wager. "I just meant I'd thought you'd invented that friend as a story to tell Mr. Young. The bookseller."

"Well, I didn't buy the book for Rand, so that much was a falsity. But he does exist. And I'd trust him with my life, although I'll admit I hesitate to let that book out of my sight." His half-smile was one of self-amusement. "I expect that's why I didn't think to call on Rand in the first place. Foolish of me—if I'd summoned him yesterday, I might know what I have already. But it never even occurred to me until Rose brought up the inconsistencies."

"You're just focused," she said. "On other things."

"You're right, you know." He moved closer. "I've always had that unfortunate trait. When I concentrate on one thing, I cannot think of another."

Finding herself backed against a table, she put her hands behind her and knocked over a flask. She whirled to right it. "My father is like that," she said while still turned away. "He thinks only of his flowers."

"My problem is," Ford whispered in her ear, "I've been thinking of *you*."

Violet's stomach did that odd flip-flop as his hands on her shoulders gently maneuvered her to face him.

"Thank you," he said, his face inscrutable as usual.

"F-for what?" Even through her gown, her skin tingled under his fingers. Her own thoughts whirled and skidded—she couldn't think at all when he was so close. When he was touching her, when she could smell patchouli, when she could feel his warmth.

This wasn't right. It wasn't fair. He was acting like he wanted her. But if he truly did want her, it was for all the wrong reasons.

And yet...she was beginning to think she might want him anyway.

His bright, bold gaze captured hers. "Thank you for forgiving me for whatever thickheaded thing I said yesterday."

Yesterday rushed back, those exhilarating moments by the river when she'd thought he'd understood, and then his words: *It is the rare fellow who'd let his wife use her fortune for such a project.*

Most husbands would expect to use a wife's inheritance for their own purposes.

She swallowed hard, hurt anew at the reminder that he thought her aspirations foolish. That she wasn't pretty enough or interesting enough to be wanted—despite her quirks—for herself.

Only for her money.

But as his hands drifted up her neck until they held the sides of her face, all those disturbing thoughts fled her mind. Her heartbeat suddenly seemed louder than the dozens of ticking clocks.

With his index fingers, he drew her spectacles forward and off. A little *click* sounded when he set them on the table behind her. Then he lowered his head and pressed his lips to hers.

A sudden rush of feeling made the blood race through her veins. Her head swam and a little thrill ran through her. He deepened the kiss, and her knees weakened, but his arms slipped around her waist to hold her up. By magic, it seemed, her own arms went around his neck in return, and she threaded her fingers into his hair.

When loud, childish voices came drifting down the corridor, Ford and Violet pulled away simultaneously. Her cheeks burning, Violet smoothed her skirts as Rowan and Jewel bounded in, chatting happily. She blinked at their blurry faces, then spun around to the table and snatched up her spectacles, shoving them back onto her face.

"Here, Uncle Ford." Jewel held out the pitcher.

Ford took it and filled the pan with water. Nonchalantly. Like nothing at all had happened.

Well, she told herself sternly, to him a kiss probably *was* nothing. Especially a kiss with her. He was obviously proceeding with the demonstration in a state of perfect calm. She shook her head to clear it, determined to pay attention.

And to appear as unruffled as he.

With a forearm, he swept aside springs and gears to set the pan on his work surface. Bright sunlight streamed through the window and glinted off the water.

He handed Jewel the small rectangle of mirror. "Put this in," he instructed, "so one end is in the water and the other end is resting on the side of the pan."

"May I do something?" Rowan asked.

"In a moment." They all watched as Jewel, looking very self-important, placed the mirror. Then Ford turned to Violet's brother. "You get to do the crucial part."

Rowan's green eyes danced. "What's that?"

"Move the pan around, and the mirror if necessary, until the sunlight reflecting off the mirror makes a patch of light on the wall."

The walls in the attic were unvarnished wood. Rowan did as he was told, gasping when a bright rectangle appeared like magic.

"What, you didn't believe it was possible?" Ford mussed the boy's dark hair.

Rowan gave him a sheepish smile. "I just wasn't sure I could do it."

"You can do anything you put your mind to," Ford told him. "Always remember that."

Violet glanced up sharply at his echoing a belief she held rather dearly. He handed her the piece of paper. "Now, hold this so the patch of light shines directly on it."

She did as he asked...and watched a brilliant range of colors bathe the white sheet.

"Holy Hades," Rowan said.

Ford's eyes met Violet's. "Do you like it?"

"A rainbow," she murmured.

"I told you I would make you one."

Thrilled, she stared at the beautiful hues. "I thought you meant figuratively."

"Now you can have rainbows without needing to prefer rain."

She felt herself blush. "I never did really prefer rain."

"I guessed that," he said with a nice smile, and any embarrassment she might have felt at being caught in that lie was lost in the shared moment.

"Why does it work?" Rowan asked.

Ford turned to him, all scientist now. "The water sitting on top of the slanted glass is a wedge shape." Violet suppressed a smile, watching as he gestured to each component. "When the sunlight bounces off the mirror, that wedge of water does the same thing a glass prism would. It's called refraction. The prism refracts the sunlight and breaks it down into all the different colors of light."

"May I try?" Jewel took the paper and held it away, then slipped it back in the beam of light.

The colors burst forth again.

"My turn." Rowan tried it himself, beaming at the results. "What do you mean by colors of light? Isn't all light white?"

"No. White light, like sunlight, is actually a combination of all the colors of light." Ford's language was simple although the concepts weren't; he didn't talk down to the children. "Isaac

Newton presented this experiment at the Royal Society last year."

Violet sighed. "I wish women were allowed to attend."

"One was, once. Margaret Cavendish, Duchess of Newcastle. But not as a member. She had written a book called *Observations upon Experimental Philosophy*, and she was allowed as a guest to observe some of our own experiments."

She gave him a wan smile. "I don't expect the Royal Society would be interested in any book I could write."

He looked contemplative. "Not as a group, perhaps. They can be a snobbish lot. But individual members would certainly take an interest." Rowan and Jewel began playing in the water, but he didn't seem to notice. "Have you heard of John Locke?"

"No." She pulled her brother's hand from the pan. "Who is he?"

"A brilliant philosopher, although he has yet to publish any significant papers. You should meet him. Perhaps he could help you achieve your dream. His ideas are quite thought-provoking." He rolled his eyes, then grinned. "I cannot believe I said that."

"I cannot believe you said that, either." Though he'd never voiced it in so many words, she'd suspected he was much too concrete and scientific to be drawn to philosophical musings.

When Rowan flicked droplets in Jewel's face, she shrieked, but Ford only smiled at them absently. "The Royal Society is holding an event next week. A celebration, if you will."

"What are they celebrating?" Violet asked, watching the girl pull a beaker off a shelf as Rowan turned away and became preoccupied by something on the cluttered table.

"Ever since the Great Fire when the City offices were temporarily set up at Gresham College, the Royal Society has been meeting at Arundel House instead."

Only half her mind on Ford's words, Violet saw Jewel scoop water from the pan, partially filling the beaker. He was oblivious, she thought. He could truly pay attention to only one thing at a time.

"But now that the Royal Exchange has reopened and the government moved out," he continued, "we've been invited back. The college is throwing a grand entertainment to welcome us."

With a victorious shout, the girl dumped the water on Rowan's head.

"Jewel!" Ford gasped, finally responding at the sound of Rowan's howl. He whirled to face her. "You must ask before you touch anything in here. That beaker could have had chemicals in it."

He didn't care that his niece had drenched Rowan's hair and shirt, Violet thought. Only that she might have ruined an experiment.

"It was empty, Uncle Ford," Jewel said.

Clearly struggling for calm, Ford dragged a hand through his hair. "Chemicals can dry and become invisible. And some can burn skin. Worse than fire."

"Oh." Jewel looked chagrined.

And Violet felt the same way, knowing she'd underestimated him.

"Are you burned?" Jewel asked Rowan. "You don't look black."

"He'd be red," Ford said.

"I'm fine." His hair still dripping wet, Rowan poked her in the stomach.

Violet opened her mouth to chide him, then decided the girl deserved it.

"I'm going to plan a prank on *you*," he promised Jewel, ruining the menace of the threat with his high-pitched giggle.

"You'd best hurry." Ford tossed him a towel. "She's going home next week."

"Home?" Rowan's grin faded. "Can't she just live here from now on?"

"I think her parents would have something to say about that." Ford took the pan and leaned out the window to dump the remaining water. "I heard from my brother this morning. There have been no new measles cases the past week, so if matters there continue to improve, I'll be taking Jewel home on my way to London for the Royal Society celebration."

He paused for a moment, seeming deep in thought, then turned to Violet. "John Locke should be there. Would you like to come as my guest?"

TWENTY-FIVE

"OF COURSE you'll go with him."

"Mum!" Violet paced the perfumery. "The celebration is in *London*."

Chrystabel looked up from the vial in her hand. "So?"

"So we're not in London, in case you haven't noticed. Parliament isn't in session, and you know Father won't leave his gardens in the summer. You don't mean for me to travel to London alone with Lord Lakefield, do you?"

Knowing Violet expected it, Chrystabel did her best to look shocked. "Of course not. But I won't have you miss this opportunity, either." It was a perfect excuse to get Violet and Ford alone together and away from the children—where their budding romance would bloom.

She was sure of it.

And she knew she needn't fret over her eldest daughter's virtue. Anyone who spent five minutes in the viscount's company would see he was a true gentleman. And Violet was far too sensible to let things get out of hand.

But Chrystabel also knew better than to reveal her strategy. "You've always dreamt of attending a Royal Society meeting, dear, and I mean to see you go."

"It's not a meeting, Mum. Only a social event."

"And as close as you'll ever get to your dream, unless you disguise yourself as a man." She set down the vial, meeting her daughter's gaze. "Don't even think of it."

"Disguising myself? I wouldn't."

No, her daughter wouldn't try that, Chrystabel supposed. Surely even Violet must realize she couldn't pull off such a ruse. Her face—which resembled her father's more than her mother's—might pass for a pretty lad's, but her figure was quite feminine.

A fact Chrystabel had observed Lord Lakefield observing for himself.

Hmm. Perhaps steering her daughter toward a more, ah, *fitted* style of gown would speed the process along. Violet might demur, but beside all the fashionable women of the court, she would still be the most modestly dressed young lady in London. It was high time she learned that dressing to her advantage was no sin.

Besides, desperate mothers sometimes had to resort to desperate measures.

Luckily, it was in tricky circumstances such as these that Chrystabel shined. Her instincts were as dependable as dew sweetening a rose. And if sometimes she found it uncomfortable to place trust in those instincts where her own daughter was concerned, she'd just have to stiffen her spine and remember what was at stake: nothing less than the future happiness of her lovely, compassionate, brilliant Violet.

Mothering wasn't always a comfortable job.

"You won't convince Father to leave his flowers," Violet insisted. Thanks to her agitated pacing, her spectacles had slipped down her nose. She pushed them back up. "He grumbles enough about spending the wintertime in London, though he wouldn't shirk his duties to the House of Lords. He'll not go in summer."

Wondering if her daughter was going to wear a hole in the

carpet, Chrystabel chose another vial. "Then we'll go without him."

"Mum! We've never!"

"There's a first time for everything, Violet." She added a drop to the bottle she was working with, swirling to mix the fragrances. "Your sisters would love a few days in the City—"

"But we cannot travel without Father—"

"Nonsense. We'll take a brace of footmen, and I am certain we'll arrive safe and sound. With Jewel leaving, Rowan will appreciate the distractions London has to offer. And your sisters have been dying to pay a visit to Madame Beaumont's establishment, to see the newest fashions. It will be a lovely holiday for all." She made a notation on Mrs. Applebee's card, then smiled up at her daughter. "Now, have you a suitable gown for this event?"

A nice, close-cut bodice would be suitable indeed.

~

*O*F COURSE Violet didn't have a gown. With all the delays, she had yet to be fitted for new clothing, and a ball gown wouldn't have been included in the order in any case.

But suddenly it seemed paramount to Mum—and to Violet, though she'd never admit it aloud—that she look as presentable as possible for the Royal Society celebration.

So the seamstress and her assistant were fetched the following morning, and Violet found herself subjected to an hour of measuring and prodding, accompanied by much babbling in incomprehensible French. This was followed by a second hour, during which Madame presented her with a mind-boggling array of fabrics, along with fashion dolls from Paris, all dressed in miniature versions of the latest gowns.

As though she could be fooled into thinking she'd ever look like one of those dolls.

They ended up deciding on a gown in pink and silver

brocade with sleeves of pink tissue. The dress would be started today, and tomorrow the women would be back for what promised to be a day full of tucking and pinning. Madame said she would have to "accomplish zee impossible" to have it ready in time for them to take it to London.

By the time the seamstress left, a headache was throbbing in Violet's temples. She wanted nothing more than to get off by herself for some quiet reading.

In the peaceful sanctuary of her lilac-hued bedchamber, the pile of new books beckoned. Between Ford's visit to talk to Rose and the afternoon in the laboratory, she hadn't found a minute to peruse the titles.

She sat on the bed and ran a finger down the stacked spines. Thomas Hobbes, *Human Nature*; René Descartes, *Discourse on Method*; *Aristotle's Master-piece*. That was the one. "'Plato is dear to me, but dearer still is truth,'" she quoted under her breath, smiling at Aristotle's words, the perfect expression of her own feelings. She couldn't imagine why she'd never heard of this book, but she was glad she'd found it.

Leaning back against a plump velvet pillow, she sighed and opened the cover. And gasped.

TWENTY-SIX

"*N*ESBITT!" Ford charged down the gravel path to meet his guest. "It's been entirely too long."

He hadn't seen Rand since leaving Oxford. Ford's life had changed so much that seemed ages ago, but criminy, had it been but six weeks? Regardless, his young friend's dark blond hair looked longer, and he'd grown a mustache.

A mustache with horrendous pointy tips sticking straight out at the sides.

King Charles wore a similar mustache, but unlike Rand, their monarch had the gravity to pull it off.

Ford struggled to keep his face neutral. He'd have to call on his former schoolmate more often. Academic prodigy or not, the poor fellow clearly needed looking after.

Lord Randal Nesbitt swung off his black horse. "This had better be important, Lakefield." His words sounded serious, but he ruined the effect by giving Ford a friendly thump on the shoulder. "So this is the place, is it?" He turned to squint up at the house.

"Well, yes." His gaze following Rand's, Ford shifted on his feet. "I'm planning some renovations."

He hadn't been, not really, since his stay here wasn't permanent and he couldn't afford renovations in any case—not without a significant change of lifestyle. But seeing his home through Rand's eyes made him wonder how Violet must see it.

The paint had worn entirely off the front, leaving bare beige stone. He'd never noticed before that it was a darker color on the left half, which had been added early this century, and a lighter color on the older half. The windows were different, too—four modern ones on the new side, five mullioned ones on the Tudor portion. The house was sound, but aesthetically...

Well, it left something to be desired.

"Rand." In an effort to draw his friend's attention from the pitiful sight, Ford touched him on the arm. "I may have found *Secrets of the Emerald Tablet*."

"*Secrets of*—?" Rand spun back to Ford. His steel gray eyes narrowed. "You're jesting."

"I'm not. At least I hope not." He ushered Rand up the steps. "I found this book in a shop in Windsor—looked like it'd been there for ages. It has five words in the title and the alchemical symbol for gold on the first page, and it looks exactly as the book has been described. But I cannot read it. Not a word." He led his friend through the entrance hall and into the study. "Violet's sister—"

"Violet?"

"A neighbor."

Rand dropped onto a faded green chair, smoothing his mustache manfully. "What happened to Tabitha?"

"She eloped with the Earl of Berrescliffe," Ford said with an impatient gesture. Somehow it no longer seemed important. "What does that have to do with anything?"

"The way you said 'Violet'..."

Wishing not to alienate his friend by sitting behind the massive oak desk, Ford sat himself on an iron chest against one wall. "I didn't say 'Violet' any special way."

He sounded sulky even to his own ears. Sighing inwardly, he

wondered for the hundredth time today whether she would agree to come to London.

And then wondered for the hundredth time today why he cared so much.

"Come on, man," Rand said. "You think you can fool me after all these years?" His quick grin emerged. "I know when you're interested in a lady."

Ford leaned back against the dark, Tudor oak paneling. "Maybe you don't know me as well as you think."

Rand seemed to consider that for a moment. He ran his tongue around his teeth, a contemplative habit of his that Ford remembered well.

"Bosh," he said finally, his smile returning. "Now, what were you saying about Lady Violet's sister? Violet *is* a lady?"

"She is." Guessing where his friend was leading, Ford sighed. "And her sister is a linguist of sorts. Her *younger* sister," he added in a warning tone, noting the interest that lit Rand's eyes.

He knew Rand every bit as well as Rand knew him.

"How young?" Rand asked, sitting up straighter. He was Ford's junior by four years—a brilliant student who had entered Wadham College early, while, due to his family's exile, Ford had started late.

"Fifteen," Ford said. "And a sheltered country miss." Though accurate, the description somehow didn't fit Rose.

"And me only just turned nineteen—that's not so big an age difference. A woman can marry at twelve with her father's consent."

Ford thought of Jewel just six years hence. "A girl of twelve is not a woman."

"Fair enough." Rand reclined in his chair, propping one foot on the opposite knee. "So what of this sister?"

"She knows a language or three, you see, and she examined the book." Ford rose, crossing to the desk to retrieve it. "She noticed a word she thought was Italian. For silver," he added significantly as he opened the bottom drawer.

"And that was enough to make you decide it was *Secrets of the Emerald Tablet*?"

"You think me so simple-minded?" He handed the book to Rand, then sat again on the iron chest. "The moment I saw this book, I suspected it might be the one. Besides the book's appearance and the clues on the title page, it includes diagrams that are clearly scientific. Other than that, though, I couldn't really say why I think this is it. It just...feels right," he added, suddenly feeling foolish.

He'd always trusted facts over feelings. Until now, at least.

"It does look quite ancient." Rand turned the book in his hands, then opened it gingerly, reverently, as such an old book deserved. "You know, Old English is so different from what we speak today, it might as well be a foreign language."

"But I would still recognize a word here or there, wouldn't I? Rose—Violet's sister—thought it might be several different languages. And patterns." His fingers worried the decorative metal strips on the chest. "I'm thinking it might be a code."

Rand looked up. "What is in there?" he asked abruptly, indicating the old iron chest.

"I don't know. It belonged to the previous owners." Ford looked ruefully at the heavy lock. The key was missing, so it would have to be hacked off with an ax. One of the many things he had yet to get around to doing here at Lakefield.

"Don't you wonder if it holds something valuable?"

"They wouldn't have left it had it contained anything valuable. Do you see anything else they left around here that was worth keeping?"

Scanning the shabby room, Rand laughed. "You have a point."

Ford wasn't at all handy with an ax, and the book was much more important. "Rose said some of the lines are written backwards. And the letters are mirror images."

"Etruscan," Rand said, glancing back down.

"Pardon?"

"Etruscan. A dead language. The people who spoke it lived in what eventually became Italy."

"Raymond Lully, the author, lived in Italy for some time."

Rand nodded thoughtfully. "The Etruscans wrote left to right and then right to left on successive lines, with the letters facing backwards and forwards." He kept turning pages as he talked. "Etruscan is phonetic and easy to read aloud, but no one's ever managed to puzzle out the words' meanings."

Ford's spirits plummeted. "Does that mean you won't be able to identify the book?"

"Not at all." Rand looked up with a grin. "Your ladylove's sister was right."

Violet wasn't Ford's ladylove, but in his rising excitement, he decided to let the annoying quip slide. "Right about what?"

"About it being many languages. I've noticed two or three ancient words here—ones I can read. But not together. I believe you're correct that it may be a code."

"And we both know how good you are at cracking those, to Alban's vexation." Alban, Rand's older brother, had been cruel to him as a boy. Rand had retaliated by constantly outsmarting him. "How is dear old Alban these days?"

"I don't know, actually," Rand said, his eyes still on the book. "I haven't been home in over a year."

"I see." Averse to the unpleasant company of his father and brother, Rand had often spent university holidays with Ford's family instead. Apparently matters hadn't improved. But Ford decided not to pry, knowing it was a sensitive subject.

He rose and moved to stand over Rand, leaning down to turn back to the first page. "Can you read the title?"

Rand stared at the words for a moment, then frowned. "If this is a code, it's a tough one." He looked up, shutting the book. "Give me some time, man. Can you not feed a fellow before taxing his brain?"

As if on cue, Hilda walked in, holding a folded piece of paper.

"We've another for supper," Ford told her.

"And what makes you think I can provide with no notice?" She walked closer, scrutinizing their guest's healthy physique. "I suppose you eat as heartily as this one?" she asked, indicating Ford.

Rand grinned. "Doubtless."

With an exaggerated sniff, she held out the paper to Ford. "Here, I came to give you this." When he took it, she added, "I'll bring your visitor some refreshments. For goodness sake, milord, you haven't offered him so much as a drink."

"Charming woman," Rand remarked when she had left.

Ford shrugged. "She came with the house. Besides, she's a kitten under the gruff exterior. Read this, will you?" He handed Rand the paper and went to the cabinet where he kept brandy.

While he poured, Rand unfolded the paper. "'Dear Lord Lakefield, The Ashcroft family would be honored to have you and Lady Jewel as our guests for supper this evening. If we do not receive your regrets, we shall expect you at seven o'clock. Yours sincerely, Lady Trentingham.'"

Ford handed Rand his drink. "You'll come along, of course. I'll have Harry take a note to warn them of the extra guest. Hilda will be relieved."

"Lady Jewel?" Rand sipped, his glance speculative over the cup's rim. "Another woman? Lady Violet isn't enough?"

"Violet isn't my woman," Ford said irritably. "And Jewel is my niece. Long story."

Rand settled back. "I'm waiting to hear it."

TWENTY-SEVEN

a KNOCK CAME at Violet's door. "Don't you want to come riding?" Lily called through the oak.

Violet's head shot up. "No, thank you!" Her voice came out squeaky. She cleared her throat. "I've changed my mind."

Rose made an impatient noise. "But you haven't come in ages."

"I...I'm just tired, that's all."

"Violet—"

When Lily pushed open the door, Violet hurried to stuff the book under her bedcovers.

Her eyes narrowing, Rose planted her hands on her hips. "What were you reading?"

"Nothing."

"I saw it. It was a little brown book." She stalked over to the bed. "Let me see."

Violet pulled it out before Rose could. "*Aristotle's Master-piece.* Philosophy. Nothing you'd find interesting."

"*Aristotle's Master-piece*?" Rose's dark eyes flashed with excitement. "Where did you get *that*?"

Violet's heart pounded. "Why? Have you heard of it?"

"Have I *heard* of it?" Rose snorted. "The ladies whisper

behind their fans about its secrets. I vow and swear, Violet, you need to get out of the house. If you came visiting more often—"

"I haven't heard of it," Lily interrupted. "And I visit as much as you."

Rose rolled her eyes. "No one would mention it in front of *you.*"

Lily pouted. "Why not? What's the book about?"

Rose turned back to Violet. "Does Mum know you have it?"

"No." Perish the thought. "You won't tell her, will you?"

"Tell her what?" Lily stamped her foot—gently, for it was Lily, after all. "What's this about?"

Rose's lips curved in a slow smile. "I won't tell Mum you have the book, Violet…if you let me read it."

"Rose!" Violet sprang to her feet, clutching *Aristotle's Masterpiece* to her chest. "You're far too young. I simply couldn't." Violet wasn't even certain she herself ought to be reading it, and *she* was practically a spinster.

Rose sighed theatrically. "In that case," she said with an elegant shrug, "I find myself forced to confess all to our dear mother. I'm sure she'll be *very* interested to hear where you got that book…" She began moving toward the door.

"Wait!" Violet made a grab for her sister's arm.

Rose paused and turned back, eyebrows raised innocently.

Violet groaned. There was nothing for it. "Come to the summerhouse." She cast a nervous glance around the chamber. "Mum won't hear us there."

"I'm coming, too," Lily announced, her expression daring them to argue. "I want to know what's in that book!"

TWENTY-EIGHT

"$\mathcal{H}$OW DID YOU get it?" Rose asked when they were safely outdoors in the garden.

Violet knew her father was in the study—they had walked right by him on their way from the house—but she was so used to seeing him out here that she couldn't help but look about, half expecting to find him lurking behind a bush.

"Lord Lakefield bought it for me in Windsor," she admitted finally.

Rose's mouth gaped open.

"It wasn't like that!" Violet rushed to add. "He thought it was a philosophy book. We both did."

"Of course," Rose said with a smirk.

Violet's fingers clenched the leather cover. "It's called *Aristotle's Master-piece*. What was I supposed to think?"

"Is it really that shocking?" Lily's shorter legs hurried to keep up with her older sisters' quick pace.

Violet shrugged. "Yes and no."

She rushed past Father's blue and yellow flower beds, breathing a sigh of relief when they reached the circular red-brick summerhouse. She yanked open one of the small garden building's four doors, and the girls scurried inside, shutting it behind them.

They huddled together on a section of the benches that ran along the wall, Rose and Lily on either side of Violet. She placed the book on her lap. Large, arched windows over each of the doors illuminated the brown leather binding, but they were placed too high for anyone to see in.

A perfect place for illicit reading.

Violet looked to her fourteen-year-old sister. "Lily, are you sure you want to stay?"

Lily's chin jutted out. "I'm staying. I'm only a year younger than Rose. If she wants to read it, so do I."

"We'll see about that," Rose said with a smirk.

Violet shook her head. "Very well. Here was my first clue that it wasn't the sort of book I'd thought," she began, and opened the cover.

"Oh, my heavens," Lily breathed. The frontispiece plate depicted a seated Aristotle with a bare woman standing beside him. Lily quickly shielded her eyes. "Is it...is the book really by Aristotle?"

"I'm sure not!" Rose scanned the title page opposite. "There's no author listed, no printer's name or date or place of publication." Even she looked apprehensive now. "It must be truly scandalous."

"It's not what you think." Violet turned the page. "I nearly tossed it in the fireplace myself when I saw the frontispiece, but then I read the subtitle."

"'The Secrets of Generation in All the Parts Thereof,'" Rose read aloud. Her brow creased. "'Generation?'"

Lily peeked from between her fingers. "It sounds like an academic volume."

"Sort of. It's more like a manual." Violet drew a deep breath. "Only the subject is..."

"The marriage bed." Rose supplied.

Lily's hands fluttered into her lap. *"Oh."* Her blue eyes were round as the moon through Ford's telescope.

Violet nodded. "Exactly. Now, are you *certain* you want to stay, Lily?"

She shook her head slowly. "I don't know. I'm not sure Mum would approve, but..." She looked down, and her hands fisted in her skirts. "But I'm going to find out one way or another, aren't I? In just a few years, I'll be old enough to marry." She lifted her gaze to meet Violet's. "I'd rather know what to expect in advance than find out on my wedding night."

"Hear, hear!" Rose cheered.

Violet couldn't argue with such a sensible way of thinking, so instead she turned the page and regarded the introductory text. "It begins with advice to parents."

"To parents?"

"Of young girls." She cleared her throat and began to read. "'It behooves parents to look after their children, and when they find them inclinable to marriage, not violently to restrain their affections, but rather provide such suitable matches for them, lest the crossing of their inclinations should precipitate them to commit those follies that may bring an indelible stain upon their families.'"

Rose giggled. "Sounds as though Father and Mum ought to make certain we marry before we get ourselves with child."

"Rose!" Lily's mouth dropped open.

"Hush," Violet said. "There's more." She swallowed and turned the page. "'For when they arrive at puberty, which is about the fourteenth or fifteenth year of their age, then the natural purgations begin to flow—'"

"They have already," Rose said. "For all of us."

"Rose!" Lily looked past Violet to glare at her.

"Just listen, both of you. '...and the blood stirs up their minds to venery: for their spirits being brisk and inflamed when they arrive at this age, if they eat hard salt things and spices, the body becomes more and more heated...'"

Violet's face was becoming heated just hearing her voice say the words aloud. But remembering Lily's understandable determination to become informed, she forced herself to continue.

"'...whereby the desire to c-carnal em-embraces'"—Violet's cheeks were positively on fire now—"'is very great, sometimes insuperable.'"

Rose crossed her arms. "So if we eat salty or spicy foods, we're doomed to become fallen women?"

"How awful!" Lily wore a look of panic, as though worried she might fall at any moment.

"I don't think it works that way," Violet said thoughtfully. "We all had salt fish for breakfast this morning. Are either of you overwarm?"

It was comfortably cool in the summerhouse, if a bit humid. They both shook their heads.

"Do you feel insuperably desirous of a man?"

"What does 'insuperable' mean?" Lily asked.

"Impossible to overcome."

"Oh. Well, no."

"Me neither," Rose said. "Not at the moment, anyway."

Violet rolled her eyes. "Well then, it seems we have nothing to worry about."

Lily's features relaxed. Rose waved an impatient hand. "If you say so, Violet. Just keep reading."

"Where were we? Ah. 'And the use of this so much desired enjoyment being denied to virgins, many times is followed by dismal consequences, as...'" Violet paused, her eyes landing on the next words: *Short breathings. Trembling of the heart. Eager staring at men, and affecting their company.*

Her stomach knotted.

Her thoughts whirling, she remembered the way her breath caught whenever Ford touched her. The strange trembling she'd felt in her chest that day on the boat. That when they locked eyes, she was incapable of looking away. And that, despite all her grumblings over having to bring Rowan to Lakefield House, she always seemed to find herself in Ford's company…

She suddenly felt overwarm.

"Violet?" She could barely feel Lily's hand on her shoulder. "Are you well?"

She wasn't well. She was very unwell indeed.

She was supposed to be the sensible one! She was supposed to be immune to gentlemen! Enjoying a kiss or two didn't change any of that—she'd thought.

But what if she was mistaken about her own feelings?

What if they were *insuperable?*

"Girls, are you in there?"

All three of them jumped out of their skins.

Father knocked on one of the doors. "Willets said he saw you heading this way—"

Violet quickly sat on the book, folding her hands angelically on her lap while Rose went to open the door. "We're just talking, Father. Do you need us?"

"Do I need what?" Looking perplexed, he scratched his head. "Your mother sent me to find you."

"Why?" Violet asked.

"Lord Lakefield has arrived for supper. With a guest. Lord something-or-other. I failed to catch the name."

"A gentleman? A titled gentleman?" Rose practically clapped her hands. "Gemini! We'd better go change our gowns!"

TWENTY-NINE

$\mathcal{A}$N HOUR LATER, Mum set down her goblet. "Violet tells me Jewel is going home tomorrow."

"Yes." Ford sprinkled salt on his spinach tanzy and returned the spoon to its little dish. "I hope she also told you I've invited her to a Royal Society event at Gresham College."

"She has," Mum said, "and she'll be delighted to attend. Monday evening, is it?"

A tiny gasp escaped Violet's lips. She'd never given Ford an answer, and she'd wanted to do that for herself.

She nudged her mother's foot beneath the table, but Mum pretended not to notice.

"Yes, Monday." Ford took an experimental bite of the rich spinach omelette, then displayed his irresistible smile. "I trust you'll be in London by then? I'll need the direction of your town house."

"More brown sauce, did you say?" Father frowned. "I don't see any brown sauce…"

Nobody paid him any attention.

"We're in St. James's Square," Mum answered again for Violet. "In the northeast corner, the house of light gray stone."

"Excellent. The celebration begins at ten, so I'll be by at half past nine."

Ignoring Rose's chatter, Violet stabbed a stewed prawn with her fork, a bit more forcefully than necessary. If her mother and Ford kept planning her life as though she weren't around to hear it, she feared she might scream.

Seated between her sisters across the table, Lord Randal Nesbitt gave her a sympathetic smile—a smile nearly as charming as Ford's. Those smiles were lethal, she decided. They should be outlawed. She wondered if they'd practiced together at school. Did boys do that? Rose and Lily practiced their smiles all the time.

Perhaps noticing the glance that passed between Violet and his friend, Ford reached for her hand beneath the table.

Heavens, what if someone noticed? She struggled to breathe normally. But she didn't move her hand away.

Feigning nonchalance, she smiled back at the viscount's friend. He did seem nice. He hadn't even mentioned her spectacles. She wondered if that was because Ford had already told him about them, or if he was just very polite.

Violet's father signaled to the maid stationed against the wall. "Dinah, could you fetch more brown sauce for Lord Lakefield, please?"

His wife plucked a grain of rice from his cravat. "No, darling, we were speaking of the *town house*. I told you we're going to London, remember?"

"Yes, to order gowns for Violet, since she's finally taking interest." Father stirred some of the butter sauce from the prawns into his rice. "From that Madame Blowfont woman."

"Beaumont," Rose clarified loudly, sprinkling cinnamon on her own rice.

Faith! Did they have to shout about her lack of fashion sense in front of Ford? Out of the corner of her eye, Violet saw him stifle a grin and straighten his smart white cravat.

She wished she could slide beneath the table. And then melt into the floor.

"Gowns?" Mum said, trying to come to Violet's rescue. "Of course she needs new gowns, but that's not the focus of our holiday. Everyone knows my eldest daughter cares more about learning than clothing." She looked to Ford's friend. "You must forgive my husband. He's a bit hard of hearing and often misunderstands."

"What?" Father asked, proving her point.

"Nothing, my love." Mum's musical laughter tinkled through the room, a sound of relief. "See what I mean?"

"Violet did order a new ball gown," Rowan said in defense of his father.

Ford squeezed Violet's hand.

Rose flashed her most sophisticated smile at Lord Randal. "What brings you to visit, my lord?"

In midnight blue silk with spills of silver lace, tonight she resembled an enchanting water sprite. She'd been fluttering her eyelashes at the newcomer all evening, reminding Violet of Jewel. Not that she blamed her sister. Like Ford, Lord Randal wore no wig, and he had a stunning mane of long, dark blond hair. He was tall and lean, with a poet's face and eyes of steely gray—the most intense eyes Violet had ever seen. When he looked at a person, he really *looked* at her, as though he could see right into her soul.

Shame about the mustache, though. Luckily, that could be fixed.

Eating single-handed, Ford used his fork to cut a bite of the tanzy rather awkwardly. "I've asked Rand to translate that old book for me, Lady Rose. He's a fellow now at Oxford—he specializes in ancient languages."

"Languages?" The cinnamon spoon slipped from Rose's fingers and clattered to the table.

When Ford squeezed Violet's hand again, she stuffed a prawn in her mouth to smother a giggle.

Rose sent her a brittle smile. "Violet," she said sweetly, lifting the salt cellar, "would you care for some *salt* on your roast chicken?"

That stopped Violet cold. She shook her head violently.

Rose turned back to Lord Randal. "I'm conversant in a few languages myself," she announced. It was the first time Violet had ever heard her sister volunteer that information to a gentleman. "Perhaps we can work on the translation together?"

"Perhaps," Lord Randal said, smoothing his mustache. "Ford tells me you've already examined the book." Violet thought his voice sounded a touch too deep, as though he were trying to sound older.

He and Rose were made for each other.

"Yes, I've examined it. But not for very long." Rose licked orange butter sauce off her lips. "Perhaps together—"

"Beatrix!" Lily stage whispered. "How on earth did you get in here?" She leaned down to scoop up a small striped cat, settling it on her lap.

"Lily," Mum said. "Not when we have company."

"She's lonely." Lily stroked the cat's fur before reluctantly setting her back on the carpet. "She had a bad day."

Lord Randal cocked his head. "Pray tell, how does a cat have a bad day?"

On his other side, Rose touched him on the arm, a clear bid for his attention. "Lily here claims she can feel her animals' emotions. She collects injured creatures. Cats, birds, rabbits, the odd squirrel. She's turned our old barn into a menagerie, or rather an infirmary for damaged critters. She even has a mouse."

Lily nodded. "His little leg was broken, poor thing."

Ford scooted his chair closer to Violet's, sending her breathing back into turmoil. But a quick scan of the table assured her no one had noticed. The others were all looking at Lord Randal, who in turn had focused his intense gray gaze on Lily.

"Cats and mice together?" he asked.

To Violet it seemed he was looking into her youngest sister's soul, but Lily, bless her, appeared entirely unaffected. "I have but three cats at the moment, and they've been with me since they were kittens. When creatures are raised side by side, they can learn to be brothers and sisters. Even cats and mice."

"Fascinating," Lord Randal said.

"Lily dreams of building an animal home," Rose announced.

"A what?"

"An animal home," Lily repeated softly. Like Violet, she'd never shared her dream outside the family. Reaching a hand beneath the table, she slipped the cat a bit of chicken while measuring their guest's reaction with her steady blue gaze. "A nice clean building where hurt or abandoned creatures can be brought to live. People who work there will care for them until they are healthy enough to return to the wild or they find a home with a family."

Lord Randal ran his tongue over his teeth, then nodded slowly. "That's a very nice idea. And innovative, too."

Violet sent him an approving smile. "Our grandfather encouraged us to be innovative," she told him, trying to ignore Ford's thumb tracing circles on her palm. "Or rather to follow our dreams. And, as he put it, leave our marks on the world."

"And what is your dream, my lady?"

Violet took a bite of chicken, stalling for time. Although she'd told Ford her dream and he hadn't laughed, it remained difficult to share with another.

Then Ford shifted his hand to lace their fingers together, and his reassuring warmth loosened her tongue. "I wish to write a book about philosophy," she blurted, shoving her spectacles higher on her nose. "My own ideas. And use my inheritance to publish it some day and distribute it far and wide. Of course," she hastened to add, "I have a lot of studying and thinking to do before then."

Lord Randal didn't laugh. "Of course. An admirable dream, Lady Violet." He turned to Rose. "And your dream, my lady?"

"I...I dream of falling in love," she said, and prettily lowered her lashes.

No one had much to say to that. Violet only just managed to stave off a laughing fit by squeezing Ford's hand as hard as she could.

Jewel broke the silence first. "Oops!" She dropped her napkin and dove to the floor to go after it. "Pretty kitty," came her voice from beneath the table.

"Jewel..." Ford warned. But she didn't come up. Instead, Rowan slipped off his chair to join her.

An alarmed *meow* came from somewhere below.

"Poor Beatrix. What are they doing to you?" Leaning down, Lily swept the cat back to her lap. She rubbed its small, furry head with a finger. "Go out now, Beatrix. I shall come to you later."

Beatrix did go out, leaping gracefully from Lily's lap to the patterned carpet, her striped tail high in the air.

"She obeyed." Admiration lit Lord Randal's eyes. "A *cat* complied with your command."

"Holy Hades," came Rowan's voice muffled from below. "Look, Jewel."

"Language, Rowan!" Mum admonished.

Jewel's head popped up. "Uncle Ford, are you holding hands with Lady Violet under the table?"

"No!" Ford yelped, raising both his hands, fingers spread to prove his point.

It was the second time Violet had seen him blush. Knowing her own face must be redder than Trentingham's roses, she was sure the truth was obvious.

Lily gasped. Rose smirked. Mum's mouth curved into a smile.

"What's that?" Father mumbled.

It was a long supper.

THIRTY

$\mathcal{L}$ ATER, FORD seated himself beside Violet at the round table in Trentingham's library. Emboldened by the wine he'd consumed during supper, he inched over in his chair until one of his knees rested against hers, then leaned to whisper in her ear. "I'm looking forward to Monday."

She turned her head slightly, her cheeks prettily flushed, and he hoped that meant she was looking forward to Monday, too. But then her eyes suddenly narrowed. She set down the book she'd been reading. "I just want you to know," she whispered back, "that I am nearly eighteen, and my mother doesn't run my life."

He wouldn't challenge that statement for all the gold in England. "I'm certain the decision was yours alone," he assured her. "I'm just glad you decided to come."

"Oh," she said, and then, "Oh!" when his arm snaked around to rest on her shoulder. Her hand drifted up to toy with the end of her plait, which he'd noticed she sometimes did when she was flustered.

Not that she had cause for worry. It was clear as the lenses over her eyes that nobody else in this room was going to take note of the two of them together.

Candles burned, warding off the dark. Reluctant to say goodbye to each other, Rowan and Jewel had fallen asleep on a corner of the patterned carpet, half twined where they'd dropped in their play. Across the table, Rand and Rose huddled over Ford's ancient book.

Violet's sister was plainly smitten.

"I'm not sure," she crooned to Rand now, "but do you think this might mean 'mystery'? It's awfully similar to the same word in German."

"Possibly." Rand flipped a couple of pages, peering at them critically. "But I don't see much else that looks to be Germanic."

Ford traced his finger along the curve of Violet's shoulder, smiling to himself when he felt her shiver.

Rand flipped back to the original page. "Do you suppose the five words might be from five different languages? I've been assuming it's only one."

"That could be." Hero worship flashed in Rose's eyes. "I hadn't considered the possibility."

"Five words?" Ford went still. "What five words?"

"The five words of the title," Rand said, frowning at the page, a finger over the text. "What if this were German, like you were saying, but an older version?" A tinge of excitement crept into his voice. "And this looks Hellenic, perhaps meaning 'emerald,' and this maybe Slavic—"

"Mystery and emerald?" Ford breathed, his heart threatening to hammer right out of his chest.

"Yes, Slavic," Rand murmured, nodding to himself. "And this one..." Quite suddenly he straightened in his chair. "Five words, five different languages. Translating to 'Mysteries of the Emerald Slab."

Ford blinked, gripping Violet's shoulder for support.

His friend leaned across the table to lightly punch his shoulder. "*Secrets of the Emerald Tablet*, you fool." He grinned. "You found the book, Lakefield. It's a blessed miracle."

All the air seemed sucked from Ford's lungs. It *was* a blessed miracle. And a marvel, and a wonder, and—

He leapt from the chair and swept Violet into a fierce hug. Then he kissed her smack on the lips, right in front of her gaping sister.

He was still beaming the next day when he showed up at his brother's castle.

THIRTY-ONE

*C*OLIN WASN'T beaming when Ford delivered his daughter, along with a still-weak Nurse Lydia they'd fetched along the way.

While Lydia crept off to her bed, Colin's wife, Amy, knelt in the entry and held Jewel close. "How did you both fare?"

"We got along famously." Pleased that Amy seemed fully recovered, Ford turned to his scowling brother. Colin looked very parental with their tiny son cradled in his arms. "What's your problem?" Ford asked.

Colin swayed back and forth in the age-old motion that soothed a baby to sleep. "You mean to tell me you were alone with Jewel all this time?"

"Of course not. Hilda and Harry were there, too."

"Those old barnacles?"

"Colin!" Amy set their daughter on her feet and took her hand, leading her from the square entrance hall. "Jewel seems no worse for the wear."

The rest of them followed. "How is Hugh?" Ford asked, referring to their other son, a lad of four.

Her raven hair shining with health, Amy smiled over her shoulder. "Much better. He's napping now."

He looked to the child in his brother's arms. "And Aidan?"

"Had a very light case," Colin said, patting the baby's back.

"I had fun, Mama." Jewel twirled in a circle, around and around under Amy's arm as they went down the corridor. "Uncle Ford bought me this necklace on my birthday!" Still twirling, she lifted the silver filigree heart she wore on a black ribbon around her neck. "And he let me sleep in his bed. And he paid me to be good!" Reaching the sitting room, she dropped cross-legged to the floor and began digging in her pockets. Shillings fell to the stone slabs with a merry sound.

Amy seated herself in a blue upholstered chair and picked up a small knife. "You're rich, poppet."

"I'm saving up to buy a mi-mi"—Jewel looked at Ford, but he knew better than to help her now—"mi-cro-scope. Uncle Ford showed me a book with pictures. Written by Mr. Heck."

"Hooke," Ford corrected, leaning an elbow against the mantel. "And the book is called *Micrographia*."

"Mr. Hooke drew pictures of big, icky things. Close-up things." Jewel collected her coins, making a neat stack. "When I buy the mi-cro-scope, I'm going to share it with Rowan."

Settling Aidan in a wooden cradle, Colin raised a brow. "Who's Rowan?"

"My friend from Uncle Ford's house. Lady Violet's brother. I'm going to marry him."

Amy's father had been a jeweler in London, and she'd been raised in the trade. Whittling away on a piece of wax that looked like it might someday become a ring, she appeared to be stifling a laugh. "Does Rowan know you're going to marry him?"

"Of course. I told him. And Uncle Ford is going to marry Lady Violet."

Ford's elbow slipped off the stone ledge. "I am not!"

"Not yet, anyhow," Colin drawled, taking the chair beside his wife's. "You'll need at least another seven years to make up your mind."

Ford ignored him, focusing on his niece instead. "What on earth gave you that idea?"

All innocence, she looked up from her spot on the floor. "I saw you kissing her."

"You did not."

"Did so."

"Did not."

Colin rolled his eyes. "No wonder you two got along. You're as childish as she is. I take it you're over Tabitha, then?"

"Did you think I was upset about her elopement?" Ford vaguely remembered being so, but couldn't fathom why. "She meant nothing to me. No more than a convenient diversion."

"Mm-hmm." Colin crossed his arms, looking less than convinced. "Tell me about this Violet."

"There's nothing to tell." Ford wandered over to gaze at a portrait of some long-dead ancestor. He didn't have anything like it in his house—nothing to personalize his living space, nothing to make it a home.

Jason, his oldest brother, had plenty of paintings at Cainewood Castle. Perhaps Ford ought to ask him if he could spare one or two for Lakefield.

"Lady Violet is merely a neighbor," he told the ancestor, a lady with shrewd blue eyes and a blond head poking out from an enormous, starched ruff. "Violet brought her little brother over to play with Jewel sometimes, that's all."

"And Uncle Ford is taking her to a ball tomorrow night," Jewel piped up. "In London."

"What ball?" Amy asked.

"Gresham College is throwing a party to welcome back the Royal Society. Lady Violet would like to meet John Locke, who will be in attendance. End of story." Ford thought his ancestress's shrewd blue eyes appeared skeptical. *Mind your own business*, he admonished her mentally, turning his back on the painting. "And it's not a ball."

"Will there be dancing?"

He walked to a chair and plopped onto it. "Yes, I suppose there will be dancing."

"It's a ball, then," Amy declared. "I'm sure you'll have a lovely time."

"Do you not think," Colin asked, drumming his fingers against his thigh, "that if you're considering wedding someone, you ought to introduce her to the family?"

"I'm not wedding her." Ford's hands clenched on the chair's arms. "I'm not wedding anyone. I'm not ready to get married."

"Jason is back from Scotland." Colin's eyes looked contemplative. They were emerald green like Jewel's, and he was just as single-minded as his daughter. "I'm sure he'll be fascinated to hear about this."

"There's nothing for Jason to hear," Ford said. "Are you deaf?"

"And Cait," Amy added, apparently deaf as well. "And Kendra and Trick." Her amethyst eyes sparkling, she smiled down at the wax ring. "They've all just arrived home last week. We'll have to arrange a family visit to Lakefield."

As there seemed to be an abundance of deaf people in his life lately, Ford raised his voice. "I'm busy working on my watch," he all but shouted. "There will be no visits."

THIRTY-TWO

$\mathcal{F}$EELING MORE lighthearted than ever in her memory, Violet twirled in her new ball gown, a veritable confection of pink brocade and silver embroidery.

Monday night had finally arrived. One of her dreams was coming true. She was going to Gresham College to rub elbows with the Royal Society, the most brilliant minds in all of England.

Feeling dizzy, she stopped and held out her skirts. "What do you think?" she asked her sisters. "Will it do for an event here in London?"

Lily beamed. "I've never seen you in anything so fancy."

Crossing the bedchamber to tweak one of Violet's ruffled sleeves, Rose shot Lily a conspiratorial grin. "She's finally coming around."

"What do you mean?" As she drew breath, Violet's ribs strained against the intricate brocade stomacher that tapered to her waist. She frowned. The cut of the bodice hadn't appeared this narrow on the French fashion doll. She didn't remember it feeling this tight during the fittings, either. Wondering if she'd gained weight, she smoothed her full brocade skirts. "Coming around to what?"

"Dressing to impress." Rose's grin turned impish. "I'd wager he'll be very, very impressed."

"John Locke?" Violet walked to the pier glass and straightened one of the fat brown curls that rested on her shoulders. Somehow, the French woman Mum had hired had managed to coax her thick, unruly hair into a stylish *coiffure*. Most of it was pulled up in the back, twisted with strands of pearls to match the ones on her necklace and underskirt. "I cannot wait to hear his ideas. But Locke is a philosopher. I doubt he cares what I look like."

"Not Locke, you goose. Viscount Lakefield."

"I'm not trying to impress *him*," Violet said. Staring at herself in the mirror, she bit her lip. "Does the dress seem rather...tight?"

"Perfectly so," Rose said with relish. "Who even knew you had such a nice shape hidden in there?

A crunch of gravel drifted through the open window, and Lily hurried to look out. "He's here, Violet. He's climbing down from his carriage. And oooh, he's dressed very fine."

Violet's stomach fluttered. "Let me see," she said, thrilled that with her spectacles she'd be able to. But by the time she hurried over to look, Ford had already ascended the house's front steps and disappeared from view.

"I'll go meet him at the door," Rose said. "Wait here, so you can make an entrance." With a swish of her blood-red skirts, she swept out of the room.

"An entrance, Violet," Lily repeated, giggling. "An entrance!"

An entrance. Contemplating her youngest, most innocent sister, Violet's heart jumped into her throat as it suddenly dawned on her that she would soon be alone with Ford. Really alone, not just sort of alone for a minute while the children's backs were turned.

She could hardly believe Mum had condoned it. More than condoned it—pushed it, in fact. But of course that was only because Mum knew how much she wanted to attend a Royal Society function.

Mum would never expect anything untoward to happen. Not to Violet. Plain Violet. Violet, who would just as soon remain invisible.

If only Mum knew that Ford had already kissed her. Four times.

Four glorious times.

As she'd done hundreds of times already, Violet couldn't help but replay those kisses now in her memory. And even though she hadn't eaten any salty or spicy food today—hadn't eaten much of anything, as a matter of fact—she felt insuperability rearing its unwelcome head.

Well, she wouldn't worry about it this night. She could sort that out tomorrow. Tonight she would simply enjoy herself.

Rose barged back in. "He's waiting, Violet. I think you should keep him waiting a little bit longer."

"No." She wasn't calculating like her sister. "I'm ready." As ready as she'd ever be.

Although the Ashcrofts' town house in St. James's Square wasn't nearly as massive as Trentingham, it was richly decorated and boasted a grand marble staircase. Violet's new red-heeled shoes clicked as she walked down it.

When Ford glanced up, his jaw went slack. "You look…" he trailed off, apparently at a loss for words.

"Different?" she supplied, gliding to a stop in front of him.

"Um…yes." As that incredible blue gaze raked her from head to toe, a grin slowly spread on his face. "And beautiful."

It had taken him too long to add that last bit, and she wouldn't have believed it, in any case. But it was nice to hear, even if it was only a polite fib. For just this night, she would pretend it was true. She'd never expected to hear a compliment like that from a gentleman.

And most especially from such a magnificent-looking one. Judging from his normal attire, she'd suspected Ford enjoyed dressing up a bit. She hadn't been wrong. His brilliant blue suit made his eyes seem even bluer. Lace dripped from the cuffs. A diamond pin winked from the folds of a snow-white cravat. The buttons on his velvet surcoat looked to be of real gold, and when he swept off his wide-brimmed hat to make her a solemn bow, a jeweled hatband sparkled in the light of the entry's chandelier.

Thank goodness Mum had loaned her the Trentingham diamonds, or she'd have felt like a pauper standing beside him.

"Shall we?" he asked.

From out of nowhere, it seemed, her mother appeared and kissed her on the cheek. "Have a lovely time, dear. You won't be back too late?"

"I won't, Mum." Violet took Ford's arm.

When he handed her into the carriage and then lowered himself beside her, her heart skittered.

They were alone. She was alone with the viscount.

He closed the door, and she immediately leapt for the opposite bench.

The carriage lurched forward as she settled in her new seat, busily arranging her skirts. "I...feel ill when I sit backwards."

"Do you, indeed?" Though she couldn't bring herself to look at him, his tone made it clear he wasn't fooled.

He moved to sit beside her.

Violet's whole body tensed. "Thank you for inviting me," she said to her lap.

"The pleasure is mine." He dipped his head, forcing her to meet his gaze. Seeing her expression, he laughed. "I won't bite. I won't even try to kiss you, I promise."

He didn't, and after a moment she relaxed. They rode for a spell in companionable silence, bouncing over uneven cobblestones and in and out of ruts.

Until a particularly large rut threw him sideways into her. He righted himself promptly, apologizing for squashing her, but somehow his arm had made its way around her shoulders.

"You smell good," he murmured.

"So do you," she replied shyly. He did, though. There was that hint of patchouli soap again, tonight overlaid by another scent—something unfamiliar and exotic. She wondered if her mother could identify it and make her a bottle, so she could inhale it and remember this evening.

As the carriage tottered through the streets, his fingers traced shivery lines up and down her arm and over the back of her neck. Her flesh prickled, and she felt warm all over.

In fact, her body seemed to be growing more and more heated.

"Oh my," she whispered.

Oh, no, she thought.

"Do you want me to stop?" His breath tickled her ear. "Tell me if you want me to stop."

She didn't tell him to stop.

The carriage's wheels bumped over the cobblestones, the springs squeaked through the traffic-clogged streets, and her breathlessness—short breathings, *Aristotle's Master-piece* had called that—sounded louder than all of it.

She wanted him to kiss her. More than anything.

Insuperably.

But as she began to lean toward him, the carriage door was jerked open.

They had arrived.

THIRTY-THREE

*V*IOLET HAD ALWAYS thought of scientific men as sober and staid, but there was an air of giddy excitement at Gresham College tonight.

Catching Ford's gaze lingering on her bodice as they made their way through the narrow gatehouse off Bishopsgate Street, she folded her arms over her chest. She'd never appeared in public in such a daring gown, and it made her nervous, despite Ford's equally showy attire. Perhaps a man could dress himself in the latest fashions and still be taken seriously, but would she be seen as frivolous and superficial?

"This was once the home of Sir Thomas Gresham," Ford said as proudly as if the mansion belonged to him. "Founder of the college."

Hand in hand—hers tingling—they crossed a simple courtyard toward the house, Violet's knees feeling embarrassingly shaky. She tried her best to relax and concentrate on what he was telling her. After all, this was a place she'd always wanted to visit.

"When did the college open?" she asked.

"At the end of the last century, following Gresham's death and that of his wife. He had no living heirs, you see, so he gifted his home to the people of London. He wished to make scholarship available free to every adult citizen." Pushing open a heavy oak door, he guided her into a large chamber that looked medieval. "Here is the Reading Hall, where the lectures are given."

"Oh, I wish I knew Latin so I could attend them." Beneath a lofty scissor-beam ceiling painted in dazzling hues of red and gold, rows of wooden benches faced a lectern, behind which rose an exquisite oriel window. "What a heavenly place to learn."

"I imagine when the Greshams lived here, this would have been their great hall." Ford walked her through the soaring chamber, their footsteps echoing on the well-worn stone floor. "The college's seven professors have lodgings here at Gresham and are each required to give one public lecture a week."

Whom might she meet here tonight? Breathless with anticipation, she peeked into some adjoining rooms, a bit disappointed when she found them unoccupied. "It just looks like a big, old house."

"It was, remember. But you will see in a moment that although his family lived here for years, and his widow afterwards, Gresham had a college in mind when he built it."

Another small courtyard lay outside the Reading Hall, leading to an arched passage that opened into a massive, grassy square with colonnaded buildings on all four sides.

"See?" Ford said. "It's essentially a college quadrangle."

Flaming torches bathed the space in a warm glow. Musicians were tuning up in one corner. Talking animatedly in small groups, guests dressed in every color of the rainbow crowded the enclosure, their chatter filling the air.

She was here. Finally, she was here. A serving maid handed her a goblet of canary, and she sipped the sweet wine, turning in a slow circle, imagining how the area might look in the daytime. Peaceful and meditative. Shut off from the hubbub of London by the buildings all around.

"I can picture it quiet," she said, "students leisurely crossing the grass, or perhaps hurrying if they're late."

"Can you picture it paved over and crammed with shopping stalls?"

She looked down at the fresh green grass beneath her feet. "Was it?"

"Until recently. After the Great Fire, the whole administration of the City moved into the buildings, and the tenants of the Royal Exchange set up here in the quadrangle until it was rebuilt. A hundred small shops."

People strolled by, men alone and some couples, nodding acknowledgments without interrupting their conversation. She and Ford seemed to be among the youngest attendees. "How long has the Royal Society been meeting here?" she asked.

"Since 1660, save during the past seven years. We were incorporated under Royal charter in 1662. On the fifteenth of July. So something good happened that particular St. Swithin's Day," he mused. "It must not have rained."

She shot him a sidelong glance. "What do you mean?"

"Never mind." A private smile curved his lips as he began walking her around the perimeter, pointing out all the professors' lodgings. There were professors of music, physics, geometry, divinity, rhetoric, astronomy, and law—and by the time she heard about all of them, she was dizzy with new information.

Or maybe dizzy with something else. It was like a fairytale, being here in this place, among these extraordinary people... with Ford.

"Do you like to dance?" he suddenly asked. The musicians had begun to play. A lilting tune wafted over the quadrangle. A temporary floor of wood had been constructed over a patch of the new grass.

Although she'd had lessons along with her sisters, Violet had never danced much. At the balls her family had managed to drag her to, she'd always done her best to fade into the background—so much so that Rose had taken to calling her a wallflower, claiming she clung to the walls like Father's flowering vines.

But this was a magical night—a night that called for her to rise above her normal fears. In her whole life, she might never see a night like this again, and she was determined to make the most of it.

"I cannot claim to have much experience," she heard herself saying. "But I wouldn't mind giving it a try."

Immediately she thought about taking back the words, but clamped her lips tight. Handing their goblets to a passing servant, Ford led her closer to the music.

The tune ended and another began. A minuet. Taking her by both hands, he swept her onto the makeshift dance floor.

She knew the steps, and for the first time, her vision sharp through her spectacles, she didn't worry about tripping. His dancing was precise if not precisely graceful, exactly as she would have pictured. She was watching him, smiling to herself, when she suddenly realized her own feet were keeping pace.

Perhaps dancing wasn't so tiresome, after all—when one happened to be dancing with the best-looking member of the Royal Society.

Cool night air breezed over her skin. She met his eyes, and her cheeks flushed at the intensity of his gaze. She wondered what he was thinking. Here beneath the stars, he seemed different, in his element. Not that he was reserved in any circumstances, but she'd expect a man of science to be more like her, preferring solitude to social occasions. Which just went to show how little she could trust her preconceived notions.

He took her hand again as they turned, and she found herself enjoying this particular social occasion more than she'd thought possible. For once, she had no desire to hide out, no wish to stay safely at home.

They rose on their toes, and he pulled her closer. Closer than the dance required, close enough to make butterflies flutter in her stomach. To make the *Master-piece's* words flash in her mind.

Pushing those thoughts away, she broke eye contact, needing a moment to compose herself.

The dance floor had become crowded. Gentlemen outnumbered ladies by double or more, and the wooden platform was surrounded by clusters of them absorbed in conversation. Violet caught more than a few glances aimed her way. She suspected people were wondering what she was doing here with Ford.

Or wondering about her spectacles. Did they look odd with her formal gown and hairstyle? A niggling thread of insecurity invaded her dreamy, perfect evening, lodging itself in her stomach.

No sooner had she and Ford made their way off the dance floor than they found themselves besieged by curious men. Instinctively, Violet crossed her arms over her chest again.

"Trentingham's eldest, are you not?" One of the gentlemen offered her a courtly bow. "I'm pleased to meet you," he added. "Christopher Wren."

She struggled to keep her face neutral. Christopher Wren! Mathematician, scientist, architect...the man personally chosen by the king to rebuild all of the City's churches that had burned in the Great Fire. She was surprised to find him no taller than she.

And she was surprised that he knew who she was. She'd thought she'd been invisible to society, hidden away on her family's estate.

"Violet Ashcroft." She bobbed a curtsy. "I'm glad to make your acquaintance."

"Are those a new sort of spectacles?" he asked without further preliminaries. Not at all the imposing personality she'd pictured, he seemed cheerful and open. She guessed him at around forty years of age. "May I see them?" Before she gave permission, he reached out eagerly.

She slipped the spectacles off and handed them to him. "Lord Lakefield made them for me."

"I'm not surprised." Mr. Wren turned them in his hands, then raised them to his own lively brown eyes and blinked. "Do they help you to see?"

"Very much. They've changed my life."

Mr. Wren nodded thoughtfully, his wavy brown periwig moving along with his head. Beneath a patrician nose, his mouth curved pleasantly, as though he smiled often.

He turned to Ford. "This frame to hold them on the face, it's brilliant. Why didn't I think of it myself?"

Ford laughed. "You've thought of plenty. Give another man a turn."

Another face peered over Mr. Wren's shoulder. "What have you there?"

"Spectacles," he replied. "Designed by Lakefield here, with a clever frame to hold them on the face." Leaning forward, he gently slid the eyeglasses back on Violet.

"Lovely," the newcomer said. "Both the spectacles and the lady." A few years younger than Mr. Wren, the man topped him by but a couple of inches. His physique somehow looked crooked, his face twisted and much less than beautiful. But his large, pale head was crowned with a wig of dark brown curls so delicate they made Violet envious.

"Robert Hooke," Ford introduced him. "May I present Lady Violet Ashcroft?"

"I've read your book *Micrographia*," Violet gushed, overwhelmed to find herself encountering yet another great name. "It's marvelous."

"I'm pleased to make your acquaintance." Mr. Hooke's gray eyes smiled along with his thin mouth, but in contrast to Mr. Wren's, his face crinkled in a way that suggested he rarely grinned. "The gardener's eldest, are you not?"

"Is my father's hobby so well known, then?" she wondered aloud.

"Legendary." Mr. Hooke shifted his awkward form. "Charming man, though," he added after a moment.

Ford touched Violet's arm. "Mr. Hooke is Gresham's

Professor of Geometry," he told her. "He lives here, right under that new observatory they're building." He indicated a corner of the quadrangle, where a small, square tower poked up from the roofline, surrounded by scaffolding.

"Convenient," Mr. Hooke said. "If I fall down stumbling drunk, I'm close to my bed."

They all laughed.

"How go the plans for St. Paul's?" Ford asked.

The two older men exchanged a glance, the kind shared by friends with secrets between them. Odd to think that such a cheerful person and a curmudgeonly one would be close.

"I'm working on a model," Mr. Wren said carefully.

Hooke let out a snort. "Twelve carpenters are working on it, and he's sunk five hundred pounds into it already. We can only pray the king likes it and the clergy give their approval."

"Approval for what?" someone asked in a voice with an Irish lilt. And before she knew it, Violet was introduced to Robert Boyle, a tall, thin man who also wanted a look at her spectacles.

No sooner had he finished exclaiming over them than another fellow walked up. Mr. Boyle handed him the lenses, and without them on her face, all Violet could tell about the newcomer was he was short and a bit stout.

"They belong to you, my lady?" he asked after examining them closely. He returned them with a bow. "Isaac Newton, at your service."

"Lady Violet Ashcroft," Ford introduced her. "The Earl of Trentingham's daughter."

"Ah, of course."

With the spectacles safely back in place, Mr. Newton looked to have five or so years on Ford. Under a broad forehead, his brown eyes were set in a sharp-featured face with a square lower jaw. He was handsome despite the prematurely gray hair peeking out from beneath his wig.

"We're pleased you remembered to attend," Mr. Boyle teased him.

Everyone but Violet laughed, and her expression must have shown her confusion. "Mr. Newton is known to be a bit absent-minded," Ford explained.

"That is an understatement of the greatest magnitude," Mr. Hooke said, eliciting more laughter. "He once entertained me for supper and went off to fetch more wine. An hour later I found him in his study, working out a geometrical problem. He'd completely forgotten I was there."

"It was an important problem," Mr. Newton protested good-naturedly. Violet couldn't help noticing that, compared to the others, he looked rather slovenly. His suit was finely made, but so wrinkled she wouldn't be surprised to learn he'd slept in it.

Mr. Wren rubbed his chin. "Tell her about that time you rode home from Grantham."

"That could happen to anyone."

"I think not." Mr. Wren turned to Violet. "He dismounted to lead his horse up a steep hill, and at the top, when he went to remount, he found an empty bridle in his hand. His horse had slipped it and wandered away unnoticed."

Even Violet had to laugh at that.

And so an hour passed while it seemed she met most every Englishman connected with modern-day science. Between examining her spectacles and regaling her with stories, they talked casually of their various projects—while Violet could do naught else but listen in wonderment.

The king's most favored architect, Mr. Wren had recently written a paper explaining how to apply engineering principles in order to strengthen buildings. He'd also patented a device for writing with two pens at once, and invented a language for the deaf and dumb, using hands and fingers to "talk."

Besides Mr. Hooke's improvements on the microscope that had allowed him to research and write *Micrographia*, he'd developed astronomical instruments that revealed new stars in Orion's belt. Ford whispered that he'd show them to her one night. Mr. Hooke had also formulated a new law of physics, asserting that the extension of a spring is proportional to the force applied to it. A lively discussion broke out over his proposal to introduce the freezing point of water as zero on the thermometer.

Since Mr. Hooke often assisted Robert Boyle, the two talked about their experiments with the new air pump Hooke had built. Using it to create a vacuum, Mr. Boyle had proven that the pressure of a gas is inversely proportionate to its volume.

"That is now called Boyle's Law," Ford told her.

Violet drank it all in, silently thrilled to be in such company. Although some of these great men were aristocrats, many were not. Here, dukes learned alongside commoners. The Royal Society was open to men of every rank and religion, so long as the proposed member held an interest in promoting discovery and science.

As each new arrival exclaimed over the genius of Violet's new spectacles, Ford basked in celebrity. And she didn't feel uncomfortable wearing them at all. Being the center of attention wasn't nearly as bad as she'd feared.

But as more eminent scientists gathered to praise Ford, she began to wonder if showing off his brilliant invention had been his real motivation for bringing her here. Disappointment took her by surprise, making the canary wine seem to sour in the pit of her belly.

True, he had never breathed a word about courting her. And she should have known better than to take his invitation as anything more than a friendly kindness.

But she suddenly realized that, somewhere deep inside, she'd begun to hope.

More fool her.

Stupid, stupid, stupid. *Of course* Ford didn't mean to court her. That wasn't how the world worked—not for girls like Violet. She'd reasoned that out for herself at a young age, and seen nothing but corroborating evidence ever since. His kisses didn't mean anything; she was simply the most convenient girl to hand.

It was slim pickings out in the country, after all.

Had displaying the spectacles been his true motivation for inviting her, or had it been something else? Sadly, if there *was* a meaning behind his kisses, it could only be one thing: that he wanted her inheritance.

She couldn't decide which option was worse.

Her insides knotted with humiliation and anger—at both Ford and herself. She couldn't seem to swallow past the lump in her throat, nor breathe through the ache in her chest. It didn't matter that she should have known the truth all along. No amount of telling herself so lessened the hurt.

"Is Locke here yet?" Ford asked the ever-growing assembly.

"Inside," Mr. Boyle said, waving to a chamber off the quadrangle. "Holding court."

"Excuse us, gentlemen." Taking Violet's hand, he drew her away.

Her other hand came up to rub her churning stomach. "I was enjoying that conversation," she protested, pleased that the words betrayed no emotion.

"And they were enjoying you." He smiled down at her, appearing as warm and sincere as ever. "We'll talk to them again later."

Her head spun with confusion.

The chamber Mr. Boyle had indicated turned out to be the refreshment room. Along one wall, long tables were laden with bottles of canary, Rhenish wine, and claret. Guests filled their plates from platters piled with fine cakes, macaroons, and marchpanes. Splendidly dressed gentlemen and ladies chatted while they ate, seated at small round tables. At one of these, a tall, slim figure stood with one foot perched on a chair, talking to a group that had clustered around him.

"John Locke," Ford said, nodding in the fellow's direction.

There was little in his appearance to suggest greatness. Although his speech was animated, his eyes looked melancholy, set in a long face with a large nose and full lips. Like Ford, he wore no wig, but his hair was straight and pale. His hands moved when he talked, his long fingers waving from the ruffled cuffs at his wrists.

As they drew close, Violet could hear his words. "Government," he said, "has no other end but the preservation of property."

A squat, balding man crossed his arms. "How can you speak such blasphemy? I've never heard such a thing."

"New opinions are always suspected, and usually opposed, without any other reason but because they are not already common."

"He's quite busy now," Ford whispered. "An introduction must probably wait for later."

"Oh, but may I stay and just listen?" *And spend a while apart from you, so I can think.* She waved an arm toward the tables bulging with refreshments. "Go have something to eat. You look starved. I'll be right here."

THIRTY-FOUR

ORD FROWNED AS he moved toward the refreshment tables. Was it his imagination, or had Violet seemed rather eager to be rid of him?

He *was* hungry, though. He picked up a plate.

"Why so gloomy, Lakefield?" Newton asked, filling a plate of his own at the heaping buffet. Gresham College was certainly welcoming the Royal Society back in style. "Are you not enjoying the festivities?"

Ford straightened his face. "I'm enjoying them immensely."

"Mmhm." Newton cast him an appraising glance as he added a strawberry to his selections. "Lady Violet sure is lovely, isn't she?"

"No. I mean, yes, of course she's lovely." Violet *did* look especially lovely tonight, what with her hair dressed in elegant curls, her ears and throat glittering with diamonds, and her new ball-gown hugging her figure in all the right places.

But even more stunning was the infectious smile that had hardly left her face all evening. The excitement in her eyes that had seemed to light up the whole courtyard. He'd never thought to meet a girl excited by science, or anything much academic. Tabitha certainly hadn't been.

Reluctant to follow that train of thought, Ford changed the subject. "I have some news I believe *you* shall find immensely enjoyable," he said, choosing radishes and slices of musk melon.

Newton bit into a macaroon. "What's that?"

"Well..." Ford was dying to share his good fortune with someone who would truly understand. He leaned close and whispered, "I've found *Secrets of the Emerald Tablet.*"

"You found *Secrets of the Emerald Tablet*?" Newton fairly bellowed.

"Hush! It's yet to be translated. I'm not ready to announce—"

But it was too late. Heads had turned, and a speculative murmur ran through the room.

Hooke rushed over. "Is it true? *Secrets of the Emerald Tablet* exists? You have it in your possession?"

"Not at the moment," Ford hedged. But at the sight of Wren and Boyle approaching, he gave up. They'd find out soon enough, anyway. "I've given it to an expert to translate. But yes, I found it, and I own it."

More men pressed close to hear the incredible news. "How much did it cost you?" someone asked.

"A shilling." As a stunned silence filled the room, he felt a grin stretch his face. "The bookseller thought it was worthless," he added.

"I'll buy it for fifty pounds," a man offered.

Hooke raised a hand. "A hundred."

Normally the most polite man Ford knew, Wren elbowed his good friend out of the way. "I'll pay you five hundred."

"I'll double what anyone else offers."

Silence reigned again as they all turned to look at Newton. His wrinkled suit notwithstanding, the fellow could well afford to honor the bid. He was wifeless, childless, and his father had died three months before his birth, leaving a tidy estate to his only son. Newton had inherited land from a subsequent stepfather as well.

He sounded sincere, and no one moved to say he wasn't; he was known to sometimes take offense when none was intended.

"It's not for sale," Ford said at last. "Not at any price."

"Well." Newton held his cup of Rhenish aloft in a toast. "I trust you'll let me know if ever you change your mind."

Conversation broke out in a deafening babble as people exclaimed over the find and maneuvered toward Ford to pump his hand and offer congratulations. The room turned hot and close as more guests made their way inside to join the crowd. Spirits were passed hand to hand from the tables to the back of the chamber, and soon everyone was clinking goblets to celebrate the discovery of the decade.

An hour flew by before Ford managed to work his way through the throng and into the corner where he'd left Violet. Along with the rest of Locke's audience, she was gone. The area had been overtaken by people marveling over *Secrets of the Emerald Tablet*.

Light-headed with success—and a bit more wine than he customarily drank—Ford hurried outdoors to the improvised ballroom. But the colonnaded courtyard was sparsely populated, and only a few couples graced the dance floor. It seemed every member of the Royal Society was in the refreshment room.

Though another chamber blazed with light, a peek into it nearly had him backing away. It was crammed with chattering ladies—all those deserted, he supposed, by the men in the other room. He pushed his way in, not really expecting to find Violet. She didn't strike him as the social, gossipy type.

He was correct.

Stopping three times to acknowledge congratulations, he crossed the quadrangle and walked through a building, finding the door to a small, deserted piazza.

The little courtyard looked dark and peaceful, especially after the excitement elsewhere in the college. He stepped outdoors, breathing deep of the fresh night air. Then, suddenly struck by an idea—perhaps not as brilliant as the spectacles, but clever nonetheless—he headed back inside to talk to one of the serving maids.

THIRTY-FIVE

*H*ALF AN HOUR later, Violet entered the quadrangle and nearly bumped into Ford. His hands went to her shoulders to steady her, which was entirely unnecessary—these days, with her spectacles, her balance was much improved.

"Fancy meeting you here," she quipped.

He didn't smile. "I've been looking all over for you."

"We had to escape that room."

"We?" he asked pointedly, his gaze flitting over her gown again.

She folded her arms over her chest. "Mr. Locke and I. Whatever was happening in there drew everyone's attention, and suddenly I found myself alone with him."

His eyes filled with an odd mixture of relief and concern. "But I hadn't made an introduction."

"None was needed." Locke had introduced himself without even making mention of her spectacles, simply accepting her as she was. "It seems he recognized a kindred soul. We wandered off and talked and talked..." She frowned suddenly. "Where were you all that time?"

"Word got out about me finding *Secrets*—"

A bewigged gentleman approached them with an

outstretched hand. "Heard of your astounding luck, Lakefield. Congratulations. If ever you want to sell it—"

"I don't." Ford pumped his hand. "But I thank you."

"Just let me know."

When the man was out of earshot, Ford sighed. "It seems everyone has to congratulate me—or make an offer to buy it. And Newton has offered to double anyone's bid. Can you imagine?"

What she couldn't imagine was him passing that up when he so obviously needed money. She measured his clear blue eyes. "You were serious, then, when you claimed you wouldn't sell at any price."

"I meant it. Considering the book went missing for so many years, it seems magical that it should end up in my hands. No matter that I don't believe in such things, it feels like fate."

She did understand how he felt. If ever she should find an ancient philosophy book, handwritten by one of the masters, she'd be reluctant to sell it as well. And she supposed it would feel like fate, too.

"Maybe it *was* fate," she said softly. "Do you believe that sometimes things are meant to be ours?"

He only smiled, a mysterious smile that for some reason made her uneasy.

She reached up to adjust her spectacles. "Well, I'm happy your announcement provided a distraction," she said by way of changing the subject. "I expect without that I'd never have spoken privately with Mr. Locke, and oh, we had the most fascinating conversation."

"Tell me about it." When another well-wisher approached, Ford impatiently took Violet's arm. "I know a place where I can listen without interruption."

He led her across the quadrangle, where the dance floor seemed to be filling now that men and women were filtering out of the buildings and meeting up with one another. She noticed Wren with an apple-cheeked, brown-haired lady. Hooke, ungainly and awkward, danced with a beautiful, redheaded woman quite a bit taller than himself.

Ford took Violet through a building and pushed open a door.

And they stepped into a veritable wonderland.

Candles sparkled everywhere—perched on the sills of the windows surrounding them, sitting on the benches around the perimeter, scattered on the patterned brick paving. Their flickering flames warded off the night, bathing the small piazza in a warm glow. In the center sat two chairs and one of the small round tables from the refreshment room, offering a selection of sweets and savories. A pair of goblets rested side by side, an open wine bottle nearby.

Gasping, she turned to Ford. "How did you know all this was here?"

"It wasn't." The door shut behind them with a soft *thud.* "I arranged it."

Though there were buildings all around, their windows were completely black. They were alone. She and her brilliant, bewildering neighbor were alone in a candlelit piazza in London. A piazza he'd had prepared especially for her.

Stunned, she shifted her gaze to meet his. "This isn't like you."

He gestured at her gown. "This isn't like you, either."

Heat rose into her cheeks as he gently removed her spectacles. She felt an arm curve around her waist, drawing her close. "Perhaps," he continued, "we bring out the best in each other." And she saw a hundred tiny lights flickering in his eyes as he bent his head.

This wasn't a stolen kiss, impulsive and rushed while their charges' heads were turned. This was deliberate and unhurried. His lips touched hers, then brushed over her cheek and across her forehead and down to her chin. He took her face in his hands and ran a thumb over her lower lip before finally covering it with his own.

Her heart trembled, then began pounding in her chest. She

felt indescribably…wanted. Unbelievably special. The feeling was warm and comforting, yet somehow shocking and exhilarating, all at the same time. She was dizzy with emotion, and with his exotic patchouli scent, and with the taste of wine on his lips, and with the heat of his body. She could have happily stayed like that forever, drowning in pure sensation with his mouth locked on hers.

When he pulled away, she just stood there, swaying for a moment, before opening her eyes. All around them, the flames glittered, gilding his features in a golden light.

"Thank you," she whispered.

As he slid the spectacles back on her face, the beginnings of a smile curved his lips. "You're entirely welcome," he said.

He sounded sincere. Was she wrong, then, about his intentions? He'd claimed to have invited her expressly to introduce her to someone who could help make her dream come true. Then he'd gone to great trouble to whisk her off to this romantic hideaway when they could be with his friends instead, showing off her spectacles and celebrating his miraculous book discovery.

And now here he was, looking at her—and kissing her—like he wanted her. *Her*, not just her money. Was he simply a good actor?

Could *anyone* be that good an actor?

She shouldn't allow herself to forget his words in the excitement of a kiss. To forget his beliefs about wives and inheritances. To forget that he was no different from all the other men where it counted.

But for this one magical night, a night of dreams come true, she would let herself live a fantasy. For just this night…

She fluffed her heavy skirts, gazing at him while she willed herself to believe she was a beautiful maiden, and he, a gentleman in love with her.

For just this one night.

"I'm famished," he said, and she laughed, breaking the tension. He led her to one of the chairs, then poured two goblets of wine. While she sipped, he moved the other chair close to hers and sat, taking a strawberry for himself.

"What did he talk about?" Ford asked, licking strawberry juice off his lips.

"Who?"

"King Charles."

For a moment, she looked around in confusion.

Then he laughed. "I meant John Locke, of course."

"Oh." A little giggle threatened to escape, so she sipped more wine. "He's brilliant."

He swiped a spear of asparagus off a plate piled high. "More brilliant than I?"

She cocked her head, making a show of considering. "In a different way." Sipping again, she warmed to her subject. "Do you know what he told me? He said all mankind should be equal and independent, and no one should have the right to harm another in his life, health, liberty, or possessions."

He bit the end off his third asparagus. "Not even the king?"

"No one." It was so radical a thought as to be startling, but so clear the way Locke had explained it. "There should be a standing rule to live by, common to everyone, and made by legislative power—a liberty to follow one's own will in all things where one does not harm another, and not to be subject to the arbitrary will of another. Arbitrary power, he said, becomes tyranny, whether those that use it are one or many."

"I wouldn't discuss this with Charles," Ford said, passing her a marchpane.

She bit into the sweet almond confection. "I've never discussed anything with the king, but if I ever get a chance, I just might."

"Criminy, what have I started?" he said with a good-natured roll of his eyes.

"Locke says every man has property in his own person, and no one has any right to that but himself. The labor of his body, the work of his hands, are his, and the only reason for men to unite and put themselves under government is the preservation of their property."

"You're excited by these ideas." Having finished the asparagus, he lifted a spoon and dug into the cheesecake blanketed in rich puff pastry. "I can hear it in your voice." He chewed and swallowed, closing his eyes, his face a mask of bliss. "Here, you have to try this."

He spooned up another bite and held it before her lips.

Though the night was crisp, she suddenly felt overwarm. But there was nothing for it. She opened her mouth and let him feed her the spoonful.

"It's heavenly," she said after she'd swallowed, though in truth, she hadn't really tasted it. She'd been too overwhelmed by the intimacy of his gesture. But she did her best to recover. "Um, yes, I *am* excited. I've never heard anything like Locke's ideas. It's a new way to look at our world." She drained her goblet, feeling woozy from both the wine and the thoughts spinning in her brain. "Thank you so much for bringing me."

"Thank you for coming." He reached to refill her cup, then leaned even closer, pressing a short, sweet kiss to her lips. "You enjoyed hearing about the scientific discoveries, too, if I'm not mistaken?"

"Very much." Her lips tingled. "I surprised myself."

"I'm surprised to find the philosophy interesting as well. So we're even this night."

"This night." Just this one night. She sighed, trying to savor the wine and the company, the candlelight, the music that drifted through the air, the stars in the clear summer sky. Knowing it had to end. "Can you hear the laughter from the quadrangle? I think everyone must be out there now." But she didn't want to join them. She didn't want to leave this magical, private place.

Afraid he might assume she wished to rejoin the party, she changed the subject. "Is Hooke really a drunkard?"

His brow furrowed in confusion. "Whatever makes you think that?"

"He said living here is convenient, because when he falls down stumbling drunk, he's close to his bed."

His face cleared. "Don't let his dry humor fool you. Far from being a drunkard, I think he and Wren are addicted to coffee, if anything at all. Best of friends they are, too."

The faint music from the quadrangle stopped. Another burst of laughter sounded. "Their wives must be proud of them," Violet said.

"Wren's wife is very kind." With one finger, he began idly tracing circles on the back of her hand where it rested on the table. "Hooke has yet to marry, though."

She hid a delicious shiver. "Well, then, with whom was he dancing?"

"Why did you assume she was his spouse? You're here with me, and we aren't husband and wife."

"Of course we aren't," she said quickly, and if his tone seemed to imply he wanted them to be, she had to remind herself why she didn't. Still, her cheeks heated at the thought, and she leaned away from the candles to hide her face in shadow.

"The Gresham professors are required to be bachelors," he explained, turning her hand over to draw circles on her palm. "Hooke calls that woman his housekeeper."

"She lives with him?"

"Mm-hmm."

"You don't dance with Hilda." Picturing it, she grinned.

He raised his hand and brushed a curl behind her ear. "Hilda is a *real* housekeeper."

"Oh." Her skin tingled wherever he touched. "Oh. You mean she's really a—oh."

"Yes. Oh," he repeated, raising a single brow.

All at once, the door was flung open and the sounds of laughter grew louder. A few couples spilled out into the piazza.

"We've been found," Ford said with a groan.

"There he is," one of the women cried, drawing a man to where Violet sat with Ford.

"Ah, yes." The middle-aged man shot the woman a rather impatient look before he addressed Ford more neutrally. "We've heard you found *Secrets of the Emerald Tablet*."

"I have." Ford reluctantly rose, bringing Violet up with him and curling an arm around her waist. "John Evelyn," he said by way of introduction. "May I present Lady Violet Ashcroft."

"I'm pleased to make your acquaintance." Evelyn had a lean, thoughtful face, shadowed by his graying hair. "My wife, Mary."

Much younger, Mary had a round, pretty face and curly hair that brushed shoulders left bare by a wide, low neckline. She smiled and curtsied, her large pearl earbobs bobbing along with her. "It's a pleasure to meet you, my lady."

"The pleasure is mine," Violet said.

Introductions concluded, the woman turned to Ford. "Would *Secrets of the Emerald Tablet* be for sale, my lord?"

"I'm afraid not." His words sounded genial enough, but Violet felt him tense. "And you'd have to fight Mr. Newton for it, anyway."

"It's just as well, my dear," Mr. Evelyn said.

The tone of his voice confused Violet. She turned to look up at Ford.

"I think," he said, "that we'd best be on our way." And he drew her out of the lovely piazza he'd created, leaving the others to enjoy it.

"What was *that* all about?" Violet asked as they walked back through the building. "I would think he'd be pleased she wanted to buy him the book."

He dropped his hand from her waist, linking his fingers with hers instead. "She wants it for herself. Her husband calls her a 'kitchen scientist.' Not fondly, I might add."

"I could tell." The quadrangle was quickly emptying, the

musicians packing up. "Does he not approve of her interests, then?"

"Mr. Evelyn believes housekeeping should be his wife's priority. His wedding gift to Mrs. Evelyn was a calligraphy copy of his own treatise on marital duties. The ladies at court think she must be the unhappiest woman in the world."

"I cannot blame her," Violet said, stepping carefully in her heeled shoes as they crossed the dew-damp grass.

"Her husband would say she has her children to console her."

"And you would say?"

He shrugged, squeezing her hand. "I know only that were I to be deprived of my scientific interests, I would be unhappy, too."

"Then let us hope your wife is more indulgent than Mary Evelyn's husband," she heard herself say.

Faith, how could she bring up his future wife?

But he only laughed, drawing her through the passage that led back to the Reading Hall and entrance. In the arched tunnel, he stopped and turned to face her. "I'm hoping my wife will be very indulgent, indeed," he said in a tone full of meaning.

"She'd have to be." A nervous giggle escaped her lips. "Are we leaving now?"

"In a minute." He stepped closer, backing her against the wall. "There will be a long line for the carriage at this time of night."

The evening had flown. "What time is it?" she asked.

He shrugged. "Not too late, in my estimation. Your mother mentioned no particular curfew. I think she must approve of me." Her heart raced as he slowly drew off her spectacles and slipped them into his pocket. "The church bells rang midnight a while ago."

"Oh. I wasn't listening."

"I wonder why," he mused with a smile, his hands moving to span her waist. She was finding it hard to listen now. Every-

216 | LAUREN ROYAL & DEVON ROYAL

where he touched felt so warm, so tingly, so aware. She glanced about, but there was no one in sight.

He lowered his head, his mouth inching toward hers, and she closed her eyes and waited, waited, her breath catching when he finally found her lips. His were soft but insistent, and despite all her reservations, she kissed him back with the same intensity.

"Violet," he murmured, and she was sure now—she heard it in his voice, sensed it in her very bones—that he felt something for her. Right or wrong, whatever his reasons, Ford Chase had feelings for *her*, Violet Ashcroft. It seemed miraculous and absurd and sublime all at once. On impulse, she pulled away, needing to see it on his face.

"Violet?" He blinked, dreamy-eyed, his lips curving in a slow smile. He looked at her as though he could look at her forever—as though he *wanted* to.

It *was* a miracle.

But what did this mean? She had to know. When he tried to kiss her again, she laid a hand on his cheek. "Ford, I—"

Laughter filled the tunnel as two other couples entered the passageway, clearly in their cups.

"'Night, Lakefield," one of the men called facetiously. "Sweet dreams."

Violet and Ford sprang apart. "'Night, Hartwell," he mumbled. His shallow breathing seemed to echo in the tunnel as he waited for the intruders to clear the other end.

When the two of them were alone again, he smiled at her, another slow, lazy smile that made her heart lurch. He leaned close, angling his head. Their lips met—

And three more men stumbled into the tunnel.

"'Night, Lakefield," they called in drunken unison.

"Let's line up for the carriage," Ford said with a sigh.

THIRTY-SIX

*V*IOLET RODE IN a carriage, crossing London on roads so impossibly smooth it felt as though she floated. The sidelight illuminated a crimson velvet interior, rich, plush, decadent. And into this upholstery she sank, beneath the weight of Ford's body.

While he kissed her senseless.

Knock-knock-knock.

A tiny sound escaped her throat, half enjoyment, half annoyance. Some very rude person was rapping on the carriage door.

Knock-knock-*knock*!

"Don't answer," she whispered to Ford. To be sure he complied, she threaded her fingers through his hair and held him captive, her lips fastened to his.

Knock-knock-knock!

With a snarl of frustration, she bolted upright, wrenched unwillingly from the dream. Her eyes popped open, but everything looked pitch black.

"Who is it?" she forced through gritted teeth.

Knock-knock-KNOCK!

"Who *is* it?" She swung her legs off the bed and pushed open the hangings, reaching for the floor with her bare feet.

Feeling blindly for her spectacles, she managed to locate them and shove them on, but of course they didn't help. Black was black.

KNOCK-KNOCK-KNOCK!

"Who is it?" she yelled, padding toward her door and fumbling in the darkness for the latch. When her fingers finally closed on it, she jerked it open.

It didn't open very far.

Bang! Like a gunshot, the noise came across the corridor, accompanied by a high-pitched shriek. Then the latch was yanked from Violet's hand, as—

SLAM! her own door flew closed.

Her frustration mounting, she opened it again.

Bang!

SLAM!

Bang!

SLAM!

She paused for a moment, shaking the last dregs of sleep from her head. After drawing a deep breath, she gingerly opened her door again, just a crack.

And heard the sound of her little brother's giggles.

"Rowan!" she scolded.

Her hand was still on the latch, and something pulled on the door, though it didn't slam this time. A steady pull.

"Rowan?" Rose's voice called.

From down the corridor came the sound of another door opening, then Lily's sleepy voice. "What's all this noise?" she said through a yawn.

"I got you!" Rowan crowed. "I got you both. It worked!"

"What worked?" Violet asked suspiciously. A soft flare of light illuminated the corridor as someone—Lily, she guessed—approached with a candle.

"Rowan, I cannot believe what you did!" Lily exclaimed. Instead of disapproval, admiration tinged her voice. "You clever boy!"

"What?" Rose snapped, apparently still trapped behind her door and as mystified as Violet. "What did he do?"

Lily's laughter echoed in the corridor. "Wait a minute." Violet heard the small *clink* of the silver candlestick landing on a table, then a rustling, scratching sound as Lily did something with her door.

A moment later, it opened wide. "He t-tied your doors together with r-rope," Lily said, the words tumbling out between giggles. "So you were slamming each other's open and shut."

Directly across the corridor, Rose opened her now-free door and glowered at their brother. "You're lucky you didn't wake Mum."

Rowan shrugged. "Mum's room is too far away in this house. Besides, she'd find it funny, don't you think?"

"I ought to murder you, you rapscallion."

His little chest puffed out proudly. "I had to knock forever to wake you. But it was worth it. Jewel said it would work. Too bad she wasn't here to see it."

Violet didn't miss the melancholy look that stole across his face. "You miss her, don't you?"

"I do. And I don't know if I'll ever see her again." A sheen of tears brightened his eyes. "I didn't think I'd like a girl, but she's not like any girl I ever knew. She's more like a boy."

Violet suspected pretty Jewel wouldn't remind him of a boy a few years down the road. "You'll see her again, I'm sure. And in the meantime, don't forget we're going home tomorrow, and Benjamin should be home by now, too."

"Benjamin!" Benjamin and he had grown up together, close as two neighbors could be. With a boy's short attention span, Rowan forgot Jewel immediately. "I'm going to sleep now, so tomorrow will come faster." And with that, he took off down the corridor, to his own room across from Lily's.

"What a rude awakening," Rose said.

Violet sighed. "He yanked me from the most wondrous dream."

"Did he?" Lily picked up the candle and swept past Violet into her room, Rose right on her heels. She lit Violet's bedside candle from her own and set them both on the night table. "What was your dream about?"

When Violet didn't answer immediately, her sisters exchanged a look, then sat in unison on the edge of her bed. "Tell us," Rose said.

Violet's cheeks flushed hot. She shut the door, cocooning the three girls together. "It was nothing, really."

Rose crossed her arms. "You said it was wondrous."

"Oh, all right." She dragged the stool over from her dressing table and sat facing them, setting her hands on her knees. "We were coming home—"

"We?" Lily interrupted.

"Ford and myself. From the Royal Society reception."

"How did that go?" Rose asked. "I tried to stay up to hear, but you got home so late—"

"Hush," Lily said. "The dream first."

Violet's cheeks warmed. "It wasn't *that* late." After all the excitement in the corridor, her dream was fading fast. She shut her eyes, reaching for the memory. "We were riding home in his carriage, but it seemed to be floating—"

"Floating," Rose echoed, and though Violet's lids were closed, she could swear she saw her sister's head nod knowingly. "Floating in a dream is supposed to be sensual in nature."

"Rose!" Violet's eyes flew open. "You are far too young to be saying such things!"

Rose raised a brow. "Yet somehow old enough for you to show me *Aristotle's Master-piece?*"

"I didn't show it to you. You barged in on me reading it, and then you blackmailed me!"

She shrugged with profound unconcern. "Let's read some more of it."

"Not now," Lily said, giving Rose a little shove. "I want to hear the rest of the dream."

"All right." Violet swallowed and rubbed her suddenly damp palms against her night rail-clad knees. "Ford's carriage is rather ancient, as you know, but instead of the old leather, the interior was all plush red velvet. And I was leaning back against a cushion, and he was kissing me—"

"Did he kiss you really?" Lily sat up eagerly.

"He already kissed her," Rose said. "In the library."

Lily turned on the bed to face her. "That doesn't count. You described it to me in detail, and it was a little peck, not a real kiss." She shifted back to Violet. "Did he give you a real kiss in the carriage?"

"Well," Violet hedged, alarmed to learn that Rose had been watching her in the library, "not on the way home. Lord and Lady Ailesbury begged a ride, and since they only live around the corner, we had no time alone together."

"But after you dropped them off?" Rose pressed.

"The street out front is very rutted, you know—the springs in that old carriage might as well be nonexistent."

"But he tried." Rose's gaze was much too piercing for Violet's comfort. "Or he kissed you earlier, didn't he? At the ball. Or later, when he saw you to the door."

Violet looked away.

"Or both!" Rose concluded. "I knew it!"

Lily laid a graceful hand on the white cotton that covered her chest. "Goodness." A theatrical sigh escaped her lips. "What was it like?"

"I never said he kissed me."

Her two very different sisters fixed her with matching, demanding glares. Rose spoke for both. "Let's hear it, Violet."

"Oh, all right." Violet crossed her legs and leaned forward conspiratorially. "It was very nice."

"Nice?" Rose folded her arms.

"It was more than nice. It was marvelous." Warming to her subject, Violet's voice gentled. "The most amazing feeling. It made my head spin and my heart beat fast. His lips felt warm and squashy—"

"*Squashy?*" Lily looked taken aback.

Rose cocked her head. "Like an overripe peach?"

"Certainly not. More like...I don't know..." Violet wracked her brains. "A hard-boiled egg?"

"An *egg?*" Lily's fingers flew to touch her own lips. "I dislike eggs."

"The white part or the yellow part?" Rose asked.

"Both!"

"No, I was asking Violet if his lips felt like—"

"Never mind!" Violet shouted over the din. "Forget about eggs. His lips were soft, all right? Warm and soft."

"Oh. That sounds nice." Lily's eyes softened to a hazy blue.

"Gemini." Rose fanned herself with a hand. "I must find someone to kiss. Tomorrow."

Violet reached out and caught her wrist. "No, you mustn't. You must care for someone before you kiss him."

Lily gave another dreamy sigh. "Oh, Violet, that's so romantic."

That was taking things a bit too far. "It's over now. We're going home tomorrow, and he's staying here to meet with his solicitor. And even after he returns to Lakefield, Jewel has gone home, so there's no longer any reason for me to visit."

"But you care for him. You just said so. And since he kissed you, he'll be asking you to wed him, will he not?"

"It doesn't always work like that, Lily. Some gentlemen don't put such store behind a kiss. The *Master-piece* says that marriage is meant to restrain man's wandering desires and affections."

Lily frowned. "Does that mean all men prefer to keep wandering?"

"I'm not sure. But he won't be asking me to marry him."

"But if he did?" Rose pressed. "That would be splendid, wouldn't it?"

"No," Violet said flatly. "If he's making a show of courting me, you can be certain it's because of my inheritance. And I won't marry for anything less than true love."

"But Violet." Concern filled Lily's earnest gaze. "You must care. Or you wouldn't have kissed him. You said a lady must care for a man before she—"

"I'm not looking for one-sided love, Lily. If I cannot have a love like Mum's, then I'd rather live life on my own." She turned to Rose. "And you can stop worrying—I don't care if you marry before me. I don't care if I marry at all." And because that suddenly wasn't true, she made a big show of yawning. "It's very late. I have much to tell you both about the ball, and especially Mr. Locke, but it will have to wait until morning."

Lily rose and placed a sisterly kiss on her cheek. "I would love to hear it all, Violet."

Rose's kiss wasn't nearly as sweet. "I don't care about Mr. Locke," she said, "but you should marry Lord Lakefield."

Long after her sisters had left, Violet lay awake, her heart and mind in turmoil.

THIRTY-SEVEN

*L*AKEFIELD HOUSE was quiet. Too quiet.

Hilda and Harry knew better than to disturb Ford when he was working, but Jewel had never quite mastered that bit of etiquette. Now Ford found his gaze straying toward the door, waiting for his niece to burst through, a grin on her heart-shaped face and a ribbon clenched in her diminutive fist.

Or a dead insect. One never quite knew what to expect from Lady Jewel.

But the one thing he hadn't expected was to feel this sudden loneliness. Emptiness. For pity's sake, he missed her.

Ford Chase missed a child.

Whoever would have thought? Wasn't a family of his own the last item on his list of priorities? Though he'd always known he must have children eventually—Lakefield would need an heir, after all—he'd never been able to envision them in his life. Having a family had seemed so dreadfully adult.

But now, instead of finishing his watch, he found himself daydreaming. A girl and a boy, like Jewel and Rowan. And a mother for them, of course.

Violet would be perfect.

Gears slipped from his fingers as that thought took root in his brain. He dropped to a crouch to reach one that rolled beneath his workbench, then bumped his head as he came back up.

Rubbing where it hurt, he sat on the floor to analyze when and how he had fallen in love with Violet Ashcroft.

He'd always thought he wanted someone like Tabitha. Effervescent, confident, a girl whose looks stopped men in the street. Violet was none of those things. But she listened to his ideas and challenged him with her own.

He'd never imagined a girl like Violet existed.

Now that he knew she did, perhaps it was logical for an academic such as Ford to find himself drawn to someone with Violet's unusual qualities.

But it would be downright illogical for him to pursue the matter. He could hardly expect Violet to marry him when his estate and finances were such a disaster. The meeting with his solicitor had not gone well. There were bills to be paid and no money with which to pay them.

The man had presented two options. One, turn Lakefield into a working estate and see that it prospered. Two, sell the blasted place. Only a small portion of the land was entailed. Selling the rest—including the house—would raise enough money to support Ford for years to come, leaving him free to pursue his own work.

As a third son, Ford should never have had a title, and while he enjoyed that part of it well enough, he wasn't cut out to be a landowner. True, he'd assisted his brother Jason with Cainewood's never-ending responsibilities—he knew the ins and outs of running an estate. But he had no love for that sort of life.

Working the land, dealing with tenants, collecting rents. It was all so tedious and trivial. At the end of a typical nobleman's life, one's legacy was naught but more of the same passed down to an heir. Nothing new to contribute to knowledge and mankind.

He'd always pictured his life in London, with his research and the Royal Society.

But now his heart was here.

Restless, he rose to his feet and tossed the gear into the mess on the table. What did it matter where his heart was? Violet's parents might appear to like him personally, but it would be highly irrational of them to allow their daughter to marry a penniless viscount. Under normal circumstances, the fact that Violet came with a sizable inheritance as well as a dowry might mitigate the situation, but nothing about Violet was normal. Knowing her feelings about husbands and inheritances, he was sure he'd have a beast of a time convincing her he wasn't after her fortune.

And knowing the reality of his finances, he'd have an equally difficult time sticking to his word.

He closed his eyes and rubbed them. It was hopeless. He might as well put her out of his mind. And he knew just how to go about that, too.

For once, his inability to concentrate on more than one thing at a time would prove an asset.

After quickly separating the jumble of gears on his work table, he lifted the gold watch to dangle by its chain. He wanted to invent a personal timepiece with two hands. That was why he had come to Lakefield in the first place. Without Jewel to distract him, he ought to be able to achieve his aim at last.

It was a good thing he'd taken time to analyze the situation, because these lofty romantic sentiments had nothing to do with his real life. Nothing to do with his aspirations.

He took a deep breath, raked a hand through his hair, and got to work.

THIRTY-EIGHT

*S*EATED IN HER customary spot in the summerhouse, Violet cleared her throat. "As I was saying..." She sent Rose a severe glance before raising the book. "'In this concavity are diverse folds, wrinkled like an expanded rose.'"

"A rose?" Rose interrupted again. "That 'concavity' looks nothing like the roses in our garden." When her sisters gaped at her, she bristled. "Well, it doesn't. I've looked. With a mirror." She narrowed her gaze. "Don't tell me you haven't."

Violet just continued reading. "'The hymen, or claustrum virginale, is that which closes the neck of the womb relating to virginity, broken in the first copulation. And commonly, when broken in copulation, or by any other accident, a small quantity of blood flows from it, attended with some little pain.'"

Silence descended on the summerhouse.

"Little pain," Lily whispered finally. "That doesn't sound too bad, does it?"

"I'm sure it's not," Violet said firmly.

But they all took a deep breath in unison.

"All right, then." Violet turned the page. "Listen to this." She swallowed. "'There are many veins and arteries passing into the womb—'"

Suddenly they heard a jaunty tune being hummed outside. "Gemini!" Rose exclaimed. "It's Mum!"

Leaping up, she ran for the door and jerked it open, Lily at her heels. The two of them pushed through at the same time, all but stumbling over each other.

"Good afternoon, Mum," Rose said. "Come along, Lily. Father is waiting."

"For what?" Mum asked, frowning at Violet as her younger daughters all but trampled her in their haste to escape.

Shrugging, Violet snapped the book closed and set it face down on the bench. "What are you doing out here?"

Unlike Father, Mum avoided the outdoors, especially on a nice, sunny day like this one. She worried for her creamy complexion. Now she was wearing a big straw hat and carrying a basket over her arm, filled with stale bread. "I thought I'd just take some air," she said. "And feed the swans."

When Violet stood, her spectacles tumbled from her lap to the red-brick floor. She bent to retrieve them, hoping her mother wouldn't notice the book on the bench. "Shall I come with you?"

"That would be lovely."

She slipped the frames on her face as they crossed the wide green lawn to the river. A multitude of daisies sprouted among the blades of grass; heaven forbid Father leave any part of his land free of flowers.

Mum bent to pick one as they went. She twirled the white and yellow posy in her fingers. "Is the book you were reading interesting?"

Faith, she'd noticed.

"It's philosophy." Well, it was. In a sense.

"What is it called?"

"Um..." Violet felt her face heat, but the title certainly wasn't a giveaway. "*Aristotle's Master-piece.*"

Stepping onto the bridge, her mother threw her an inscrutable look. "And is it?"

Her heart stuttered. "Is it what?"

"A masterpiece."

"Oh." Halfway across the bridge, Violet stopped and turned to the rail. She focused out over the river. "It's Aristotle, you know. I'm sure you've heard me jabber enough about him." She reached into her mother's basket and broke off a bit of bread, tossing it out to the lone swan nearby. "I don't expect you'd find it very interesting."

"You might be surprised."

Violet wondered what her mother meant, but she didn't want to ask. She had a feeling she was better off not knowing.

More swans glided near, and her mother tossed a few crumbs. "You miss him, don't you?"

Him. Mum had to mean Ford. But Violet had never admitted to any regard for him, so how could Mum know?

"Miss whom?" she asked.

"Lord Lakefield, of course. Don't be coy, Violet. For weeks you saw him every day, but now that Jewel is gone, you have no excuse to visit. I know you're fond of him."

"He's very nice," Violet said carefully.

"You don't allow a gentleman to kiss you just because he's nice."

Violet's jaw dropped open. She closed it, along with her eyes, then opened them and turned to her mother. "Wherever did you get the idea he kissed me?"

"One of your sisters." Mum held up a hand. "No, I won't tell you which one, because it doesn't matter."

"It matters to me! It was Rose, wasn't it?"

"I won't be saying."

Violet was more frustrated than embarrassed by Mum's revelation. She knew her mother must have kissed her father before they were married—how else could they have been caught in a 'compromising position'?

But that was beside the point. "I'm not marrying him, Mum."

Below them, the swans squawked, and Mum broke off more bread. "Why not?"

"Well, for one thing, he hasn't asked me. And for another, I wouldn't agree if he did."

"Can you explain why?"

"Why?" To avoid meeting her mother's eyes, Violet took a hunk of bread and faced the graceful white birds. "Why should I? With or without my spectacles, I'm not blind. I know I'm no beauty. If he asked for my hand, it would only be to get my ten thousand pounds—heaven knows he needs it, as Rose has pointed out countless times. And I won't marry for less than true love, Mum. I...I suspect marriage isn't all it's purported to be, anyway."

She wished she could still believe that with the certainty she once had. But she wasn't quite so sure any longer, not since attending the ball. Now, late at night, she lay in her four-poster bed alone, wishing to feel that feeling again. That feeling of being wanted—cherished, body and soul—that she'd felt in that candlelit piazza.

Mum threw the last of her crumbs to the swans. "I see."

Violet didn't care for her mother's tone. Tossing the rest of her own crumbs, she turned to face her. "You're not going to try to match me up with him, are you? Because—"

"Goodness, no! I want you to be happy, Violet. Married or not—whatever makes you happy."

Mum sounded sincere. But as they strolled hand-in-hand back to the house, Violet couldn't help but wonder.

THIRTY-NINE

*C*HRYSTABEL LOVED the nighttimes.

In the quiet of the master chamber, her dear Joseph could always hear her. It didn't quite make sense, which was why she sometimes teasingly accused him of selective listening. But he said it had to do with competing sounds. That during the daytime, there were noises, always noises: servants going about their work, animals in the fields, birds in the skies, dishes and silverware at mealtimes, and the children all talking at once. With more than one sound, he couldn't distinguish any of them.

But within the thick, solid walls of their room, the nighttimes were blessedly quiet. And he also declared that her voice was the one he could hear most easily, especially when there were no competing sounds. The perfect pitch.

That *did* make sense to her. Because they'd always, always been perfect together.

But now he had nodded off, though she'd expressly asked him not to. She closed the door behind her with a smart *thump* that startled him awake. "I told you to wait up."

He yawned and rolled over. "Has Violet fallen asleep yet?"

"Yes. Finally." She deposited a leather-bound book on the counterpane. "I got it."

"What?" He rubbed his face, then struggled up onto his elbows to see better. "What is this all about?"

She untied the sash around her waist. "*Aristotle's Master-piece*," she said in a deceptively casual tone.

"Holy Hades. The marriage manual?" He bolted upright. "Where on earth would Violet get such a thing?"

"Language, Joseph! No wonder Rowan has learned such habits." Shrugging out of her dressing gown, Chrystabel straightened her chemise, then went to work on unpinning her hair. "And I've no idea where Violet got the book. But I mean to give it back to her before she realizes it's missing—we've this night only to peruse the material and ensure it's appropriate."

"*Appropriate?*" He cast the ordinary-looking tome a thunderous glare. "How could it possibly be—"

"Ah, Joseph, don't be so old-fashioned. I know the book is supposed to be scandalous, but Violet is old enough to learn the facts—and if half of what's said about the *Master-piece* is true, it will explain things much better than we could ever bring ourselves to do."

Chrystabel saw no need to mention their younger daughters were reading it as well. Her beloved Joseph wasn't always as open-minded as she. Often he needed some time and guidance to come around to her way of thinking.

Settling herself in the soft feather bed, she retrieved the book in question and laid it on her lap. "Frankly, I'll try anything to discourage her preposterous commitment to spinsterhood."

"Spinsterhood! Why, she's not even eighteen."

"I know, darling. But Rose has been hard on her. Violet has tremendous strength of character, but she's not without her weak points. And clever Rose knows exactly how to exploit them."

Joseph crossed his arms. "I still don't see how letting Violet read this unseemly book will improve matters."

Chrystabel sighed. Men. They had to have everything spelled out for them. "What does Violet love more than anything else in the world?"

"Learning, of course."

"Indeed. And what knowledge might she hope to gain from a marriage manual?"

"Um…knowledge about marriage?"

"Precisely. She's taking an *interest*, Joseph. Will you be the one to quash that interest? Don't you want to see your daughter happily married?"

"Of course I do—but not at the expense of her innocence."

Chrystabel rolled her eyes. "Her innocence will remain intact. We'll make sure of it." She took a candle from the side table. "Or do you not plan to read it with me?"

Joseph's eyebrows quirked with sudden curiosity. "I suppose it *is* my fatherly duty…"

Stifling laughter, Chrystabel leaned over and planted a kiss on her husband's cheek. Then she opened the book.

"Oh my," they said in unison.

FORTY

*A*N IMPATIENT KNOCK came at the laboratory door before Hilda's voice called through it. "Will you be wanting breakfast, milord?"

Ford blinked and then carefully, reverently, set aside his watch. Still in somewhat of a daze, he rose and went to admit her. "Is it morning already?"

His housekeeper's hands went to her hips. "Have you not bothered to look out a window lately?"

He turned to the one right over where he'd been working. The sky was blue. Birds were chirping, the perfect accompaniment for a beautiful, sunny day.

"Did you stay up all night again?" Hilda demanded.

"What is it with the questions?" Ford shook his head, refusing to let her disapproval ruin his exuberant mood. "Come, I have something to show you."

She followed him to his workbench, weaving around a water bath and flicking her dust rag as she went. "If you'd let me in here to clean once in a while, this wouldn't be such a skimble-skamble mess."

Accustomed to her lectures, he ignored this one and lifted his watch, dangling by its gold chain. "Here it is," he said with a broad smile. "I'm finished."

"It's very nice." She raised a glass funnel and wiped it off.

Nonplussed, he stared at her. "I know it's not fancy, but do you see here? It's different from other watches. It has a minute hand, like a clock. So you won't have to guess how far into the hour it is by looking at only the single hand."

"Well, that is very nice, my lord." She smiled, but her faded blue eyes didn't sparkle with the enthusiasm he was seeking. "Although you have clocks enough around here for me to tell the time, I expect many individuals will appreciate the convenience." She set down the funnel and glanced around the attic, sighing at the clutter and dust. "Will you be wanting breakfast now, then?"

He was silent a minute before mutely ordering himself to shrug off the disappointment. "Breakfast would be nice. I'll be down shortly."

He watched her calico-clad back as she picked her way through the maze that was his sanctuary. *Convenient.* She'd called his watch convenient. Although he supposed it was, that hadn't been the reaction he was hoping for.

After months and months of analysis and experimentation—not to mention years of schooling and an entire childhood's worth of tinkering—he'd finally managed to create something that could benefit mankind. He wanted awe, excitement. Criminy, a bit of hero worship wouldn't be amiss, either.

Suspecting Jewel would have expressed all those sentiments and more, he found himself missing her all over again.

Luckily, another enthusiastic girl lived not so far away.

FORTY-ONE

*A*N HOUR LATER, having bathed, shaved, and gulped down some breakfast, Ford found himself in the galleried entry of Trentingham Manor, proudly holding up his watch for Violet's inspection.

"Oh my," she said, her brandy-colored eyes wide with unabashed admiration. "It's amazing. I cannot believe it! Can I just stand here a while and watch it work?"

Ford laughed, finally feeling that rush of success, wanting to kiss her for giving it to him. "If you'd like. But if you'd care to invite me into a room with chairs, you can sit and watch it instead. That would be more comfortable, don't you think?"

"Oh. I'm so sorry." Holding the book he'd just given her, she turned and started down the corridor. "I've forgotten my manners."

He walked beside her. "I'd forgotten how lovely you are."

In his single-minded focus on his watch, he *had* forgotten. Intentionally forgotten. But she blushed prettily at the compliment.

"Besides," he added, "I'm the one who's socially inept. I should have exchanged pleasantries before shoving my invention in your face. Your manners, by contrast, are impeccable."

She flashed him a smile that might as well have been a fist in his gut. He shouldn't have come. Neither she nor her parents would ever agree to a match, and here he was, falling in love all over again.

How was it that he could he be so clever in some ways, and yet so entirely harebrained in others?

She was wearing a yellow gown today, and her red heels clicked on the corridor's polished oak floor. "Would you show my family the watch? I'm certain they will be just as impressed as I."

Thinking of Hilda's reaction—or rather, lack of one—Ford wasn't so sure.

"Mum is in her perfumery," Violet told him, and he shrugged and followed her to the left, through a study he hadn't seen before. Unlike the pretty feminine desks in the library upstairs, this room's desk was heavy and utilitarian. There were papers all over it, and a pile of ledgers that looked ready to topple. He figured this was where Joseph Ashcroft ran his estate. It was obviously hard work—a demanding job Ford had no desire to tackle for Lakefield.

But that's exactly what he'd have to do if he ever hoped to be worthy of a girl like Violet Ashcroft.

He looked away from the desk, preferring instead to watch Violet as he followed her through the house. The yellow silk nipped in at the waist before flaring out over her curved, feminine hips. Well, he couldn't see her hips beneath her ample skirts, but he remembered placing his hands on them as he'd kissed her once, and he wanted to do that again.

He sighed. He didn't want someone *like* Violet—he wanted the genuine artifact.

But all the hoping he could muster wouldn't make a blasted bit of difference. He couldn't magically transform himself into the sort of husband she deserved.

His watch was finished. He really ought to go back to London.

Like many old houses, Trentingham had few corridors, most of the rooms simply opening on to the next. The adjacent chamber was tiny, more or less a closet. But it would do as the storeroom for a laboratory. The walls were lined with row upon row of shelves, upon which rested vials of liquid. Chemicals.

He stopped dead, looking around.

"Mum is through here."

He blinked. Violet was gazing at him, the red-covered book he'd given her clutched to her chest. "I'm coming," he said.

The next room *was* a laboratory.

True, it was nothing like his. While his had but a single small window over his work space, Lady Trentingham's large windows afforded glorious views of the gardens and the river. While his had only one wooden chair for him to sit and work, hers had six upholstered ones, arranged in pairs with elegant inlaid tables between them. Clearly this room was used for socializing as well as work. But it was a laboratory nonetheless.

Forgetting the watch in his hand, he found himself drawn to the center of the chamber, where Lady Trentingham stood at a large, rectangular table, plucking flower petals and tossing them into some sort of contraption.

"Good morning, Lord Lakefield," she said, beaming at him as though he were her long-lost son.

He wished.

"A pleasure to see you again," he told her.

"Yes, it's been a while, hasn't it?" If he wasn't mistaken, her tone was slightly scolding. "What is it you've brought us?"

"He hasn't brought it for us, Mum, not exactly. Just to show." Violet twirled the end of her plait around a finger, looking a bit flustered. Ford wondered if that was due to her mother's warm welcome. It had certainly surprised him.

Perhaps the Ashcrofts would be more amenable to a match than he'd thought.

Violet set the book on a table. "Give me a moment to fetch the rest of the family."

The room seemed immeasurably emptier after she left. Listening to her fading footsteps, Ford set his watch on another of the small marquetry tables. "What is *that*?" he asked Lady Trentingham, indicating the peculiar device.

Favoring him with a smile, she tossed a final few petals into the bowl. "Joseph has given me the last of this year's roses. I'm about to make essential rose oil. Would you care to help?"

"Certainly." He wiped his palms on his breeches, approaching the crude apparatus. "What is it you'd like me to do?"

"Just hold the bowl while I pour boiling water, then quickly set this other bowl on top. Upside down." She demonstrated. "Ready?"

"Pour away," he told her, gripping the bowl while she turned to take a kettle from the fire. He watched while she poured, noting how much steam escaped before she finished and he was able to place the second bowl over the rising vapors.

"It's called distillation." Replacing the kettle, she swiped the back of a graceful hand across her brow. "When the drippings cool, they separate into water—rosewater, in this case—and essential oil." She indicated the tray below.

"I see," he told her. It was a still. But although he could tell it would work, it was like no other still he'd ever laid eyes on. Her process would be more efficient with the heat supply directly beneath, the water and petals contained in a flask so the vapors couldn't escape. And with tubing and a water-cooling method, the oil—

"Violet said you invented a new watch," Rose said, walking into the room with her two sisters in her wake. Rowan came close behind, making a beeline for the table where Ford's invention waited.

"Uh-uh-uh," Violet said before he could touch it. She reached to clasp his wrist. "Wait until Father arrives."

"But, Violet—"

"Here." She fetched the book Ford had given her. "Lord Lakefield brought you this from London."

"*Micrographia*," he breathed, opening it to the middle. "Look at this." He shoved a picture in Rose's face.

"Ewww." She wrinkled her nose. "What is that?"

"A blue fly up close."

Violet smiled. "I met the author at Gresham College."

The sudden blush on her cheeks made Ford suspect she was remembering other parts of their evening at Gresham College.

"That was *very* nice of Lord Lakefield," Lady Trentingham said. She was beaming in Ford's direction again. "What do you say to him, Rowan?"

Before Rowan could offer his thanks, Violet's father barged in, his hands full of colorful flowers.

Lilies? Violets? Ford could only recognize roses, and he saw none of those.

"What's this all about?" Lord Trentingham asked.

"Lord Lakefield has designed a new watch," Violet said.

"Lord Lakefield has resigned? Resigned from what?"

The three sisters giggled.

"Quiet, everyone." Lady Trentingham set down the bottle she was holding and glided over to her husband. "Thank you, darling." She accepted the flowers and stuffed them into a vase she took off a shelf, one of many. "Lord Lakefield has an invention to show us. Would you care to see?"

"A new sort of watch." As Ford lifted the pocket watch's lid, everyone else moved to huddle around.

"Look," Violet said. "There's an extra hand to mark the minutes, so you no longer have to guess. Isn't it amazing?"

"Very impressive," Lord Trentingham said.

"Brilliant." His wife's smile looked so genuine that Ford found the tiniest, most fragile sliver of hope that she might secretly approve of him.

"I want one," Rowan said.

"Let me see," Rose demanded, and Lily chimed in more softly with "Me, too."

Ford handed over the timepiece, watching to make sure they'd be careful with it. But then his gaze was drawn to Violet. He hadn't seen her in a week. Hadn't touched her in a week.

Their eyes searched, met, locked. Sparkling behind the lenses he'd made, hers were brandy-brilliant and beautiful. An unspoken message passed between them.

"If you've no objections," he said carefully, "I would like to take your daughter for a walk."

"Go ahead, dears," Lady Trentingham said. "We're watching the time pass!"

FORTY-TWO

ATCHING TIME. How much time, Violet wondered as they strolled toward the river, until Ford returned to London?

This last week had been so monotonous while he'd been holed up working on his invention. She could hardly remember what she used to do with her days before he'd arrived with Jewel in tow. But now his niece had gone home, and he was finished with what he'd come to do. Soon, he'd be leaving. He'd probably asked her out here to tell her that.

She crossed her arms.

"Cold?" he asked.

"Not really." The August day was breezy yet warm, and the grass felt springy beneath her shoes. Violet tossed her plait over her shoulder, wondering if she should have allowed Margaret to spend the entire morning coaxing her hair into the fashionable ringlets she'd worn to the Royal Society event.

Faith, next she'd be fretting over her complexion!

Feeling self-conscious, she turned away and bent to pick a daisy as they approached the bridge. Her fingers idly plucked the white petals.

He loves me, he loves me not.

But of course he didn't love her. She might be decked out in fancy new clothes, but who did she think she was fooling? Such finery couldn't hide the deficiencies underneath.

Violet had always found things to dislike about herself, but today, for the first time ever, she found herself genuinely wishing she were a different person. The thought made her want to cry.

Instead, she changed the subject. "Have you missed Jewel this past week?" Dropping her mangled daisy at the foot of the bridge, she started across.

Keeping pace, he gave a rueful smile. "Yes—to my great surprise. I've written her two letters already. She loves getting mail."

In the middle of the bridge, she stopped and turned to face him. "How thoughtful."

He shrugged. "It's selfish, mostly. I'm hoping for letters in return." Water flowed under the boards beneath their feet, and two swans glided near, but they had no bread to toss to them. "I missed you this past week as well," he said quietly.

Had he? She searched his fathomless blue eyes. "It felt odd not to be heading for Lakefield in the afternoons."

"Then you missed me, too?"

She couldn't deny it. But what good would it do to confess? Admitting her feelings would change nothing.

Reaching to raise her chin, he looked straight into her eyes. Keeping his own wide open, he leaned in and pressed a soft, measured kiss to her lips. "I care for you, Violet. I've been trying to analyze why. But I think—no matter how much it pains me to admit this—there are some things one cannot analyze."

She didn't know how to respond, but her lips tingled. His fingers felt warm on her skin. When he moved toward her again, her gaze darted up to the perfumery's windows. Her family lurked behind the glass, probably still exclaiming over Ford's invention. A pale oval appeared behind a pane, then disappeared. She'd bet the *Master-piece* it was Rose, spying.

"Afraid we're being watched?"

She sighed. "I wouldn't put it past my sisters. Or Mum, come to that."

He nodded, and they strolled across the bridge and along the far bank of the river. Cattle grazed in the fields beyond, and a hawk circled lazily overhead. As Ford slipped his hand into hers, her gaze flicked once more to the window, and he chuckled beside her.

They walked in silence, listening to the whinnies of the horses in the field and the songs of two lovebirds in a tree. Violet focused on the sensation of their joined hands, startling when he slipped his thumb inside to circle her palm. A little thrill rippled through her.

If only she could believe it was the same for him.

A small wooden gate marked the entry to the woods, and they paused only long enough to open it.

Here were new sounds: twigs crackling beneath their feet, leaves rustling overhead. Still playing with her hand, Ford led her to the thick trunk of a fallen tree and sat upon it, drawing her down beside him.

Though they weren't actually far from the house, the canopy of trees made this place feel secluded and private. She shifted to look at Ford, noting faint circles under his eyes. "Looks like someone's not sleeping," she said quietly.

"I was up all night finishing the watch." He raised their joined hands to brush his lips over her knuckles. "Didn't even realize it was morning until Hilda offered me breakfast."

"You should have slept, then, after you were done."

"I couldn't. I was too excited. I wanted to show it to someone." He paused, slanting a glance up at her. "I wanted to show it to you."

Her breath caught. Faith, she wanted to believe him. "I'm sorry, then, that I brought my family—"

"No. I enjoyed showing it to them, too." Still holding her hand, he used his free one to brush a loose strand of hair behind her ear. "But you were the one I truly wanted to share it with." He scooted closer until their faces were mere inches apart.

He was all but daring her to kiss him. And insuperable as she'd become, she couldn't bring herself to refuse.

So, after a deep breath, she leaned forward and pressed her lips to his. He tensed, as though surprised, but then his body relaxed and his hands came up to skim along her arms, slide over her shoulders, pull her closer. She still wore her spectacles, but he didn't seem to mind. He moved closer still, until he was pressed against her, just like in her dream.

Well, except for the tree bark digging into her bottom. But other than that, it was just like the dream.

In fact, it was better. She couldn't have imagined the sensation of his chest against hers—hadn't had any notion that his body would feel so solid and muscled and different from hers. Nor could she have dreamt up the feeling of his lips trailing soft kisses across her throat. She'd never realized her skin was so exquisitely sensitive.

Suddenly she could understand, at least a little, how fallen women succumbed to that temptation.

There was nothing about neck kissing in the *Master-piece*, she thought dazedly, winding her fingers into his hair. "Ford," she heard herself whisper, "do you think it feels like this for everyone?"

He stilled, then pulled back enough to meet her eyes, a hazy expression in his own. "No. I think…"

He fell silent. Shaking his head, he reluctantly backed away from her—slowly, as though he didn't want to—until they were once again sitting side by side, turned toward each other. He plucked a leaf from her shoulder, smiled at it, then suddenly sobered.

"I think I may have fallen in love," he confessed in a rush.

Her world skidded. It wasn't quite *I love you*…but it was close.

She removed her spectacles and wiped them on her gown,

stalling for time. Trying to wrap her mind around the meaning of his words.

He was saying all the right things, in just the right way to make her question all her old insecurities. When he looked at her like that, with those incredible blue eyes, she wanted to believe him more than she'd wanted anything, ever. She just didn't know whether she could.

She slipped her spectacles back on, determined to regain control, to refocus her mind on something less confusing. Something safe and practical. "Where will you sell it?" she asked quietly.

His eyes changed, darkening with concern, with hurt at her lack of response. "Sell what?"

"Your watch."

"My watch?" He sighed, then bent his head, his hair flopping forward like a young boy's.

A desperate streak of longing shot through her.

"I'm not planning to sell my watch," he said. "I'm not equipped to manufacture watches."

Stunned, she sat up straighter and saw him tense in response. "Well, then," she asked, "what do you plan to do with it?"

He straightened, too. "I'll bring it to the next Royal Society meeting. I'm certain it will be a sensation."

"And then…"

"That's it. I have other projects I'm working on—"

"You're serious, then?" She couldn't believe it. "You're not going to patent it? You have no plans for the watch?"

"I invented it. That was my plan." He made to rise, but she gripped his shoulder and held him in place. "I'm not a business-man," he said through gritted teeth. "I have no knowledge of that world. The creation was a satisfying end in itself."

"I don't understand you," she said. True, aristocrats tended to think trade beneath them, but only a rich man had the luxury of doing what he pleased without considering his income.

Or a man who planned to rely on his wife's fortune.

She didn't want to think that of him. His confession had sounded too sincere, his explanation of his motivations too uncalculated. She'd seen how much he cared for Jewel; she knew he had a good heart. And though his eyes held many indecipherable emotions, she felt instinctively that none were deceit.

Yet she couldn't help wondering.

He stared at her for a long, silent moment. A bird fluttered from one tree to another. A cow lowed in the fields beyond the woods. She heard her blood pounding in her ears.

"I don't understand me, either," he said.

FORTY-THREE

"AVE YOU AND the viscount had a fight?" Sitting cross-legged on Violet's bed that night, Lily patted May-dew on her face from a bottle she'd purchased in London. "He didn't seem very happy when he came back for his watch."

Violet paced her bedchamber, restlessly touching things at random. "No, we didn't fight."

She had no idea how to explain what had happened in the woods, because she hadn't yet figured it out. The two of them had walked back in silence, as though they had nothing left to say to each other. But Ford hadn't seemed angry. Before they'd reentered the house, he'd even brushed a kiss across her forehead at the door. And then sighed before he opened it.

She sighed now. "I still cannot believe he isn't going to do anything with the watch."

Rose played with her hair, examining herself in the mirror at Violet's dressing table. "Not everyone is as ambitious as you are, Violet." Holding her tresses twisted up high, she turned from her reflection. "Do you prefer it up or down?"

"Up," Lily said at the same time Violet said, "Down."

"Some help you two are." Rose stood, fluffing her white night rail. Violet was struck anew by her younger sister's stunning beauty, but quickly suppressed the stab of envy. "It's not like you can change him," Rose told her. "And why would you want to, anyway? You keep insisting you're not interested in him."

Violet plopped on her bed so hard the ropes creaked a protest beneath the mattress. "I just find it hard to believe he can invent something so important and not be interested in selling it. Or patenting it, at least. At the Royal Society event, I heard that Christopher Wren patented a device for writing with two pens. If anyone uses his idea, they have to pay for it."

Lily scooted nearer and wrapped an arm around her shoulders. "Why is this bothering you so, Violet? It's not your invention."

"I just hate to see such brilliance go to waste."

Blinking, Lily shifted to face her. "Perhaps Lord Lakefield isn't motivated by money, but it's not as though he's lazy. It's only that he does things for other reasons than you would. He might invent something to make someone happy, or create something he hopes will be a benefit to mankind. His values may be different than yours, but that doesn't mean they're wrong."

Violet wondered when young Lily had become so wise. "I never thought of it that way," she murmured, more confused than ever.

Her two sisters exchanged a glance. "Did he kiss you again?" Rose asked.

"Maybe." Violet stood and resumed pacing—then stopped, wondering if it were a habit she'd picked up from Ford. Feeling her sisters' gazes on her, she turned to face the wall. "Very well, he did."

"And was it as marvelous as before?" When Violet failed to answer, Lily rose and came up behind her, placing a hand on her arm. "If you love him," she said softly, "why won't you consider marriage?"

"He hasn't asked me." Violet twisted out of her sister's grasp.

And because Ford had as much as said he loved her, something in her middle twisted as well. "And even if he did ask me, I would wonder if it were only for my inheritance. I'm not the type of girl who inspires love."

Compassion flooded Lily's deep blue eyes. "*We* love you, Violet!"

"You're my sisters. That's different."

"Now I see why you're so upset," Rose said. "You wish he would sell watches and make a lot of money. Because if he still kissed you then, you'd know it was for yourself."

That could be so, Violet realized. Rose was far too shrewd for her comfort.

Lily stepped closer. "Or is it your dream of publishing you don't want to give up? Are you afraid that if you marry, your money will go to your husband instead of your dream?"

"No. Not that." Maybe she would have agreed with Lily last month. But although she still wanted to write a philosophy book, she had new dreams now.

Yet she was sure, deep down, that if Ford were suddenly showered with gold—or figured out how to make gold himself—those new dreams still wouldn't come true. And it irritated her that she'd even begun dreaming. She used to be content with her lot, and that had been much easier.

"My own money has nothing to do with it," she said. "I just hate to see wasted potential. It disagrees with the practical in me."

"But Violet," Lily said quietly, "what is it you really want?"

Good question, Violet thought. She didn't know anymore. "Maybe we should talk of something else."

Rose shrugged, then grinned. "We could read more of the *Master-piece*." She snatched the book off Violet's bedside table. "Where did we leave off?"

"Here, give it to me." With a sigh, Violet took the book and climbed into bed.

Lily ran around to the other side, and the three of them

huddled together beneath the covers. "Just like old times," Lily said. "Do you remember when we couldn't read yet, Violet, and you used to read to us at night?"

"Read to us again, big sister," Rose lisped, stretching her mouth wide in a silly, babyish smile.

Giggling, Violet turned to the next chapter. "'Chapter Seventeen: A Word of Advice to Both Sexes, Being Several Directions Respecting Copulation.'"

Rose rubbed her hands together. "Sounds like a good one."

"That's strange..." Violet flipped a page, fingering the book's binding. "It appears most of the pages in this chapter are missing."

"Oh, no!" Rose looked crestfallen.

"I can't believe I never noticed before." Violet closed the book and examined the tailband at the bottom of the spine. "Look, you can even see a little gap."

"Could they have fallen out just recently?" Lily asked. "Maybe the pages are somewhere in your room, or in the summerhouse."

"No, it looks like they were cut out." Violet turned back to Chapter Seventeen to show them the skinny strips of paper still attached to the binding.

"Hang it!" Rose leapt out of bed with an angry huff. "Someone ruined the book!"

Lily shook her head. "Who would do such a thing?"

"It must have happened before Mr. Young sold it." Violet shrugged. "I'm sure he didn't know the book was damaged."

"I suppose," Rose said with a pout. "I bet they were the best pages, so someone decided to take them."

"Maybe." Lily looked disappointed, too.

Violet raised her chin. "Get back in bed, Rose. We've got plenty more to read."

"Very well," Rose grumbled as she climbed back under the covers. "Let's get on with whatever's left of Chapter Seventeen."

FORTY-FOUR

*F*OR THE DOZENTH time, Ford turned over in his bed. Though his project was finished, for some exasperating reason he still found himself sleepless in the wee hours of the morning. Or perhaps it was *because* his project was finished.

It was time to leave Lakefield.

Tabitha's elopement was behind him. Far behind him. So far behind him, he wondered what he'd ever seen in her—on the rare occasions he thought of her at all.

His watch was completed, and although he had another idea to add a chime to wake the watch's owner at a certain time of the day, he could work on that at Cainewood, or even in London. With the Royal Society settled back in its old home, the meetings would be more regular. He wanted to attend them.

But though he knew he'd ruined things with Violet—though she'd made it perfectly clear in the woods this afternoon that she neither welcomed nor returned his feelings—he still found himself irrationally reluctant to leave. The very thought seemed to cause a painful squeezing sensation in his chest.

So he decided not to think.

Instead he climbed from the bed and wrapped himself in a

robe. As long as he couldn't sleep, he might as well start designing the wake-up bell.

On his way up to the laboratory, he bumped into Harry coming down. "Pardon, my lord." Holding a candle in one hand, Harry scratched his bald head with the other. "I was just sneaking down for a midnight raid. I wouldn't be averse to some company."

"Midnight raid?"

"On the kitchen." The houseman patted his round belly. "Hilda is always nagging me not to eat, so I don't much. Not so she can see it." He grinned. "She baked bread before retiring."

As usual, Hilda's offerings this evening had been less than enticing. Feeling his own stomach rumble, Ford followed Harry downstairs and drew a stool up to the big table in the cavernous kitchen.

Harry swiped a fresh loaf off the counter and reached for a knife. "Quiet around here since Lady Jewel left, if I may say so."

"It is." Ford watched him slice the coarse brown bread. "She's a charmer."

Scooping butter from a crock, Harry slathered it onto a piece. "She is that. And Lady Violet, too."

"Lady Violet?"

"Don't pretend there's nothing between you two."

Ford accepted the buttered bread. "Criminy, you're as meddling as your wife." But unlike Hilda, Harry managed to probe without asking a single question. "What business is that of yours?"

The houseman didn't so much as bristle. "Just wondering how long you'll stick around here is all, my lord."

"As I've no excuse to stay, most likely I'll be heading to London soon." He bit into the chewy bread. "Or not," he added around the mouthful.

"Just as I thought," Harry said, buttering his own hunk of loaf. He took a hearty bite. "Those Ashcrofts have made you feel right welcome."

"They have," Ford admitted. In a few short weeks, he'd begun to feel like Violet's family belonged in his life. Even her parents, which surprised him.

His oldest brother had been fairly simple to manipulate, and he'd always imagined real parents would be a nuisance. But Violet's were rather amusing.

He swallowed and nodded. "I find myself shouting at Lord Trentingham with the rest of them now. And earlier today, I helped Lady Trentingham make essential oil."

Harry drew a pitcher of ale and grabbed two goblets off a shelf. "Sounds like a messy business."

"Not particularly, although she has a disaster of a distillery." Ford watched while the man poured. "Perhaps I ought to make her a new one," he mused. After all, Lady Trentingham had been the soul of kindness and had even tolerated Ford's pursuit of her daughter, never mind that Violet had ultimately rejected him. He owed the woman a world of thanks—and a new, sophisticated distillery would be just the thing.

"Sounds like a good enough excuse to stick around," Harry observed.

Ford raked back his hair. "It has nothing to do with that. Lady Trentingham deserves it, as a token of my thanks for her hospitality."

"Of course." Harry's brown eyes twinkled as he raised his cup. "Drink up, my lord."

Ford did, his mind already occupied by how to best arrange the copper tubing.

FORTY-FIVE

OTHER THAN THE odd squeaks and groans emitted by any old house, Trentingham was deathly quiet. By candlelight, Violet sat at her desk in the library, chewing on the end of a quill.

Nodding to herself, she dipped it into the ink and began writing.

Dear Mr. Wren,

It was a pleasure meeting you at the Royal Society function last month, and it is my hope that we renew our acquaintance sometime in the future.

The quill's scratch sounded loud in the empty room.

In the meantime, I am requesting your assistance with some information. You had mentioned patenting an invention, and I would be grateful to know how to go about doing so. A few lines of instruction would be most appreciated.

Yours truly,

Violet Ashcroft

Simple and straightforward. She read it over twice before folding it, then added a seal and addressed it to the Royal Society for delivery. Surely someone there would see it reached Christopher Wren's hands.

Now to the more important letter. She had already addressed the backside of the paper to *Daniel Quare, Watchmaker, Fleet Street, London.* She'd found the information engraved on the backs of two of her father's gold pocket watches.

Dear Mr. Quare,

I have invented a new watch with an additional hand to mark the progress of the minutes. I am querying your interest in producing and selling the design, a vast improvement on all current watches. I am certain you can envision the profits as patrons must replace their old watches with this newer one, which could very well allow you to domi-nate the market. I have patented the design—

She removed her spectacles and rubbed her eyes. That wasn't quite a lie—she *did* intend to see it patented.

—so there is no sense in your own craftsmen attempting to duplicate my idea. I am asking—

She hesitated again, then took a deep breath.

—twenty-five thousand pounds for my sketches and the working sample, plus a royalty percentage to be negotiated. You have two weeks in which to answer, after which time I will offer my invention to Mr. Thomas Tompion. I hope to hear from you in the affirmative, with a contract ready to be signed.

Yours truly,

For a third time she stopped and closed her eyes. Then she opened them, redipped her quill, and etched the name.

Ford Chase, Viscount Lakefield

If he had no ambition for trade, she figured she had enough for them both.

FORTY-SIX

"**M**OVE ASIDE, if you will. Please. This is heavy."

At the sound of Lord Lakefield's voice, which she hadn't heard for far too many days, Chrystabel looked up to see Violet scurry into her perfumery. The viscount and a footman followed close behind, an enormous machine held between them.

At least, she *thought* it was a machine.

"What *is* that?" she asked.

With some effort, the men maneuvered it to her worktable and set it down. "My thanks," Ford said to the footman, who bowed and took his leave. "It's a distillery, my lady."

"A distillery?" The machine wasn't like any distillery Chrystabel had ever seen. Well, besides her own, she hadn't seen any distilleries other than the one her aunt Idonea had used to teach her how to make perfume. Which had looked very much like the one she owned now. Two wooden bowls, a wooden block, a wooden tray beneath it all.

But *this…this* was all metal and glass and copper tubing. It positively gleamed.

And she hadn't a clue how it would work.

"You're sure that's a distillery?" she couldn't help asking.

He stroked the thing, very much like Lily petted her beloved stray animals. "I'm certain. I assure you there's nothing radical about the design."

"He has a much bigger one in his laboratory," Violet said.

Ford nodded. "And at Cainewood, yet another that dwarfs that one. But they all work on the same principles." He smiled at Chrystabel. "I hope you'll enjoy using it."

"Enjoy using it?" Her head swam with confusion, an unusual state of mind for Chrystabel. "Do you mean...can you mean to give it to me?"

He blinked. "Of course. I made it for you. Why else would I bring it here?"

"Why..." She felt speechless, another atypical condition. "That's so generous, I...I don't know how to thank you."

"No thanks are necessary. I saw a need, I filled it. One does that for friends."

Unsure which she appreciated more, his declaration or his gift, she came forward to take both his hands. "Then I'm fortunate to be counted among your friends," she said warmly, her gaze drifting to Violet.

Chrystabel hoped to be more than the young man's friend; she hoped to be his mother-in-law. But she was clever enough to keep her mouth shut lest she thwart her plans. One wrong word from her lips, and her skittish daughter would go running the other direction.

Her best bet was to keep throwing the two of them together until Mother Nature did her work. Chemistry...she'd wager that was how the viscount thought of it. And she knew it was only a matter of time before those feelings—those *insuperable* feelings, as the *Master-piece* put it—overcame her daughter's stubborn and over-particular nature.

Hopefully Violet was still studying the marriage manual— minus those few unsuitable passages which had had to be removed, of course. Chrystabel meant only to open her daughter's eyes to the institution of marriage, not to give her *ideas*.

She squeezed the viscount's hands before dropping them. "I do thank you, whether you feel that's required or not."

Violet circled the large table, ostensibly examining the distillery. "Will you show us how to use it?"

"Of course," he said, following her.

A courtship dance, Chrystabel thought with an inward smile.

"This container down here is for oil." He lifted a lid. "Not your essential oils, but fuel, if you will. I've filled it for now, but you'll need to add more as you use the still."

"That makes sense," Chrystabel said, watching her daughter move away again.

Lord Lakefield shifted closer to replace the lid, which had a hole in the middle. "Make sure the wick is thick and long at the top," he instructed, inserting one he pulled from his pocket. "You'll want the flame high enough to boil the water. At home, this part of my still is brick—a proper oven. But for your purposes, this should do fine."

Violet's next tactic was to cross back to Chrystabel's side of the table. "It looks very complicated."

A large glass bulb sat in a frame, and a second glass bulb was attached by a tube. Smaller, it was designed to rest on the tabletop.

"Put your petals in here," Ford said, coming halfway around again to indicate the larger bulb. "Then fill it with water. There's room here beneath the cover for the steam to collect, you see, but not too much room. Soon it will be forced down the tube, and on the long way down, away from the heat, the essential oil will condense and collect in this second receptacle." He showed them how to remove it. "Does that make sense?"

Still overwhelmed by his gift, Chrystabel nodded. "It does!"

"It will take a bit longer than your original method, but you won't be losing any steam. Your oil will be purer and stronger."

"It will," Violet said with a smile. "That's quite obvious, and quite brilliant."

"I simply can't begin to express my thanks," Chrystabel said, shaking her head in wonder. Impulsively, she rounded the table to wrap Lord Lakefield in a hug. "You're a genius!" she exclaimed. "And so generous."

And so perfect for her Violet.

His face was pink when she released him. "It's nothing, really."

"It's everything," Violet disagreed from across the table, leaning forward on both hands, though she still wouldn't meet the viscount's eyes. "Few men would take a woman's hobby seriously, let alone devise ways to improve it. Most would be like John Evelyn with his 'kitchen scientist' wife Mary."

Chrystabel hadn't the slightest idea who John Evelyn was, but Violet's voice was filled with admiration. Her daughter was falling for Ford, she was sure of it. However, things weren't progressing as quickly as she'd like. The fellow had a disconcerting habit of disappearing for days at a time while he invented one thing or another.

"Violet's birthday is tomorrow," she told him. "We're having a family celebration. I'd be pleased if you would join us."

"Mum—"

"I'm delighted to accept." He hesitated, then added all in a rush, "But I was planning to ask if Violet might take supper in my company tonight."

A little gasp came across the table. "Alone?" Violet asked.

"Well, Harry will be there, and—"

Violet opened her mouth.

"I'm sure she'd be pleased," Chrystabel rushed to say before her daughter could decline the invitation. She just managed to suppress a grin.

"Shall I come for her at six, then?"

"Wait." Violet raised both hands, palms forward, looking thoroughly indignant. "Have I no say in this?"

"Of course you do, dear." Chrystabel fixed her with a steady gaze. "I just couldn't imagine you refusing such a request after Lord Lakefield went out of his way to make this new distillery."

Ford walked around the table, stopping nose to nose with her daughter. Or they would have been nose to nose, if he wasn't so much taller. The dance had ended. When their gazes finally met, Chrystabel's heart sang to see her daughter's eyes softening.

Surrender.

"Would you rather not come?" he asked quietly.

"I..."

"Please say you will."

Silence for a heartbeat. "All right."

A less than enthusiastic response, but Ford looked as happy to receive it as Chrystabel was to hear it. If she hoped to speed up this courtship, a supper alone together would be just the thing.

"I'm looking forward to it." He bowed to both ladies. "Until six, then."

FORTY-SEVEN

*N*O SOONER HAD Ford cleared the door than Violet's sisters rushed in to see what he'd brought.

"He made this?" Rose dumped an armful of flowers on the table. "He really and truly made this without you even asking?"

Mum laughed. "How could I ask? I had no idea such a thing even existed."

"That was nice." Lily ran a finger down the gleaming copper tube. "*Very* nice." She turned to Violet. "You should marry him."

Violet's mouth gaped. Though she'd discussed the subject with her sisters, she had trusted them to be more discreet. Especially in front of Mum. What of their pact to maintain a united front against any matchmaking?

"Has he asked you to marry him?" her mother asked with widened eyes.

"No," she said shortly. That, at least, was true.

Lily bit her lip, looking to Violet in apology. "I was just teasing her, Mum. But it was very nice of him to make this. I cannot wait to see you use it."

"And she should marry him," Rose put in.

"Oh, do hush up," Violet said, dropping onto a chair. She raised her spectacles and rubbed her eyes, then pushed them back into place to focus on her mother. "Why did you invite him to my birthday celebration? It was supposed to be a private party. Family." The day would be disconcerting enough without celebrating it in public. "You're not trying to match me up with him, are you?"

"Of course not." Mum waved a dismissive hand. "He'd just brought me a gift. I felt it necessary to reciprocate in what little way I could."

That made sense. Maybe. "Then what is your explanation for encouraging me to join him for supper? Alone, Mum? Harry and Hilda don't count."

"You're eighteen years old now, a woman grown. I'm certain I can trust you."

Violet wasn't sure she could trust herself. Not around Ford Chase, anyway.

"Besides, it was very much like I said, dear. He'd just done me an enormous favor, and I didn't feel it would be right to refuse him a boon. It's naught but a couple of hours in his company—surely you cannot find that too onerous."

"But you really should marry him," Rose said again.

Violet rounded on her. "Why, so you can start your own husband hunt?"

"No." Rose actually looked hurt, which made Violet feel badly for lashing out. "You just seem perfect together. Mum, don't you agree?"

Their mother's fingers played over the flowers scattered on the table, picking out the white jasmines. "I promised you girls I would allow you to find your own husbands."

"That doesn't mean we don't want your opinion," Lily said.

"Yes, Mum," Rose agreed. "What's your opinion?"

Violet didn't want to hear anyone else's opinion. If she thought she could get away with it, she'd have slunk from the room.

Mum lifted the lid off the new still and began plucking

jasmine petals, tossing them in as she talked. "I think he is brilliant."

Rose began collecting carnations, doubtless planning another floral arrangement. "Which makes him perfect for our Violet, doesn't it?"

"I didn't say that, Rose."

"But you thought it."

Violet gritted her teeth. "Rose, would you hush up?"

"Girls. Stop bickering. It's up to Violet to choose her own husband. I said from the first I thought Lord Lakefield was too much of an intellectual, and I haven't changed my opinion."

"But he's so nice," Lily said.

Violet's fingers clenched on the chair's arms. "You think so? Then would *you* marry him?"

"I'm not looking for a gentleman like him," Lily protested. "I'm looking for a gentleman who shares my love for animals."

"You're too young to be looking at all," Mum said.

Rose rubbed a pink bloom across her lips. "I like looking."

Violet snorted. "We all know that by now."

"Viscount Lakefield is nice to look at."

"Despite his horrifying lankiness?" Violet said dryly.

Rose tossed her gleaming chestnut ringlets. "Indeed. But I want a gentleman who appreciates my femininity. Lord Lakefield looks right through me."

"Not too difficult, since you're so shallow."

"Violet!" Her eyes wide, Mum stopped plucking.

"I'm sorry," Violet muttered. She hadn't meant to be mean; she was just tired of being pestered. "It's only that Rose is so intelligent, yet she tries so hard to hide it."

Rose turned to pull a vase from the shelf. "I've told you, men aren't interested in intelligence."

"Lord Lakefield is," Lily said.

"And that," Rose declared, plopping the carnations into the vase, "is why he's so perfect for Violet."

Violet wanted to press her hands over her ears. Instead she

massaged her temples. *How long will you abuse my patience?* she paraphrased Cicero in her head, but the familiar quotation did nothing to help her regain her own.

This discussion was going nowhere at all, and if she heard one more time that she should marry Ford—from her mother, her sisters, *anybody*—she was certain she would scream.

She rose and headed for the door. "I need to go get ready."

Lily came to block her way, her blue eyes concerned. "Don't you want to see the distillery work?"

"Perhaps tomorrow," she said, skirting around her sister. "Today I have no time."

Thanks to Mum's meddling, she had a supper date in less than three hours.

FORTY-EIGHT

"*V*IOLET!" HER father called from over by a border of pink candytuft. "Where are you going?"

Walking through the garden with Ford, she cast him an apologetic glance. "I'm off to Lakefield House for supper!" she shouted. "Did Mum not tell you?"

As they drew close, Ford tucked her hand in the crook of his elbow. Father's gaze landed on their linked arms, and a smile tugged at the corners of his lips. Apparently *he* wanted her to marry Ford, too.

Faith, just what she needed. More family pressure.

"Have a pleasant time, dear." Father leaned to kiss her on the cheek. "Be back by supper."

"Supper?" Ford repeated. "Lord Trentingham—"

"Forget it," Violet told him. "We could stand here all night. Mum will explain when I'm not at the table." She gave her father's hand a squeeze, knowing he hadn't heard her low comments. "I'll see you later, Father."

"What?"

"I'll see you later!" she shouted and drew Ford away. "Sorry about that," she said to him once Father had turned back to his gardening. "We yell a lot in this family, but we never mean anything by it."

"If you're thinking that will put me off, you're wrong. My family yells, too. And none of us are deaf." Ford led her around the corner of the house.

And there was that silly, old-fashioned barge.

She stopped in her tracks. "Where is your carriage?"

"It's a beautiful evening," he said, coaxing her along. "I thought to spend it on the river."

He unleashed that brilliant smile of his, rendering her speechless as they crossed the lawn. And although she hadn't tripped in weeks, she nearly did as he handed her onto the barge. Nodding to Harry and the stable hands to cast off, Ford drew her into the cramped, unsuitable cabin that contained nothing but a bed.

Only it wasn't quite so unsuitable now. The bed had been removed, and in its place sat a little table and two chairs. The entire space was lit by dozens of flickering candles.

He'd made a wonderland for her again, this time on his elegantly decrepit barge. The table was covered with a soft pink cloth, and silver domes covered two plates. While she stood gaping, he leaned forward and swept off one of the domes.

"Supper," he said. "Since Hilda's culinary skills are a mite lacking, I had Harry fetch it from the cookshop in the village. I only pray it hasn't all gone cold."

Overwhelmed by the unsettling trembling in her heart, Violet laid a hand on her blue moiré stomacher. Her other fingers toyed with the end of her thick plait. Countless cheerful little flames warded off the approaching evening chill. And Ford's expression of nervous hope warmed her as well, in an entirely different way.

But suddenly she felt small and silly, like a schoolgirl playing dress-up. This couldn't be *her* life. These sorts of things weren't supposed to happen to plain, sensible girls—they were supposed to happen to irresistible wood nymphs!

Something was wrong.

"Is something wrong?" he asked, looking concerned.

"No!"

She chewed her lip. Each time she and Ford met she only grew more confused. She knew now that she wanted him, and she sometimes felt that he wanted her. But she couldn't be sure he wanted her in the way she wanted him to want her, *if* she even wanted that, considering where it might lead.

What if marriage wasn't all that the *Master-piece* claimed? What if she traded her grand aspirations for a life full of heart tremblings and short breathings, only to discover it was all a horrible mistake—

Oh, hang it! This was ridiculous. For heaven's sake, how could she hope to ever call herself a philosopher when she couldn't even puzzle out her own feelings?

Two goblets sat on the table, the red wine in them gently swaying in rhythm with the barge's movements. She raised one to her lips and took a long, unhurried sip, trying to slow her whirling thoughts. "Nothing's wrong," she finally said. "It's only that I...I thought we were dining at Lakefield."

He drew out a chair and waited for her to sit, then pulled the door shut. "I never said that. I only asked if you might take supper in my company tonight." He seated himself across from her. The table was so small their knees touched. "Don't you think this is more romantic?"

She wasn't used to being romanced. She didn't know how to react. "Where are we going?" she asked to change the subject. They were moving at a good clip already.

He shrugged one blue-velvet-clad shoulder. "Nowhere. Up, then back. We scientists call that perpetual motion," he added with a smile.

She shifted uneasily. "Nowhere?"

"Just you and me and the river, food, wine, candlelight...is it not enough?" In the flickering light, his eyes looked dark and earnest. He reached across the table and took one of her hands, his lace cuff spilling over their joined fingers. "I want to apologize for the other day, for how our conversation went in the woods. And especially for how it ended." He took a deep breath. "I care deeply for you, Violet."

He cared deeply for her. Did that mean...?

"But I understand if you don't care for me—yet," he added quickly. "We've only been acquainted a scant few months. All I'm asking for is a chance to change your mind. To court you properly."

She raised a brow. "You call this"—her gesture took in the intimate quarters and the two of them crammed together at their tiny table—"a *proper* courtship?"

He grinned. "Well, not *too* proper. But if you don't like it—"

"No, I like it."

He chuckled. "I'm glad. Does that mean you'll give me another chance?"

She looked away, considering.

A proper courtship.

Other gentlemen had tried to court her as her eighteenth birthday approached—the same gentlemen who'd ignored her at every ball she'd ever attended, letting her hide in the corners without ever trying to coax her out. The same boys who, when she was younger, had huddled around her little sisters after church on Sunday, while she sat nearby with a book and pretended not to care. Faith, even when she was just five and Rose and Lily still babies, those same boys' parents cooed over them while Violet stood by unnoticed.

Was Ford just a more convincing version of those boys?

When she failed to respond, he rose and turned to stick his head out the window. "Johnnie, my lady requires a bit of persuading. Music, please."

Almost at once, the strains of a violin reached her ears.

Despite her distress, a laugh bubbled out of her. "You've thought of everything, haven't you?"

"Nearly everything. I forgot about the cold night air.

Wouldn't want you to be chilled." He closed the window's shutters and reseated himself with an innocent smile.

He was smooth, too smooth for her to handle. And he'd gone to so much trouble to make this evening special. As if he honestly believed *he* was the one who needed to impress *her*.

For such a brilliant fellow, he was oblivious when it came to women. He was wasting his time trying to persuade her to care for him.

Because she already did.

Ford Chase was a study in contradictions. Part serious academic, part dashing romantic, part responsible uncle, part irresponsible adolescent. And she adored every confusing facet.

He dressed like a prince and lived like a pauper. He was the most generous person she'd ever known. He'd made her spectacles; he'd made her mother a distillery.

He'd made her fall in love with him.

She loved him.

She loved him! Dear heavens, when had she come to love him?

But she did.

And yet...

Just before he'd closed the shutters, she'd glimpsed Lakefield House as they'd sailed by, twilight's shadows throwing its crumbling facade into stark relief. Now, the image of Ford's neglected estate lodged itself in her mind. Despite her love for him, despite all the good she saw in him, she couldn't help wondering if his sudden wish to court her was only because...

She didn't want to think about that now. She didn't want to ruin this night, her last night before she turned eighteen. Tomorrow, according to Rose, she would officially become a spinster.

But tomorrow could wait until tomorrow.

"Are you hungry?" he asked, reaching to uncover her plate. His knees moved away from hers and didn't return, to her vast disappointment.

As she'd expect from a country cookshop, the supper was

simple and hearty. A wedge of lamb pie, sweet potato pudding, parsnips, and asparagus.

"It's all quite good," Violet said after sampling each dish. The sweet potato pudding was smooth and fluffy, swimming in butter with eggs, nutmeg, and dark sugar. The lamb pie was flaky and rich. As they dined, they discussed the books they'd recently read—excluding the *Master-piece*—and the latest news from Ford's friends at the Royal Society.

Violet savored both the food and the still-novel experience of conversing with a gentleman who spoke to her as an intellectual equal. It dawned on her that those weeks without Ford, when he'd gone off working on one project or another, it wasn't just kissing him that she'd missed. Even more so, she'd missed talking with him.

He didn't touch her during supper, didn't so much as nudge her foot with his. But all the time he talked, he gazed straight into her eyes in a way that set her heart to trembling just the same.

When his plate was empty and she was only picking at hers, he refilled her wine cup. "Violet?" He reached across the tiny table and gently removed her spectacles. "May I kiss you?"

He'd never asked before, and she didn't know what to say. In the guttering candlelight, he looked blurry. But he must have seen her answer in her eyes, because his face came into focus as he leaned across the table, and she sucked in a breath as his lips met hers—

And his pewter plate crashed to the floor.

"Everything all right in there?" came Harry's voice through the shutters.

Violet jerked away.

"We're fine," Ford called to Harry, looking a bit startled as he bent to retrieve the plate. He set it back on the table, then ran a hand through his hair. Raggedly.

"This won't work," he told her, gesturing to the table

between them. "Do you suppose you might...would you like to dance?"

"What, in here? Wouldn't we need, um, music?"

He raised a single brow. "Is that not what Johnnie is currently providing?"

"Oh. Right." She cocked her head, listening. "I don't recognize the tune. It doesn't sound like a minuet, or a—"

"Oh, it's not any of the usual dances." Unconcerned, Ford took Violet's hands and drew her up and away from the table. "We'll just make up a dance of our own."

Violet cocked her head in bewilderment. "Make it up?" They now stood at the exact center of the bed's former position, the thought of which made her cheeks heat.

"Why not? No one's watching." Placing his hands at her waist, he began to sway in time to the music.

"Um...what should I...?" Violet stood stock still. Dancing made her nervous even when she knew exactly what she was supposed to do, having had every motion drilled into her by the dancing master. Now she was expected to both devise the dance and perform it? Simultaneously? And in front of the man she'd just realized she loved?

Was he mad?

"Just follow me," he said, his hands nudging her body to and fro. After a few clumsy beats, she was swaying along with him.

All right, this wasn't so difficult.

Still, it was a very odd sort of dance.

And she had no idea what to do with her arms. She let them hang stiffly in front of her, then clasped her hands together, then crossed her arms over her chest. No matter which position they were in, she knew she looked ridiculous. She was thankful Ford hadn't returned her spectacles, so she didn't have to observe the amused expression he surely wore.

Her hands came up to cover her flaming cheeks. "I don't know what to do with my—"

Her sentence ended in a squeal as the boat made a sudden sharp pivot and she pitched forward.

"Turn, ho!" Harry's voice carried into the cabin.

"We could have used a little more warning!" Violet shrieked in reply.

"Apologies, m'lady!"

Violet huffed. Luckily she'd managed to avoid taking a tumble, her fall having been broken by Ford's body. Her right hand had been caught by his left, while her left hand had landed on his shoulder. She couldn't help noticing the solid muscle beneath her fingers.

Now, incredibly, he resumed swaying—"dancing"—once again, taking her along with him.

"Are you enjoying yourself, my lord?" she asked tightly.

"Very much so." He pulled her closer. "Are you not?"

"I..." All at once, she noticed their bodies were a hair's breadth apart. She could feel the heat of his skin, smell his patchouli scent, see his clear blue eyes in sharp focus. His right hand slid around her waist, settling gently, deliciously on the small of her back.

Lanky, she scoffed, thinking of Rose's foolishness. *If he's lanky, then I'm Socrates.*

"I suppose I don't mind," she admitted, surprised to realize she truly was enjoying the dance. Ford's left hand was doing an admirable job of steering her around the tiny cabin, relieving her of any responsibility for her own coordination. And the swaying motion was rather soothing.

"Yet another brilliant invention," Ford said with a lopsided grin. "Shall I patent this one, as you once recommended?"

"Of course," she quipped. "The patented 'hold hands and sway' technique will revolutionize the art of dance, becoming popular the world over."

"Undoubtedly." Ford drew her even closer, until her head lay against his shoulder.

Mmm, she thought.

And that was the only thought she had for a good long while.

Enfolded in Ford's arms, lulled by soft music, surrounded by dwindling candle flames…something about that combination seemed to make her melt in his embrace.

"Violet?"

She glanced up. The look in his eyes made her heart leap.

"May I kiss you now?"

Swallowing hard, she nodded.

Their dance ground to a halt. And when his mouth met hers, everything changed.

He had kissed her before, but never like this. This kiss was wild. It stole her breath, her thoughts, her will to resist. Her heart racing, she threw her arms around him, holding tight. And the kiss led to more kisses, so many frantic kisses.

Earlier tonight, when she stepped foot on the barge, she'd known exactly how many kisses they'd shared, could remember and relive and savor each and every one of them. But within minutes she knew she would never be able to keep count again.

"Violet," he breathed.

"Faith." She was feeling those short breathings she'd read of again, and tremblings of the heart, and— "Ford?"

"Mmhm?" he said through another kiss.

"I love you."

FORTY-NINE

"*J* LOVE YOU."

With Violet pressed against him, Ford had felt the words reverberate in his chest. But he couldn't have heard them correctly.

He kept kissing her, although more absentmindedly than he'd ever thought possible. Her words kept buzzing through his brain.

I love you.

It was the exact phrase he'd resolved not to utter, fearing he'd startle Violet even worse than he had with his boldness that day in the woods. This time, he'd been determined to proceed with caution, knowing he needed to win her over—needed to convince her they belonged together—before venturing anywhere near that word again.

I care deeply for you, Violet, he'd said instead. A sentence carefully planned in advance, because he'd been so afraid to say anything that included the word *love*.

Love. Love led to marriage, and he hadn't wanted to risk reminding sensible Violet of all the reasons she shouldn't marry him.

But now everything had changed. Violet loved him back.

She loved him!

His heart soared. He'd brought Violet here hoping to start their courtship anew, but this was more, so much more than he'd dared hope for. She would be his wife, and, someday, the mother of his children. They would be together all their days. Somehow, despite his woeful financial circumstances, beautiful, brilliant, extraordinary Violet had found it in her heart to love him back.

When had that happened? He didn't know. He knew only that, slowly but surely, she'd woven her way into his life, until she was as much a part of him as his hands and his feet and his analytic brain. Until he found himself building distilleries as an excuse not to leave her side.

His arms tightening around her, he broke the kiss and buried his nose in her hair. She smelled of flowers, sweet Violet flowers...

"I love you, too, Violet," he said.

When he heard her happy sigh and felt her face turn toward him, her warm breath on his neck, nothing had ever been so perfect.

He thought—he hoped—her parents would approve. He was positive Lady Trentingham liked him, at least, and the earl had smiled when he'd seen them walking arm in arm. But in truth, whether or not they objected didn't matter now. Ford would convince them, whatever it took. He simply had to.

"Violet?"

"Hmm?" Keeping her eyes closed, she rubbed her nose in his neck.

Criminy, she was adorable. A grin stole over his face. She was everything he hadn't known he wanted. And needed. And she loved him. He was the luckiest fellow in the world. "I cannot wait to get married," he whispered in her ear.

Quite suddenly, he felt her stiffen in his embrace.

"Pray pardon?" Her eyes snapping open, she raised her head. "I never said I would marry you. You haven't even asked me."

"Oh." Of course. She wanted to be romanced. He took her

face in both his hands, brushing his thumbs gently over her soft cheeks. Then he gave her his famous smile. "Will you do me the greatest honor I can imagine and become my wife, Violet Ashcroft?"

Her eyes looking bare without her spectacles, she blinked. "No."

"What?" Taken aback, he jerked away from her. "I…I thought you said you loved me." It had never occurred to him that she wouldn't wed him after admitting her feelings. No matter what she claimed, she was a romantic at heart. And the only girl he'd ever met who didn't make him feel thickheaded.

Until now.

"I didn't mean it like that." He saw her jaw set and felt a pit of blackness opening somewhere in his gut. "Was that tonight's true objective, then?" she asked. "Not a courtship, but a betrothal?"

"No!" He scrubbed his hands through his hair. "I intended to begin a courtship, but you said you loved me, Violet, and I thought that meant we would marry—because I love you, too. Isn't that what two people in love ought to do? Get married?"

"If they're a suitable match," she said.

The blackness expanded to engulf his heart. "It's my estate, isn't it? I know things look bad just now, but—"

"That's not it, Ford."

The words were said much too calmly. If she truly loved him, shouldn't her heart be breaking? Just as his was?

"I'm a bit more enlightened than you give me credit for," she went on. "Money has nothing to do with this. And before you ask, I wasn't lying about my feelings for you. But my feelings alone aren't enough. I don't want to marry for the wrong reasons."

At least *I don't want to marry for the wrong reasons* wasn't an outright refusal. And though he knew what she meant, he would never understand how she could love him and yet not agree to marry him now. Not if love felt the same to her as it did to him.

"Question Convention," he quoted woodenly.

He was beginning to understand what she'd meant when she said the Ashcrofts weren't a conventional family...but he wasn't at all sure anymore that he liked it.

FIFTY

ORD WAS SITTING at his desk the next morning, struggling to make sense out of a mound of Lakefield's neglected paperwork, when his family showed up.

And showed up, and showed up—three carriages worth of them.

He'd known, of course, when he'd ordered Colin and Amy not to visit or bring the rest of the family, they were going to ignore him. But that didn't mean he had to be happy about it. Especially on a day like this.

Lucky for him, most of them stayed outside while his twin, Kendra, came into the study, wearing an all-too-cheerful yellow gown.

"We're here!" she announced, as though they'd sent notice ahead.

"I deduced as much when I heard the children shrieking." All seven of the precious angels. For the first time in weeks, he was pleased with the sorry state of his garden—at least there was little they could do to harm it.

Kendra stopped beside his chair, her dark red hair glimmering in the too-bright sun that streamed through the window at his back.

He scowled up at her. "Who invited you?"

She leaned down to give him a hug. "I've missed you, too."

"Right," he grunted without rising.

Backing off, she went to find a seat. He'd piled ledgers on the only extra chair, so she perched on the old iron chest he'd never managed to open.

"How was Scotland?" he asked her grudgingly.

"Beautiful. Hamish is in good health, and Niall has done wonders with Duncraven." He'd never met these people—her husband's family—but felt he knew them from her lively descriptions over the years. "And Cait's family is well, too. Cameron and Clarice had another baby."

"That's good." And no surprise. Everyone connected to the Chases seemed to have plenty of babies. Assuming it would be the same for him, he thought amidst another round of shrieks that perhaps Violet's refusal had been for the best.

"Well." Kendra crossed her legs, the foot on top swinging up and down with its red-heeled shoe. "We've come to meet Violet, so enough of the pleasantries."

"Have I been pleasant?" Ford wondered.

Her green eyes flashed with all-too-familiar annoyance. "What's wrong with you, anyway?"

"Besides the fact that the woman I love won't agree to marry me?"

"Colin said you were over Tabitha," she said, frowning, and then, "Oh. Oh! It's this Violet, then, isn't it? Od's fish, I cannot believe you admitted that. Ford Chase in love, and ready to marry?" The annoyance faded from her eyes as they filled with compassion instead. "Why on earth won't she have you?"

"Look around," he said, gesturing toward the peeling walls. "I believe you'll begin to get the picture."

"Well." Now her eyes filled with outrage. "If she values gold above love, then she doesn't deserve you, anyway."

"It's not like that," he said with a long-suffering sigh. "She's more interested in books than material comforts. But she has money of her own, and she's convinced herself no man would want her save to have it. I'm afraid the condition of this place has done nothing to reassure her my motives are otherwise."

When Kendra came to hug him this time, he rose and let her wrap him in her arms.

"Poor Ford. You've always managed to get everything you've wanted before, haven't you?"

Torn between taking comfort and bristling at his sister's patronizing view of him, he opted for the comfort. "I guess so," he mumbled into her flower-scented hair.

"Where is she?" Kendra demanded, pulling back. "I'll talk to her and explain that your intentions are sterling. The sort of fellow you are—"

"She's busy today," he said quickly. The last thing he needed was his family poking their noses in—which was exactly why he hadn't wanted them here. Violet's family might be unconventional, but his was mad as a cell full of Bedlam inmates.

Violet was already dubious about the prospect of marrying him. One glimpse of the family she'd be marrying into, and her answer would change to an unequivocal *no*.

"Are you sure?" Kendra asked. "We've come all this way—"

"I'm positive." He plopped back onto his chair, willing to discuss anything to get off the subject of Violet. "Sit down and catch me up on the gossip."

She wandered back to sit on the chest. "Cait is with child again."

"What took her so long?" he asked dryly. Jason and Caithren had two boys already. "And you?"

"Oh, two girls are enough."

"Trick isn't wanting an heir?"

"If one comes along, he wouldn't mind, I suppose..." The faint blush on her cheeks told him she and her husband, Patrick, were trying to conceive. She looked down, her fingers tracing the decorative metal strips on the chest. "You know," she said, also a master at changing the subject, "this chest has always reminded me of the treasure chest Trick and I found and brought to King Charles. Every time I see this one, I wonder what might be in it."

"I've always wondered that myself."

Her head whipped up. "You don't know?"

He shrugged. "It came with the place, and there's no key for the lock, and—"

"I'll have Trick open it, you fool. Let me go get the others." Before he could respond, she'd shot out the door.

While he waited for the invasion, he leaned his elbows on the desk and dropped his head into his hands, shutting his eyes against all the paper. Bills, letters, a notice from his mortgage holder that a payment was overdue. If only he had enough money to settle it all, get a fresh start...

He would have to see how Rand was coming along with the translation. But even if *Secrets of the Emerald Tablet* did hold the key to making gold, it could take months or possibly years to get the formula to work...

He jerked upright, staring at the chest across the room. He'd always assumed it wouldn't have been left here if it contained anything valuable, but what if Kendra were on to something? The chest she and her husband had found for King Charles had been filled with precious metal and jewels, and for all Ford knew, this one could be stuffed to the brim with gold.

The solution to his problems might have been sitting here all along: the means to pay the debts, the proof to convince Violet he didn't need her for her inheritance.

His heart was racing by the time the family trooped in. Colin led the regiment with Amy, who was holding their baby son Aidan in her arms. Ford's oldest brother, Jason, followed behind with his wife, Caithren. Kendra brought up the rear, her husband, Patrick—or Trick, as they all called him—by her side with their one-year-old girl.

Their remaining collective five offspring burst in after them, racing around Ford's desk, hanging on his back, climbing on the chairs and the iron chest.

Whatever had made him think he might want one of these wild creatures? Then Jewel climbed up on his lap in greeting, and as she pressed a damp kiss to his cheek, he suddenly remembered why.

"Here it is," Kendra said, leading her tall, golden-haired husband to the chest. She plucked her nephew Hugh off of it and plopped him on his feet.

The boy looked up. "Can you open it, Uncle Trick?"

Trick grinned, displaying a front tooth with a slightly chipped corner. "I wasn't a smuggler in my prior life for nothing, you know." Handing his baby daughter to his wife, he pulled out his knife and dropped to one knee to get to work.

While his brother-in-law probed the heavy lock, Ford rose and set Jewel down, taking her hand as he walked closer. As though the chest were a magnet attracting metal shavings, everyone else drifted near and gathered around, until they were all hanging over it in anticipation. An expectant quiet descended on the room. Even the children stopped playing.

Ford's heart hammered against his ribs. This could be the answer—

A rusty *click* shattered the silence. Trick twisted the old padlock from the hasp.

Ford moved in, holding his breath as he stooped to raise the iron lid.

As one, the family exhaled.

Jewel tugged on Ford's breeches. "It's empty, Uncle Ford."

"I can see that."

It would have been such a nice, neat solution. But he'd always known there was nothing of value in that chest. Otherwise, he'd have hacked off the lock years ago.

He might be desperate, but he wasn't stupid.

Kendra reached to touch his arm. "I'm sorry."

At that, Colin sighed. "Were you expecting this to solve all your money problems?"

Ford's jaw tensed. "What makes you think I have money problems?" He let the heavy lid close with a *slam*.

A rotting wooden panel detached itself from the wall and tumbled to their feet.

Followed by a sprinkle of plaster.

Colin shot Ford a sarcastic look.

Jason lifted a squirming niece off the trunk and set her back on the floor. "You're always looking for the easy way out, Ford." The compassion in his brother's voice didn't cut the sting of his words for Ford. "One of these days, you're going to have to give in and face your responsibilities."

Ford raked his hands through his hair. Would his family forever see him this way? In the past few weeks, he'd proved himself capable of caring for a child. He'd completed his first significant scientific achievement. He'd fallen in love and wanted to get married. Hadn't he changed?

"Who invited you here to pick on me?"

"We need no invitation. We're family. Do you ask for an invitation before coming to Cainewood?"

"That's different. I live there."

"Do you?" Jason raised a brow. Maybe he sensed the changes in Ford, after all.

And Ford wondered: where *did* he live? At the Chase town house in London? Or the big castle at Cainewood? Or here?

He wanted to live here, he realized. Not in bustling London near the Royal Society and all his friends, not at his brother's castle with his family. Here, in the staid countryside. With Violet.

Criminy, love changed things more than he'd thought possible.

Amy and Cait exchanged a sympathetic glance. "Ford—" they started together.

"Milord, do you not think you should have left for Lady Violet's celebration already?" Hilda bustled into the room, a steaming pie in her hands. "I've made a tart for you to bring. Cherry, the young viscount's favorite."

"A celebration?" Kendra's eyes lit. "What is it for?"

"Her birthday," Ford said shortly. "And none of you are invited."

"But Uncle Ford." Jewel turned her little face up, her eyes pleading. "Mama promised I can see Rowan."

In the face of an argument like that, there was no hope in fighting this battle. Already, he had lost.

FIFTY-ONE

*E*IGHTEEN. IT FELT no different than seventeen, which Violet found amazing, especially considering she'd now experienced her first—and probably last—love.

Standing before her dressing table, she peered into the mirror and straightened one of the bright green ribbons that Margaret had woven through her plait. She squinted and moved closer, removing her spectacles. Shouldn't there be new creases around her eyes? A slight maturation in her features? Anything?

When a knock came at her door, she shoved the spectacles back on. "Come in."

The door opened a crack. "Violet?"

"Yes, Mum." She swiveled on the stool to face her. "Is it already time for the celebration?" A glance at the clock on her mantel—an old one with just a single hand—told her only in the vaguest terms. "It would be nice to have one of Ford's new pocket watches, wouldn't it?"

"It would. And yes, it's time." Mum came in, closing the door behind her. "I've come to tell you that your father spotted Ford's barge heading down the river."

"That silly barge again?" Memories flashed of last night on that barge, and her face heated.

"Are you quite all right, dear?" Oh, no. Could Mum tell he'd proposed? Just by the blush on her cheeks? "You've been hiding up here all day," she added, much to Violet's relief.

Violet forced a laugh. "You know we older women take longer to get ready. To create the illusion of youth."

She rose and wandered to the window, nervous about seeing Ford, half surprised he was still coming after she'd refused him.

The barge hadn't arrived yet. "I'm fine, Mum. It's only that these fancier gowns take forever to get on properly."

Clearly not falling for those excuses, her mother joined her at the window. "Did something happen last night? I waited up for you, but you went straight to bed without saying goodnight."

"Well…"

Violet had never hidden things from her mother—at least not anything that counted.

She paced back to the center of her room, more comfortable with some distance. "Ford asked me to marry him."

Mum turned to face her, hope in her eyes. "And what did you say?"

"I told him no," Violet said, and watched that hope fade.

Faith, she wished she'd said yes. At the moment she'd refused him, she'd been feeling closer to him than she'd imagined possible. Closer to him than she'd felt to any other person ever. She'd wanted to believe his feelings were real, that he truly loved her as he claimed.

More than anything, she'd wanted to say *yes*. A huge, enthusiastic *yes*.

But he was too good to be true. Too handsome, too charming, too perfect. Even his perfectly sincere response to her embarrassing confession of love had given him away. It was just utterly impossible that someone as incredible as Ford would fall for someone as average as Violet. At least, not without some additional motivation.

"I told him no, Mum," she repeated. "Don't you see? I want a marriage like you and Father have, or none at all."

"What makes you think you wouldn't have that with him?"

She wished she could explain it, but it was all too confused in her head. Maybe she *could* have that with him. She just didn't know for sure, and until she did…

Mum was gazing at her, waiting for an answer. An answer she didn't have. "You and Father won't make me marry him, will you?"

"I'm a good judge of people," Mum said quietly, "which is why I'm so good at arranging marriages. I believe Ford is a good person. I also believe that he truly loves you. I've seen it in his actions and on his face. However, your father and I would never make you marry anyone. I thought you knew that."

Tears sprang to Violet's eyes. She felt relieved and frustrated all at once. A tiny part of her *wished* her parents would make her marry Ford, but that wasn't the thinking part, the part of herself she trusted.

"Your father and I raised you girls to think for yourselves," Mum continued, "a folly for which we've suffered ridicule all our days. But heaven knows, after all these years, we'd be fools to make you do anything now. You're not likely to put up with it, and your sisters would stand beside you."

Despite Violet's mood, she felt a half smile curve her lips. No matter their constant bickering, her sisters would always be there for her. It was comforting to know some things never changed.

Tomorrow all this fuss over turning eighteen would be finished. And now that she'd refused his proposal, soon enough Ford would leave for London, probably not to return for months or years.

Everything would go back to the way it had been—except for Violet herself.

Mum turned back to the window. "He's here. No, *they're* here."

"Who?" Violet demanded. "Mum, have you invited someone without telling me?" She didn't even want to see Ford today, and not only because she was sure she'd feel awkward with him after last night. She didn't want to face anyone but her family on this, the official first day of her spinsterhood.

"I would never have invited anyone else without asking you first. But there are others on the barge, too."

"Harry," Violet said with not a little relief. "And the stable hands." She headed for the window. "He uses them as crew—"

She broke off, staring toward the river.

"Faith," she breathed, horror-struck. "Who *are* all those people?"

FIFTY-TWO

$\mathcal{B}$Y THE TIME she made it downstairs and into the gardens, Violet was shaking—from frustration, anger, fear, or maybe a combination. She wasn't sure. But when she saw Ford, she stopped dead in her tracks.

A little girl clung to his leg, a toddler rode on his shoulders, and an infant squalled in his arms.

He would make such a good father, she realized, and then wondered where that bizarre notion had come from. She'd never really pictured herself raising children, being that spinsters didn't have any. But somehow she could see herself raising Ford's children.

Her heart suddenly hurt.

Her mother was right. She should have said yes.

The shaking stopped, replaced by trembling of another sort. If only he would still have her, she *would* say yes. And she wanted to tell him so. Whoever they were, she wanted all of these people gone. Despite her fears of awkwardness between them, she had to talk to Ford now. She had to know if she'd lost him forever—

"Violet!" Spotting her, Ford approached with an apologetic

smile, dragging the attached little girl behind him. "This is my family."

His family. If she'd been thinking clearly at all, she would have realized that, of course. He proceeded to introduce everyone—loudly, to be heard over the baby—and she smiled and exchanged pleasantries, trying to memorize names and faces.

The two dark-haired gentlemen were his older brothers, the redhead his twin sister. Although Ford was the only one of the four siblings blessed with those spectacular blue eyes—the rest had eyes of green—they all bore a marked resemblance to one another, and she thought she might be able to keep them straight.

Their spouses and all those children, however, were another matter altogether.

And she wanted to make a good impression. Suddenly that seemed very important.

"Are those spectacles?" one of the ladies asked. The raven-haired one. Faith, who was she?

Feigning unconcern, Violet removed the eyeglasses and forced a smile. "They are. Ford made them for me and designed these frames to hold them on my face." She handed them to the lovely violet-eyed woman. "The members of the Royal Society were all very impressed."

As had happened at Gresham College, they passed the spectacles around, exclaiming over them and trying them on and praising Ford for his brilliance. Watching with a plastered-on smile and a growing feeling of dread, Violet realized she couldn't remember who anyone was except Jewel. Too many names, too many faces. Too many people at a party that was supposed to have been private and painless.

She wasn't happy about that, but she was happy to be by Ford's side. Belying her expectations, he was treating her with the same mix of teasing regard he always had. Did that mean he still cared for her?

She needed to know. She was desperate for an excuse to slip away to somewhere the two of them could be alone. Perhaps she'd take him to their hidden spot in the woods. She'd tell him she would be honored to become his wife. And then she'd let him kiss away all her lingering fears and misgivings—every last, lingering doubt—until she was filled with nothing but certainty that marrying him was the right choice.

But she couldn't do any of that, because his entire family was here. Not to mention hers.

The sun was hurting her eyes, or maybe it was all these people making her head ache. Her blurred gaze wandered to the summerhouse. One of the doors stood open, and it looked blessedly dim and peaceful inside. Maybe…

Her mother rang a bell, and everyone looked to her. "My husband wishes to speak," she called.

Faith, Violet thought, Father was going to embarrass her in front of Ford and all his family.

One of Ford's sisters-in-law returned her spectacles, and she shoved them back on her face. Everyone began making their way over to her father, who stood by a table laden with who-knew-what, all hidden beneath a bright white cloth.

As they walked, Ford slipped an arm around Violet's waist, and she glanced about to see if anyone noticed, catching the eye of one of his brothers. The marquess? Or the earl? Whoever he was, he winked at her, and despite everything, a smile spread over her face.

With all her heart, she wanted Ford's family to like her.

When her father cleared his throat, she turned.

"Due to the terms of my own father's will, the age of eighteen holds unusual significance in our family. And I've two special surprises," he announced, "to celebrate our Violet's special birthday."

Theatrically he whipped off the cloth, revealing a table covered in an artistic arrangement of fruits and fancy sweets, plus one homely cherry tart set off to the side.

"A pineapple?" Lily gasped, staring at the centerpiece, a prickly brown fruit raised on a pedestal. "Is it real? Wherever did you get a pineapple?" Pineapples were so rare in this part of the world, King Charles had had himself painted with one.

"May I try it?" Rowan yelled. "Oh, please, please!"

"Please, please!" four other children echoed, taking up the chant. "Please!"

"There isn't enough for everyone," Ford said loudly, sweeping his siblings with an accusatory glance. "You weren't invited here, remember?"

"Nonsense," Father said. "Yes, it is real, and yes, everyone may try it. A bite, at least. But first"—he paused and looked toward the door—"here comes the second surprise." Four housemaids and two footmen approached, each holding a thick green bottle in one hand and stemmed glasses in the other. "The new French champagne. Who will have a taste?"

"Me!" Rowan yelled. "Me! Me!"

"Me! Me!" Ford's nephews and nieces joined in.

"You're too young," Rose told Rowan. "Champagne is too costly to water down."

Father looked to Mum. "Wash her gown in champagne?"

"Water down the champagne, darling. But we won't be doing that." Mum scanned the gathering. "Rowan may certainly have a taste," she announced, "as may any other children whose parents agree."

The maids poured while the footmen bore the esteemed pineapple back to the kitchen to be sliced.

Father handed the glasses around and raised his in a toast. "To our Violet, on the anniversary of her birth." The center of attention, Violet felt her face burn. "May she live in health and happiness another eighteen years times four."

"Hear, hear," everyone said, smiling in her direction.

Whoever they all were.

She looked down and took a cautious sip. "It's like drinking stars," she breathed. She'd never tasted anything like it. It tickled the back of her throat.

Rowan spewed his mouthful onto the grass. "Zounds, I've got bubbles up my nose. Ick." Violet cringed at her brother's lack of manners, but at least no one had to worry about him drinking too much, since he immediately set down his glass.

"It's an acquired taste," a golden-haired gentleman told him. The duke, Violet remembered, congratulating herself. Though Ford had introduced him as Trick.

Well, that was one memorable name.

Lily looked awed. "Have you tried it before, your grace?"

Trick nodded. "It's all the rage at court."

"Have you been to court, then?" Rowan asked.

Jewel elbowed him. "Of course he has, you goose. He's a duke!"

Rose sighed. "I've never been to court. Father won't allow it. He says it isn't a place for nice, unmarried girls."

"A wise decision," Trick said dryly.

Ford bent down to whisper in Violet's ear. "The bucks at court would have an innocent like Rose for supper."

Though she suspected her sister could handle herself, Violet's eyes widened at this news.

"Have you never been, either?" he asked.

Sipping the sparkly drink, she shook her head. "Is it beautiful?"

"Whitehall is magnificent. Court itself can be amusing or boring, depending on who deigns to show up that particular day. But I was raised with the court in exile...I imagine you would find it exciting."

She'd felt more at home among the Royal Society than she'd expected. "Maybe now that I'm eighteen, Father will take me someday."

"I was thinking *I* could take you," he said with that winning smile of his. "After we're wed."

He sounded terribly confident, which normally would have

irked her. But today, her heart sang instead. He hadn't given up on her, after all! Held fast by his gaze, she remembered how it had felt to dance with him in their own little wonderland, holding each other close. A rush of warmth shuddered through her.

She wanted to tell him yes. Here. Now. Her gaze went wistfully to the summerhouse again, but this was no time to sneak away, not while she was the center of attention.

Yet she was dying to tell him, and if he had whispered a private message to her, she could do the same...

She raised up on her toes. "Ford—" she began quietly.

"The pineapple!" Rowan squealed, and the moment was lost. They all turned to see a footman approaching, bearing a silver bowl filled with small cubes of yellow fruit. "I hope I like it better than the champagne," Rowan said as the man put it down.

"Have you tried *this* already, your grace?" Rose asked the duke.

Trick shook his head. "Never."

"I've seen pineapples before at parties, but only as a decorative centerpiece," Ford's sister said. "I suspect someone is making a fortune renting the things so people can impress their friends."

Mum laughed at the idea. "Do you expect they actually spoil before anyone eats them?"

"I imagine so," said one of those dark-haired brothers. Jason, the marquess, Violet thought as he curved his arm around the waist of the sister-in-law that had long tawny hair. "From what I understand, most of them rot on the way from the islands. But this one looks perfect."

"I hope it is," Father said. "I've heard it said that if I dry the crown for a couple of days, I may be able to plant it and grow pineapples, providing I can keep the bush warm during the winter. They're supposed to have pink flowers that look like a pine cone." He lifted the bowl and held a spoon out to Ford. "As our guest, will you honor us by trying it first?"

"But this is Violet's day." Ford took the spoon, scooped up a cube, and moved it toward her lips.

He'd fed her in the piazza at Gresham, and now, as then, it seemed an almost shocking act. Her gaze darted around to see how their families were reacting, but everyone just looked expectant. And the moment the fruit touched her tongue, she forgot to be self-conscious. Flavor burst in her mouth.

"Oh my," she said, chewing slowly. "It's the sweetest thing I've ever tasted!"

Everyone else scrambled to try it.

"Do you like it?" Violet asked Rowan.

He grinned, yellow pulp in his teeth. "It's much better than champagne."

"Oh, but the champagne is so light and delicious!" Lily daintily sipped from her glass. "The pineapple is sweet but…"

"Acidic?" Ford suggested.

"Well, I'm not exactly certain what that means, but it sounds about right."

He smiled and grabbed a bottle to refill her glass. "Acids react with a base to form a salt."

Jewel looked up to the sister-in-law with the beautiful raven hair. "Uncle Ford is smart, isn't he, Mama?"

"I assume your Uncle Ford is *very* smart," the woman said with a smile, "since I understand only half of what he says."

Jewel's mother. Violet committed that to memory, trying to figure out which gentleman was her husband. Probably the one who laughed now, then leaned down and pressed a kiss to the top of her head. Colin. She remembered Ford telling her Colin played practical jokes, so of course he would be Jewel's father. It was all coming together.

Rowan grinned at Jewel. "I'm glad Violet had such an important birthday."

"Me, too," Lily said, sipping more champagne.

"Me three," Rose added, all but gulping hers.

If Violet didn't miss her guess, her sisters were getting a bit tipsy.

Doing her best to relax, she looked around at everyone drinking champagne and chatting amiably. The sister-in-law with the straight tawny hair caught her eye and smiled. Jason's wife, she thought happily, glad she was finally figuring out who was who. She liked them. They seemed friendly.

Then once again, Father cleared his throat. When nobody took heed, he raised Mum's bell and gave it a shake. Violet winced, sure something else embarrassing was about to come out of his mouth.

"This is quite a momentous occasion. As the oldest, our Violet is now the first to come into her inheritance. I hope you will save it and spend wisely, my dear daughter."

Violet sighed. She'd been right. Sometimes Father could be so—

"She can use it to buy a husband!" Rose announced with a tipsy giggle.

Violet wished the earth would open up and swallow her.

"Now, Rose," Mum chided, reaching to brush a bit of pineapple off Father's surcoat.

"It was but a jest!" Rose poured herself more champagne. "Can you people not abide a jest?"

But Rose was absolutely right: most young ladies would use a large inheritance to buy into a highly ranked family, and most gentlemen would be happy to accept that bargain. Looking around again, Violet no longer saw a warm, good-natured gathering; she saw an assembly of prestigious and powerful men and women.

She took a gulp of her own champagne, but she wasn't feeling tipsy, just sick.

To think, mere minutes ago, she'd nearly told Ford yes. Now all her doubts came flooding back. She tilted her head back, letting the the bubbly drink run down her throat, wishing it could restore her world to balance.

She was so confused. If she could just spirit Ford away from this crowd and talk to him, really talk to him, maybe she could tell whether he was sincere. A grown woman of eighteen ought to be possessed of some feminine instincts, oughtn't she?

With a sigh, she reached to pour herself more champagne.

"I think you may have had enough," Father said, gently prying the glass from her clenched fingers. "Come with me to the summerhouse for a moment."

"Not now, Father."

"Always arguing." He shook his head. "Chrysanthemum, Violet, Rose, and Lily…my lovely flowers always argue. Except for the ones in my garden. No wonder I like them so much."

Violet couldn't help but smile. He scooped a bunch of grapes off the table and started toward the summerhouse, leaving her to follow.

After shutting the door, he gazed at her fondly and wrapped her into a hug. It was quiet inside the structure—quiet enough that he could hear without her yelling. Quiet enough that she could hear her own heartbeat as she felt herself calming in his arms.

"How's my eldest flower?" he asked, pulling back. "You looked upset there, for a bit."

She couldn't stay vexed with him. His speeches might have been embarrassing, but they were well intended, after all. To outsiders, he might seem rather addlepated, but that was only because he couldn't hear well enough to participate in many conversations. Those close to him knew he was wise.

She gave him a wry smile. "I'm well, Father. Sort of like fine, old wine, aged but better for it."

"You're not so old," he said, sitting down on one of the benches that lined the curved red-brick wall. "Don't go consigning yourself to spinsterhood yet."

She saw the truth in his face. "Mum told you Ford proposed."

"You know we share everything." He pulled four grapes off

the bunch. "That's what I want for you, Violet. Someone to share your life with."

"I was sure I'd never have that. But now…"

"Yes?" He popped one of the grapes into his mouth.

"I don't know. I'm confused. Socrates said the unexamined life isn't worth living. But I'm driving myself mad examining and reexamining."

Chewing on the grapes, he rose and wandered back to the door. "Sometimes," he said quietly, "we just have to take a leap of faith. When the time comes, you'll know."

Would she? She felt inadequate to make such a decision. Philosophy, after all, taught one to question everything. And the single thing she'd been sure of all her life—that she would never find true love—she'd now caught herself rethinking.

She felt like she didn't know anything anymore.

He handed her a grape. "Now go back out there and smile at your guests."

They weren't *her* guests, but as he opened the door, she decided that, for once, she'd be the flower that didn't argue.

Besides, she really wanted to get Ford alone here in the summerhouse.

She stepped outside, blinking in the bright sunshine. Everyone had scattered. The children had organized themselves into a game of duck-duck-goose, and Jewel was "it." On the far side of the garden, Ford was picnicking beneath the giant oak with his brothers and their wives, both of the women with babes in their laps. He looked over and waved, and she waved back, noting the others watching. They were discussing her, she was sure of it. She'd give up *Aristotle's Master-piece* to hear what they were saying.

Fairly certain one of the two babies belonged to Ford's sister, Violet scanned the other end of the grounds, then blushed to see the fiery redhead and her husband in the shadows of a tree-lined path, locked in a rather tender embrace.

She politely averted her eyes, though the sight made her

smile. They reminded her of her parents and of the love she wanted for herself…and that she'd be daft to allow Rose's thoughtless remark to hold her back. She wouldn't let her old insecurities haunt her. No matter what her sister said, she wasn't buying a husband. Ford had said he loved her, and she believed him.

She was ready to take that leap of faith.

With a new determination, she headed past the children toward Ford.

"Duck, duck, duck—" Rounding the circle, Jewel broke off. "Rowan, why do you keep scratching?"

He scraped his fingernails on his shirt. "I don't know," he said, raking his leg, then the back of one hand.

Jewel stepped into the circle and gasped. "Gads, you have red spots all over your face! Measles!"

Violet detoured into the circle, knowing her brother was entirely too lively to have measles. "Let me see." She bent and peered into his face, wiping the remnants of cherry tart from his chin. "Rowan, did you drink chocolate?"

"Just a little," he squeaked. "The champagne was icky."

"Oh, Rowan!" Exasperated, she hauled him to his feet. "You know chocolate gives you hives. Now you'll be scratching for days."

"He looks funny," a little girl said with a giggle.

"Funny, funny!" The other children took up the chant.

Jewel stepped closer and poked him on the chest. "You goose!" She burst out laughing.

Clearly mortified, Rowan ran for the house. All the adults rushed over to see what had happened, except for Mum, who followed Rowan.

This birthday was turning out every bit as miserable as Violet had feared.

She just wanted to be alone with Ford. Over the giggling children's heads, she met his gaze, and a silent communication passed between them. She inclined her head toward the summerhouse, signaling him to meet her there.

Seeming to materialize out of nowhere, his sister touched her arm. "May we have a word with you, Violet?" Her two sisters-in-law stood behind her. "Do you mind if we call you Violet?"

"I...of course not. Not at all." She sent Ford a questioning glance, but he just shrugged apologetically.

There was nothing for it, she thought with an inward sigh. She couldn't rebuff his family. Her answer to his proposal would have to wait a bit longer.

She tried to muster a smile. "Shall we talk in the summerhouse? It's quiet in there."

As they followed her silently, she braced for what she was sure would be an unpleasant barrage of questions as they assessed her worthiness for their brother.

When the door closed behind them, Ford's sister returned her tentative smile. "I'm Kendra, in case you don't remember. And this is Amy and Cait."

Violet nodded, feeling rather outnumbered as she mentally noted who was who, hopefully once and for all.

She didn't want to make any mistakes.

Dark-haired Amy was Jewel's mother and Colin's wife. And she was a jeweler, Ford had said. Colin had rescued her after her father's London shop burned in the Great Fire.

Cait, Jason's wife, had lively hazel eyes. Her straight wheaten hair, while less than fashionable, seemed to suit her perfectly. She stood with a hand on her middle, and although her stomach looked flat, Violet wondered if she might be with child.

She wondered if she would ever have a child. With Ford.

"My brother has a good heart," Kendra announced without further ado.

"A very good heart," Amy added.

"A very, very good heart," Cait echoed in a distinct Scots accent.

Ford had told Violet that Cait was Scottish, so she was sure she had the right names with the right faces now. But she was stunned. She backed up and sat on a bench. "I know he does," she said slowly.

This wasn't the grilling she'd been expecting. Were they trying to talk her into marrying him?

"He loves you," Kendra said.

"Very much."

"Very, very much."

They were trying to talk her into marrying him.

She didn't know whether to laugh or just hug them for caring so deeply for Ford's happiness. What they were doing was so very sweet. "He's told me he loves me," she assured them.

Kendra crossed her arms. "But you don't believe him." It was a statement, not a question.

Violet opened her mouth to disagree, but Kendra cut her off.

"Look," she said, dropping to sit beside her. "Let me tell you something. If Ford were looking for money, he could have married Lady Tabitha ages ago. She had pots full of it."

Lady Tabitha?

Her mouth still hanging open, Violet blinked. "Who is Lady Tabitha?"

FIFTY-THREE

*A*T LADY TRENTINGHAM'S invitation, Ford walked with her in companionable silence along a path that took a meandering route to the river. All afternoon, her speculative looks had been convincing him Violet had told her something.

He just wondered exactly *what*.

"She told you, didn't she?" he finally asked, unable to bear the suspense.

In the dappled light that came through the trees, she stopped on the path and nodded. "Yes, she told me you proposed. We're a close family. Some think us a bit odd."

Ah. Well, Violet's rejection had been devastating—not to mention humiliating—but if she'd had to share the experience, he supposed Lady Trentingham was one of the kinder souls Violet could have confided in.

He shuddered to think how Rose might have broached the subject.

"Your family seems close, too," Lady Trentingham added.

"We are," he said, knowing it was true, no matter how irritating they could be sometimes. "We lost our parents long ago at Worcester, so we've always leaned on one another." By tacit agreement, they resumed walking, the gravel crunching beneath their shoes. "I'm hoping to have a close family of my own soon," he said carefully.

Still strolling, she met his gaze. "Violet fears you're only pursuing her in order to get your hands on her inheritance."

Lady Trentingham was direct—in that way, she reminded him of his twin sister. But the news hurt, even though he'd suspected as much from the start.

"How can she think that?" he wondered aloud. "I've told her I love her." Despite everything, hearing those words from his mouth prompted an embarrassed half-smile. "I never thought I'd admit as much to her mother."

"And I'd suggest you not tell her you did. If Violet knew I was doing anything to encourage this marriage, she'd run the other way. I've something of a reputation as a matchmaker, and my daughters are all dead set against becoming one of my statistics."

"I won't breathe a word." *Encourage this marriage* still rang in his ears, making his spirits rise with premature glee. He'd hoped Violet's parents weren't an obstacle, but now he knew for sure. That left only the lady herself. "What can I do to persuade her?"

"It won't be easy," Lady Trentingham warned. "My daughter decided she was unmarriageable long before she met you. Old convictions are difficult to overcome." She discreetly cleared her throat. "And I'm afraid the condition of your estate is doing little to convince her you're not in need of her funds."

He'd known that, too. "What if I told you I *am* short of funds, but that's not the reason I want to marry her?"

They reached the river and turned, her brown eyes reminding him of Violet's as she met his gaze for a long, silent moment. "I'll give you points for honesty," she said at last with a nod of approval. "But I fear it will make your task even harder. Lakefield's sad state isn't only due to neglect, then?"

"Mostly. I am not in dire straits." Heading back toward the

house, he sighed. "The place was unoccupied long before it was deeded to me, but...well..."

He supposed since she was giving him points for honesty, he might as well follow through. If his situation would make him unacceptable as a son-in-law, he'd as soon learn that now rather than later.

Though that didn't mean he was obliged to make things sound worse than they were.

He raked his fingers through his hair. "It's true I've never made Lakefield a priority. I understand the estate was prime horse-breeding property before the Civil War, but nothing remains of that now save a few decrepit stables. And I imagine you're aware there have been several disastrous agricultural years since I took ownership in '61. However," he rushed to add, "I assure you I've always made certain no one dependent on the property has suffered as a result." Indeed, in order to see that none of the tenant farmers went hungry a few years ago, he'd been forced to mortgage the estate. Those payments were proving to be his downfall now.

"I'm sure you have," Lady Trentingham said soothingly. A touch of understanding infused her voice, making his pulse leap with hope. Could it be possible he still had her support? "But I understand there were few tenants left by the time you took over."

"True enough. If the estate is to produce a decent income, I must attract more people to move here." And repair the housing meant to shelter them. Dozens of crumbling cottages—more costs he was too strapped to bear. But perhaps Rand was finished with the translation by now, and regardless, somehow he would work it out.

He just hadn't cared enough before this. Loving Violet made all the difference.

He smiled at her mother, thinking having parents of this sort mightn't be such a bad thing. "I just need to put my mind to it."

"And you've got a brilliant mind there." She smiled back.

"Perhaps Violet's dowry will ease your way. You do know it's three thousand pounds?"

"No, I didn't. It's very generous." More than he'd expected.

But it wasn't enough. No amount of money would be enough. Oh, he supposed there was some number of thousands that would dig the estate out of debt—to his disgrace, he had no idea how much—but he was coming to realize that without his ongoing efforts to ensure that Lakefield produced sufficient income to support all the people who depended on it, it would soon sink back into the morass.

He was ready to take on that responsibility.

Lady Trentingham was waiting for more of a reaction. "I'd have to win Violet first, and even then her marriage portion wouldn't be enough," he admitted, then realized she could take that the wrong way. "I mean, my own hard work—"

"I understand." She touched him on the arm. "My husband is an expert estate manager. I'm sure he'd be happy to counsel you."

Ford wasn't too proud to accept help. "I'd be pleased to accept any guidance he's willing to offer."

"You may have to shout a bit in the process." Her smile this time was the same warm smile she'd given him the first day in his garden. "I have faith in you, Ford. And despite what she may think, I know my daughter well, so I'll tell you this: She wouldn't mind that you need her inheritance, as long as she were convinced you weren't marrying her for it."

He wasn't sure he believed that, and in any case, he didn't want to take Violet's money. Her dowry was one thing, her inheritance quite another. Having aspirations of his own, he'd think twice before jeopardizing her dream of publishing.

No, he'd think ten times. Twenty. Surely there was another way to solve his difficulties.

Lady Trentingham peered through the trees. "I think your family may be ready to leave."

Indeed, they were all gathered by the barge, shifting from

foot to foot. A quick glance at the sun told him if they didn't get back to Lakefield and their carriages soon, they wouldn't make it to their homes by nightfall.

But ahead of him, at the end of the path, stood Violet. Looking upset.

Ignoring his siblings' shouts, he hurried to meet her.

FIFTY-FOUR

ATCHING FORD approach, Violet took a deep breath.

She was determined not to jump to conclusions. She'd had enough of that today—enough of indecision. She would talk to Ford calmly...and she wouldn't let him touch her until afterward. She needed to keep her head clear.

But before she managed to say a word, he took her hand. And the next thing she knew they were in the summerhouse, and he was pulling off her spectacles and dragging her into his arms. And clear thinking went right out the window.

When he crushed his lips to hers, her knees weakened so, she feared she would tumble to the bricks beneath her feet. They clung together for a long, searing moment before he finally drew back.

"I love you," he said.

She searched his eyes, still close enough to see. "So you've said."

"What else do you need me to say? Tell me, and I'll say it." He set her away, backing up until he looked blurry, until the backs of his knees hit the bench. "I know my life is a shambles," he said, rushing on as though he'd prepared a speech, "but everything will get much easier after Rand completes the translation. I'm going to Oxford to see him tomorrow. And I know my home isn't good enough for you, but I'm going to fix it up. Either way, whether Rand is done or not. I never did before, because... well, I'd never planned to live here. But now I want to."

"Just like that?" she asked, still feeling dizzy from the kiss. And heaven help her, still wanting more.

"Just like that," he said.

It was exactly what she'd wanted to hear. If only she could believe it.

Faith, how she wished she'd never heard Lady Tabitha's name! She knew the Chase ladies' interference had been well-intentioned. They hadn't meant to trouble her, and they certainly hadn't meant to give her yet another reason to question their brother's motives.

"I like your family," she said, because she did.

"I like your family, too. I want to live here, near your family."

"Ford—" She paused, then forged on. "Tell me about Lady Tabitha."

"What?" The shock in his voice worried her. "Where did you hear about *her*?"

"Your sister. And Amy and Cait—"

"Criminy, what did they say?"

That an heiress you'd planned to marry—despite never truly loving her—jilted you right before you came to Lakefield...

...where he'd conveniently found himself another heiress.

She sighed, suddenly exhausted with her own suspicions. Too exhausted to confront him. "Just that you expected to marry her," she mumbled.

"That was before I met you." He stepped closer, so close the scent of patchouli overwhelmed her. "She meant nothing to me, Violet. *Nothing*." His eyes burned into hers, willing her to believe.

And perhaps she had meant nothing. But Violet had been too buffeted by emotions today to think straight.

He loved her, he loved her not.

She felt like she'd been through a war.

He switched tactics, running a hand down her arm, and, predictably, she weakened all over. It was uncanny, this effect he had on her. And not only was her body weak, her heart was weak as well. Slowly but surely, Ford was conquering it, conquering her, robbing her of her of her good sense.

"Marry me, Violet," he said in a fierce whisper.

Because too much of her wanted to blurt out yes, she took a step back before once again searching his eyes. Which meant she couldn't really see them. In vain she willed them to give up his secrets. Perhaps feminine intuition skipped a generation?

She loved Ford—of that she was certain. But as for the rest, she was only confused.

"Marry me, Violet," he repeated. "Please."

And before she could answer, she was back in his arms.

When he kissed her this time, she forgot why she wasn't sure she could marry him. She forgot she'd decided not to touch him. She forgot her own name.

And when he finally released her, she grabbed her spectacles from him and ran.

Out the door, through the garden, across the wide lawn to the portico and front door.

"Violet!" Mum called. "Dear heavens, what has happened?"

"He asked me to marry him again, the wretch!" she screamed before slamming the door.

∼

"*T*HE LAST OF the champagne." Joseph handed Chrystabel half a glass before climbing into bed beside her. "How is our dear eldest doing?"

"She'll survive. She didn't want to talk at first, but she was glad I returned her spectacles." Chrystabel sipped, letting the sparkling liquid slide down her throat and soothe her frayed nerves. "He shouldn't have proposed again so quickly. His timing couldn't have been worse."

Joseph took the glass from her and drained it. "What do you mean?"

She sighed. "Following *your* ill-timed announcement of her inheritance, and Rose's subsequent comment—"

"Ouch."

"Yes, but it wasn't only that. His sister also spilled past history, confusing Violet. It reinforced her fears that Ford's true motive is money rather than love."

"She could be right." He grinned, clearly not understanding the gravity of this situation. "You married me for *my* money."

Well, he was just a man, so she shouldn't expect him to understand. Giving in to his playfulness, she punched him lightly on the shoulder. "I did not. I married you for your flowers. How else would I make my perfume? And without my perfume, I'd have no excuse to visit and chat with all the neighbors—and find out Nancy Philpot's son has left the army and is living with a Parisian courtesan."

"Ah, I see where that outrageous bit of gossip could be much more important than money." He set down the empty glass and took her hand. "But are you certain that was the only reason you married me?"

She pretended to consider. "I suppose insuperable desire may have also played a part. But it definitely wasn't the money."

"It won't come down to money for Violet, either," he told her, and turned to blow out the candle, plunging the room into darkness.

While he burrowed under the coverlet, Chrystabel remained upright, thinking. "You agree with me, then? That they're well suited?"

"Of course, darling." Joseph's arm snaked around her waist and pulled her down to nestle against him. "When have you ever been wrong?"

FIFTY-FIVE

*S*OME PLACES never changed. The King's Arms, a tavern in Oxford where Ford and Rand had whiled away many an evening during their university years, was one of them.

Occupying their usual spot at one of the long tables, the two friends supped on pigeon pie and ignored a loud argument about radical politics taking place just behind them. That was nothing new, either. John Locke's challenging ideas had germinated here in Oxford, after all, while he was an undergraduate at Christ Church College.

His pie disposed of, Ford nursed a tankard of ale, trying to be patient while Rand detailed his father's latest transgressions against him. The two had never seen eye to eye, which explained why a marquess's son would choose an unglamorous academic career in Oxford over a life of leisure and luxury at home.

Not that Rand wasn't happy here. Only nineteen years of age and already gaining notoriety in his field, he was on track to become the youngest Professor of Linguistics in the university's history. And he was doing it all with no help or encouragement from his family.

After finishing both his tirade and his ale, Rand stared

pensively into the empty tankard, fingering his mustache. "If you've come to ask about the translation, I'm afraid I have no good news for you."

Ford's heart sank. "What seems to be the problem?"

"It's more difficult than I had anticipated. There are words—and symbols—that seem unrelated to any language I've ever encountered."

"Symbols?" Ford frowned. "I saw a few formulas, which was one of the reasons I thought it might be *Secrets of the Emerald Tablet*. But those were just numbers, mathematics—"

"Not that. There were a few pages stuck together—"

"I opened a couple and saw nothing special, and I was afraid I might tear the paper."

"I steamed the rest open. Most were stuck from age, I imagine. But one...one, I believe, was on purpose."

"On purpose." Ford sipped, swallowed, tried to tamp down his rising hopes. "Are you thinking it might be the page that reveals—"

"No, nothing like that. I see no indication the secret you're searching for will be found on a single page. It's not going to be that simple." Rand's words reminded Ford of his family telling him something similar. "But this page is at the end, and it seems to be a legend for part of the code—perhaps for the author's own use. There are words—most of which I cannot read—with other words beside them, like a list, you understand?"

Ford nodded. "Go on."

"Well, that's the page that has some odd symbols." Rand tipped his tankard, letting the dregs of his ale run onto the table. "One of them, I think, looked like this." He used a finger to scribble in the wet, a design like a triangle with a three-branched candelabra perched on top.

"Air," Ford said.

"What?"

"That's the alchemical symbol for air. Or one of them. There are hundreds of similar symbols, some common, some not.

Many whose meanings have been lost, but I can identify a number of them."

Excitement lit Rand's gray eyes. "So even though I cannot read the word beside that symbol—which is gibberish, I suspect—when I find it in the text, I'll know it means air." He smeared the puddle, then used a finger to draw another mark. "How about this one?"

Ford frowned at the squiggle. "I don't recognize that."

"And this?"

A circle with three dots that suggested eyes and a nose. "That's a human skull."

Rand grimaced. "You mean a dead person?"

"Yes. A skull can be powdered and—"

"Never mind. I'd rather not know." He smoothed the liquid and sketched another design. "What's this?"

It looked like the letter *I* with an arrow curving up through it. "That's an instruction, not an ingredient. It means to filter."

After four more tries, one of which Ford could identify and three which he couldn't, Rand gave up. "I cannot remember any more. We'll fetch the book later, and you can write down the ones you know. But, Ford..."

His friend's gaze looked serious. "Tell it straight, Rand."

"Don't get your hopes up, will you? It's a single page of clues, and the symbols are few compared to all the other things I find undecipherable. Even with this help, the rest of it could take years."

Something fisted in Ford's middle. Or rather, the fist tightened—it had been there for days already. "I don't have years. Not if I want Violet."

"Ah. It's like that, is it?" Rand signaled for another round. "Tell me."

Though Ford normally wouldn't, his tongue was loosened by ale—and something akin to desperation. "My family approves. Her parents approve. But Violet refuses to marry for anything other than—"

Rand perked up when a comely serving maid arrived with two more ales. Smoothing his mustache, he flipped her a coin. "My thanks," he said in a deepened voice. After watching her retreat, he turned back to Ford and his speech returned to normal. "You can't mean Lady Violet refused you? Most women would leap at the chance to wed a Chase, given your family's connections to King Charles. And most fathers would insist on it."

"The Ashcrofts are not 'most' people. Their daughters are allowed to make their own decisions. And they have the most preposterous family motto: *Interroga Conformationem.*"

"Question Convention?" Rand's lips quirked with amusement. "Regardless, she should choose you. For security." He took a gulp of ale. "Even without the Philosopher's Stone, you're hardly a pauper. Take her to Cainewood if she wishes to live in luxury."

"I don't want to live at Cainewood." He was tired of being a guest in someone else's home. He'd much rather be in charge of his own life. "Anyway, it's not luxury that Violet wants. She's not a frilly sort of girl, and she has her own money."

"Ah. I remember. Given to her by the eccentric grandfather. To 'leave her mark on the world.'"

"Yes. And being familiar with Lakefield's, um, deficiencies, she's convinced herself I must be after her inheritance—which I'm not! I love her."

Rand's eyebrows shot up. "Did you tell her that?"

"Repeatedly. In every way I know how." Closing his eyes, Ford lowered his head and raked both hands through his hair.

When he looked up, Rand wore an expression of sympathy. Or disbelief. Or maybe both.

"Man, you've got it bad." Rand drained the rest of his ale. "I've never told a girl that."

Ford eyed his young friend with skepticism. "When would *you* have had occasion to?"

"Pah!" Rand lobbed a bit of pie crust in Ford's direction. "I've been involved with many women, I'll have you know."

"Oh? In the few months since I left here?" Dusting pie crust off his cravat, Ford raised a brow. "Do any of these women have names?"

"Of course they do," Rand said, his face going slightly pink. He jutted out his chin. "But a gentleman doesn't kiss and tell."

Ford snorted. "That's what I thought."

FIFTY-SIX

*S*O HE WASN'T going to be making gold anytime soon. Their minds muddled by several more ales, Ford and Rand had concluded that didn't mean he had to give up on marrying Violet. All he had to do was convince her he loved *her*, not her money, which shouldn't be an impossible task.

First, they decided, he had to keep *showing* her how he felt. He'd made a good start there, Ford declared in a drunken boast. Enough stolen kisses ought to eventually wear her down. It was only a matter of time before he became part of her the same way she had become part of him.

Rand groaned at that sentimental slop and ordered another round.

Second, Ford would change his priorities, put managing the estate first and relegate his science to a hobby. He'd already decided he was willing to do that and told both Violet and her mother as much. And it was infinitely more palatable than the alternative, which was losing Violet.

Love changed a man.

Of course, it would be a good while before the estate earned an income sufficient to pay off all the debts, but in the meantime, Ford and Rand had reasoned, if he fixed up Lakefield, it wouldn't keep reminding Violet of his temporary lack of finances.

Which was why he was now outside, hacking away at his garden.

Hilda approached, bearing a tankard of fresh lemonade.

"A gift from heaven." He thunked his ax into the ground and held the cold drink against his forehead.

Hilda settled her hands on her wide hips. "Just what do you think you're doing out here?"

"Cleaning up." He gulped greedily. "Then I'll plant."

"Plant what?"

"I'm not sure. I'll think about that when I get there." He knew zero about plants, other than what some of them looked like extremely close up, thanks to *Micrographia*.

She eyed a ladder propped against the wall. "Are you planning to plant vines?"

"Excellent idea." He sipped again, letting the sweet coolness flow down his throat. "That would save me from painting, wouldn't it?"

"You're going to paint, too?"

"That's the plan. I sent Harry off for paint. Didn't he tell you?"

"Since when does Harry tell me anything?" She took the empty tankard from his hand. "What was the ladder for, then?"

"I tried to fix the roof." Turning away, he lifted the ax. "If you wouldn't mind going into the laboratory—"

"Into your private domain?" She laid a hand on her pillowy bosom. "Be still my heart."

"—you may find some foreign matter has fallen from above." He whacked at an overgrown bush. Or vine. He wasn't sure which, but he was fairly certain the thing wouldn't be termed a tree. "I'm going to have to ask Harry to find a roofer." He whacked again, then turned sharply when he heard a chortle. "Are you laughing at me, Hilda?"

"Of course not, milord. That would be terribly disrespectful, wouldn't it?" She cleared her throat. "You know, some of that may be salvageable if you prune it instead of killing it."

He ran a grubby hand back through his hair. "Is that so? I had no idea you were knowledgeable about vegetation. Perhaps you could—"

"I most certainly could not." She drew herself up to her full height of five feet. "I'm a housekeeper, not a gardener. It's dirty work, that is."

It certainly was, if the state of his clothing was any indication. Deciding he'd done as much to destroy that plant as possible, he moved to the next one.

"Why are you limping?" Hilda's eyes narrowed. "Your breeches are torn."

He started to wave the ax in a dismissive gesture, then changed his mind and lowered it. He was reasonably proficient with a sword, but an ax was another matter. "It's nothing," he said. "Just scratched myself a bit up on the roof."

"Fell through, you mean, do you not?"

On second thought, if his housekeeper failed to curb her tongue, the ax could come in handy. His hand tightened on the hilt. Or the grip. Or whatever one called the wooden part of an ax. "Perhaps my foot did slip. I told you there might be foreign matter in the laboratory that needs to be cleared away."

"Well, I hope your blood isn't mixed with it. That'll stain the floor." Shaking her head, she walked away, leaving him in peace at last.

As soon as she disappeared around the corner, he plopped onto a stone bench, swiping a hand across his brow. He eyed his handiwork.

He'd been chopping away for nigh on four hours, and the job looked bigger than when he'd started.

FIFTY-SEVEN

"*V*ERY INTERESTING," Violet said, staring at the dried top of a pineapple.

Lily smiled sweetly at their father. "What an exciting project."

"It's an ugly thing," Rose said.

Father gave her an indulgent smile—or perhaps he hadn't quite heard her. All plants were beautiful to him, and he'd been known to take offense on their behalf. "I'm going to plant it in a big pot and keep it here in the Stone Gallery at nights and all winter."

Violet didn't find the plan surprising, since he was already trying to grow oranges indoors. The long, narrow chamber, which was lined with windows and occupied the entire ground floor of the west wing, had been used in Tudor times to take exercise in inclement weather. But now one could hardly walk two steps without bumping into a plant.

Rowan's foot tapped on the black-and-white marble floor. "How many pineapples will it grow?"

"I'm not sure." Father frowned. "Maybe only one."

"One? We'll eat it in a trice!"

"But then I'll have another top, and I can grow more—"

"And by the time Rowan is married with children," Rose

finished for him, "we ought to have a decent crop. Anyone want to go riding?"

It seemed a long time since Violet had exercised anything but her heart. "I'm game," she said.

"Me, too," Lily added.

"Me three." Rowan scratched his head. "No, make that four."

They all laughed.

"Be back in time to dress for supper!" Father called after his children as they trooped outside.

A few minutes later they were mounted on their horses and riding along the river. Violet took the lead and automatically headed toward Lakefield, hoping Ford was back from Oxford. She wanted to see him, to talk things through now that she'd had time to think. She hoped she could get him alone somehow, away from her siblings where they could speak in private.

The sun felt warm on her skin, and Socrates's white hide was tickly against her legs. She leaned into a turn, loving the wind in her hair, the effortless movements of the animal beneath her. Suddenly she felt like she'd been cooped up in the house entirely too long. The fresh air was marvelous. She decided she should leave her books behind and go out more often.

"We should ride the other way," Rowan said.

Lily pulled up alongside him. "Why is that?"

He shook his head ruefully. "I don't want to see Jewel."

Three days had passed since he'd drunk the chocolate, and he was still scratching. And doubtless still hearing Jewel's laughter in his ears.

Rose laughed now. "Jewel went home with her parents, you goose."

"Rose!" Seeing their brother flinch at the word *goose*, Violet sent her a warning look. "But she's right, Rowan, Jewel is nowhere near..."

Her words trailed off as Lakefield House came within sight.

"Oh my," she said, staring at the decimated garden. "What do you think happened?"

"A storm," Rowan guessed. "With lots of blowing."

Lily's eyes sparkled with amusement. "I expect we would have felt the effects of that at Trentingham."

Rose shaded her eyes with a hand. "Is that a hole in the roof?"

They drew nearer. "Oh my," Violet said. "Is that—oh my."

"On the ladder there." Lily cocked her head. "Is that the viscount?"

Rose drew breath and released a very unladylike holler. "Lord Lakefield! Is that you?"

Her voice carried so well, even their father would have turned his head. Which the fellow on the ladder did, to reveal a face splattered with paint. His clothing wasn't faring any better. As they rode closer and came to a stop near the house, Violet watched a white blob roll down Ford's hair and land on one of his boots.

She burst out laughing.

He backed awkwardly down the ladder and limped over to gaze up at her on her horse. He crossed his arms, then dropped them, grimacing at the white handprints he'd just made on his clothing. "What's so funny?"

At that, her sisters burst out laughing, too.

With a supreme effort, Violet got herself under control. "What on earth," she asked, "do you think you're doing?"

"I told you I was going to fix this place up."

Another little giggle escaped. "I didn't think you meant to do it yourself."

But her heart melted a little. Was he doing this for her?

Clasping her sides, Rose gasped, "It looks worse than when you started!"

Ford's jaw tightened, but he ignored her and addressed Violet. "May I speak with you for a moment? In private?"

She looked to her sisters, but this, after all, was what she had come for. So she shrugged and handed her reins to Lily, slid off Socrates, and followed Ford around the corner of the house.

The moment they were out of sight, he pinned her against the stone wall.

Her gasp of surprise was covered by his lips. The familiar weakness stole over her, and her muscles went limp as his mouth slanted over hers. He smelled of Ford and paint, and his body pressing her against the house reminded her of that day in the woods, and how he'd felt crushed against her…

Breathless, nearly senseless, she pulled back, then looked down at her gown and let out another gasp.

"Sorry," he said. "I'll buy you another."

"I'm more concerned with what my family will think."

He ran a paint-stained finger down her arm. "They'll think I couldn't help myself, because I'm in love with you. Which is true."

She heaved a frustrated sigh. "It's not that I don't want to believe you. But I need to feel certain, and I can't seem to do that because every time we're together, you make me feel so…"

"In love?" he suggested.

"Confused. I can't think straight when…when you touch me," she finished in a whisper, her cheeks heating. "And I—"

"Oh, Violet!" Rose's voice called sweetly from the front of the house. "Are the two of you all right back there?" Lily's and Rowan's giggles drifted around the corner.

Violet's flush deepened. It was bad enough having to admit such personal things aloud to Ford. She couldn't bear the humiliation if her siblings overheard.

"It seems," Ford said dryly, "that we can't talk in private here. Will you take supper with me tonight?"

"I can't tonight. We're having my favorite, chicken and artichoke pie, to celebrate…" She trailed off, realizing she'd almost revealed to Ford that she'd spent the last few days pleading illness and hiding out in her bedchamber, so her special birthday supper had had to be postponed until tonight. "Um, never mind. At any rate, I'm having supper with my family tonight."

"Will you come after supper, then? Once your family is

abed?"

Her mouth fell open. "Are you...you can't be suggesting I sneak out of my house and come to you? Alone? In the middle of the night?"

"Not alone, no. I'll wait below your window."

"You want me to climb out a window? That would be highly impro—"

"Yes, highly improper. But nothing will happen, I promise. I won't even touch you." To demonstrate, he retreated a step and clasped his hands behind his back. "I want you to be able to think clearly—clear enough to realize the truth."

She crossed her arms over her chest. "Can't I just call on you tomorrow? *With* my parents' permission? Or can you call on me?"

He shrugged. "Wouldn't you rather talk in private—truly in private? We're always getting interrupted by your family, or mine, or my nosy servants. Wouldn't it be nice to have just one conversation without anyone else getting in the way?"

As if to prove Ford's point, Harry suddenly appeared out of nowhere. "Is this the right color, milord?"

Violet jumped.

"Beg pardon, milady." With a heavy grunt, Harry set down two buckets of what looked like paint. "Didn't mean to startle you. Am I interrupting something?" His gaze flicked between Ford and Violet with interest.

The two exchanged a look. Silently, she nodded her assent.

"Not at all, Harry. The color's perfect." Ford clapped his houseman on the shoulder. "Will this do for all the trim?"

Harry laughed. "Not hardly. There's more in the cart." He left, presumably to retrieve the rest.

As Ford walked Violet back to her siblings, she noticed he took care not to touch her. "I'll be there, waiting, at midnight," he said quietly. "Beneath your window."

Under her breath, she muttered, "I am *not* climbing out a window."

FIFTY-EIGHT

*I*N THE END, she didn't climb out a window.

Instead she sneaked out a back door.

Thanks to the state of her gown, Rose and Lily had teased Violet mercilessly all the way home from Lakefield. No matter that she had a reputation for tripping, they'd refused to believe her excuse about stumbling and falling against wet paint.

After bathing and donning a fresh gown, she endured yet more teasing through three courses of supper. Even Father and Mum had joined in. Violet had stared daggers at her siblings, wondering which of them had told their parents about the paint.

By the time she retired to her bedchamber, she was in a stormy mood. This was all Ford's fault, the scoundrel. He'd sent her off in her paint-stained gown with nary a second thought. He'd fed her to the wolves.

Well, he'd pay the price, she vowed, diving into bed and yanking the covers up to her chin.

On no account would she go along with his scheme. Not after what he'd put her through. She was taking the sensible course of action and staying right here. Why should she risk her parents' wrath, not to mention her reputation, for *him*?

When the first faint *tap* of a pebble hitting her window startled her from her vengeful thoughts, she rolled over and closed her eyes. She wasn't going anywhere.

At the second *tap*, her eyes popped open.

When a third pebble hit, she leapt out of bed, fully clothed except for her shoes. Odd, that—she'd honestly meant to go to sleep. But this incessant tapping was keeping her wakeful. She'd just slip back into her shoes, go downstairs, and tell him to leave.

On her way out into the corridor, she snatched up a cloak. Just in case she had to go outside in order to give him a piece of her mind.

It wasn't until she was tiptoeing past Father and Mum's chamber that she admitted the truth: She was going with him.

She was in love. Hopelessly, tragically, insensibly in love. And though she suspected all that would come of it was one more night in Ford's company before her heart broke forever, well, she supposed she'd take what she could get.

Faith, did love make everyone pathetic? Or only her?

Had she not seen, just this afternoon, the very proof of his desperate need for her money? Ford Chase, who'd refused to sell his watch because aristocrats didn't go into trade, was reduced to painting his own house, tending his own gardens. If that wasn't dire straits, she didn't know what was.

Yet some gullible part of her still held out hope that his circumstances were coincidental to—and not the cause of—his suit. Knowing how unlikely that was, dread coursed through her even as she trembled with anticipation.

They had a whole night ahead of them.

Whatever happened, Violet was determined to make her decision by the end of the night. If she couldn't convince herself of his sincerity by then, she never would. And if she remained unconvinced...she would walk away. She could never pledge herself wholeheartedly to a man she didn't trust.

Better to spend the rest of her days lonely in the arms of her family than lonely in a tarnished dream.

She'd only just slipped out the door when she found herself

caught up and swung in a wide circle. "I feared you weren't coming!"

"Hush!" she admonished in a sharp whisper. "We'll be caught."

"Then you'll be forced to marry me." Sounding not at all displeased with that possibility, he set her on her feet. "Apologies, my love—I promised not to touch you. It won't happen again."

"Um, right." She cleared her throat. "I appreciate that."

"Do you?" His smile let her know her disappointment was obvious.

She decided not to dignify that with a response.

"I'm cold," she said instead, hoping he'd mistake her trembling for shivering. "Let's go."

～

*U*PSTAIRS, CHRYSTABEL let the curtain drop closed. "She's not alone, Joseph. Ford was waiting."

"I told you Violet was too smart a girl to go wandering off by herself. Even if she wasn't bright enough to realize we'd notice. Now come back to bed."

"Should we go after her?" She perched herself on the mattress, wrapping her arms around one raised knee as she faced her husband. "Are we doing the right thing?"

"She'll be safe with him."

"My immediate concern is for her virtue, not her safety. Like the *Master-piece* says, she's at that age—"

"Oh, Chrysanthemum, you said yourself we can trust in her good sense." He took one of her hands. "And though I was skeptical at first, I have come around to your way of thinking. I know how overwhelming first loves can be—"

"You remember how it was with us," she interjected with a smile.

He chuckled, his emerald green eyes crinkling around the

edges. Those deep, expressive eyes were the first thing Chrystabel had noticed about him. And they hadn't changed a whit since the day they'd met.

"Indeed. But *unlike* us," he continued, "Violet has kept her head. Instead of rushing into marriage, she's taking time to consider the wisdom of such a choice."

"Too much time, if you ask me," Chrystabel grumbled.

"I know you're frustrated, darling." Joseph tugged gently on the tail of her nighttime plait. "But I, for one, am proud of her."

When Chrystabel didn't immediately respond, he poked her shoulder. "Oh, all right," she conceded, "I'm proud of her, too. I suppose."

"Good. And you agree she's earned our confidence?"

Chrystabel shrugged helplessly. "If seeing Ford alone will help convince her...and you're certain nothing unseemly will happen..." With a gusty sigh, she settled back beneath the covers. "I would't have to fret over her virtue if she'd just see sense—"

"She will. Lakefield is a clever fellow." Joseph planted a kiss on his wife's cheek. "He'll think of something."

FIFTY-NINE

"THIS ROOM doesn't have a door," Violet whispered.

"It's a drawing room," Ford said at a normal volume, rising from the faded red couch. "Most of them don't."

"Shh!" Violet kept picturing Hilda lurking in the corridor, and just her luck, Mum was planning to deliver more Spiced Rosewater perfume tomorrow.

"Relax." Ford crossed to a side table where a jug and two goblets sat at the ready. It seemed he'd prepared for her arrival. "Hilda's and Harry's rooms are at the other end of the house and two floors up. They cannot hear us."

Violet flinched at the clink of drinkware. "What if one of them comes downstairs to use the privy?"

"They won't. They are neither of them used to strong drink, and I insisted on sharing a bottle of sherry sack with them after supper—of which *I* drank very little." Ford grinned, crossing back to the couch with a cup of wine in each hand. "I guarantee no interruptions."

Only somewhat reassured, she accepted her goblet and sipped the white Rhenish wine as Ford settled himself beside her. He sat rather close, although true to his word, no part of them actually touched. Her gaze strayed down to the scant inches that separated them.

After a stretch of silence, she cleared her throat. "Well. Shall we begin?"

"Begin what?"

"The conversation." At his blank stare, she rolled her eyes. "The one where you talk me into believing you're in love with me?"

He looked amused. "What could I possibly say that I haven't already said?"

"Faith, how should I know? This was all your idea." Too irritated for manners, she took a gulp of wine and wiped her mouth with the back of her hand.

Now he looked even more amused. "I had something other than talking in mind."

She narrowed her eyes. "What's that supposed to mean?"

"Telling you that I love you hasn't worked. I was thinking perhaps I'd show you instead."

It took her a moment to grasp his meaning.

Then she leapt off the couch. "Is *that* why you brought me here?" She'd spilled wine on herself, but she hardly noticed in her state of shock.

"What?" Looking equally shocked, Ford rose and cast about for somewhere to put down his own wine. "Violet—no, I—"

"Was your plan to ruin me so I'd have to marry you?" Her voice wobbled, but she held on tight to her outrage, determined not to cry in front of him.

Some new emotion stole over his face, though Violet couldn't make it out until he stepped closer, into the glow from the branch of candles behind her.

White hot rage.

Never in her life had she seen such anger on a person's face. Eyes blazing a brilliant blue, mouth set in a twisted line, he spoke in a voice of deadly quiet. "How dare you?"

She gasped, astounded at his nerve. "How dare *I*?"

His eyes burned into hers for a moment that felt like an eternity. Then he turned away, as if he couldn't bear to look at her anymore, and Violet's heart sank to the vicinity of her stomach. She suddenly feared she'd made a dreadful mistake.

"I don't understand how you can think these things of me," he said toward the wall. He didn't sound angry anymore. He sounded ill. Exhausted. "You call me a liar—yet you must be one yourself, for you once claimed to love me. And you couldn't possibly love someone you believe capable of such cruelty and selfishness."

She opened her mouth to defend herself, but no words came out.

Because he was right.

She did love him, of that she had no doubt. And all the things she loved most about him—his warmth, his generosity, his desire to help people—were the exact opposite of the devious motives she'd just ascribed to him.

How could Ford Chase ever hurt another for his own gain when it was in his very nature to sacrifice his own gain for others? As he'd done with the watch.

And how could she, Violet Ashcroft, aspiring philosopher and lover of reason, have failed to notice such a glaring contradiction?

Well she'd noticed it now, thank heavens. How close she'd come to turning her back on the love of her life. Unless it was already too late…

"Ford?" Cautiously she reached to touch his shoulder. Though his face was still turned away, somehow his posture radiated pain and disillusionment.

He shrugged her off. "I'll take you home."

Tears flooded her eyes. "Ford, I'm sorry." She winced at the inadequacy of the words. "I didn't mean it. I know you would never hurt me—or anyone. You're far too good and honorable for that. And I…"

When she hesitated, his shoulders tensed. He suddenly whirled to face her, and her heart jumped into her throat.

But the fury was gone from his eyes. All she saw there was love. And desperate hope.

Answering hope rose inside her. She wanted to tell him how wrong she'd been about everything, how much she loved him, that she'd be honored to become his wife. But she couldn't seem to find the words. After all she'd put him through, she wanted her declaration to be perfect—

Seeing the light in his eyes begin to fade, she seized his hands and said the first thing that came to mind. "What was it you wanted to show me?"

Some distant part of her observed that his palms felt rough. From the day's renovation work?

Staring down at their joined hands, he made no response.

She looked down, too, and realized she was breaking her own no-touching rule. But she wasn't about to let go of him, not for anything. "You said you didn't want to talk," she prompted him. "You wanted to show me something."

He measured her a moment, then shrugged. "I wanted to show you my plans for the house."

"For fixing it up?" She blinked at him, nonplussed.

"Yes. You see"—he cleared his throat—"I've put a lot of thought into making the place a comfortable home for us. For our family. And perhaps if I could show you how I envision our life together..." He trailed off, his eyes searching hers for a reaction. Violet thought he might be holding his breath.

Her heart melted. "Show me. Please."

SIXTY

"**IS THIS WHERE** you sleep?" Violet asked.

"Yes." Ford gave her hand a squeeze. "This will be our bedchamber. Unless, that is, you prefer your own—"

"No," she said emphatically, making him grin. She blushed and added, by way of explanation, "My parents have always shared a bedchamber."

Leaving her at the threshold, he took the candle around the room and lit others. "I know it doesn't look like much now," he said, watching her take in details as they became visible.

He was trying to see his home as she would. Dominating the chamber was a four-poster so enormous it couldn't possibly fit through the doorway—the bed had to have been built in the room. Fashioned of heavy oak, it was dark with age and smoke from the blackened brick fireplace. Grayish bed-hangings draped from a wooden canopy overhead, looking as though they might once have been rich and possibly blue.

A very long time ago.

Violet's gaze moved over the walls paneled in plain smoke-stained oak divided into squares with simple molding, then paused again on the bed. Another, deeper blush staining her cheeks, she averted her eyes. Ford bit back a smile, presuming the sight had turned her thoughts to their wedding night.

Unless, of course, she was just mortified by the bed's shabby state. But considering they'd been through most every shabby room in the entire shabby house, he doubted an old piece of furniture could shock her now.

She ventured farther into the bedchamber, her head tilting back to examine the beamed ceiling coated in peeling white paint. "It's very...interesting," she said politely.

"I believe it's the ceiling of the original great hall, retained when the floor and fireplace were added some years later."

"Fascinating." After glancing around a bit more, she pointed to an open door across the chamber. "Where does that lead?"

"An attached sitting room. And over here, in this corner, that door leads to a smaller chamber I was thinking could be your dressing room."

Her lips curved in a smile. "That sounds...quite..." She broke off amidst a violent yawn. Her third in the past ten minutes.

"You're tired. Would you like me to take you home?"

"No, I can't leave yet. I need to..." She bit her lip. "Um, see the other bedrooms."

"All right." Ford suspected she'd been about to say something different, but any inclination to remain had to be, in his estimation, a very good sign. It had been a gamble revealing to Violet the full extent of the repairs this house needed. Most women would run in the other direction.

But as he well knew, Violet wasn't most women.

And he could think of no other way to show her what she would be giving up by refusing him. Not only his love, but the home they would make together. The library he'd build for her in the space currently occupied by his study, where she would someday write her book. The enormous dining room—two rooms he was planning to join together—where their big families could gather for Christmas dinner each year. The nursery where their babies would sleep, and extra bedrooms they could move into as they grew older.

Their whole lives together, here in this house.

When he looked around the place now, he didn't see decay and neglect. All he saw were years of love and happiness ahead of them.

Could Violet see it, too?

When he noticed her stifling another yawn, he took her elbow. "At least lie down for a few minutes," he said, steering her toward the bed.

"Oh, I couldn't." Dragging her feet, she eyed the four-poster with trepidation.

"Of course you can. There's nothing improper about it if I'm not in the bed with you. I won't even pull down the covers—don't think of it as a bed, think of it as a handy horizontal surface for resting. Here..." Relinquishing her arm, he dashed to the sitting room.

"Ha!" she called after him. "There's nothing that *isn't* improper about this!"

Returning with a scarred wooden chair, he set it next to the bed and sat on it. "See? I shall sit right here—at a safe distance—while you rest. Please. Otherwise I fear you'll tumble over."

When she still didn't move, he rose and went to her. Ignoring her noise of protest, he lifted her easily into his arms and deposited her on the bed, then pulled off her shoes. She made more noises. But she didn't get up.

"There," he said, reseating himself. "Isn't that more comfortable?" She snorted. He grinned. "Now imagine how comfortable it will be after all of the improvements. Refinished oak, a fresh mattress, new bedhangings—do you like blue?"

"Ford," she said, her voice suddenly serious. Her fingers toyed with the end of her plait. "How will you pay for all of this? Even with my dowry—"

"I'm going to turn the estate around," he rushed to assure her. "My financial position isn't stellar; that much is true. But nor is it dire. If I pour all my funds into the estate instead of my research, I can make it productive again." Raking a hand through his hair, he rose from the chair again and paced. "I'm afraid, love, that we won't be able to fix up the whole house right away. We'll finish the exterior and our bedchamber first, then the main living rooms. And once the estate is turning a profit, we'll be able to pay for the rest. But, Violet—"

He turned and knelt beside the bed. Reaching for her hand, he captured her gaze. In the dim, flickering light, her eyes behind her spectacles looked as dark and fathomless as the night sky.

"Violet, no matter what happens, I will never take your inheritance from you. Not a penny of it. Not ever. You have my word."

Something in those beautiful eyes softened. Shifting onto her side to face him, she set aside her spectacles before lifting her hand to his cheek. Fingertips grazed his jaw so delicately he felt their warmth more than their touch. "Thank you for saying that," she breathed.

Then her hand curled around the back of his neck and dragged his head to hers, and their lips met with an intensity he'd never felt from her before. Or from anyone. Burying her hands in his hair, she rolled onto her back, urging him onto the bed with her.

He hadn't the strength to resist that wordless invitation. Though he'd promised not to touch her, he went. He was touching her already, after all—and she had touched him first.

To lie on a bed with his love was a dream come true, even though they were both fully clothed. He molded the length of his body to hers, feeling fire everywhere they made contact, every nerve he possessed buzzing with overwhelming sensation. Still, he wanted to be even closer, wanted nothing between them, not even a single particle of air. His arms burrowed beneath her, enfolding her, holding her to him as hard as he could while he kissed them both senseless.

A long time later, they finally calmed, then stilled. Lying side by side, facing each other, their ragged breathing was the only sound Ford could hear over the blood pounding in his ears. For a moment, he just drank in the wonder of being here in his bedroom with her. Her gown was all rumpled, and her lips looked deliciously pink and slightly swollen from their kisses.

"I love you," she said quietly, "for what you said. About my inheritance. But it's not necessary."

I love you, she'd said. That had to be a very, *very* good sign. He smoothed back some hair that had escaped her plait. "What do you mean by it's not necessary?"

"When we marry—"

"*When?*" A fist seized his heart. Had he heard correctly? He struggled up on an elbow. "Does that mean you'll agree to marry me?"

Her well-kissed lips spread into that wide, infectious smile that had first made Ford notice her all those weeks ago. She nodded.

Then he could've sworn he died, because his heart exploded with joy. But he didn't care. He was too busy kissing Violet all over again. She felt soft and incredible in his arms, and she smelled like flowers, and she was all his.

"I love you so much," he whispered fiercely, pressing his forehead to hers. Because it was true, and because he wanted to hear her say it again.

"I love you, too," she whispered back, and those three little words warmed him from the inside out, like the strongest, richest brandy imaginable.

They shared one more extraordinarily gentle kiss. "Marry me tomorrow," he said against her lips. "I'll ride to get a special license as soon as the sun comes up—I'll be back with it by nightfall, and we can wed the next morning."

He felt her smile. "I can tell you my mother won't consent to that. She loves weddings—she'll want to invite everyone she knows."

"If she makes us wait, she may not get a wedding at all. I shall expire from anticipation."

She laughed giddily. "Is that so?"

"Quite so. It must be tomorrow. Do you think you can convince her?"

"I doubt it." Pulling back, Violet shrugged. "Why such a hurry? What will happen if we don't get married tomorrow?"

"Nothing will happen—except I'll miss you every single second we're not together."

Her laugh was muffled by the pillow. "I won't be far. Just next door."

"Next door is much too far." Sighing, he rolled onto his back, taking one of her hands with him. His thumb slowly stroked her palm. "Will you try talking to your mother?"

"I'll do my best."

He hoped her best would be enough. How long did it take to plan a large wedding? A month? Two? Even one more night alone in this bed sounded like torture, let alone a few dozen.

"Violet?" he called softly, but there was no answer.

She was sound asleep.

SIXTY-ONE

"JOSEPH?" CHRYSTABEL called softly, shaking her husband's shoulder. Outside their window, the pre-dawn sky was just beginning to turn pink.

He grunted.

"Did you hear Violet come back?"

Another grunt.

Chrystabel's stomach lurched. "Neither did I."

When she climbed out of bed, he cracked one eyelid. "What are you doing?"

"Getting dressed."

Sleep-addled and blinking, he finally sat up. "You don't think...?"

"That she's still at Lakefield?" Pulling a pair of stockings from the clothespress, Chrystabel looked to Joseph with a tight nod.

His jaw slackened. "Oh, Chrysanthemum..."

She realized her hands were shaking. "Darling, I think we've made a terrible mistake."

"*F*ORD, WAKE UP!" Violet shrieked, shaking his shoulder. "I must get home!"

His glorious blue eyes fluttered open, and for a moment all she could think was she wanted to stay in this ancient bed with him. Somehow they'd got under the covers, and he felt impossibly warm and wonderful curled around her.

But *impossible* was the operative word. "It's morning already!" Rolling out of bed, she was relieved to find herself still fully dressed. She had only to step into her shoes and hook her spectacles over her ears.

Groaning, he pulled the covers over his head. "Are you sure?"

"Of course I'm sure!" She yanked the counterpane from his grasp and threw it back. "I cannot believe we both fell asleep."

Heaving on his arm, she eventually managed to maneuver him into a sitting position. He looked boyish and adorable, with his hair all rumpled and the imprint of one of the counterpane's tassels on a cheek—

Faith, there was no time to notice how he looked!

"Ford," she said between gritted teeth, "if I don't get home before my parents wake, there's no telling what they will do. You must take me home! So get up!"

"Criminy, I'm up!" Rubbing his eyes, he staggered to his feet. "Just let me…um, get dressed—"

"You *are* dressed," she protested. "I know you're fastidious about your appearance, but this is no time to fret about fashion—"

"But I have to—well…" His voice trailing off, his gaze strayed toward the chamber pot.

"Oh." Violet blinked. "Oh!" She looked to the window to gauge the time. "We've less than an hour before my parents rise. I'll wait for you downstairs in the entrance hall. Please hurry!"

On her way down the stairs, she smiled at the worn boards that creaked under her feet, at the paneling on the walls that so badly needed refinishing, at the peeling paint on the beams over-head. None of it bothered her. The truth was, the condition of Ford's home didn't overly concern her. She'd just needed to know, deep in her bones, that the man she chose to wed truly loved her. *Her*, Violet, not the financial boon that would come along with her.

And now she did know that, all the way down to her marrow. Though Ford's love had always appeared sincere, she hadn't been able to trust that appearance when it seemed to contradict all reason. But now that she'd realized Ford was inca-pable of committing selfish or evil-intentioned acts—and deceiving her into marriage to get his hands on her inheritance would certainly be a selfish, evil act—she was forced to conclude that Ford was not deceiving her, and therefore his love must be real.

It was deductive reasoning, pure and simple—as practiced by Aristotle himself.

Of course, the conclusion would invalidate one of her other premises: if Ford loved her, the premise that she was unworthy of his love must be false. Though she was having trouble accepting this particular reversal, she had to remind herself she'd been wrong before—about Ford. So very, very wrong.

Perhaps she'd been wrong about herself, too.

Thankfully, the route to the entrance hall proved clear. It seemed Hilda and Harry were still abed. She finger-combed the top of her hair using a spotty old wall mirror with a rusted-out frame, then paced the entrance hall while she waited for Ford and thought about her new life—the wonderful new life the two of them would have together, here at Lakefield.

The life that could begin tomorrow—if she could somehow persuade Mum to forego the extravagant wedding. Which was an enormous *if*.

But even if she had to wait several weeks or months—and even apart from her profound feelings for Ford himself—she was excited by the prospect of moving to Lakefield House. She felt a growing kinship with the queer old manor. She supposed in some ways the place reminded her of her eccentric family—a little disregarded, a little misunderstood. She couldn't wait to help restore it to its former glory.

She expected her dowry would cover the immediate renovations. That ought to leave more of his funds available to improve the estate, which in turn would allow it to run more profitably. She was anxious to go over Ford's plans. Since she wouldn't be publishing her book for many years, she planned to suggest they use her inheritance to accelerate the improvements. The investment would surely come back to her long before she needed it.

Now that she knew Ford wasn't marrying her for her inheritance, she wouldn't mind him making use of it. In fact, it made little sense to let all that money sit idle for years.

Her gaze went up the empty staircase. What was taking him so long? Wondering if the sun was over the horizon yet, she jerked open the front door.

A shocked face was on the other side. Violet screamed, and the young boy turned tail and began running.

"Wait!" she called.

He stopped and pivoted back. "I have a letter, madam." Rather cautiously, he approached the door, holding forth a rectangle of sealed parchment. "Will you give this to the lord?"

"Of course. Let me just...wait." Below the mirror, she'd noticed a bowl of coins sitting on a marble table that needed a serious buffing. Dashing inside to retrieve a coin, she pressed it into the boy's hand on her return. "Thank you."

He touched his cap and took off.

She slowly closed the door, turning the letter in her hands. It looked long and very official. There was no return address, but she hoped...could it be from Daniel Quare, the watchmaker?

Her heart pounded at the thought.

She sent a furtive glance up the stairs before slipping her fingernail under the seal.

My dearest Lord Lakefield, she read. *It is my sad duty to inform you that I have received a foreclosure notice on your estate.*

Her blood seemed to freeze in her veins as her eyes skimmed down the letter.

…you have thirty days…

…mortgage in arrears…

…tenants may face eviction…

The parchment fluttered to the floor, her heart sinking along with it.

"You've dropped something."

Startled, she whirled around to see Ford reaching the bottom stair. He approached and knelt to retrieve the fallen letter. "What's this?"

"A letter—" Her voice came out hoarse. She cleared her throat. "A letter for you."

Frowning, Ford turned the sheet over. She watched his expressions change as he read the first few lines. Surprise. Anger. Horror. Finally raising his eyes to her, he opened his mouth.

But she jumped in first. "You lied to me."

He looked genuinely confused—but then, she already knew he had a talent for pretending. "What did I lie about?"

"I believe the term you used was 'not dire.' In reference to your estate—the estate you're apparently about to lose."

"I didn't know!"

She gave a dry, brittle laugh. "How stupid do you think I am? You met with your solicitor less than a week ago, yet you expect me to believe he didn't mention any of this?"

"I swear to you, I didn't realize—"

"Save your breath." She sucked in her own breath as another realization hit her. "This is why you were so insistent about marrying quickly, isn't it? You knew you'd need my money soon. Or you meant to secure my vows before I caught wind of the truth. Or both."

What will happen if we don't marry today? she'd asked him.

Nothing will happen…

Another lie.

Your tenants may face eviction.

With this letter, the last puzzle pieces fell into place. She'd believed it was logically impossible for Ford to be both a well-meaning person and a selfish liar. And she'd been right. But if he was in fact a *selfless* liar…if he sought her fortune for the purpose of saving his tenants from eviction, rather than merely enriching himself…

Well, that wasn't a contradiction at all. It was perfectly in line with his character.

And what's more, it was a better explanation than Ford loving her, since it also left that one troublesome premise intact. She'd been right there, too: a man as handsome and brilliant and good as Ford Chase—and despite her pain and fury, she still thought him good at heart, for his deception was meant to serve the good of others—could never love someone like Violet.

"I knew it was too good to be true," she whispered, her soul splintering into a thousand pieces.

She whirled to leave, but he seized her arm. "Violet, *stop*. I…I know this looks bad. But I swear to you, on everything there is to swear on, that I love you. *I love you.* Isn't that all that really matters? Please—whatever else you may think of me, whatever lies you think I've told—at least say you still believe my feelings are real. If you believe that, I know everything else can be fixed." Incredibly, his eyes brimmed with unshed tears.

He'd missed his calling with science; he belonged on the stage.

"I let you fool me once," she said, wrenching her arm from his grip. Finally she was able to reach the door latch. "But rest assured, I'm a fast learner."

"Violet—"

She was already out the door.

But she didn't make it far. On the last step down, she stopped dead in her tracks, though she suspected Ford wasn't far behind.

Which was worse, she wondered…the heartache behind, or the carnage ahead?

"Are those your parents?" Ford had reached the step above her.

Violet couldn't seem to move. Wonderful. Apparently she'd be forced to manage both nightmares simultaneously.

Barreling forth from the Trentingham carriage, Father and Mum advanced with more menace than a thousand-strong army. Violet didn't know whether to cower or weep. She felt rather inclined to both.

"*What* have you done to my daughter?"an enraged Mum hollered.

While at the same time Father bellowed, "Lakefield, you're marrying my daughter *tomorrow!*"

SIXTY-TWO

*F*ORECLOSURE.

The single word was like a jab to Ford's gut. More than an hour after receiving the blasted letter, he still frantically paced the laboratory, reading and rereading it. He'd had no idea his situation was this bad. Never again would he allow himself to stay ignorant of his finances.

He'd thought if he put his mind to the task—and the funds he usually spent on his science into the estate—he could make Lakefield profitable and dig himself out of debt. And that was true, according to his solicitor. But now it would be much more difficult than he'd imagined.

Foreclosure.

In lieu of selling or surrendering the estate, his solicitor had outlined an emergency plan to save it, but it certainly didn't include funds for the cosmetic restorations Ford had promised Violet. All of his income would have to go into the fields, purchasing livestock, fixing the stables, and repairing crofters' cottages so new tenants would have a place to live.

And foreclosure wasn't the worst of his troubles...

The scene with Violet's parents had been bad, but the way he'd left things with Violet herself was unbearable.

In the wee hours of the morning, he'd finally managed to earn her trust. He'd seen it in her eyes, felt it in her touch. Before, there had always been a part of her holding back from him, measuring his actions, questioning his motives, although he hadn't realized it. Not until last night, when he'd watched the mistrust begin to melt away.

But now her faith in him was destroyed, and Ford was back to square one. Worse than square one. Square *negative* one. Square negative *one hundred*. He saw approximately zero chance of Violet ever trusting him again.

And she would be forced to marry him tomorrow. He should be riding toward London right now, not pacing and stewing. Westminster and the Archbishop of Canterbury were a long ride away, and he needed that special license before the wedding.

How would it feel to be wed to someone who despised him? Even though her accusations were false—he really hadn't known foreclosure was imminent—he couldn't deny that he had let her down. He'd promised to care for her, provide her a decent home, and leave her inheritance untouched. But now he couldn't do any of those things, thanks to his own wretched shortsightedness. And incompetence.

"My lord?"

Ford whirled to face the door. "Please leave me alone, Harry."

"But I have a letter for you. Just delivered from Trentingham."

A letter from Violet! His heart leaping with hope, Ford dropped the loathsome foreclosure letter and paced over to retrieve the one from Violet.

Except it wasn't—instead of her tidy hand, a masculine scrawl marched across the page:

Lakefield,

I hope this missive finds you before you ride for London, because you won't be marrying my daughter tomorrow. Or ever. Violet explained everything. While I thank you for not compromising her virtue—and I thank our Lord that no one else knows she spent the night in your home, leaving her reputation intact—it is clear she feels the two of you aren't suited.

Trentingham

"My lord? Are you all right?"

"I told you to leave."

While Harry complied, Ford stumbled over to lean against the wall. Then slid down it to sit on the floor, because his legs refused to hold him up even one second longer.

Violet was gone.

She wouldn't be married to him and despise him.

She wouldn't be in his life at all.

And given his current circumstances—circumstances he'd brought upon himself—he saw no way to win her back.

He could tell her he loved her a thousand more times, but as long as he remained low on funds, she would never stop wondering if he wanted her for her money. And it would take years of careful management to fill Lakefield's coffers. Surely by that time, she'd have accepted someone else's proposal.

The loss was a physical ache deep inside him. Empty years yawned ahead. Usually he'd fill them with scientific pursuits, but for now—and the foreseeable future—he couldn't afford to do that. Besides, pouring all those hours into such tiny advancements suddenly seemed pointless. He knew, with a certainty that crushed him, he'd never again find the same satisfaction in his experiments and innovations. Not without Violet here to share his successes. Not even if Rand managed to—

His thoughts whirled and skidded, his fist closing around Lord Trentingham's letter. After a moment, the crumpled parchment fell to the floor.

SIXTY-THREE

*V*IOLET LOOKED UP from her philosophy book, muttering under her breath. She'd read the same page four times and still didn't understand it. It had been three days since the morning her parents hauled her home from Ford's house—three days during which she couldn't concentrate on anything and snapped at everyone within earshot.

"Violet?"

Exasperated, she swung toward the door. "Yes?" she spit out, then bit her lip. Her mother didn't deserve her misplaced ire. Especially considering how sympathetic and forgiving she'd been about Violet's midnight escapade—once she'd calmed down enough to hear her daughter's account.

Of course, Violet had had to endure quite a bit of hollering first. She could still detect a faint ringing in her ears.

Regardless, it wasn't Mum's fault that Violet was too plain and odd to find true love.

She closed her eyes momentarily, then opened them, drawing on her last reserve of patience. "What is it, Mum?"

"There's a gentleman here to see you. Not Ford," she added in a rush, and Violet was chagrined, knowing the leap of hope must have shown in her eyes. "His friend," Mum said gently. "Lord Randal Nesbitt."

Rand? Why would Ford's friend want to see *her*? "Are you sure he isn't here to see Rose, Mum? She's the one who likes languages."

"He asked for you. He's waiting in the drawing room."

Sighing, she reached for her spectacles. In a fit of melancholy that terrible morning, she'd tried to put them away in a drawer, because they'd reminded her too much of Ford. Of her dreams, dashed and broken. But after three or four hours of walking around half blind, she'd decided that was ridiculous. She wasn't going to forget him anyway, and there was no point in bumping into things for the rest of her life.

She slid them on and made her way downstairs to the drawing room.

When Violet entered the chamber, Lord Randal stood. "Ford doesn't know that I'm here, my lady, and I'd prefer to keep it that way."

"As you wish." She waved him back to the cream-colored chair and took the matching one for herself. "What's this all about?"

Mum had served him tea and left another cup on the table for Violet. Rand raised his cup and sipped. "Ford wrote to me two days ago, and I thought you should know."

"Know what?" Taking a biscuit from a tray, she nervously broke off a piece. "I'm confused. I can't imagine what you mean."

He inclined his head. "My apologies. I'm just so shocked, I wasn't sure how to...well...he asked me to sell *Secrets of the Emerald Tablet*. To take bids on it and then contact Mr. Isaac Newton."

"Sell *Secrets of the Emerald Tablet*?" Unheeded, crumbs sprinkled her lap. She remembered Ford clutching the book the day he found it. His declaration that he'd never sell it. His eyes glittering with excitement every time another bit was deciphered. "It's his favorite thing in the world, his chance to discover the Philosopher's Stone and bring it to all of humanity. He'd never sell it."

"Never say never." Casting her a wry look, Lord Randal used his napkin to dab a drip of tea from his mustache. "According to Ford, Newton has offered to pay double the highest bid, and he wishes to collect. It's the only path he can see clear to winning your heart."

That heart skipped a beat. Involuntarily, Violet pressed a hand to her chest. "I don't understand…"

Appearing thoughtful, he passed his tongue over his teeth. " I've known Ford since we were lads together at Oxford, but never have I known him in love. Until now."

"You're mistaken, my lord."

"What makes you think so?"

She rolled her eyes. "Look at me, Lord Randal. Really look. I'm not a girl who inspires love—"

"What are you *talking* about?" he interrupted.

She lifted her cup and sat straighter in her chair. "I have a mirror, and two good eyes." Her free hand went to her beloved spectacles. "Well, bad eyes, actually, until Ford made me these, but—"

"Two good eyes and half a brain," he interrupted again.

She must warn Rose he had terrible manners, she thought absurdly.

Then his intense gray gaze pierced hers, demanding her attention. "Ford loves you, Lady Violet. And no matter what you think, you're a fine-looking girl, but that's not the reason why. He loves your spirit and your intelligence and the way you listen to his ideas. And the way you have ideas of your own."

"And he loves my money."

"No. That he hates. Because it's the reason you won't take him at his word." He gave her a moment to digest that. "Ford is a third son, the third son of a man who squandered the family fortune fighting the king's war. Under the circumstances, he's doing all right for himself. He's in a bit of financial trouble now, but nothing he cannot handle if he moves carefully, except—"

"His estate is being foreclosed upon."

Lord Randal grimaced. "The foreclosure is a fact, but beside the point. He's working with his solicitor to resolve that."

She looked down at her cup, held between trembling hands. Could that be possible? She hadn't read the entirety of that long letter.

"Ford's problem, Lady Violet"—he waited for her to look up —"is he's lacking enough funds to both rescue his estate and remodel it for you as he promised."

"Which is the reason he wants my money."

"No. He's convinced you won't wed him unless he has enough money that you'll be forced to believe he doesn't need yours, which is why he's selling the book." He paused to let that sink in. "He's trading the book for *you*, Violet."

"Oh, good heavens." Her cup clattered to the table, and she dropped her head in her hands.

Ford loved her.

He'd told her so, over and over, and she'd stubbornly rebuffed him. She'd questioned his honor at every turn, taken any excuse to keep her defenses raised. Not even his extraordinarily charming tour through the home he'd dreamed up for her could make her admit what she knew in her heart...

Ashamed, she felt hot tears prick her eyes. That he would go to the point of selling his most cherished possession...

"I cannot let him do it."

Lord Randal stood and, raising her from the chair, wrapped his arms around her shuddering form. "I was hoping you'd say that."

SIXTY-FOUR

"FATHER," VIOLET said loudly, "I'd like the use of my inheritance."

Seated across from her at the library's round table, Joseph glanced at Chrystabel before looking back to their daughter. "Have you an investment in mind?"

"No. Well, yes." She lifted her chin. "An investment in my future."

Chrystabel barely suppressed a smile. "Can you explain yourself, dear? This is very confusing."

"Ford is planning to sell *Secrets of the Emerald Tablet*. I wish to buy it."

Joseph frowned. "You hardly need your inheritance to buy a book."

"This book costs ten thousand pounds."

Watching her husband's jaw drop open, Chrystabel reached beneath the table to take his hand. "Why do you want to buy it?" she asked Violet calmly.

She thought she knew the answer. She *hoped* she knew the answer. And when tears sprang to her daughter's eyes, she knew she knew the answer.

"He's s-selling it," Violet stuttered out, "so he can fix up his house and win *me*."

"Then let him do it," Joseph said. "You don't need to spend your—" He broke off when Chrystabel kicked him under the table. "What the—"

"What your father means to ask," she interrupted, laying her free hand on Violet's arm, "is what you intend to do with the book once you have it?"

Her daughter's eyes cleared, and she drew a deep breath. "Why, give it back to him, of course. As a wedding present."

"Oh, dear." Chrystabel's own eyes glazed over. Her eldest was getting married. "I was hoping you'd say that."

~

*H*ER PARENTS watched while Lord Randal handed Violet the book. She clutched it to her chest, wishing she were clutching its owner instead. But she hoped to be holding Ford soon enough.

"Father's solicitor will send the money tomorrow. You won't tell Ford who really bought it, will you? Even though he's your friend?"

"My best friend. But I wouldn't dream of it. Your secret is safe with me."

"You're a good friend, Rand."

He nodded toward the book. "So are you."

She sent him a tremulous smile. Ford would have her inheritance now, but if she felt a tiny pang at the loss of her own dream to publish a book, it was completely eclipsed by the joy of finding love. True love. A lifetime of love was so much more precious than any academic goal she might reach as a lonely old lady.

"Thank you, Rand. For everything."

"You're more than welcome." He turned to leave, then swiveled back. "Where's your sister Lily?"

"Oh, outside, I'm sure. Tending to her poor, bedraggled menagerie."

His eyes lit, and he looked to her father. "May I have your permission to stop and visit with her?"

Father blinked. "What?"

"Joseph," Mum explained loudly, "Lord Randal is asking if he might visit with Lily."

"I have lilies in the garden."

"Of course you do, darling." She smiled at Rand. "Go ahead. I expect Lily will be pleased. But she's young yet, Lord Randal. So visiting is all that will happen."

Wide-eyed, he nodded and left.

Slack-jawed, Violet turned to her mother. "Lily?" she asked. "What about Rose? If she hears of this, she'll be furious."

"I'm not telling her," Mum said. "Are you?"

"Absolutely not."

"Tell who what?" asked Father.

SIXTY-FIVE

THREE WEEKS LATER, Ford paced Lakefield House, satisfied with the progress of the renovations. Not that everything was complete—even with an army of skilled laborers, there was only so much one could accomplish in three weeks. But the roof was sound, and the exterior was a gleaming white. The garden had been cleared, and if it couldn't yet rival the lush beauty of Trentingham, at least it was tidy.

Ford could easily find his sundial now. A quick glance told him it was nearly noon—nearly time for Violet to arrive.

He felt as though he'd waited his entire life for this moment. Thanks to the sale of *Secrets of the Emerald Tablet*, Lakefield shone not only in ways that showed, but behind the scenes. The latest farming implements were on order, and tenants were moving into the newly refinished cottages. The estate hummed with productive energy and the promise of more to come. The threat of foreclosure was behind him, and despite spending a prodigious amount of money to accomplish his goals, he had enough funds remaining to live well for a few months until Lakefield started producing the respectable income it should.

He'd been surprised to discover he didn't mind the labors of a landowner, either. It seemed to him that striving to improve a theory or technology was not so very different from improving the land. Both required experimentation, innovation, and highly specialized knowledge—the last of which Ford was currently acquiring from a very patient Lord Trentingham. He'd never been given to think of agriculture as a science, but he was finding it every bit as complex and fascinating as the other branches. Perhaps someday he'd propose a lecture on the subject to the Royal Society.

Ford knew now, beyond any doubt, that selling the book had been the right decision—and, perhaps for the first time in his life, the *responsible* decision. He no longer faced the months and years ahead with dread, but rather with anticipation of watching his efforts and investments pay off.

While he wouldn't be renowned for bringing the Philosopher's Stone to the world, Violet meant the world to him, anyway. If he could only see that look of approval return to her eyes, he'd know her love for him had endured.

He'd know all his sacrifices had been worth it.

His stomach knotted at the sight of an approaching carriage.

Here was his moment of truth.

He'd done right by Lakefield and all its people. He'd secured a future for his tenants and his children, and his own future along with it.

But if Violet refused to share it with him, it would be a bleak future indeed.

SIXTY-SIX

*A*FTER WAITING what seemed an eternity while she wondered what, exactly, Ford was doing with the money from her inheritance, Violet had been unnerved when a note arrived inviting her entire family to dine at Lakefield House this afternoon.

Now on their way, she twisted her hands in her lap, not really listening to her sisters' and Rowan's chatter filling the carriage.

As they approached Lakefield, she leaned to part the carriage curtains, spotting bright white repaired and repainted cottages along the way. They had been so dilapidated she'd hardly even noticed them before, but now children were playing outside of them and at least two dozen workers were reroofing and painting yet more.

Ford's tenants were not being evicted. Instead, it seemed many more had moved in.

Mum placed gentle fingers over Violet's busy ones. "Are you ready?"

"For what?" Rose asked.

Violet exchanged a glance with Mum. "Just to visit," she said in as offhand a manner as she could. "You needn't read something into every sentence."

"What are you reading?" Father asked.

"Dear heavens." Violet took a deep breath as the carriage rolled to a stop. They were here. Whatever was going to happen would happen now. She'd never considered herself much of an actress, but she had a role to play today, and she intended to do it well.

Ford greeted them outdoors with a formal reserve that did nothing to relax her, inviting them all for a tour of the house before dinner. Violet followed him, wondering what her parents would think, whether they would still bless this possible marriage when they saw his shabby surroundings.

But then she stepped inside.

The old dark paneling in the entrance hall was now a honeyed tone, and their first tour stop was the drawing room, where the floor had been stripped and polished, the walls painted a soft turquoise in place of the faded red.

"This is lovely," Rose said in awe.

Had Rose seen the place last month, Violet thought, she'd be making one of her saucebox remarks instead.

But the room *was* lovely. Unbelievably lovely.

"I still need to order furniture," Ford explained, "and draperies." He looked to Violet. "I've no eye for decor, so I'm hoping for help with that."

She nodded, hoping he was hoping for *her* help.

His study was similarly refurbished, done in shades of cinnamon and olive green. New, empty bookshelves lined all four walls.

"A library," she breathed.

"That's a rather feminine desk," Rose pointed out.

"Indeed, it is," Ford agreed. "I've moved my own desk upstairs, to the back of the laboratory."

Gone was the ugly brown decor in the dining room, replaced with walls of deep burgundy to set off the refinished cabinetry. A wall had been removed to include the room next door.

Hilda was setting the old table, which now looked too small

for the expanded space. "It will be half an hour or more before dinner," she told Ford, "but I've set out some victuals in the garden."

"We're going there straight after our tour," he assured her.

"The garden?" asked Father.

Hilda smiled and raised her voice. "If you'll but wait a moment, Lord Trentingham, I'll show you outside."

The rest of them headed upstairs. The staircase had new, polished balusters, and the steps didn't creak. "I've hired a cook," Ford told Violet as they climbed, "so Hilda is just a house-keeper now."

In Ford's bedchamber, the peeling ceiling had been stripped, revealing dark beams with colorful painted designs from some fanciful former owner. "It's changed so much," Violet marveled.

Lily's eyes went wide. "You've been in here before?"

Violet's face burned. "Not *here*. I meant the house in general."

The chamber looked entirely different. The massive oak canopy bed had been refinished to a warm tone, and the old bed-hangings were gone. The attached room had been opened to combine with this one, providing a spacious sitting area.

"What is this?" Rose asked, opening a door on the other side of the chamber.

The small room beyond was clean and painted but yet empty. "It will be a dressing room," Ford said, looking to Violet and making her blush again.

"'You cannot conceal love or a cough,'" Rowan read slowly, and she turned gratefully to see an inscription above the door.

"That was there already," Ford rushed to explain, looking a little uneasy at hearing the romantic sentiment aloud. "We found it beneath layers of paint."

Mum smiled. "It's a clever turn of phrase."

He nodded, shooting Violet a significant glance. "I suppose I agree with it, too."

"You should marry him," Rose whispered to Violet as they left the room. "He even has a nice house."

For once, Violet wasn't tempted to slap her middle sister. And if she was reading Ford's silent messages correctly, she had reason to hope he would ask her to marry him again.

Buoyed by optimism, she practically floated into the next room, a small one painted pale green.

Ford told them it was "Jewel's room."

"Will Jewel come to visit and sleep here?" Rowan asked.

"I hope so."

"Me, too." Now that Rowan was no longer scratching, it seemed he'd forgotten that Jewel had laughed at him. "May we go to the laboratory?"

First Ford walked them through two more bedchamber-sized rooms with new walls that weren't painted yet. Then they all trooped up to the attic. The old desk at the far end was the only change in the laboratory, but Violet wouldn't have wanted it to see it any different. The room was Ford, plain and simple.

She didn't remember drifting down the stairs, but a few minutes later they'd joined her father in the garden, where he was in the middle of explaining the newest pruning techniques to poor old Harry.

Leaving her family to the refreshments Hilda had set out, Ford drew Violet aside. "Come with me," he whispered. "I've something else to show you." And he walked her around the corner of the house.

There, hanging from three oaks, were three swings: two regular swings and one wider version that was more than just ropes and a board. It had a back and armrests as well.

A swing for two.

"For us," Ford said softly, taking her hand to lead her toward it. "I remembered how you like to swing."

"Not too high," she reminded him, suddenly nervous. "I notice you didn't hang them on trees near the river. Are the other two for Jewel and Rowan?"

"For now." His hand squeezed hers. "But I hope other children will use them someday. Our children."

"Ford..." Faith, how did one tell someone she wanted to spend the rest of her life with him? She had no experience with this sort of thing.

But he didn't seem to be expecting an answer now. Reaching the double swing, he smiled and said, "Sit," just like that day on the riverside.

Slanting him a glance, she did so, and he stepped behind her. She waited for him to push, but instead he tilted her back, drew off her spectacles, and lowered his mouth to hers in an upside-down kiss.

A kiss that made Violet's heart turn upside down, too.

It was a good thing she was seated, she thought as he drew away and the swing bobbed upright. She doubted her weakened knees could have supported her.

He gave her a gentle push. "What do you think of the house?"

"I think..." Here came the acting. She wouldn't dream of ruining the surprises—either his to her now, or hers to him later —by revealing she'd been the one to buy the book. Even though the white lie weighed a bit on her conscience, that wouldn't be fair to either of them.

"I think I'm confused," she said, thankful he couldn't see her face. Without her spectacles, the river looked blurry in the distance.

He pushed her again. "Confused about what, my love?"

The endearment filled her with a cautious thrill. "About everything. Why was this place so run down if you could afford to fix it up? Just because you couldn't be bothered?"

"No," he said without hesitation. He wasn't going to try to hide anything from her, and she loved him all the more for it. "I thought I could afford to fix it up, but that turned out not to be true. Until I asked Rand to sell *Secrets of the Emerald Tablet* for me." He walked around to face her. "He got ten thousand pounds."

She gasped. "Ten thousand pounds! Why...that's as much as

my inheritance!"

"I know." Gripping one rope, he stopped the swing and slid onto it beside her. "It's amazing, isn't it? I suspect the buyer was Isaac Newton, since he'd pledged to double any other bid, but Rand told me the purchase was made on condition of anonymity."

"I wouldn't want anyone knowing I owned such a valuable thing, either." That much, at least, was the truth. "I expect it would make him a target for robbery."

"Perhaps." Raking a hand through his hair, Ford scooted closer, close enough to be in focus. He captured her gaze with his glorious blue eyes. "I hope this will change your mind."

"Ford, I must apologize—"

"In a matter of months, Lakefield will be earning a tidy profit. And in the meantime, I have more than enough funds to finish the improvements I told you about." He pushed off with his feet, setting the swing to swaying. "You can marry me now without fear that I'll spend your inheritance and rob you of your publishing dream."

Her heart throbbed in her chest. "Is that what you thought? That I valued a philosophy book over you?"

Suddenly she could see where he could have inferred as much, and her shame escalated beyond bearing. Her throat tightened painfully.

"I would never put a book before you," she choked out. He hadn't valued a book over her, either. He'd sold his precious alchemy book for her. "Never. It's just...well, I couldn't bring myself to believe any man would want me for myself." She gave a mournful shake of her head, her gaze trained on her lap. "It was my failing, not yours. And I'm so very sorry."

Tears welled, and one rolled down her cheek.

She wasn't acting now.

He reached to wipe away the teardrop, his fingers soft and warm on her skin. "Egad, don't cry. Please. Just say yes." As the swing slowed to a halt, he pulled in a deep breath. "Will you marry me, Violet?"

This time she didn't hesitate. "I'd be honored."

He caught her up in a hug so tight it threatened to crack her ribs. "I love you," he said. "Have I told you I love you?"

"Most generously." She laughed through her tears. "I must catch up."

His eyes looked anxious. "Please do."

She graced his lips with the softest, most cherishing kiss she could contrive. "I love you, Ford Chase." Missing the feel of his warm, tender mouth on hers, she sought it again.

As he pulled her closer and deepened the kiss, she sank into a heartfelt embrace that told her she was his—and his alone. She hadn't known it, but she'd been waiting for this all her life. This love, this trust, this acceptance of her just as she was.

She loved him. Here, now, today, tomorrow, for all time.

"I love you," she repeated breathlessly when he finally pulled back.

A smile curved his lips as he toyed with the end of her plait. "Before you change your mind, I expect I should ask your father for your hand."

"Is that why you invited my whole family? Planning ahead?" she teased, reaching to his pocket for her spectacles. "All right, then. Just don't forget to shout."

~

"SIX MONTHS," Mum said after the congratulations and the hugs and the kisses. "It will take that long to arrange everything and allow people time to make plans to attend."

"Tomorrow," Ford countered loudly, evidently remembering Violet's instruction to shout.

"Tomorrow!" Rose snorted. "That's preposterous! It's too late in the day to get a special license in time for tomorrow. And

Madame Beaumont cannot make a wedding gown by tomorrow, either."

Ford turned to Violet. "Tell me you're not going to London to order a gown."

She shrugged. She was a newcomer to caring about fashion and knew nothing about planning events. "Three months?"

"One week."

At that point, her father pulled her mother aside for a whispered conversation. Mum's feminine laughter trilled over Ford's neat new garden.

"Two weeks," she said, "and that's final."

SIXTY-SEVEN

*T*WO WEEKS LATER, in the wee hours of the night before her wedding, Violet found herself wide awake for the last time in her childhood bed.

The house was quiet, but her mind was whirling with anticipation, excitement, and plans. Unable to sleep or read with her thoughts in such disarray, she was absently flipping through the pages of the *Master-piece* when she noticed something odd.

In one particular section, the pages felt different.

She shut the book. The section *looked* different, too. Its pages didn't lie as flat as the rest.

Dragging the candle on her night table nearer, she reopened the book—then blinked and peered closer.

The pages looked as if they'd been cut out and then reattached, messily stitched back onto the cut edge, as if the job had been done in haste.

How had she not noticed this before? Her brow furrowed, she paged back to the beginning of the section. *Chapter Seventeen: A Word of Advice to Both Sexes, Being Several Directions Respecting Copulation.*

"Hang it!" she remembered Rose saying. *"Someone ruined the book!"*

And Lily: *"Who would do such a thing?"*

Violet gasped in sudden horror.

Mum!

~

*T*HE NEXT MORNING, Margaret finished threading a pale blue ribbon through the back of Violet's hair and tweaked one of the fat, springy curls she'd so painstakingly created.

At last, Violet's wedding day had arrived.

The days since her betrothal had been excruciating. All of a sudden, her parents had become oddly vigilant, when earlier they'd seemed so permissive. She hadn't found more than five minutes alone with Ford at any one time. They'd scarcely stolen a single kiss.

"Why are you smiling?" Rose asked, watching Violet's face in her dressing table mirror. "Brides are supposed to be nervous."

"I'm not," Violet told her. In truth, she was a bit nervous— but only a bit. This marriage was so *right*. How could Mum have ever imagined Ford was too intellectual for her? Was her mother losing her matchmaking touch?

When her maid left, she stood and turned to face her sisters.

"You look beautiful," Lily breathed.

Today, in her pale blue satin wedding gown, Violet *felt* beautiful, whether she actually believed she was or not. Smiling to herself, she absently traced the pearls embroidered in scrolling designs on her bodice—which was every bit as tailored to her form as the gown that had riveted Ford the night of the Royal Society celebration. But this time she didn't feel self-conscious. She was seeing herself in a new light. What did it matter if she'd never be as pretty as her sisters? The man she loved wanted her, and that was all that counted.

"You should leave off your spectacles," Rose said. "At least for the ceremony."

"No." She wanted to see everything clearly, especially Ford's eyes when they exchanged vows. "Ford said I look fine in them. And I believe him."

"I told you that you should marry him," Rose gloated. "Just think," she continued, her tone changing to one of half awe, half envy. "Tonight you're going to experience the secrets of *Aristotle's Master-piece*."

"Oh, Rose," Lily started, but then a knock came at the door and she went to answer it.

"A delivery," the majordomo said, holding out a small, long box. "From Lord Lakefield to Lady Violet."

"Thank you, Parkinson." Lily shut the door and carried the wooden box over to Violet. "What do you suppose it could be?"

"Diamonds, I'm sure," Rose said. "It's a wedding present, after all."

"I think not." Generous though he might be, Ford was focused on the estate these days, and Violet doubted he had enough of her ten thousand pounds left to feel comfortable spending money on diamonds.

The box was tied—very crookedly—with a purple ribbon Violet thought she remembered seeing in Jewel's hair. "Open it," Rose said, reaching for it. "I'm dying to see what he gave you."

Violet pushed her sister's hand away and untied the bow herself. The object inside was wrapped in blue brocade fabric, which she quickly unfurled.

"Oh, how lovely," Lily gasped.

"Gemini!" Rose's mouth hung open. "Even I would wear those!"

With trembling fingers, Violet lifted an exquisitely crafted pair of eyeglasses. Around flawless lenses were elegant gold wire frames, worked all over in the most delicate, intricate tracery imaginable, and studded with tiny purple stones. They were more beautiful than any piece of jewelry Violet had ever owned.

Removing her plain spectacles and placing them in the gift

box, she slowly, reverently slid the gold spectacles into place and moved to the mirror. And gasped.

They looked beautiful. *She* looked beautiful. For the first time in her life, she felt like the prettiest girl in the room.

Lily was beaming. "I told you eyeglasses suit your face," she reminded Violet. "Do you believe me now?"

Violet nodded without turning her head. She couldn't seem to tear her eyes away from the mirror.

But eventually she had to, because it was time to go to the chapel. She tucked the box with the plain spectacles into her satchel, alongside her night things and her own wedding gift to Ford. She planned to present it to him later, when they were alone.

On their wedding night.

During which, as Rose had helpfully pointed out, Violet would be initiated into the secrets of the marriage bed. She was glad she'd had the *Master-piece* to help prepare her for the evening ahead, even if she remained horrified that Mum knew she'd been reading it.

Yet somehow she still felt entirely unprepared. She pressed a hand to her chest, wondering when her heart had begun thumping.

Perhaps she was more nervous than she'd thought.

SIXTY-EIGHT

*A*S EVENING FELL, it began to rain. Violet stood with Ford and her family within Trentingham's covered portico, watching the last of the guests sprint to their carriages while she waited to say good-bye to her father.

"It was a nice wedding," Mum said, "wasn't it?"

Violet sighed. "I can hardly remember it."

"Perhaps you've had too much champagne?" Ford flashed a mischievous smile. "I remember it perfectly. A rather solemn ceremony, right here in Trentingham's chapel." It hadn't been solemn at all. Violet's lips twitched as he continued. "I have lingering impressions of much Tudor woodwork and jewel-toned stained glass, with my beautiful bride a glorious vision in blue."

Lily giggled. She'd definitely had some champagne. "I cannot believe so many people showed up with only two weeks' notice! All of Father's friends from Parliament, and your friends from the Royal Society—"

"And everyone Mum knows," Rose cut in. She was *still* drinking champagne. "Which means everyone who lives within a twenty-mile radius."

Ignoring her middle daughter, Mum smiled at Ford. "You have very nice friends."

Although Violet would swear her mother had once referred to Ford's friends as "that odd group of scientists," today she'd seemed to hang on their every word. "I saw you chatting with Mr. Hooke's 'housekeeper,'" she teased Mum.

"I enjoyed chatting with Rand," Rose said dreamily, taking another sip. "And dancing with him."

Rand had danced with Lily more often, but apparently Rose hadn't noticed. Meeting Lily's guilty gaze, Violet decided to hold her tongue on that subject. "I think at least two hundred people tried on my spectacles. My face hurts from smiling."

"My poor wife." Ford pulled her close. "You're not used to being the center of attention," he teased, kissing her softly.

"Ewww." Rowan made a face. "More kisses."

Everyone laughed. Earlier, Jewel had informed Rowan her Auntie Cait said kissing was encouraged at weddings, then planted one smack on his lips. Violet had never seen anyone turn quite so red as her brother.

"Here we are," Father announced, coming out with a footman bearing the last of Violet's trunks. He kissed her on the cheek. "I hope we'll still see you around here."

"Oh, it's time," Mum said with a sniffle, and wrapped her in a hug.

Rose drained the last of her champagne. "I want a full report on your wedding night. Tomorrow."

"Oh, Rose," Violet said, exchanging an embarrassed glance with Ford. But she kissed her sister anyway. Tearing up, she gathered Lily and Rowan close.

"Enough," Ford said, straightening his blue velvet surcoat. "Any more of this, and you'll all turn to mush and be washed away by the rain."

He took Violet's hand, and they made a dash for the carriage. She barely had time to gather her skirts before he grabbed her by the waist to swing her up and inside.

"I thought we'd never get out of there," he complained as the door shut behind them and he yanked her into his arms. She'd been dying to be alone with him, too, and when he crushed his lips to hers, a delicious warmth spiraled through her, all the way out to her fingers and toes.

But when the carriage lurched to begin the short, jarring journey to her new home, they bumped noses and then teeth. She laughed, smiling up at him as she nestled closer.

Rain beat on the carriage's roof, a soothing tattoo that made her feel even more warm and cozy and safe with her new husband.

"I've decided," Ford said, "that rain brings me luck."

"Because it sent everyone home early?"

"That, too," he said cryptically.

She felt entirely too drained to figure out what he meant. This day had been the most exhilarating and exhausting of her life. Surrounded by all their family and friends, Violet had felt such an outpouring of genuine affection that she was left stunned and profoundly moved. Never had she imagined there were so many people who loved her and wished her well.

Perhaps she was a girl who inspired love, after all.

"Mum was right," she said with a happy sigh. "It was a nice wedding."

"You can thank me for that. I extracted Colin's vow, under pain of death, that there would be no practical jokes."

"He wouldn't," she protested. "Not at a wedding."

"I can see you don't yet know my brother. Ask Kendra and Caithren about *their* weddings sometime."

"I will," she said, very much looking forward to that. "I like your family."

"I was sure they'd scare you away. They're loud, and meddlesome—"

"And they love you."

"I know," he said. "And now that I've married you, I think

they might approve of me, too. I even overheard Jason boasting of my watch design to the Lord Chancellor."

"He must be proud of you." It was obvious his brother's praise was of special significance to Ford. Though Violet wasn't sure why, she sensed it was a conversation best left for another day.

Seeming lost in thought, Ford made no response. His arm tightened around her. Resting her head on his shoulder, she closed her eyes.

Contented silence reigned for a while before he spoke again. "Do you like your new spectacles?"

She touched the golden frames. "More than I can say. Truly, Ford, I've never received such a lovely gift. They sparkle so."

"Amy insisted on the stones—violet-colored gems for Violet."

"Oh! I was wondering if she'd made them." Violet was relieved. It would have cost him a fortune to special order such a trinket from London.

"I'm so glad you're pleased." He pressed a slow kiss to the top of her head. A kiss so cherishing, she felt tears spring to her eyes.

What had she done to deserve him?

"Speaking of wedding gifts," she said, moving to reach for her satchel, "I've one for you, too." She was rummaging through the open bag when another great lurch sent it flying, scattering its contents. "Oh, hang it!"

"Blast this road. Here, let me—"

"Wait, don't—"

But it was too late. Ford straightened, raising a leather-bound book that had landed face up, its cover flung open.

A book with a very shocking illustration on the frontispiece beside its title page.

"What's this?" When she failed to respond, he turned disbelieving eyes on her. "Violet...?"

For a bare instant, she seriously considered leaping out of a moving carriage.

But she was rooted to the spot. "*Aristotle's Master-piece*," she mumbled, her tongue feeling dry and heavy. "You bought it for me that day in Windsor, remember?"

His brow furrowed. "I thought it was philosophy."

She gave a mournful shake of her head.

Remaining silent, her hands clasped in her lap, she watched him page slowly through the book, pausing here and there to read a passage. His eyebrows rose higher and higher, until they nearly encountered his hairline. "It's a manual," he breathed in sudden realization.

She nodded, her gaze dropping to her clenched hands.

"Some of the pages are marked," he observed. "And there are notes written in the margins. Is this…Violet, have you been *studying* for our wedding night?"

"I—" Feeling his stare, she hid her flaming face in her hands. "I'm an idiot. I just wanted…" Swallowing hard, she fought off nausea and released a shuddering breath. "I just didn't want to do it wrong," she finished lamely. "I'm sorry."

She wondered miserably what would happen next. Would he laugh at her? Could he bear to go through with the night ahead, knowing what a naive fool he'd married? Or would he take her straight back to Trentingham and have their vows annulled forthwith?

She heard the book snap shut. "You're *sorry*?"

Tasting bile in her mouth, she braced herself for the worst. She could survive this. She could go back to her old life. Somehow.

"I can't imagine," he went on, "why you think you need be sorry."

Bewildered, she peeked through her fingers. A wisp of hope rose within her.

Until he began to laugh.

She lunged for the carriage door.

"Violet, no!" He caught her by one arm, then the other, and held her in her seat. "I'm sorry," he choked out. "I shouldn't be laughing. I'm not laughing at *you*." He sucked in a breath, trying to calm himself.

Her blood roared in her ears. If she couldn't escape outside, she wished she could sink into the floor or fade into the walls. Or turn invisible. Anything.

"It's just the thought," he continued, "of treating tonight like an exam..." Shaking his head, he slid his hands up her arms and over her shoulders to cup her cheeks. "It's the sweetest thing I've ever heard."

"Pardon?" The roaring diminished.

"But you needn't worry, my love." His famous smile stole over his face. "Tonight is going to be absolutely perfect."

She swallowed again. "How do you know?"

"Because it's the two of us together." Bright and full of promise, his eyes bore into hers. "How could we ever be anything but?"

SIXTY-NINE

*I*T WAS PERFECT.

Later that night, Violet lay nestled under Ford's arm, admiring the lovely blue brocade canopy overhead. "The bed-hangings are new," she remarked.

He laughed. "Have you only just noticed?"

Smiling, she thwacked him with a matching blue cushion. "Perhaps I was a bit preoccupied."

That was an understatement. By the time they'd entered Lakefield House, she'd been a bundle of nerves and anticipation. But Ford had said it would be perfect, and she'd known she could trust him.

And now she knew she would never doubt his love again, not for a single second as long as she lived.

His love was a part of her now. Everywhere he'd touched, she'd felt him sinking into her skin, washing over her soul: a sense of belonging so sure and so right, it was truer than any truth she'd ever known.

Now she settled into Ford's arms, and for long while he held her close, kissing her hair and drawing in its flowery scent. He didn't want to let go, didn't want to move, didn't want to break the spell. Usually one to turn over and go to sleep, he decided she must have enchanted him.

"I never gave you your wedding present," she finally said softly.

"It can wait until morning," he protested, but the moment was lost. He held her fast for one more kiss before letting her go.

When she slid from the bed, his gaze followed her all the way across the room and back. With her hair trailing down her back, her skin aglow in the dying firelight, she was the most beautiful thing he had ever seen. He could hardly believe she was all his.

"Stop," he said. "Right there."

"What?" Her eyes darted furtively around. "Is there another hairy spider?"

"No." He laughed. "I just wanted to look at you. You're perfect."

"I am not." Self-consciously she folded her arms across her chest. "I'm neither tall like Rose, nor petite like Lily. Neither plump nor slender."

"Exactly. You're perfect. Now, what have you brought me?"

"Just this." Slipping back into bed, she handed him a package wrapped in fabric, gathered and tied with ribbons on both ends.

He felt its shape. "Another book?"

She blushed prettily. "Just open it."

He pulled off the ribbons, letting the fabric fall open.

And the breath left his body.

He stared down at the old book a moment, then raised his gaze to meet hers. "*Secrets of the Emerald Tablet*. How—how did you get this?"

"I bought it. With my inheritance."

"From Newton?"

"From you."

He pushed it into her hands. "Give it back. I won't have you sacrificing your own dreams for this book. I've already given it up, and I'm not sorry for the bargain." His voice sounded rough to his own ears, and he forced himself to gentle it. "It's not that I'm ungrateful, my love. It's just that—"

"No. You're not understanding. *I* bought it, Ford. In the first place. Rand told me you'd instructed him to sell it, and I couldn't allow that to happen. I couldn't let you sacrifice your prized possession just to convince me of your love."

His heart squeezed painfully in his chest. It was a moment before words would come, and when they finally did, he had only three.

"I love you."

SEVENTY

*I*T WASN'T THE first morning Ford had awakened next to Violet, but it was the first time he'd awakened next to his wife.

He just lay there a while, watching the rise and fall of her breathing, admiring the color in her cheeks, her lips still rosy from their kisses. Finally, unable to help himself, he reached out, brushing the side of her face with the backs of his fingers.

"Ford?"

"Hush, my sweet. Sleep."

With a sigh, he rose so she could do so. Quietly he padded to the washbasin and splashed his face, then reached for a towel.

He stared at himself in the mirror.

What kind of a man was he? He'd thought he was doing the right thing, the responsible thing, when he'd sold the book to save Lakefield. He'd been so pleased with himself when he'd managed to make his home livable and still have money left to last for a while until the estate could turn a profit. It was the first time in his life he hadn't spent every shilling the moment he laid hands on it.

Last night, when Violet returned the book, he'd been stunned and thrilled to discover the depth of her love and generosity. But as he studied himself this morning, reality set in.

Criminy, her money had paid for everything. And would continue to pay their expenses for the next few months, at least.

He closed his eyes, guilt battering his newfound happiness. Never mind that he was accustomed to living hand to mouth, he now had a wife. Shouldn't he be the provider?

Society said not necessarily, but his heart told him yes. Especially because he'd been telling Violet that all along.

Straightening, he looked in the mirror again and ordered himself to come to terms with it. Like it or not, his new wife had been his anonymous benefactor. At this point, all he could do was resolve to work even harder, and not in his laboratory, but on his land and at his desk. He would do whatever it took to ensure her investment was returned to her.

As he tossed the towel to the washstand, his gaze fell on *Secrets of the Emerald Tablet*. He would ask Rand—the scheming rascal—to resume the translation, too. But he would no longer depend on an ancient book to rescue him. Gold wasn't waiting at the end of rainbows. Or in an alchemy crucible, either.

Someday, somehow, he would provide Violet with the funds to publish her book. But the way it looked now, he thought with a resigned sigh, "someday" was far in the future.

A knock came at the bedroom door. He hurried into his breeches and went to answer it.

"Will you be wanting breakfast, milord?"

He looked from Hilda to Violet. "In an hour," he whispered. "My wife is still abed."

My wife. His heart swelled at hearing his own words.

"She'll wake, will she not? It's hot and ready now. Eggs and cheese. This new French cook certainly is fancy." Hilda shoved a heavy tray into his hands. "Your mail is there, too."

Openmouthed, he watched her sway down the corridor before he shut the door. "If I cannot control my servants," he muttered, "how will I deal with my children?"

"You never did manage to control Jewel."

"Too true." He turned and put the tray on the bed. "You're awake."

"And famished." Violet spooned up a bite of eggs, puffed from oven baking and redolent with the scent of sharp Italian cheese.

He sat beside her and sipped coffee from a steaming cup. Setting it down, he took the first letter and snapped open the seal.

"'Dear Lord Lakefield,'" he read aloud, thinking it might be a congratulatory note on their wedding. "'I am writing on behalf of my client, Daniel Quare, Watchmaker, who is very interested in buying the rights to produce your patented watch. Please find enclosed a contract—'" He looked up. "What in heaven's name...?"

Violet's face had gone white. "Oh my. They've responded. I gave them two weeks, and it's been far longer, so I thought—"

"You gave them two weeks to what?"

"To agree to buy your watch before I took my offer else-where. Your offer, I mean." Some color rushed back into her cheeks. "I signed your name."

His wife was obviously confused from lack of sleep. "I haven't patented my watch, love. I haven't even shown it to the Royal Society yet—"

"*I* patented it. I wrote to Christopher Wren and asked for instructions. I remembered him saying he'd patented a device for writing with two pens at once."

"You sold my watch?" It was all beginning to click into place. Shaking his head in disbelief, he scanned farther down the page. His heart stopped. "You sold my watch for twenty thousand pounds? *Twenty* thousand pounds!"

His heart had started again, but it was about to hammer right through his ribs.

"Twenty thousand?" She grabbed the letter from him. "Is that all they've offered?" she said, sounding disgusted.

"All? All! Violet, it's twice the amount of your inheritance!"

She looked up from the page. "But I asked for twenty-five. What makes them think they can get away with a contract for twenty?"

He started laughing. And laughing. "T-t-t-twenty-five," he forced out. "You asked for twenty-five."

"And royalties. Was it not enough?" she asked. "I know your design is revolutionary, but I thought twenty-five thousand pounds was...well, you're worth more than that, of course. You're priceless."

"*You're* priceless," he said. "Give me that contract."

"You're not going to sign it, are you? I hope not. They didn't offer enough. We need to negotiate."

"Oh, I'm signing it, Violet." To make certain she wouldn't stop him, he rolled the paper and stuck it in his breeches. "I wasn't planning to do anything with the watch, remember? Now, thanks to you, it shall make me wealthy beyond comprehension."

Thanks to his clever, ambitious, practical wife—a woman who embodied all the things he'd once thought unimportant in women—"someday" had just come a lot sooner than he'd ever dreamed.

His mind raced with plans. "I can sink more money into Lakefield or buy a second estate. Or both." He grinned. "I can finance the publication of my brilliant wife's book."

She cracked a small smile, a smile that stole his heart. "Do you suppose that can wait a while?" she asked. "I mean to raise some children first, if you're amenable."

She made him happy. Criminy, he was happy. Happy with his wife, happy with his life.

"Hmm," he said, watching her speculatively. "After careful consideration, I find I am indeed amenable. But won't we have to *make* those children first?"

Her smile widened as she set aside the breakfast tray.

When their lips met, he poured all his love into a kiss.

EPILOGUE

Seven months later

$\mathcal{V}$IOLET WAS READING in bed when Ford burst into the chamber. "I've just had a message from Jason. Cait is delivering their babe, and the family is gathering at Cainewood to celebrate. If we leave soon enough, you may even witness the birthing."

"That would be nice," she said dreamily, toying absently with the cover of her book.

"What's that?" He walked closer, and his lips curved in a half-smile. "*Aristotle's Master-piece* again?"

She sat up against the headboard and grinned. "I've suddenly become interested in this particular chapter. Listen." She patted the bed beside her and waited for him to sit. "'Signs taken from the woman are these. The first day she feels a light quivering or chillness running through the whole body; a tickling in the womb, a little pain in the lower part of the belly—'"

"What on earth?"

"Just listen." She turned the page. "'Ten or twelve days after, the head is affected with giddiness, the eyes with dimness of sight...'"

"Violet—"

"'…the belly soon sinketh, and riseth again by degrees, with a hardness about the navel,'" she pressed on. "'The heart beats inordinately, the natural appetite is dejected, yet she has a longing desire for—'"

Ford's hand clenched her arm. "What's the title of this chapter?"

She turned back to the previous page. "'Of the Signs of Conception.'"

When she looked up, his heart was in his brilliant blue eyes. "Does this mean…?"

"Yes," she whispered. "I hope you're pleased."

And a moment later, he gathered her into his arms, telling her without words just how very pleased he was.

Apparently being with child had some effect on her responses. When his mouth met hers, her head was affected with giddiness and her heart beat inordinately…

Wait, she thought, with what little sense she had left. He always made her feel those things.

Always.

They were going to be late to Cainewood.

AUTHOR'S NOTE

~

DEAR READER,

It goes without saying that Ford didn't invent frames to hold spectacles on the face—credit for that goes to a London optician named Edward Scarlett, who came up with the idea in 1730. The first spectacles for reading were made in the late 13th century (and the first ones for distance about 300 years later), but before Scarlett's innovation they were simply held to the face or balanced on the nose—momentarily helpful, but not something one could wear all day long. I like to think that if Ford Chase had really lived, he'd have been brilliant enough to invent eyeglass frames half a century earlier.

Although the minute hand began appearing on watches around 1675, it's not clear who managed it first. Obviously someone missed a chance at a profitable patent! Everyone agrees the two-handed watch was developed in England, but some historians claim that Daniel Quare was the first to sell such a timepiece, while some say it was Thomas Tompion or others. But what *does* seem to be clear is that the minute hand was made possible by Robert Hooke's 1660 invention of the spiral spring, which brought watches from a totally unpredictable performance to within two or three minutes' accuracy a day.

A true genius, Robert Hooke did much more than revolutionize timekeeping; he also made important contributions in chemistry, meteorology, astronomy, and physics. Other scientists of the time are much revered today, including Isaac Newton, Christopher Wren, and Robert Boyle. Yet Hooke has been largely forgotten. Newton and Wren were both knighted, so why not

Hooke, arguably a greater scientist? In 2003, Gresham College marked the 300th year of Hooke's death by a series of lectures designed to resurrect his reputation.

Gresham College has provided free public lectures in London for over 400 years. Over time, it's occupied several different locations. The lectures currently take place at Barnard's Inn Hall, in a building that dates from the late 14th century. To see the upcoming schedule, visit the college's website at www.gresham. ac.uk.

The Royal Society really was welcomed back to Gresham College in 1673, "with six quarts of each of canary, of Rhenish wine and of claret, and with fine cakes, macaroons and marchpanes," as the City Archives describe an account of their entertainment. But the actual date of the celebration was Monday, December 1. I took the liberty of tweaking history a bit in moving the event to the warm summertime, so Ford could decorate the piazza. All of the people I mentioned at the ball were members at the time, including John Evelyn, best known for his diary that has given us a window into the Restoration period, and John Locke, whose ideas were a powerful influence on the subsequent history of the Western world. Thomas Jefferson called Locke one of "the three greatest men that have ever lived, without any exception," and drew heavily on his writings in drafting the Declaration of Independence.

Along with these men of note, I enjoyed bringing Hooke and the other scientists—and yes, alchemists—to life. Although the mere idea of making gold from base metals is a laughable one today, up until the mid-18th century it was considered a serious science. During the 1600s, most of the luminaries of the day practiced alchemy, King Charles included. Ironically, it was his chartering of the Royal Society that eventually led to alchemy's decline. In that ordered environment, modern chemistry and the new scientific methods taught men to free themselves from the old traditions and question theories that had prevailed for centuries.

Although I invented the title *Secrets of the Emerald Tablet*, Alexander the Great did claim to have discovered the Emerald Tablet in the tomb of the legendary Hermes, and medieval alchemist Raymond Lully was said to have written a treatise about it that subsequently disappeared. No one knows the title, however, and although other writings attributed to Lully survive, that particular one was never found.

A combination marriage manual and advice to midwives, *Aristotle's Master-piece* first appeared in the late 1600s and by the turn of the century was a veritable bestseller—likely to be found in any newlywed couple's home. All of the words Violet read were actual passages from the book. Reflecting the attitudes of the time, this book presented marital sex as an act of pleasure without sin or guilt. In later years, of course, society became much more strait-laced about such matters... although the *Master-piece* saw countless reprintings up until about 1900, in Victorian times the chapter Chrystabel cut from Violet's copy was completely removed from the book!

As usual, the homes we used in this story were based on real ones that you can visit. Though we moved it to the Thames, Lakefield House was loosely modeled on Snowshill Manor in Gloucestershire. Snowshill was owned by Winchcombe Abbey from the year 821 until the reign of Henry VIII in the 16th century, when, with the dissolution of the monasteries, it passed to the Crown. Thereafter it had many owners and tenants until 1919, when a man named Charles Paget Wade returned from the First World War and found it for sale. The house was derelict, the garden an overgrown jumble of weeds, including—of course!—a sundial. Wade bought Snowshill and restored it, removing the plaster ceilings, moving partitions back to their original places, unblocking fireplaces, and fitting Tudor paneling to many of the rooms to recapture the original atmosphere. He scorned the use of electricity and modern conveniences, so the house appears today much as it would have during Ford's time. Wade never lived in the house, instead using it to showcase his amazing collection of everyday and curious objects, literally thousands of items including musical instruments, clocks, toys, bicycles, weavers' and spinners' tools, and Japanese armor. The home is now owned by the National Trust and open April through October to view the house and collection.

Trentingham Manor was inspired by another National Trust property, The Vyne in Hampshire (which we also relocated to sit on the banks of the Thames). Built in the early 16th century for Lord Sandys, Henry VIII's Lord Chamberlain, the house acquired a classical portico in the mid-17th century (the first of its kind in England) and contains a grand Palladian staircase, a wealth of old paneling and fine furniture, and a fascinating Tudor chapel with Renaissance glass. The Vyne and its extensive gardens are also open for visits from April through October.

I hope you enjoyed *The Viscount's Wallflower Bride*! Next up is Lily's story in *The Baron's Inconvenient Bride*. Please read on for an excerpt!

Always,

Lauren Royal

Read on for an excerpt from

The Baron's Inconvenient Bride

Book 6 of the
Sweet Chase Brides series
by Lauren & Devon Royal

Lily Ashcroft fell for dashing Oxford scholar Lord Randal Nesbitt as a schoolgirl. Four years later, her older sister Rose wants him—and what can soft-hearted Lily do but help her sister land the man of her dreams?

Read an excerpt…

❦

Trentingham Manor, the South of England
August 1677

HE'D FORGOTTEN about her.

Well, maybe he hadn't quite forgotten about her, but he'd certainly put her out of his mind.

Well, maybe he hadn't put her *all* the way out of his mind, but he'd banished all thoughts of her to the outskirts. She was only fourteen, after all. And Lord Randal Nesbitt was far too honorable to let a girl of fourteen anywhere near his…well, thoughts.

But it had been four years since they'd last met, and now, he'd just realized, Lady Lily Ashcroft must be eighteen.

A fetching, dark-haired, blue-eyed eighteen. A marriageable eighteen.

Marriageable? Having never really considered marriage in all of his twenty-three years, Rand found the notion jarring. Perhaps being in a chapel put ideas into a fellow's head. Though truth be told, he hardly knew where he was or what was going on around him. All his awareness was focused on Lily standing beside him at the altar, her month-old niece cradled in her arms.

"Having now," the priest continued, sounding distant to Rand though the man stood right in front of him, "in the name of these children, made these promises, wilt thou also on thy part take heed that these children learn the Creed, the Lord's Prayer, and the Ten Commandments, and all other things which a Christian ought to know and believe to his soul's health?"

"I will, by God's help," Lily replied softly. Gently, gazing down at the babe she held close.

A smile curved Rand's lips. In four years she had changed, of course. But her gentleness, that unfailing sweetness, hadn't changed. Couldn't have changed. It was what made her Lily.

Ford Chase, Rand's friend—and father of the children in question—elbowed him in the ribs.

"Hmm?" Startled, Rand looked down at the month-old boy squirming in his own arms, its bald little head colored by the sun streaming through the chapel's stained-glass windows. Ford's son, he thought, surprised by a rush of tenderness. Rand's godson...or at least the tiny fellow and his twin sister would soon be his godchildren, provided he made it through their baptism.

"I will," he answered, echoing Lily's words.

"By God's help," the priest prompted.

"By God's help."

A few titters rose from the crowd, but Rand ignored them, shifting on his feet. Sweet mercy, he felt as though he'd been standing for a week. Mass, and then a lesson, and now this ritual at the font—delivering a two-hour lecture at Oxford wasn't nearly so exhausting. He suspected his knees were now permanently locked.

But even more than he wished to sit down, he couldn't wait to speak to Lily. Never mind that she'd barely noticed him. He'd scurried into Trentingham's grand, oak-paneled chapel at the last minute and had no chance to greet her before the ceremonies began.

The priest turned a page in his *Book of Common Prayer*. "Wilt thou take heed that these children, so soon as sufficiently instructed, be brought to the bishop to be confirmed by him?"

"I will." Rand and Lily said the words together this time. Their voices, he thought, sounded good together.

"Name these children."

The bundle in Rand's arms chose then to begin wailing. "Marcus Cicero Chase," Rand hollered over the squall.

"Rebecca Ashcroft Chase," Lily said more softly and with a smile, even though the girl's cries had joined her twin brother's, seeming to fill the chapel all the way up to its sculpted Tudor ceiling.

Whoever would have thought such tiny creatures could make such a huge racket?

The priest scooped water into his hand, letting it trickle through his fingers. It ran in rivulets down the backs of the two babies' heads and landed on the colorful glazed tile floor. "I baptize thee in the name of the Father, and of the Son, and of the Holy Ghost." He made crosses on the children's foreheads. "Amen."

Amen. It was over. Well-wishers crowded close. Still holding his bawling godson, Rand turned to Lily.

She was gone.

How could she have disappeared so quickly? Using his height to advantage, he peered over heads. But she'd vanished.

Nearby, Ford held little Rebecca and spoke with an older gentleman Rand recognized. Or rather, Ford was shouting at the gentleman, since the Earl of Trentingham, Lily's father, was hard of hearing.

Marveling that his friend looked so natural holding a baby, Rand jiggled little Marc uneasily. Rebecca had stopped crying, apparently content in Ford's arms, but in Rand's, her twin brother still howled.

Glancing around for help, Rand was relieved to see Ford's wife, Violet, moving close. When she reached for her son, Rand offered a grateful smile. But then he found himself oddly reluctant to hand Marc over. Loud little thing though he was, he smelled good and had a soft, warm weight.

When Violet took him, Marc quieted immediately. Resisting the urge to run his fingers over that fuzzy little head, Rand crossed his arms and leaned on one of the intricate carved oak stalls. "I assume you chose his name, Marcus Cicero, for the philosopher."

Violet bounced the babe in her arms, her brown curls bouncing along with him. She looked more motherly than Rand usually pictured her. Did children change people so much? "It was only fair," she said. "Ford had the naming of our firstborn."

"Nicky? Ah, Nicolas Copernicus," Rand remembered. "Well, I suppose it's a better choice than Ford's other favorite scientist."

"Galileo Galilei?" She laughed, her brown eyes sparkling behind her fancy gold -rimmed spectacles. "Yes, thank heaven Ford had already bestowed *that* name on his horse."

"And Rebecca? Who is she named after?"

"No one. I just like it. And there's never been a major female philosopher."

"Yet," Rand added, knowing Violet hoped to publish a philosophy book of her own someday.

"Yet," she confirmed with a nod, clearly appreciating his support. She touched her husband's arm, claiming his attention. "We'd best be heading home," she said when he turned, "or our guests will arrive there before us."

When Ford smiled at her, Violet's return smile transformed her face. Perhaps she wasn't as pretty as her sisters, Lily and Rose, but she was lovely in her own way. A way that was enhanced by her obvious delight in both the occasion and the magnificent purple gown she'd donned to celebrate it.

Moreover, she made Ford happy. A sort of happiness that glowed from his eyes whenever he looked at her. Through six years together at university, Rand had never seen anything close to that look on Ford's face.

It was incredible how much his friend had changed.

Ford was still holding his new daughter, her tiny fist tangled in his hair. Giving in this time, Rand skimmed his fingers over Rebecca's dark curls. "They're so soft," he murmured.

Violet nodded. "All babies are soft."

"I wouldn't know. I cannot remember holding a baby before."

"Really?" She looked surprised to hear that. "Well, someday you'll have babies of your own."

"Perhaps," he allowed. "I never say never. But should it happen, I can assure you it won't be any time soon."

Her laugh tinkled through the nearly empty chapel. "That's always what a man says just before he falls in love."

Ford rolled his eyes. "If you say so, my sweet." He turned to his friend. "Now, come along—I want to show you the water closet I built. It's much better than the ones imported from France."

Rand smiled as he followed his friends out the door. Perhaps Ford hadn't changed that much, after all.

"WHAT?" LILY demanded as her friend Judith Carrington pulled her toward a carriage. "What's so important you couldn't wait until we got to Violet's house to tell me? So important you nearly made me drop my niece, not to mention almost dislocated my arm dragging me out of there?"

Before climbing inside, Lily searched out her family in the crowd. Her father was easiest to spot, tall and trim with deep green eyes, his real hair still as jet-black as the periwig he wore for his grandchildren's baptism. Mum and Rose were both dark-haired and statuesque. They looked elegant in their best satin gowns, her mother's a gleaming gold and Rose's a rich, shimmering blue. Lily waved to them, then pointed at Judith, signaling that she would ride with her friend.

The Ashcrofts were a handsome family, in truth. Looking at them, one would never guess they were so eccentric.

Mum waved back distractedly, holding her two-year-old grandson, Nicky, as she busily ushered guests out the door to their waiting transportation.

Feeling Judith's hand on her back, Lily laughed and lifted her peach silk skirts to duck inside the carriage. "What?" she repeated.

"Oh, just this." Even though they weren't ready to leave, Judith pulled the door shut. Then she settled herself with a flounce. "I'm betrothed."

"Betrothed?" Lily seized her friend's hands. "As in you're planning to wed?"

"Well, Mama is doing the planning. But it's ever so exciting. Come October, I'm going to be a married woman. Can you believe it, Lily?"

"No, I cannot believe it," she confessed, squeezing Judith's fingers. The third of her friends to marry this year. Yesterday they'd been children; now suddenly they were supposed to be all grown-up. "Who will be your groom?"

"Lord Grenville. Didn't your mother tell you she'd suggested he offer for my hand? Father says it's a brilliant match."

Grenville was wealthy, but thirty-five years old to Judith's nineteen. "Do you love him?" Lily wondered aloud. She hoped so. Judith was plump and pretty, but even more important, she was genuinely nice. A good friend who deserved happiness.

"I barely know him. But Mama assures me we'll grow to love each other—or get along tolerably, at least." Her hands slipped out of Lily's, moving to worry the embroidery on her turquoise underskirt. "It will all work out fine, I'm sure of it."

"I'm sure of it, too," Lily soothed, wishing she were as certain as she sounded. Lily's parents had promised their daughters they could choose their own husbands, but she knew it didn't work that way for most young women.

Her family was different. The Ashcroft motto—*Interroga Conformationem*, translated as Question Convention—said it all.

The Carringtons, on the other hand, were as conventional as roast goose on Christmas Day. Judith forced a smile and pushed back a lock of bright yellow hair that had escaped her careful coiffure. "Who was that gentleman who stood as godfather?"

Lily sat back. "One of Ford's old friends. Lord Randal Nesbitt."

"Wouldn't it be fun to be newly wedded together, have babies together?" Some of the color returned to Judith's cheeks. "You should marry *him*."

"Wherever did you get that idea?" Lily crossed her arms over the long, stiff stomacher that covered the laces on the front of her gown. "I barely know Rand."

"Rand?" Judith repeated significantly, and Lily blushed to be caught using the over-familiar name. But somehow she'd always thought of him as Rand, though she'd never realized it before. How odd.

"So what if you barely know him," Judith argued. "I hardly know Lord Grenville, either. And believe me, he doesn't look at me the way *Rand* was looking at you."

"Looking at me?" Lily echoed weakly. She'd hardly looked at him at all. She'd been focused on the cooing baby in her arms, her sister's first daughter. Her first niece. Nicky was great fun, of course, but now she'd have a little girl to play house with, to fix her hair, to—

"Upon my word, he didn't take his eyes off you the entire time." Judith's lips curved in an impish grin. "Watching him was more entertaining than the baptism."

Lily felt her face heat and wondered if Judith could be right— if instead of watching the ceremony, everyone had been watching Rand watch her.

But surely that hadn't been the case. Why would Rand be interested in *her*? The two of them had nothing in common. Her friend had seen something that wasn't there. "You just have the wedding fever," she said lightly, rubbing the back of her hand left hand. "Besides, if he's interested in anyone, I'm sure it's Rose. They share an interest in languages."

"Ah," Judith said with a tilt of her pert nose. "You know more about the fellow than you're willing to admit."

Ignoring that, Lily leaned to look out the window. But there was a long queue of carriages. They were going nowhere.

"Who's that?" her friend asked, following her line of sight. "The girl in pink, coming out of the barn with your brother?"

"That's Jewel, Ford's niece. Rowan and she have been friends forever."

"What sort of friends? And what do you suppose they were doing alone together in a barn?"

"Goodness, they're but children of ten! Your mind is too much on romance these days. Knowing those two, they were probably planning a practical joke."

"In a *barn*?"

Lily laughed at the expression on her friend's face. "I doubt there's an inch of Trentingham that hasn't seen one or another of their schemes. And Lakefield, too."

Judith looked likely to say more, but the door popped open and her mother poked her head in. "Were you leaving without me, dear?"

"Of course not, Mama." Judith scooted over to make room. "We just came inside to talk."

A large, jolly woman, Lady Carrington wedged herself beside her daughter and tucked in her voluminous coral skirts. Before her footman could shut the door, Lily's striped cat nimbly leapt inside.

Lady Carrington sneezed. "Shoo!" she exclaimed, waving an elegant hand at the creature.

"Beatrix," Lily said softly, "you cannot ride in this carriage."

The cat gave her a hurt look before hopping out.

"Much better," Judith's mother said as the door shut. She turned to Lily. "This afternoon, I'm hoping your father will advise me about flowers for Judith's wedding."

The Earl of Trentingham was nothing if not an expert on flowers. "I'm certain Father will fancy being consulted," Lily assured her.

The carriage began moving at last. "I've my heart set on

yellow flowers," Lady Carrington told Lily, "because Judith looks best in yellow. But she wants to be married in blue. What color will you wear for your wedding?"

"Blue is nice," Lily said with a vague smile.

She wasn't ready to think about weddings, and most certainly not her own.

Rose was a year older—her wedding had to come first.

∼

AVAILABLE NOW!
Learn more about *The Baron's Inconvenient Bride* at
www.DevonAndLaurenRoyal.com

ENTER FOR A CHANCE TO WIN
the sterling silver filigree heart pendant Ford gives Jewel in this book!*

Visit the Contest page on Lauren & Devon's website
at www.LaurenandDevonRoyal.com
and answer a question to be
entered in the monthly drawing.

No purchase necessary. See complete rules on the site.

*Please note: Depending on when you enter, the prize may be another piece of jewelry
associated with one of Lauren & Devon's books. The authors reserve the right to discontinue
this promotion at any time.

ABOUT LAUREN & DEVON ROYAL

∾

LAUREN ROYAL decided to become a writer in the third grade, after winning a "Why My Mother is the Greatest" essay contest. Now she's a *New York Times* and *USA Today* bestselling author of humorous historical romance novels. Lauren lives in Southern California with her family and their constantly shedding cat. She still thinks her mother is the greatest.

DEVON ROYAL is the daughter of romance novelist Lauren Royal. After attending film school, she wrote an award-winning TV comedy pilot and worked in digital video production before turning her focus to fiction writing. Devon lives in Southern California with her husband and son. She also thinks her mother is the greatest.

ACKNOWLEDGMENTS

∽

OUR HEARTFELT THANKS:

To Al Stewart, for writing "House of Clocks," a song that sounded so eerily like Ford Chase that it inspired us to rewrite the beginning of his story to make it start on St. Swithin's Day (check out Mr. Stewart's album *Down in the Cellar* if you'd like to hear it).

To Geoff Pavitt, Facilities Manager at Gresham College, for finding an incredible amount of information for us, including stuff we didn't even know we needed until he sent it.

To librarian Claire Andrews, at the Heritage Park Library in Irvine, California, for all her hard work finding obscure 300-year-old books and arranging inter-library loans for us.

To Peter Do and Martha Altieri, for the Latin translation.

To Herb Royal, for *attempting* the Latin translation.

To all the honorary Chase cousins in our Chase Family Readers Group, for their enthusiastic support.

And, as always, to all of our readers, especially the ones who have taken the time to write and let us know how you feel about our stories.

Thank you, one and all!

CONTACT INFORMATION

~

Newsletter

littl.ink/News

Facebook Readers Group

facebook.com/groups/ChaseFamilyReaders

Website

www.DevonAndLaurenRoyal.com

Email

royall.ink/Email